DR. DECLAN MURPHY CONFRONTS ESCALATING TERROR AND MURDER WHILE INVESTIGATING ENVIRONMENTAL TOXINS AND THEIR REPRODUCTIVE HEALTH EFFECTS.

"Unfortunately, Paris Laveau has escaped and is on the loose," Rosemary said.

"I know. That bothers me a lot. Paris is a predator and has the survival instincts of a cockroach. I don't think either the Louisiana state police or the F.B.I. is going to catch her."

"She can't hide forever. The Laveaus are just glorified trailer trash. I don't know how she was able to get over on Marcellus, but she doesn't have the resources that are necessary to stay off the F.B.I.'s radar. Sooner or later, they're going to roll her up."

"I hope so, but I'm not so certain. Paris is an excellent chameleon, which actually makes her more reptilian than a cockroach. Sociopaths don't have an identity of their own, so they become great mimics. Finding her isn't going to be easy. She's got a lot of tricks."

"I'm not as worried about her as you are. Somehow she got the better of Sheriff Greene, but I don't think there's any chance that she's coming back here. Right now, Paris needs a deep hidey hole. That hole is deepest in the bayous of southwest Louisiana. Coming back to Charleston only makes her more visible and vulnerable."

"You're probably right, but you should've seen the look in her eyes when you slapped her face. She hates you, and she hates me. Paris isn't the kind to forgive or forget a slight."

"... *What Becomes* is Newman's best novel to date. His latest page turner is a medical thriller, a mystery, and a love story, all wrapped in one, highly enjoyable, fast-paced adventure, a must read. That's one thing I'm certain of." — ***Bill Noel, author of the best-selling Folly Beach Mystery series including the award-winning Boneyard Beach.***

"A medical eco-thriller that crackles with wit and colorful, brainy characters. The environmental misdeeds and their chilling implications for human health are utterly, alarmingly believable. With the unerring talent of a gifted storyteller, Roger Newman layers on the suspense, holding us willingly captive to the final, disquieting line."—***Donna Cousins, author of The Story of Bones***

"The further adventures of amateur detective Dr. Declan Murphy, Ob-Gyn, is threatened when a suspect in a previous novel escapes police custody and vows revenge. Author Roger Newman weaves his narrative into a tapestry of real people, real places and real events so artfully done, the reader soon forgets *What Becomes* is fiction. And that's writing at its very best."—***Roger Pinckney, author of Blue Roots, Reefer Moon and The Mullet Manifesto***

WHAT BECOMES

Roger Newman

Moonshine Cove Publishing, LLC
Abbeville, South Carolina U.S.A

FIRST MOONSHINE COVE EDITION
July 2018

This book is a work of fiction. Names, characters, places and incidents are products of the author's imagination or are used fictitiously. Any resemblance to actual events, locales or persons, living or dead, is entirely coincidental.

ISBN: 978-1-945181-39-9
Library of Congress PCN: 2017948982

Front cover photograph by Dr. Lou Guillette, used with permission, cover design by Moonshine Cove staff.

About The Author

Roger Newman, M.D. is a nationally known leader in Ob-Gyn; selected as one of the "Best Doctors in America" by Woodward and White each year for the past two decades. He is the Maas Endowed Chair for

Reproductive Sciences at the Medical University of South Carolina (MUSC) in Charleston. He has been the South Carolina Chair for the American Congress of Obstetricians and Gynecologists, President of the South Carolina Ob-Gyn Society and an editor for the *American Journal of Obstetrics and Gynecology.* Dr. Newman was also the national president of the Society for Maternal-Fetal Medicine and served five years on the Scientific Advisory Board for the NIH-NICHD Maternal-Fetal Medicine Network. He has written more than 170 peer-reviewed scientific publications and book chapters. Dr. Newman is considered an expert on the care of women with twins, triplets or higher order gestations. He has written the chapter on multiple gestations in most of the major Ob-Gyn textbooks and co-authored a book entitled *Multifetal Pregnancy: A Handbook for the Care of the Pregnant Patient.* In 2017, Dr. Newman co-authored along with Dr. Barbara Luke and Tamara a the 4th edition of the award-winning self-help book *When You're Expecting Twins, Triplets or Quads.*

What Becomes follows the publication in July 2014 of *Occam's Razor* and *Two Drifters* in 2016. *Occam's Razor* introduces the character of Dr. Declan Murphy and his involvement with the Charleston Jackpot drug smugglers of the early 1980s, abuse of political power and the risks of an inappropriate physician-patient relationship. *Two Drifters* continues the story of Dr. Declan Murphy- literature's only obstetrical action hero- as he becomes involved in a treacherous malpractice allegation.

Roger Newman is married and has three inspiring children. He and his wife, Diane, have lived in Charleston for the past 30 years following completion of his Ob-Gyn and Maternal-Fetal Medicine training at MUSC and the University of California, San Francisco, respectively. Besides medicine and writing, Dr. Newman is passionate about sports and his other "job" is coaching the Women's Varsity basketball team (Raptors) at the Academic Magnet High School and rooting for the Seton Hall Pirates.

For news about Roger Newman, visit his website:

http://rogerbnewman.com

For the dozens of teachers and mentors that have guided my career, represented herein by Homer Lahr, M.D. and Louis J. Guillette, Jr., Ph.D.

Acknowledgment

Most importantly, I want to acknowledge the two people who are playing themselves in *What Becomes*. Dr. Homer Lahr was an Obstetrician – Gynecologist that I met early in my residency training at the Charleston Naval Hospital. We worked together for 3 memorable months. I have never seen him since, but his influence on me has been lifelong. The full scope of a man like Homer Lahr cannot be captured in a believable fashion, even in a work of fiction. The Homer Lahr character in this book only paints around the edges of the man that Homer was. As outlandish as my fictional character may seem, I can promise you that his characterization is based on true stories, and is presented with at least a 30% discount.

Homer Lahr was the proverbial "man-in-full." Homer taught me the difference between life and livelihood, to never compromise who you are for professional gain and the simple joy of painting red, orange and black racing strips on white surgery shoes. Despite more lifetime experiences than Forest Gump, Homer never lost his moral compass or belief in himself. Boss man, wherever you are, your lessons have not been forgotten. It's still "a blessing to be underestimated."

Louis J. Guillette, Jr. Ph.D. is a mentor that I had the great privilege to befriend late in my career. I was asked by the Dean to serve on a search committee for an Endowed Chair in Marine Sciences. From the moment I met him, I was fascinated by both the man and his work. Lou had spent most of his career at the University of Florida and was internationally known as the "alligator man." Lou had researched the links between environmental contamination with endocrine disrupting compounds (EDCs) and reproductive abnormalities in non-football playing Florida Gators. Lou was convinced, as I am now, that alligators are sentinel species for human health risks, and that maternal exposure to even small amounts of EDCs at critical periods of fetal development can have life-long health effects.

After a successful recruitment, I sought Lou out, and we began a collaboration to translate his alligator research to human health. We believed that environmental EDCs were relevant to the field of Obstetrics and Gynecology. The epigenetic effects of in-utero exposure to EDCs, such as the well understood Diethylstilbestrol (DES), may be responsible, at least in part, for current "epidemics" in reproductive health such as prematurity, PCOS, infertility, endocrine responsive tumors and cancers, obesity, autism and learning disabilities. The research described in this novel is a synthesis of many projects initiated by Louis J. Guillette. Jr., Ph.D.

For his work, Lou received the prestigious Heinz Medal in 2011, awarded by the Heinz family of Pittsburg, which is the equivalent of the Nobel Prize in the field of Environmental Science. Louis was lost to us prematurely in 2015 due to a disease that may well be linked to environmental toxins.

With his death, I lost far more than a friend and mentor. We all lost a visionary who pioneered scientific concepts that describe the impact of environmental toxins on human health. These concepts will ultimately inform us more about human disease than the Human Genome Project. We also lost a magnificent teacher of the next generation of environmental scientists. I think about Lou every day and wanted to include his story in this book. Lou once spoke to a Special Congressional Committee regarding the impact of unregulated environmental and industrial pollution on our growing burden of reproductive and chronic disease conditions. His was a voice for environmental and societal protection that we cannot allow to be lost.

In addition to a career as a renown Reproductive Biologist and Environmental Scientist, Lou was also a world-class naturalist and wild-life photographer. The cover art for this book is one of my favorite of Lou's photos. I have this picture in my office with the caption, "Lou making evening rounds on his patients." If you are interested in looking at some more of Lou's brilliant nature photography, his favorites, and many others, can be accessed at www.musc.edu/mbes-ljg/CVPubl/ or at www.flickr.com/photos/lou_guillette/ .

To some extent, Homer and Lou are bookends to a great treasure of family, friends, teachers and students that have filled in the time between them. Many of these friends have enriched my writing. Most of the characters in my books borrow in whole, or in part, from these many relationships. Even if not a character, remembrances or conversations with these friends worm there way into my stories. I thank Bill "Cat" Staats for letting me call "heads" and for reminding me about the story of the sinking of the Lusitania.

I would also like acknowledge all those who have encouraged and advised my writing. First among them is Dr. Richard Berkowitz, a Maternal-Fetal Medicine mentor, from Columbia University who again offered generous and thoughtful suggestions to improve the manuscript. A similar helpful critique was provided by my long-time assistant and friend, Ms. Becky Nida, who shares my love for the writing of the late Hunter S. Thompson. Thanks to Dr. Tripp Nelson who shared his fear and loathing of the MUSC autopsy suite, Dr. Rebecca Wineland for being simpatico and to Dr. Mark Bland who agreed to let me shape an alternate persona for him, different than "the new face of compassion in Charlotte." I appreciate that my real lawyers, Barbara Wynne Showers of Charleston, and Larry Nodine of Atlanta helped me understand the resources and moves that Rosemary Winslow had available to her.

Elizabeth "Buzzy" Guillette, Ph.D., Lou's wife, generously agreed to read the manuscript and offered insights and anecdotes about Lou's life and passions. Her contributions were beautiful, and helped me shape and improve my story. She helped me capture the force of nature that was Lou, as best I possibly could. I cannot thank Buzzy, and the entire Guillette family, enough for their help with this story.

I also want to acknowledge the natural beauty of the South Carolina coast. I've said in my books, and believe, that South Carolina is "too small to be a state, but too large to be an asylum." That said, South Carolina is also one of the most naturally beautiful places in the world. I have endeavored to include some of our Low Country beauty in this book from the Angel Oak, to Bowen's Island, to Captain Sam's Spit, to dolphin stranding, to Winyah Bay and the Yawkey Wildlife Preserve. These are environmental treasures that are under attack on multiple fronts from short-sighted governmental regulators, self-serving land developers, and real, and imagined, environmental polluters.

Professionally, I owe a great deal of thanks to my editor, Gene Robinson, at Moonshine Cove Publishing. He has taught me and helped me with each of my books. Finally, I need to acknowledge the unfailing support, love and non-negotiable suggestions of my wife, Diane, and the encouragement of my children, Bryan, Taylor and Sarah who represent my marketing, IT, and sales team. Maybe the only people who never underestimated me, and that turned out to be a blessing as well.

What Becomes

Chapter 1.
GYPSY SUMMER

It was a wisp of a breeze at most.

I doubt I would've noticed, except for the first time in months, it seemed to be at my back.

Since the death of my wife, Helene, my apathy and anger had been all-consuming. Helene's death had been horrific. The Human Immunodeficiency Virus remorselessly destroyed her mind, and then her body. It was the price she paid for seeking sanctuary from her powerful and abusive father with the Jackpot drug smugglers. My vacillation between outrage and indifference, over the loss of Helene, stripped away my friends, colleagues and any professional respect I had left. Worse, it dulled my sense of caring. Attempts at reflection devolved into destructive self-recrimination. Recollection only reminded me of what I no longer was. That wind had been much stronger and was perpetually in my face.

Then I met Rosemary Winslow. She gave me reason to be wishful. It'd been a long time since I'd wished for anything other than the end of the day. Hope had been lost to me. More than most, I appreciated how rare and effervescent a commodity hope could be. The inability to put Rosemary Winslow out of my mind sparked an interest in personal redemption which previously repulsed me. Choosing to follow the subtle aroma of optimism was dangerous. Anger and isolation were easier, safer.

The previous July fourth, my academic career as a professor of Obstetrics and Gynecology at the Medical University of South Carolina was jeopardized by a pair of events that both occurred on the same night. Two drifters from Alabama turned up in my examination room on Labor and Delivery with a well-rehearsed litany of symptoms and wild accusations. Finding nothing other than a normal pregnancy, and frankly, suspicious of domestic violence, I discharged them home with a recommendation to follow up in our outpatient clinic to establish her prenatal care. Several days later, she represented with an intrauterine infection, fetal distress, an emergent Cesarean and a dead newborn. All fingers pointed at me, and my waning obstetrical skills, for missing the warning signs days earlier. *Res ipsa loquitur*, as the lawyers say.

The resulting medical negligence lawsuit looked to be a slam dunk. The university planned to cut me loose, leaving me individually libel, because of what they described as callous indifference. Only two people believed that the case may not as open and shut as it appeared; myself and my lawyer, Rosemary Winslow. The background provided by the two drifters could not be confirmed. They revealed a level of medical sophistication which failed to match their dull and pitiful presentation. With Rosemary's help, I tracked the drifters' trail of hideous criminality.

It cost me a drugging and near fatal beating in Lake Charles, Louisiana, but Paris and Hector Laveau were exposed. The daughter and son of an infamous Cajun Voodoo princess, they incestuously conceived commodity babies from Korea to Charleston. They presented their feticide, in carefully constructed tableaus, to look like medical malpractice. A settlement was collected, and Hector and Paris moved onto the next unsuspecting community and a resumption of her menstrual cycling. Without Rosemary's help, and a few lucky breaks, their unimaginable crimes would have continued until Paris' ovaries ran out of eggs.

Rosemary cornered the Laveaus at one of their depositions and, at long last, they were caged, like the hideous beasts they were. Their lawyer dropped the lawsuit without ever realizing how close he'd come to ineffable wickedness. Without Rosemary, their negligence lawsuit would've ruined me both professionally and financially. The lawsuit challenged one of the few things left to me. Professionally, I was redeemed. Whether the Medical University of South Carolina felt the same way was an unresolved question.

On the same night that Paris and Hector Laveau showed up in my life, I staffed an emergency Cesarean on a Hispanic woman named Ramirez. Her baby's umbilical cord fell out during labor. We handled the emergency perfectly. One of the nurses elevated the baby's head off the cord and Ms. Ramirez was on the operating table in minutes. Obstetrically, we were ready to go. However, the anesthesia attending never showed up, and the senior anesthesia resident, Arthur Crumpler, refused to intubate the patient. As Crumpler waited for his attending to arrive, we listened to the fetal heart rate chronicle the baby's loss of oxygen and future. Ms. Ramirez's baby girl remains unfeeling and unblinking in our hospital's neonatal intensive care unit. She'll remain attached to life supporting tubes and wires until the day she dies.

As we waited, I pleaded, demanded, berated and belittled Arthur Crumpler's lack of action. It was simply an unethical failure to provide a duty in the face of a life-threatening emergency. Following the case, I documented Crumpler's and anesthesia's failure in the medical record as the direct cause of the newborn's catastrophic brain injury. Crumpler stood behind an anesthesia department policy that residents were not allowed to intubate in the absence of an attending anesthesiologist.

I took the fight directly to the anesthesia department chairman, Dr. Kenny Leslie. Leslie gave me nothing but double talk and eventually asked Dean Shriver to intervene. The Dean was supportive of staffing changes that would improve the obstetrical anesthesia service. However, these changes would need to wait until several new anesthesiologists could be hired to cover a long-anticipated expansion of the main operating rooms. The Dean couldn't tell me when that might be. I'd heard more than my fair share of false promises from hospital administration, and I have a good sense of when I'm being played. I tired of their excuses, I didn't believe the promises, so I kept raising sand.

At some point, I went too far, and Dr. Leslie and Dean Shriver initiated a Peer Review complaint against me. The bad outcome of the Ramirez case was regrettable, but rules were rules. My behavior towards Arthur Crumpler, and my inflammatory documentation of the case, sealed my fate. The Dean suspended me from the only job I'd ever known with a recommendation to terminate.

Next week, the Medical University Board of Trustees would hear my Peer Review appeal. They would decide my academic future. I didn't fault the medical university for being tired of my act. To be honest, I thought my act was tired. Still, I struggled with a lot of unanswered questions. If they upheld my termination from the medical staff, what would I do? Where would I go? What would happen to my relationship with Rosemary Winslow? I surprised myself that I cared most about the answer to that last question.

My career and life stood at a crossroads. Important choices needed to be made. I decided to take a day for myself.

Charleston is blessed with more than its fair share of sunny and crisp autumn weather. Today was a sapphire jewel of a perfect October day along the South Carolina coast. The Eastern European term is "gypsy summer," which we didn't deserve, but had become accustomed. Being marsh-born, I instinctively knew this would be one of the last opportunities for a beautiful beach day until April or May. Sullivan's Island was the closest. The high sun and crystalline Wedgewood sky made it unseasonably warm, but comfortable, compared to the mid-summer sear. The honey-coated sun and riffling sea-breezes made the beach a perfect wellness retreat. My mind was tied in knots and needed to unravel. A day at Sullivan's Island wouldn't solve my problems, but it couldn't hurt.

I unfolded a beach chair on an uncrowded stretch of sand near a wash. I tried out the ocean for a few minutes, but a stinging chill had replaced the bath tub temperatures of high summer. The waves were breaking sideways against the disappearing beach; cresting too close to shore for good body surfing. I returned to my beach chair. The sun and wind made a towel unnecessary. I pulled my Seton Hall baseball cap down low, shielding my eyes.

I slumped half-awake in my chair. Advancing micro surf periodically washed over my feet. I imagined I could perceive a pattern, but each time I anticipated another wash, and receding sand around my feet, I was proven wrong. I smiled at my naivety. The interplay of the sun, moon, wind and waves was far more complex than anything I could decipher. I was okay with that. I relaxed and allowed all five of my senses to be rewarded.

Besides the warmth of the sun against my skin, I could feel the salt encrusted hairs on my legs and chest being ruffled by the gentle breeze off the ocean. In my ears, I could hear the rhythm being beaten out by the waves slapping against the sand and the melody of children's laughter drifting on the wind from down the beach. A little girl in white linen and lace spun in circles on the sand, while her father wrangled a kite bouncing around the sky. For just a second, I caught the smell of a thick sirloin grilling over charcoal on the sun-porch of one of the beach houses across the dunes. Two college-aged girls walking down the beach in one size too small bikinis, and the taste of a cold Abita Purple Haze beer I'd hidden in my beach bag, made for just about a perfect afternoon on the island.

I allowed myself to become caught up in fanciful thinking. I imagined, or perhaps fanaticized, that the dismissal of the Laveaus' malpractice suit against the University would somehow sway the Board of Trustees. I'd been identified in the *Post and Courier* as being responsible for exposing the stomach-turning truth of the Laveaus. Their serial feticide had rapidly become a national story. Paris Laveau's incestuous children had been self-aborted in exchange for a cash pay-out. Incest is one of the oldest cultural taboos. There're some isolated and inbred countries that struggle with the idea of third degree relatives, but there isn't any debate about a relationship between brother and sister.

The Laveaus were the most unsettling thing that had happened in Charleston since the Operation Jackpot drug smuggling busts. I wondered what were the chances that one person would become so deeply involved in both. The blue hairs south of Broad Street got the vapors when they heard the Laveau story. The Saint Cecelia Society members were simultaneously titillated and aghast. Charleston's politically savvy D.A. was going to ride the case all the way to the Governor's mansion. Paris and Hector Laveau now shared the podium with Pee Wee Gaskins as the most notorious killers in South Carolina history.

Each news cycle brought new revelations, and salacious details, of the Laveaus' inhuman behavior. I became a local celebrity. That had to count for something. Rosemary Winslow believed that my celebrity would help me with my Peer-Review suspension, and upcoming Board of Trustees appeal. It's difficult to fire the local hero. At Rosemary Winslow's insistence, I'd done multiple newspaper and magazine interviews, and had been on local television several times already. I didn't particularly enjoy these publicity events, but I didn't want to argue with Rosemary. Even if it didn't sway the MUSC Board of Trustees, it was helping to rebuild an ego that had taken a lot of hits over the past two years.

In my fantasy, I would receive an apologetic letter from the hospital lawyer, Vincent Bellizia, announcing the dismissal of the Peer-Review complaint. I would be excused from my appearance before the Board of Trustees. I would receive a heartfelt thank you note from the University. In reality, I knew no such letter was coming.

Setting fantasy aside, I spent the next hour on the beach trying to sort out fact from fiction. There wasn't going to be any last second reprieve. Next week, I would have to sit before the Board of Trustees and answer for my actions during the Ramirez Cesarean. For the past three months, I had been startled out of a deep sleep, once or twice a week , by nightmares of Ms. Ramirez's prolapsed umbilical cord and emergency delivery. The background images were unclear, but the auditory never changed. I would hear a nurse's voice counting off the minutes, while the unmistakable beeping of a fetal heart rate monitor trailed off from normal, to slow, to agonal and then absent. As the fetal heart tones disappeared, I would be jolted back to wakefulness with cold sweat on my neck and searching for breath.

Back to reality, however, the Board of Trustees wasn't going to care that the anesthesia attending didn't show up until it was too late. They weren't going to care that the illegal brown-skinned baby in the NICU would never be able to control its' own drool. They certainly weren't going to care about my nightmares. They would care that I'd lost my religion on a pathetic anesthesia resident. They would care about the inflammatory language that I'd used in my delivery note.

Mostly, they would care about the fact that I'd fucked with their plans to expand the number of operating room, and I'd disrespected the Dean.

As much as everyone seemed to think I should, I didn't feel bad about any of it. More than anything else, I was pissed at being hung out to dry over the Ramirez delivery. What had happened to her baby was completely foreseeable and preventable. The Medical University of South Carolina did not have dedicated anesthesia coverage assigned to the Labor and Delivery Unit. The residents, who were assigned, had to call for anesthesia attending back up from the main operating rooms whenever an emergency occurred. It was an awkward arrangement for anesthesia coverage with more holes than Swiss cheese and a vestige of previously segregated obstetrical services.

A high acuity obstetrical service like ours demanded a dedicated anesthesia attending. Good medical care demanded it, and the Dean, who was an anesthesiologist, knew it. What made my conflict with the Dean both understandable, and simultaneously unresolvable, was articulated years ago by "Deep Throat." Just follow the money. Dedicated anesthesia coverage for Labor and Delivery would require several full-time equivalent salaries. Those salaries were needed to staff the on-going expansion of the main operating rooms. A main operating room churning out endless appendectomies, cholecystectomies, cardiac revascularizations, bowel resections and cancer debulking generated more profit in a day than epidurals and Cesareans generated in a week.

The outcome of next week's Board meeting was not a mystery to me. I'd read the updated Hippocratic Oath that came with an asterisk at the bottom mentioning financial exigencies. I knew exactly what Dr. Leslie and the Dean were going to say. I'd screwed with a lot more than the Dean's sense of order. I'd screwed with the university's fiscal solvency. That was the transgression the Board of Trustees understood best. It didn't take a genius to know how things would go down.

My day with the Board of Trustees would be a far different sensory experience than my visit to Sullivan's Island. At the end of the day, I'm a trouble maker. I knew it, and the Board of Trustees certainly knew it. There isn't anything in the definition of trouble maker that is qualified by whether you're right. Rosemary believed that righteousness made a difference, but she is a lawyer, and they're taught to think that way.

I'd been in this spot before. I'd seen up close what can happen when you throw a monkey wrench into the gears of the money-making machine. Plenty of well-intentioned trouble makers had been grist for the mill before me, and plenty would follow. It's foolish to get this close to the remorseless maw of what I knew to be a bureaucratic and voracious meat grinder. How could I have not seen this coming?

How things were going to go before the Board of Trustees was as certain as another wave breaking at my feet. The Board of Trustees already had the answers to the questions that were important to them. I wish I knew the answers to the questions that were important to me.

When my cell phone rang I had no interest in answering. It insisted seven or eight times before I finally picked it up. As soon as I flipped it open I realized I'd made a mistake.

Chapter 2.
TOMMY PETRUS

Becky Nida, my administrative assistant, wanted to let me know that the department chairman, Dr. Tommy Petrus, was hoping to talk with me. It was a conversation that I'd been dreading. I told Becky that I'd come by the office tomorrow and asked her to set up an appointment. I'd known Tommy Petrus as a mentor from the time I'd been a resident. He'd gone to Duke to be their Vice-Chairman which we all believed to be field training for the inevitable call back home. When the Dean finally fired our former chairman, his replacement was a no-brainer. Tommy was a breath of fresh air following the lethargy of the Templeton years. Under Tommy's leadership, Ob-Gyn was enjoying a re-birth of respect and university support.

Tommy knew about every meeting I had with anesthesia. He understood that anesthesia coverage needed to be upgraded. Tommy and I had an unwritten working relationship. With Tommy's tacit approval I did much of the department's dirty work. My role was to be the shock troops when there were inter-departmental wars to be waged. In both high school and college, I'd been a champion debater. When I got fired up, I didn't mind going toe-to-toe with anyone. I relished the opportunity to loudly point out empty promises, illogical arguments or hypocrisy and I was relentless. I specialized in a mocking tone that most people found unbearable. The more exasperating, the more concessions Tommy could win at the negotiating table. On more than one occasion, Tommy promised to simply keep me out of somebody's office if we could just get an agreement on one thing or another.

Tommy had been heavily invested in my battle with Dr. Leslie and the anesthesia department. The up side was high. Tommy wanted dedicated anesthesia coverage for Labor and Delivery and didn't want

Obstetrics and Gynecology to pay for it. Tommy and I both believed we had the upper hand. We'd been decrying the inadequacy of our anesthesia coverage for years. We previously warned Dr. Leslie about the potential for just such a tragedy. Sometimes, however, the tide of battle doesn't go your way. Once the Dean got involved, Tommy realized the battle was unwinnable. He advised me to drop it, without telling me that I had to. He knew that I wouldn't. I should have known better.

Tommy congratulated me on the resolution of the Laveau lawsuit. He told me that I'd looked good on Channel 5. Tommy was interested in what really happened down in Lake Charles. I gave him the Cliff Notes version. I could tell we were in the middle of some painful small talk. I opined that maybe my newfound celebrity from exposing the Laveaus might help me with the Board of Trustees. Tommy said he was glad that I brought that up.

"It can't hurt, Declan, but I don't think it's going to be enough."

Tommy told me that he'd met with the Chair of the Peer Review Committee a couple of days ago. Based on that conversation, Tommy was pessimistic about the outcome of my appeal to the Board of Trustees despite my recent legal success. He'd put his finger on the pulse and determined that nobody on the Board was interested in either my detective work or discussing anesthesia coverage. My insubordination to the Dean and the malpractice risk that I'd created for the hospital trumped those issues.

Tommy had also talked twice with Dean Shriver. If I admitted my sins to Dean Shriver and asked for forgiveness, Tommy believed I'd be able to save my career. The Dean wanted the anesthesia issue set aside until the College of Medicine had the resources to resolve it properly. Dean Shriver expected me to grovel a little bit before he would be magnanimous. Despite Tommy's conviction, I knew in my heart that groveling would only delay the dagger insertion until I was safely out of the publicity spotlight.

"I appreciate what you've done, Tommy, but I'm not doing that. I'm right about the deficiencies in our anesthesia coverage. My gosh, you know it too. Sooner or later, lack of full-time coverage will jump up and bite us in the butt again. Shiver and Leslie are just trying to sweep this under the rug, so they can get the new operating rooms on line. Once again, OB ends up getting the shit end of the stick. I just don't see the reason to roll over, and go belly up, when we're in the right."

"Sometimes you just have to survive to fight another day."

"I have no illusions that my meeting with the Board of Trustees is going to be anything other than my long overdue comeuppance."

"Don't take offense, but the reason to go belly up is to keep the Board of Trustees from eviscerating you. That's what's going to happen if this comes before them. I can set up a meeting with the Dean this afternoon. If you're contrite, we can make the Board meeting disappear. There are things that we need to get done around here and I need you to help do them. They won't get done if you're working on an Indian reservation in Tuba City, Arizona."

It occurred to me that people always say "don't take offense" right before they say something offensive. I looked at the floor and let out a sigh.

"They're going to do whatever they feel like doing. Going into Shriver's office, and begging for my job, isn't going to save my career. If they want to take my head, they're going to have to do it in the bright light of day. When it happens, I want to be standing on my on my own two feet. I'm not getting down on my knees in front of those treacherous bastards."

Tommy looked at me like I was crazy. He had no frame of reference for what he was dealing with. Tommy was at Duke when I last went to the President's office. I'd been called in to account for myself , when Helene Eastland and I fled to Garden City to keep her from being involuntarily admitted to the State Mental Hospital. I knew exactly what to expect sitting across an oval mahogany table from hypocritical pricks with unrestrained power.

There was a major difference this time. This time, I really didn't care.

Tommy was clearly irritated. I couldn't tell if his exasperation was over losing me, or the time and effort he'd put into lobbying the Dean. Tommy liked his work to be appreciated. Apparently, I wasn't being appropriately thankful.

I nodded my head as Tommy continued to talk strategy. I had no intention of heeding his advice. I realized that I'd lost track of the score a long time ago, a realization that came too late.

I understood the need to pick your fights, but, my God, sooner or later, you must stake out the ground where you're going to make a stand. Otherwise, you're doomed to being scattered before the prevailing winds. Sometimes you can't back up any farther. Tommy wasn't going to have my back in the coming fight. He'd negotiate for me, but he wasn't going to fall on his sword. For the first time ever, I wondered what Tommy might be saying behind my back.

I told Tommy I'd think about apologizing. I was lying. I thanked Tommy for his advice. I felt deep disappointed.

I left Tommy's office and headed over to see Becky. Walking down the hallway, I passed the Gynecology-Oncology team with students in tow. The Gyn-Onc attending nodded, but didn't speak. The residents looked away. The students were clueless as to who I was. I was a dead man walking. I hadn't been to my office in more than two weeks. Becky was happy to see me, and shared all the departmental gossip that I'd missed. It was remarkably bland. It dawned on me that Becky's gossip was so mundane because I was the subject of the really juicy stuff.

Nobody in the department was as smart as Becky. She managed my academic affairs beautifully in my absence. Multiple piles of papers covered my desk, segregated by subject matter. Becky distilled two weeks' worth of catch-up into about two hours of work. Clinical charts that needed to be signed, arranged from oldest to newest. Student grades that needed to be checked off, signed and submitted. Becky summarized each student's performance on the wards, on their exam and on their other rotations and ghost-wrote my resident evaluations. They only needed my signature. The other faculty would be horrified by this delegation of responsibility. The truth was that Becky did better resident evaluations than I did.

There were a few invitations to speak at various continuing education conferences or at other hospitals. Becky tentatively rejected a couple and had given the others a tentative yes. I agreed with each of her decisions. The *American Journal of Obstetrics and Gynecology* sent a letter acknowledging that my manuscript revisions had all been accepted. That was great news, except for the fact that I couldn't remember doing any of those revisions. Becky grinned.

The administrative pile included a letter from the Dean's office instructing me on where and when to present myself for the Board of Trustees meeting. It emphasized the seriousness of the allegations against me and the liability risks that I'd brought to the doorstep of the Medical University. The Dean was personally sympathetic, but these were issues identified by my peers as egregious. My future would be placed in the hands of the Board of Trustees. Pontius Pilate could not have said it more eloquently.

After working my way through Becky's paper piles, I gathered up all the Ramirez records and letters related to my Peer Review. Rosemary Winslow had given me precise instructions. She wanted to see everything I had regarding the Ramirez case. It was a small, but ugly folder. I knew what every piece of paper said. I didn't plan on dragging myself over those pages again.

I went by and spoke to Becky one more time. I thanked her for everything that she'd done for me. Her assistance had been indispensable. She wished me luck on Friday, and we gave each other a hug. I promised to let her know which way the winds were blowing. Becky told me that she had one more piece of mail, but she didn't want to leave it out on my desk. She reached into her top drawer and pulled out a post card addressed to me.

"This arrived yesterday. I was going to call you but then you said you were coming in. I wasn't sure what to do with it."

She handed me the postcard which was a scene from Bourbon Street at Mardi Gras. It had a Louisiana postmark. The scrawled inscription on the back was succinct.

"Fuck you, your nigger sheriff friend and your bitch lawyer. *Laissez les bon temps rouler.* Paris"

"Well, that's the cherry on the cake of my day. Nothing warms the soul like a note from an old friend."

Paris Laveau's escape from Sheriff Marcellus Greene during her extradition back to Louisiana had been front page news in Charleston. Becky understood that Paris Laveau was a fugitive.

"I wanted to tear it up, and not show it to you, but I got worried that it might be important."

"You're probably right. Let's put it in a manila envelope, and I'll call the Lake Charles police. They'll tell us what they want us to do with it."

"Well, I'm still sorry. I know it's upsetting to hear from that witch."

"To be honest, Paris Laveau isn't my biggest concern right now. If she wants to fuck with me, pardon my French, then she's going to have to get in line. Right now, my colleagues are a bigger threat than that inbred Cajun."

Becky nodded sympathetically. "I know everything is going to work out. I can't imagine things around here without you."

"Thanks , Becky. I hope we can work all this out on Friday. How's that for a Pollyanna?"

"Well, if things aren't going the way you think they should, then you call me. I'll come over there and give that Board a piece of my mind."

"They don't stand a chance. I've got the two smartest women in Charleston on my side. By the way, you might be interested to know that Ms. Winslow and I are going on a date tonight." I couldn't suppress what, I'm sure, was a silly looking grin.

"Good for you, Dr. Murphy. I'm glad. I hope this doesn't offend, but it's been too long. You need some companionship. Be nice and don't mess it up."

"Yes, ma'am. I'll do my best."

I'd been asking Rosemary to go out ever since the Laveau's arrest. She finally agreed, if I brought her the Ramirez records. She especially wanted to see the Peer Review Committee report. I would've promised Rosemary anything. I called and told her that I'd drop off the file when I picked her up tonight. I spent the rest of the afternoon planning the greatest first date ever.

Chapter 3
PEPPERMINT DIPPED ICE CREAM

Rosemary's apartment was in the historic Printer's Row building, south of Broad Street, where Charleston's Confederate currency had been printed. Its antebellum exterior contrasted with the sleek interior updated with a modern minimalist style. Rosemary's few furniture pieces were glass, chrome and angular. The only exception was a mahogany king-sized rice bed, a gift from her mother. The bed had intricately carved rice sheaves on each of the four posts. Rosemary's work area was dominated by an oversized stainless steel industrial desk surrounded by stacks of law books, notebooks, plastic covered depositions and piles of yellow legal pads with no apparent organization. I felt like the guy in the Beatles' song, "Norwegian Wood." I looked around and noticed there wasn't a chair. I placed the folder with the Ramirez records on her industrial work bench illuminated by a small library lamp.

We went to the kitchen and Rosemary opened a bottle of wine. The kitchen was Rosemary's crown jewel. She had a Jenn-Air gas stove with a grill top and a down draft. The countertops were five-star Italian marble and the refrigerator was a Sub-Zero. Rosemary's mother had a Ph.D. in American history but chose to teach at the high school level to remain a fixture in her children's lives. Rosemary's happiest childhood memories were watching her mom prepare family dinners. To Rosemary, the family kitchen was a holy place. Rosemary hoped to someday be as good in the kitchen as her mother. That information added to an ever-lengthening list of things I found fantastic about Rosemary Winslow.

Rosemary and I drove up East Bay Street on a festive, fall Friday night. The early evenings were still warm enough to justify a strapless dress, while the late evenings were cool enough to demand an arm wrapped around the shoulder. After months of blistering, energy sapping heat, the arrival of cool, crisp nights renewed Charleston's vitality. The intersection of East Bay and Market was the epicenter of Charleston nightlife. It was at maximum volume as Rosemary and I drove uptown. Lucky couples, and small packs of hopefuls, roamed in and out of the street from bar to bar. Carnal anticipation was the tune; over-mixed with a pulsating rhythm hammering out of the open doors of each public house flaunting the city's seductive virility.

Driving up East Bay Street, you paid less attention to the lights and signs, and more to the short skirts and long legs that were apt to dart or stagger out in front of your car at any corner. Navigating through crowded streets, I felt sad for the cautious loners and social dilettantes, chasing the promise of romance in the neon beer lights. They'd burnish all their worn-out lines, drink until they could drink no more, and exhaust themselves maintaining the forced smile and bravado that disguised their anxiety and disappointment. For most, Saturday morning would bring no comfort, only another small quantum of emotional wreckage to be packed away.

After crossing Calhoun Street, I cut across to Meeting Street and merged onto Interstate 26 heading north. That got Rosemary's attention who, so far, had not asked me about my plans.

"Where the hell are we going?"

"It's date night. I've planned some big fun."

"We're headed to North Charleston. There's no big fun in North Chuck. It's the land of the great unwashed."

"Don't be such a snob. Besides, we're skipping North Charleston and heading to Summerville. Cool weather means only one thing. It's Coastal Carolina Fair time."

"Are you crazy? I'm wearing four-inch heels, black stockings and a pencil skirt that I poured myself into."

"And I appreciate the effort."

"Thank you very much, but I don't think its appropriate dress for the Coastal Carolina Fair."

"No worries; as opposed to downtown, there's no dress code at the fair. You'll feel like a local."

"I'll feel about as local as a fish in a tree. The lack of a dress code at the fair is exactly what I am worried about."

"Trust me. You're going to have the time of your life. Wait till you see the chicken that plays the piano."

"Oh, Jesus."

The Exchange Club of Charleston started the Coastal Carolina Empire Fair in 1957 and it returns to town every October. Almost a quarter million Charlestonians make the trip to the fair each year to see the daredevils, high wire walkers, fire-breathers, knife-throwers, past their prime entertainers, and the "world's brightest midway." As a boy, you never forget the night you first saw a mustachioed dandy flinging knives at a scantily clad assistant spinning on a round wooden board.

The original Charleston County Fair started downtown on a parcel of land leased from the city near the Citadel across from Johnson-Hagood Stadium. In 1959, the new Coastal Carolina Fair moved from Johnson-Hagood to a thirty-eight-acre plot of land at Spruill and Meeting Street which had previously been a race track. The fair only stayed at the racetrack for a few years before moving to a site off Dorchester Road. Interstate construction required a final move to the current Ladson location in the mid-1970s. While Ladson is a time warp from downtown, the re-location allowed the fair to thrive with hundreds of acres and parking for ten thousand cars.

What Ladson really offers is neutral turf for all of Charleston's various gangs. The fair's assemblage included high-roller downtown doctors and lawyers, south of Broad Street debutants, dope-smoking College of Charleston students, Bible thumping Baptist College students, drunken Citadel cadets, Summerville middle-class families, North Charleston gang-bangers and poor blacks and red-neck whites from rural Dorchester and Berkeley Counties. The only thing scarier than the Coastal Carolina Fair patrons were the carneys who showed up on trucks from Florida to assemble the rides, fry the elephant ears and flimflam patrons up and down the midway. The rides became even more exciting when you considered that they'd been constructed by a crew of cretins whose last job was picking up trash along the highways of the Florida panhandle in orange jumpsuits. The Coastal

Carolina Fair isn't nearly as large as the South Carolina State Fair in Columbia, but it makes up for that with a seediness, and element of danger, that the State Fair can't touch.

"Wasn't someone killed at the fair last year?" Rosemary asked.

"Yeah, but it wasn't premeditated; probably deserved. Isn't 'he needed killin' still a legitimate legal defense in South Carolina?"

"I don't do criminal law, so I wouldn't know. But, I do know that there's a lot of shady stuff that happens at the Coastal Carolina Fair."

"Not that much. Last year there were only a handful of beat downs, a statutory, some runaways and petty pilfering. With a world-class eclectic event like the Coastal Carolina Fair, you must expect modest collateral damage. Sometimes it attracts a few ne'er-do-wells and profiteers. As long as you know going in, that nothing's straight, you'll get along fine with the carneys. Whatever you do, just don't take a swing at one of them. The carneys are like the Hell's Angels. If one's in, they're all in."

"I'll try to keep that in mind." Rosemary's disdain for the fair was obvious. "After dealing with Paris and Hector Laveau, it's such a treat to go to the fair, and rub shoulders, with all their goober cousins. I would've thought that you'd had enough peckerwood time in that bar parking lot in Lake Charles."

"Sulfur, not Lake Charles, to be precise. Plus, I'm taking my lawyer with me. I'm sure you won't let me get beat-up again." Rosemary wasn't in the mood for levity. Still, I knew it would all work out, if I could just hang on long enough to get Rosemary to the parachute drop and a peppermint dipped ice cream cone.

"So, back to my original question, how do you expect me to walk through the cow pasture they're calling a parking lot in these four-inch stilettos? I'm going to stick in the ground like a butterfly on a cork board. Barefoot isn't an option either."

"Okay, that's going to be a problem."

"No shit, Sherlock."

The shoe situation seemed like a deal-breaker. I hadn't anticipated footwear issues. I thought for a second that maybe I could win Rosemary a pair of fake Air Jordans on the midway with a ring toss. But, the chance of my winning them was slim, and, if I did, the chance of Rosemary wearing them was none. Amid an evolving panic, I had a date-saving epiphany. "I've got some flip-flops in the trunk. Nice ones."

"You know that flip-flops are tough to wear with panty hose."

The footwear issue was surprisingly complex. I didn't have an answer. Check-mated, all I could manage was to stare at Rosemary, a clueless expression on my face.

Rosemary stared back at me, completely exasperated. "Well, isn't this turning out to be a special evening. I don't usually shame myself like this on a first date, Murphy. You're lucky that I'm feeling pretty damn fierce after taking down the Laveaus. Keep your eyes straight ahead."

As I drove, Rosemary slid her dress up and over her hips, and pulled off her panty hose. After wadding them up and stuffing the hose into her purse, Rosemary gave me a look I'm sure she saved for hostile witnesses. "Were you glancing?" she asked, with an accusatory tone.

"No, ma'am."

"And don't ask me to ride the mechanical bull, or any other bullshit ride, that involves wrapping my legs around something."

"That's disappointing."

"Watch yourself smart guy. You're on thin ice. You know don't you, that the membership of the Exchange Club is all male."

"You're not going to bring political correctness into a trip to the fair?"

"I'm just saying."

"Hey, no matter how hard you try to avoid it, you're going to love the fair. It has a way of getting under your skin."

"I'm afraid of that, too. I suspect that the fair gets under a lot of people's skin, like chiggers or ring worm. I'm afraid that my lasting memory of the fair will be an itchy, scaly rash that won't go away."

"Very funny. Despite your poor attitude, this is going to be great. We'll do some rides, and at ten o'clock we'll go over to the Lakefront Stage."

"I can't wait. Which long-forgotten band from the sixties have they brought out of mothballs tonight? Herman's Hermits? Paul Revere and the Raiders? Little Anthony and the Imperials? The Original Drifters, which, by the way, is an ironic name since almost all the Original Drifters are now dead? There is a chance, that by the end of the evening, we will be too."

"Do I sense some sarcasm, counselor? Those are great acts. A few years ago, I saw Percy '*When a Man Loves a Woman*' Sledge. He was fabulous. No music tonight though. Tonight, we've got the funniest man in America, James Gregory. 'How far can a plane take you with only one engine? All the way to the scene of the crash! It'll make good time too. Will beat the emergency vehicles by thirty minutes.' I've seen him twice. James Gregory makes everybody laugh their ass off."

"He sounds like a hoot. How else can we disgrace ourselves?"

"We can skip the petting zoo if you want, but we've got to hit the Agricultural barn. That's where the chickens are. Besides the piano player, there's another one that shoots baskets, and one that kicks a soccer ball into a net. They also have the world's largest hog which is a must-see. At midnight, there's a huge firework show."

"We'll still be here at midnight?" The contempt in Rosemary's voice was undeniable.

Ignoring Rosemary's negative Nancy act, I continued, "However, I can't ride the rocket ship. It's embarrassing, but I get motion sickness. A couple of years ago, things went horribly wrong on the Swinging Pirate Ship. The people on the other side of the ship hated me."

"You're a manly man, now aren't you?"

"Whoa now, counselor. No need to get personal. We'll see how fierce you are after the parachute drop. That'll take some of the wind out of your sails. We've also got to do the bumper cars. I can't wait to get you in the bumper cars. You'll see then what kind of manly man I am."

"I look forward to the challenge. I hope your delicate tummy can handle some bouncing around." The condescension was dripping from her pouting lower lip.

"No need to give me that tone and that boot lip. We'll see when we get there. If you give the operator an extra ten bucks, he'll turn up the power. The bumper cars usually run at a four or five, but the knob goes all the way up to ten. When it's turned up to nine or ten, the cars really fly. Moms start crying and children start screaming. It's a rush. I'm Richard Petty, king of the bumper cars. I'm going to knock you right out of your new flip-flops."

"We'll see about that big boy."

We cruised over a rise on Highway 78. Showers fell earlier in the day, but the sky was now clear. There were a million stars twinkling brightly against the inky blackness of a cloudless rural night. As we cleared the rise, we watched the night stars descend and mix with the majestic aurora of the multicolored carnival lights of the Coastal Carolina Fair.

Chapter 4.
ROY BEAN

A small army of volunteers, in reflective yellow tape, helped us find a parking space in a field that was about an eighth of a mile from the fair. The past week of traffic had torn up all the grass. The rain earlier in the day turned the torn-up turf into slop. Here and there plywood boards covered the particularly impassable parts. We'd have to pick our way to the fairgrounds carefully. There wasn't a single landmark that we'd be able to use to help re-find my car at the end of the night. I retrieved my flip-flops out of the trunk.

"Orange. Are you kidding me?"

We walked in silence to the fair entrance, but with every muddy flop of her flips against her heel, I felt myself sinking deeper and deeper into trouble. A group of teenage boys came running past, all wearing ridiculous, tall, striped "Cat-in-the-Hat" headwear. Rosemary looked at them, shook her head and glared at me. Thank goodness the fair had my back. I could turn all this around in a minute, but I needed to find some big fun right away.

We bought a pocketful of coupons and headed into the heart of the beast. In rapid succession, we knocked out the Himalaya, the bumper cars, the sea lion splash and then the parachute drop. As Rosemary dropped ten stories, she had her orange flip-flops clutched to her chest and joy on her face. She wasn't even bothered by the pimply-faced "Cat-in-the-Hat" boys on the ground, desperately trying to see up her skirt. I tried to interest Rosemary in the fair's culinary delights, but she turned up her nose at the pepper and onion sausage dogs, barbecued turkey legs and fried Twinkies. Her weak spot was a fried elephant ear, smothered in enough powdered sugar to look like the final scene from *Scarface.*

We finished our elephant ears just in time to catch James Gregory at the Lakefront. It took Rosemary a few minutes to sync up with James' rural Georgia red clay twang. By the time James explained that there should be two story mobile homes, for people "whoooo've got muny, "she was completely locked in. When he took us to the church-sponsored covered-dish supper, and the controversy as to whether the ham was homemade or Kroger-bought, he had Rosemary laughing hysterically. It's a no-brainer really. If the ham's covered with pineapple rings and clove buds, it's from Kroger.

When the show ended, Angie Peel, Elizabeth Yung and their husbands approached Rosemary and me. They spotted us from the other side of the stadium stands. Angie and Lizzie were best friends and the odd couple of our residency program. Angie had been born and raised in Texas. However, her father was British, and Angie had somehow completed a Dallas public school education with a posh British accent. Listening to Angie's "hook'um horns, don't mess with Texas" bravado coming from a woman who looked, and sounded, like Lady Di in snakeskin cowboy boots was odd, but always interesting. Angie had a well-deserved reputation as being the hardest partier in the residency program. She'd been genetically gifted with a boundless alcohol tolerance. Stories of Angie drinking people under the table were legion. Angie reigned as the unchallenged champion of beer pong, or any other drinking game you could devise.

Elizabeth Yung was a second-year resident from Columbia, South Carolina, who attended the Medical University and stayed for her Ob-Gyn residency. Lizzie was remarkable for being the most highly functioning obsessive-compulsive that I'd ever met. When things were hectic on Labor & Delivery, there wasn't anyone better to be working with than Lizzie. It never got so busy that Lizzie couldn't keep it all organized. Lizzie's mastery of Labor and Delivery was obsessive-compulsive disorder at its highest iteration. I worried that, sooner or later, Lizzie would get overwhelmed by the chaos of the delivery floor. Obsessive-compulsive personalities can break down dramatically when their structure fails. In two years, however, I'd never even seen a crack. In fact, Lizzie was known for her clinical efficiency, which was surprising, since obsessive-compulsive disorder is usually characterized by its repetitive and time-consuming rituals.

Lizzie's constant companion was her red Day Runner which surprisingly was not in her hand tonight. Nothing demanded an organizational chart and a flow diagram more than the Coastal Carolina Fair. I'm sure Lizzie probably kept it safely snugged away in her purse, where she could reach it for reassurance whenever necessary. Lizzie's Day Runner was a magnificent compilation of circles, squares, arrows and triangles with a Crayola box of highlighting color codes. I've watched Lizzie study her Day Runner on many occasions, placing her hands on the pages for comfort, while her mind melded with the intricate maze of lines, shapes and colors. That red Day Runner soothed Lizzie's chaotic neural network in a way that clinical psychopharmacology would never be able to match.

Residents typically get to work about six in the morning, if not earlier, to round before the attending arrives. Rumors are that Lizzie gets up at 4 a.m. to make it out the door in time. I've been told that her walk-in closet is arranged by item and color-coded, in much the same way as her Day Runner. The closet is reorganized each night before bed, and then again after the selection of any clothing in the morning. Her daywear choice creates a flaw in the gemstone which must be recut to re-establish perfection. Choosing breakfast from the refrigerator creates another round of critical decisions and needed rearrangements.

Lizzie fully embraced her demand for order. She was the most upbeat resident we had, and unquestionably, the funniest. If her obsessive-compulsive disorder ever distressed or disturbed her, she'd left that well in the past. She liked to make fun of herself and loved to tell OCD jokes. Her favorite was why did Christopher Robin have hand washing OCD? He was always playing with Pooh.

Letting things get out of control was about the last thing that Lizzie Yung enjoyed. That's what made her friendship with Angie Peel so unusual. Angie's idea of fun didn't begin until things started getting out of control. Seeing Angie at the fair was expected, but it had to be a nightmare for Lizzie.

Both Angie and Lizzie were married to anesthesia residents. Angie's husband, Charles, and I were good friends. We played soccer together on the DoubleFootlings. I'd never played any soccer in my life and didn't even know all the rules. However, my size and reflexes made me a pretty good goalie. Charles had played soccer all his life and was an impassable central defender. He stepped up to every challenge. A half-lit Angie would come to our city league soccer games wearing provocative short, pleated cheerleader outfits. She ran up and down the pitch performing one-person cheers, chants, and tumbles during the match. The DoubleFootlings became used to the inappropriateness of the whole thing, and Charles seemed to get turned on by it. Our opponents, their families, and friends however, were always disconcerted by Angie's overly erotized cheerleading. Without a doubt, Angie got us two or three extra goals each season.

Jai Ho Yung was Korean, and I didn't know him as well. People said he was an excellent resident. He and Lizzie married during medical school and his devotion to her was unquestioned. Lizzie joked that all Koreans were OCD, and that her behavior was culturally acceptable. Lizzie claimed that Jai Ho would divorce her if she didn't stay obsessive-compulsive. "Whenever there's a mess in the house, Jai Ho starts pacing, sweating and burying money in the back yard," Lizzie claimed while laughing at her own joke.

As the two couples approached, both Lizzie and Angie were checking out Rosemary. A potential romance involving a faculty member was invaluable fodder for resident gossip. Lizzie fixated on Rosemary's oversized, orange flip-flops; a fashion incongruity that would set off urgent alarms in Lizzie's head. Rosemary could see it too. I introduced them both to Rosemary and told them that she was a friend. They nodded, but their silence told me they wanted more details. I wasn't forthcoming. We exchanged opinions on our favorite parts of the James Gregory show. We all agreed that Gregory was, indeed, the funniest man in America.

Angie finally turned it real when she asked me when I'd be returning to work.

"I'm not sure, but I hope it's soon. I have a meeting with the great and powerful next Thursday morning. I'll probably know then."

“This is about the anesthesia coverage on Labor and Delivery, isn’t it?”

“Yeah, I guess I’ve been pushing too hard. I’m told that I’ve been way out of line.” I turned slightly to address Charles and Jai Ho. “I want you guys to know that I don’t have anything personal against Dr. Crumpler. He just happened to be the anesthesia resident in the room. Despite what you’ve might’ve been told, this was never about him. The fact of the matter is, I couldn’t care less about Dr. Crumpler. This has always been about the policy that anesthesia residents can’t intubate in an emergency. It’s a dangerous policy.”

Charles spoke for Jai Ho. “Dr. Murphy, you’re preaching to the choir. We couldn’t care less about Art Crumpler either. He’s a dick. We had a resident meeting last week. Dr. Leslie informed us of policy changes. All residents except the interns are allowed to intubate in an emergency, as long as it isn’t a high-risk intubation.”

“Well, that’s a hopeful bit of progress.”

“Not really. When we asked for the definition of a high-risk intubation, we were given a short list. It was the usual things like abnormal jaws, head and neck tumors, severe asthma, or morbid obesity. However, the list also included pregnancy. When we asked, we were told that all pregnant women were to be considered a high-risk intubation. Intubation of a pregnant woman, without an attending present, would jeopardize our residency position. The mood was drop dead serious.”

I thought about that for a minute while Jai Ho and Charles waited on my response. “That’s a Catch-22 even Joseph Heller would be proud of. I’m sorry I’ve put you guys in a tough spot. That wasn’t what I intended. I thought if I pushed the point, everyone would do what was right. I was too gullible.”

“You don’t have to apologize to us, Dr. Murphy. We’re married to Ob-Gyns, so we have a different perspective than most of the other anesthesiologists. It’s a stupid rule. If we’re upper level residents, and can’t intubate for a Cesarean, then we’re in the wrong line of work.”

“Thanks. I appreciate that. You guys can play sweeper and stopper in front of me anytime.”

They seemed to appreciate the odd compliment. I turned my attention back to Angie and Lizzie who were still silently checking out Rosemary. "Great seeing all of you. I hope to be getting back to work soon."

Lizzie told Rosemary that it was nice meeting her. She hoped to see her again soon. It was an obvious fish. Rosemary just smiled and nodded, which wasn't the depth of information that Lizzie was hoping to record in her Day Runner.

Lizzie turned to the others, "I'm hungry, but I'm not eating fair food. Did you see those grills? The fresh peppers and onions are all mixed up with the ones that've been simmering for hours."

Jai Ho mentioned that there was a Waffle House just about a mile away.

"Wonderful," Angie chimed in. "Some bangers and mash would be brilliant."

"Really, Angie?" Lizzie said. "You're in the wrong hemisphere again. Waffle House serves smothered and covered, not bangers and mash."

"It just depends on what you see in your minds-eye." Angie danced away to a musical tune only she could hear.

After leaving Angie, Lizzie and their husbands, we hit the midway to try out the games of no chance. It turns out that shooting a clown in the mouth with a squirt gun is a skill rapidly lost in adulthood. After losing a couple of shootouts to the Jiffy-Pop "Cat-in-the-Hat" kids we moved on to the ring toss game which seemed impossible to lose. It wasn't.

Rosemary became fascinated with betting on the hermit crab races. Twenty hermit crabs, with numbers painted on their shell homes, were set down in the middle of a round wooden table. The first crab to fall off the edge of the table is the winner. Rosemary believed that she could handicap the hermit crabs. After five races, it became clear that there are several other less obvious, but important variables. Rosemary pronounced that the races were fixed. We moved on.

Instinctively, my eyes locked on the basketball game of skill. Two shots for two dollars. Sink one and win a small prize; sink both for a big prize. The game is designed to appeal to all self-imagined, former high school basketball hot shots. Simultaneously, the game is impossible for all self-imagined, former high school basketball hot shots. Basketball muscle memory tells your body exactly how to sink a shot on a ten-foot basket from ten feet away. It's a muscle memory that cannot adjust to a ten-and-a-half-foot basket, nine feet away. The geometric theorems that govern the trajectory of the ball in flight also don't hold true when the ball is overinflated, the rim bent into an oval and the backboard reinforced by cinderblocks. The carneys had scientifically made sinking a free throw no longer a game of skill.

The 20-something barker with his oversized leather jacket, and University of Miami ball cap turned backwards, had no trouble sinking the shot he'd already taken five thousand times that day. An idiot savant, when his eyes caught mine, he immediately knew my life's story. He would use my desire to impress Rosemary to his advantage.

"Hey player, you've made this shot a million times. Show your woman what a jock you are. You know she wants a big teddy bear."

Knowing better, I waved him off with a smile and we tried to walk on. The carney turned his back, sank another shot, then smiled back at us over his shoulder. "Maybe I can show your lady how it's done." The carnal undertones in his pimply arrogance were unmistakable to everyone within earshot.

My only two options were to punch him out or pay for two shots. By this time of night, especially on a Friday, the wholesome families had cleared out. The fairgrounds took on a decidedly edgier feel. A throw down would end up with me on the ground, behind the midway, with six hyenas on top of me. I reached for my wallet just as the dip-shit knew I would. Five minutes later, and down fourteen dollars, I found the rhythm and sank two straight. Rosemary and I walked away with a three-foot-tall red, white and blue striped elephant named Petunia.

"We've got one more stop."

"It's almost midnight. It's been a long day. A girl couldn't ask for anything more than a striped elephant, named Petunia. I'm good with calling it a night."

"Come on, just one more stop. It's the best thing at the fair."

We walked to the end of the midway, and across a small barnyard, to the Agricultural building. We headed around the long aluminum barn to the opposite side. We could hear the commotion even before turning the corner. On the other side of the barn was a small boxing ring measuring approximately ten by ten feet, enclosed in a metal cage. The light poles encircling the cage provided insufficient amperage, the murky brown light casting all the principals in long shadows.

Beyond the light poles, the boxing area was surrounded by a half-dozen fifty-five-gallon burn barrels. The burn barrels were open at the top, and two square holes had been punched at the bottom to feed oxygen to the fire. In addition, the metal plates around the center of the barrel had been pried open, creating vents that caught the wind to further feed the flames. The side vents created a cyclonic flow of air that swirled the fire and created intense heat. Virtually all the trash from the fair eventually made its way to these burn barrels. The hotter the fire, the more completely the fuel is converted to its elemental carbon form. The elemental carbon then forms tiny particles that absorb all light creating a black smoke against the sky. We approached, breathing in both the fire and soot.

The caged boxing ring was at the edge of the fairgrounds where the lights and colors of the carnival began to bleed into the blackness of the periphery. The heat, swirling fire and cinders, along with the scorched black smoke, brought images of *Dante's Inferno* to mind. The crowd, five deep surrounding the ring, were screaming and pumping their fists.

The star of the sideshow was a seven-foot brown bear, named Roy Bean. Roy was sitting on a stool in the corner of the ring, drinking beer from a bottle that he tossed after gulping it down. I'd seen Roy for years, or at least, a brown bear that looked a lot like Roy. Rosemary had a look on her face like she'd stumbled onto the backstreet debauchery of Hanoi, just before the fall of Vietnam.

It was a simple and perfectly constructed deal. For five dollars you got into the ring. If you could stay on your feet for two minutes you won fifty. Before each fight, the bear's mouth was muzzled, and oversized boxing gloves were strapped on his clawless paws. When the bell rang, Roy Bean would stand up, spread his arms and roar. The muzzle made the roar more guttural, and human-like, which drove the crowd into a frenzy. I'd seen more than a few hopefuls go to the canvas as soon as Roy Bean roared to life. It was damn impressive, even if Roy was muzzled, de-clawed and drunk.

If Roy's opponent didn't go down immediately, and leave a piss-burnt canvas, he'd have about one minute to dance around the ring like Mohammad Ali, while Roy played to the crowd. After a minute, Roy's handlers rang a handheld clangor which signaled game-on. With a ten-foot ring, and Roy's size and reach, it was easy for him to trap his quarry in a corner. One swipe of Roy's immensely powerful gloved paw was more than enough to send all opponents, tumbling ass over applecart. After each KO, Roy gave his defeated opponent a gentle hug followed by a well-earned adult beverage.

As the next up scrambled to avoid Roy's advance, the jeers and curses grew louder. When each wannabe was eventually knocked silly, the cheers and hoots erupted. It was bloodlust elevated to sport. It was primitive, feral and emulated the great Roman gladiatorial spectacles. Rosemary was utterly revolted, yet transfixed, as we all were.

Rosemary shouted at me over the din. "This is Lord of the Flies. How stupid do you have to be to get in the cage with that brute?"

"I've been watching Roy Bean knock people over for years. It's almost always the same opponent. Look around. What do you see?"

Rosemary looked again and recognized that the guy being dragged out of Roy's cage, the next guy up, and most everyone else surrounding the cage were Citadel cadets. With a big game tomorrow against Western Carolina, the Commandant gave the entire corps a pass for the night. They swarmed out of the Citadel gates in their butternut gray uniforms and headed for the fair. The Citadel is all about Southern machismo. Proving to your daddy that you're more of a man than he thinks you are. Legend has it that Brian Ruff, a Citadel All-American linebacker, once knocked Roy Bean down in the late sixties. However, since then, I'd personally seen hundreds of Citadel knobs, and upperclassmen, get knocked into next week trying to create their own legend. People claim they've seen an occasional mongoose of a cadet keep out of Roy's reach for two minutes and collect their fifty dollars. However, that was rare. The best chance seemed to be late at night when a drunken Roy didn't care that much anymore.

Every now and then, there'd be a newspaper article about Roy Bean and animal cruelty. The writer had obviously never been to the fair to see Roy in action. From what I'd seen, Roy never experienced any cruelty, and his winning streak rivaled the Harlem Globetrotters' dominance of the Washington Generals.

The best fights were when a burly, size-small cadet, filled with Napoleonic zeal , decided he could stand in the middle of the ring and trade with Roy Bean. Rosemary and I got to see one of those, and a couple of failed scrambles, before she grabbed my arm and told me that she'd seen enough Neanderthal behavior for one night. She was leaving with, or without me. I preferred option one.

"You know, that's me in there," I told Rosemary.

"What are you talking about?"

"I'm not any different than those damn cadets. I'm trying to prove something to someone who doesn't care. I must have a hole in my ego somewhere. I've been poking the bear over this OB Anesthesia thing. Next week, at the Board of Trustees meeting, they're going to ring the bell, and the bear is going to knock me silly. You can't beat the bear."

"From what I understand, you hold the high ground. Even those anesthesia residents think that you're in the right."

"Yeah, I know I'm right, but how much does that matter? You heard what Charles and Jai Ho said. They've already 'solved' the problem with their new Catch-22. Being righteous is a luxury that I don't have. People with power can be righteous, but if you aren't powerful, taking a righteous position often comes at a steep cost. Just like those amped up cadets, my pissing contest with the Dean is just me trying to convince myself that I'm more of a man than I think I am."

"Declan, you're more of a man than I've met in a long time. You proved that tracking down the Laveaus."

"That's different. My professional reputation was all I had left. I had to know if I'd really screwed up that badly. I had to know the answer. What's going on between me and the University has been going on for years. It's not about answering any questions, it's about trying to prove a point. I get sanctimonious about something and create a lot of fuss. When they tell me to sit down and shut up, I give up and slink away. I have a lot more respect for that little cadet who tried to trade punches with Roy, than I do for myself. At least, he didn't go belly up as soon as Roy got off his stool."

"I doubt that you've ever gone belly up."

"More times than I care to admit. Not next week though. I'm going to finally stand up and face the bear. I'm going to stand in the center of the ring and trade. If they want me to go down, they're going to have to knock me down."

"What do they want from you?"

"They want my apology first, and then my obedience. They aren't going to get either."

"They may fire you."

"They probably will. I used to consider that the worst thing possible, but it doesn't bother me much anymore. Even when you're thick as a brick, like me, you eventually get the message. They don't want me around anymore. I know a nice hospital in Sulphur, Louisiana, that could use an obstetrician."

"I know the place. It's a hot, humid and horrid little town. The biker bars are also a little rough for my tastes."

We both laughed. "Let's get out of here."

Finding our car wasn't as hard as I thought it would be. The Coastal Carolina Fair had proven to be a huge success, just as I'd expected. The walk back to the car was hand in hand. There was a smile on Rosemary's face that hadn't been there three hours earlier. I hadn't been on a date in years, but I think I did okay.

Rosemary tossed the mud-caked flip-flops into the back seat and sat Petunia up like a passenger. She placed her feet up on the dashboard, putting her magnificent legs on full display. With my defenses down, Rosemary began her interrogation. "Let's talk about this Peer Review thing."

Rosemary was familiar with the background of my Peer Review suspension. She couldn't imagine my receiving anything more than a reprimand for what was admittedly inflammatory documentation. As a lawyer, Rosemary always trusted in the power of being right. Reason would eventually win the day. Rosemary reminded me that she'd already studied my *curriculum vitae* for the Laveau case. I'd been on the faculty for more than a decade. An MUSC graduate with an exemplary record of achievement. Beyond that, I was now a local hero, who'd just saved the medical university several million dollars.

Rosemary was wrong. This wasn't going to end with just a stern talking to. I reminded Rosemary that I'd been in this spot before. Few good things happen when you're called up to the big house. The Old South plantation mentality was still alive and well at the Medical University of South Carolina. My fatalistic attitude irritated Rosemary. She had no tolerance for my whining.

"I'm not whining. I'm just being realistic. Things are going to go bad for me next Thursday."

"Don't take this wrong, Declan, but I have clients who've been physically battered, emotionally ravaged and financially stripped. They are desperate people with crushed spirits, little hope, and for whom, I'm their final option. I know real problems when I see them, and, frankly, yours don't measure up."

Rosemary rattled off, in rapid succession, all the reasons they should apologize to me, rather than the other way around. Her closing argument was impressive, but no one on the Board was going to have any interest in her points and sub points. There wasn't anything she was saying which would sway my upcoming kangaroo court, but her enthusiasm and belief in me, meant more than she'd ever know.

"Don't smile at me like that. I know a patronizing smile when I see one. I'll smack that supercilious grin right off your face."

"That'll help get me ready for next Thursday. Make it a backhand if you wouldn't mind."

"Seriously, you've got to stand up for yourself, not let these administrative pimps push you around."

"That's what got me into trouble in the first place. I made an issue out of the OB anesthesia coverage. The biggest administrative pimp of them all told me to drop it, and I wouldn't do it. I don't see how I help my position by going in front of the Board of Trustees and continuing to argue why I'm right, and they're wrong. They've heard it, ignored it, and now they're using the Peer Review process to punish me for it. I don't think I'm being passive. I just know that they've already made up their mind."

"What you have to say, is what the Board of Trustees needs to hear."

"Sure, I can go in there, and use my five minutes to light the room on fire with self-righteous indignation. What will that accomplish? The Board is going to back up the Dean. Nothing I can say is going to change that. I'm not going to lay down again for these guys, but I'm not going to waste my time arguing with them. Definitely not going to plead with them. Whatever they decide to do, I'll be standing on my feet and they'll have to look me in the eye. My objective isn't to walk out of that meeting with my job intact. My objective is to walk out with my dignity intact."

Rosemary wasn't going to give up that easily. "The Laveau case has got to be a game changer. MUSC had significant exposure. If you hadn't figured things out, Hector and Paris were going to walk away with serious cash. The Joint Underwriters Authority had already approved a million five in settlement dollars. That number would've gone up if the remaining depositions had gone poorly. Barry Banther knew he had the upper hand. He would've squeezed every penny out of MUSC."

"I know."

"You should also know that the Joint Underwriters Authority settlement approval was for the hospital only. They were prepared to cut you out. You would've been individually libel. If the Laveaus had pushed craven indifference, they were going to waive your Sovereign Immunity. If the University had instructed us to drop you, we would've been obligated."

"Yeah, I'd heard that. It kept me motivated. But, when things were darkest, what really kept me going, was knowing that you would've stuck with me, even if the state and university had cut me loose."

"You can believe that little fairy tale if it makes you feel better. I'm a lawyer, not a social worker. The day they tell me that the hours are no longer being reimbursed, I'm gone like a puff of smoke. It's a cute notion though. It makes me smile."

"That was a little sarcastic, wasn't it?"

"Look at you. Everyone over at the hospital says you aren't a very bright bulb, and then you turn around and come up with a perceptive observation like that."

"Okay, there it is. That was sarcastic."

"You're a god-damned idiot savant."

"What can I say? Even a blind hog can root an acorn every once in a while. But, one of those acorns is the knowledge that the Board of Trustees is going to do whatever Dean Shriver says he wants done. I'm having a hard time convincing myself that it's even worth going next Thursday."

"Don't be chicken-shit. What are you going to do if they vote to terminate you?"

"Nothing, and I know that disappoints you, but I've thought this over a hundred times. Why would I want to stay? They've worked extremely hard to get rid of me, not once, but twice! I'm never going to get a leadership position in either the department or the hospital. Since Helene died of HIV, our friends, my colleagues and even the residents have drifted away. Celebrate might be the right answer to your question. A better question is what I should do if they don't terminate me."

"I understand what you're saying, but doesn't it ruin your career if you get terminated? Are you willing to give all that away to those milksops?"

"Well, it doesn't look good on a resume, but it's not lethal. I'm well trained and, as you said, I've got a good *curriculum vitae*. I'll find something. I've got friends all over the country. They'd go to bat for me. If I can't find anything academic, I could do private practice. Lots of places need somebody. I'm not above trading prenatal care for a sack of corn, a couple of live chickens or an oil change. To tell you the truth, it's almost an exciting prospect."

"You can't go back to Lake Charles, though."

"No, definitely not. I was bullshitting about Lake Charles. I'm never going back to that suppurative boil of a city."

Chapter 5.
BOARD OF TRUSTEES

Rosemary insisted on accompanying me to the Board of Trustees meeting. On one hand, I didn't want Rosemary to see what I knew was going to happen at the Board meeting. On the other hand, I embraced any opportunity to be with her. I counted the Board meeting as our second date. Rosemary dressed in another of her magnificent black pencil skirts with a white silk blouse and a Navaho silver and turquoise squash-blossom necklace. She completed the outfit with an immaculate white leather jacket with a Nehru collar. Rosemary's fashion sense was exquisite. She must be fabulous in front of a jury. I'd believe anything she said.

I picked her up at eight thirty. I decided to make one last effort to dissuade her. "Look at you. All dressed up, but no place to go."

"You think I'm not going to this Board of Trustees meeting? I took the day off. I wouldn't miss this for all the tea in China."

"I'm not sure if I'm allowed to bring a guest."

"I don't give a tinker's damn. I'm not letting you go in there by yourself. You don't have enough sense to go in there alone."

"I told you my mind is made-up."

"I know, big boy. All the more reason why I'm going with you."

"Jesus, this is going to be a long day. Do I have any choices here?"

"No." Rosemary's hands were uncompromisingly placed on each hip.

"I'll bring you, but only on one condition." The tone in my voice was more pleading, rather than the desired insistence. "You have to let me do the talking. It's my fight, and I'll fight it. Can I trust you to keep quiet?"

"Absolutely."

Rosemary and I headed over to the Medical University. The Board of Trustees meeting would be in the President's conference room on the second floor of the Administration building. Memories flooded back from the last time I'd been in that room. There was, however, one dramatic difference. Last time in the President's office, I was terrified and desperate to retain my job. This morning, I was certain about what was going to happen, and was at peace with it. I didn't say anything to Rosemary. She'd never accept that the outcome of the upcoming inquisition was unalterable. I didn't feel like being accused of cowardice again, especially by someone whose opinion I greatly cared about. Soon, I'd be called much worse. I wasn't happy that Rosemary was going to hear it.

Vincent Bellizia, the hospital's attorney, met Rosemary and me as we entered the President's conference room. "Dr. Murphy, Ms. Winslow, a pleasure to see both of you again."

It was the most insincere welcome I'd ever heard. "That's why I'm here, Vince. It's been so long, it's just inexcusable. If I didn't see you again soon, I wouldn't be able to forgive myself. How are the wife and kids? Give them my best." I tried to match Bellizia's insincerity. I didn't know if I hit the mark perfectly, but I was close.

"Declan, it brings me no joy to be meeting in this room with you again."

"I don't know about that. Time will tell. I know it didn't bring you any joy the last time I was here."

"Quite right, but this is an entirely different situation."

"Is it?"

"Yes, it is. The last time you were here, everything was queered up by Governor Eastland. He was out for your blood. Everyone was dancing to his tune. Several people paid dearly for not standing up to the Governor."

"It always surprised me that you weren't one of them."

"We all knew that you were being railroaded. That's not to say you weren't guilty of everything you were accused of. You were lying. We all knew it. To be honest, that episode did the university a lot of good. Our house had a lot of rotten wood in its foundation that needed to be replaced."

"Well, I'm glad I was able to help." I replied as sarcastically as I could. "Is it really necessary to do this all over again?"

Vincent Bellizia paused for few moments before answering. "This time you called this tune. This is about insubordination. The Dean is pissed. That isn't a good thing when you're an associate professor without tenure in an underperforming department. I'm sure that you don't want any unsolicited advice but being a little penitent might help."

"You're first instinct was right. I'm not interested in any unsolicited advice. Especially from you." I didn't know why I was even talking to Vincent Bellizia. My antipathy towards him made me splenetic. He was a weasel, but I wasn't smart enough to walk away.

"If I might add, people don't usually come to the Board of Trustees meeting with legal representation, although Ms. Winslow is excellent."

Just hearing Vincent Bellizia say Rosemary's name, while squinting at her squash-blossomed chest through his wire-rimmed pince-nez glasses, made me want to smack him upside the head. "Ms. Winslow is here as my friend, not as my legal representation. She's always told me how much she's wanted to see you work," I said, as derisively as I could. "She never gets to see you down at the courthouse. Don't disappoint her. She wants to eventually become a partner at the Holmes Law Firm. I promised that you'd show her how to expertly suck-up without actually getting down on your knees." I looked at Vince and waited for the insult to really set. Recognizing that Bellizia wasn't going to take my bait, I ended the conversation. "Okay, let's go in. It's almost show time."

Rosemary smiled coyly and shook Vincent Bellizia's hand. "I'm looking forward to seeing you work," she said, as primly as she could. We left Vince steaming. I couldn't care less. That Rosemary had fallen right in step with my belittling of Vince Bellizia thrilled me.

The Board members were seated around the grand mahogany table in the center of the President's conference room. They were joined at the table by President Charles Lockwood, Dean Shriver and a few other dignitaries I didn't recognize. The Board members were a collection of physicians from around the state, local politicians, prominent businessmen and a couple of community leaders. They were all white, politically appointed, and rarely did anything other than rubber-stamp the wishes of the medical leadership. The Board had very little accountability for the rising or falling fortunes of the University, so why sweat the small stuff. I also noticed that the current composition of the MUSC Board of Trustees didn't include a single woman. That didn't bode well for an Obstetrician-Gynecologist.

Sort of like a Senate hearing, there were chairs lined up behind the Board members. Those chairs were reserved for the knights, bishops and rooks. Vincent Bellizia took a seat behind President Lockwood. I noticed Kenny Leslie, chairman of the Anesthesia department, seated across the room behind the Dean. I hoped to see Tommy Petrus on one of the back benches, but he wasn't there. At the back of the room, three rows of folding chairs had been set up for guests coming before the Board. Rosemary and I took two chairs on the back row.

The first two hours were unbearable; a classic dog and pony show. A seemingly endless parade of researchers and clinicians presenting fifteen minute capsule summaries of how they, and MUSC, were going to change the world. A microchip for the retina that restored vision to rabbits, a raspberry extract with anti-oxidant properties that was going to cure cancer, a new vaccine for Dengue fever, a computer program that learned from its mistakes and would eventually become the best clinical diagnostician almost-alive, and, best of all, a new anti-viral medicine that could be impregnated on Kleenex tissues to cure the common cold. That's right. An assistant professor from the Infectious Disease division at MUSC was going to cure the common cold.

In no case did the evidence support the rhetoric. That wasn't a concern for the Board. This was the feel good, self-aggrandizing morning that would precede the serious bloodletting scheduled for the afternoon. Worse, after every mini-presentation, the Dean received congratulations from the Board members for his wonderful stewardship of clearly one of the most fabulous academic medical centers in the country.

During a working box lunch President Lockwood presented a Power Point covering the University's finances and benchmark activity numbers for the various colleges. No other way to describe it but riveting. After that, Vincent Bellizia announced that the Board would be going into Executive session to discuss disciplinary issues. A murmur of excitement circulated around the table. The part of the meeting they liked best.

Vincent Bellizia took responsibility for the various case presentations, each of which was followed by comment from the Dean of the involved College. The first case involved a member of the dental faculty who'd been accused of sexually molesting one of his patients. An assistant caught him red-handed fondling a woman he'd "relaxed" with an excessive amount of nitrous oxide. The dentist had been arrested weeks ago and had already been reported to the State Board of Dentistry. He didn't bother coming to the meeting. The Dean of the College of Dental Medicine said nothing, other than to reassure the Board that this was an isolated event. Everyone else in the University, and on the street, knew that wasn't true. The dentist was terminated without much fanfare.

The second case was more interesting. A microbiology professor ensnared by sexual harassment allegations. Bellizia made him sound pretty slimy, but they really couldn't nail him to the wall until the Director of the Gender Equity took the floor. The primary allegation boiled down to a "he said/she said" involving an offer of an outstanding student grade in microbiology in exchange for a graphic extra credit project. The student had no evidence other than her complaint. The professor believed his tracks were well covered. He also believed that his academic rank would buy him the benefit of the doubt. What the professor didn't know, however, was that he'd been on the Gender Equity watch list for almost two years. When the Director of Gender Equity began to itemize the dreaded "pattern of behavior," his goose was cooked.

Rosemary whispered, "I would've buried him eighteen months ago."

I reminded Rosemary of her promise to keep quiet.

The douchebag gave a pitiful, tear-filled response. His accuser, and the others, were just a handful of entitled students who were dissatisfied with their grades. He would not apologize for being a demanding taskmaster. He'd been a respected, and partially funded, faculty member for almost twenty years. However, now that he was aware of how small things could be misinterpreted, they would never happen again.

I promised myself there wasn't any way that I'd grovel like this pathetic pervert. The Microbiology Chair gave a brief and uninspiring defense of his faculty member. The professor's student evaluations were about average. Five years ago he'd been nominated for a teaching award. Rosemary leaned over and whispered, "I wonder if he's ever received a perfect attendance ribbon?"

I gave her the stink eye.

The Board terminated him as well. They advised the Microbiology Chair to be very careful with his discharge letter of recommendation. It was an interesting comment and it wasn't clear what it meant. Was the Chair supposed to make sure this incident was included or covered up?

Rosemary knew. "They're going to cover it up. They're afraid of being sued. They really don't have any hard evidence. That "pattern of behavior" stuff sounds pretty good in this little Spanish Inquisition, but out in the real world, it's not going to cut the mustard. A good plaintiff's lawyer won't have any difficulty squeezing a wrongful termination settlement out of MUSC. They'll write him a nice letter of reference so that he'll go away quietly."

I couldn't argue with her.

The third case involved a Urology attending who'd been cited by the Peer Review committee for repeated episodes of unprofessional behavior in the operating room. Dr. Fairchild lacked impulse control. When anything went wrong in the OR, he completely lost it. Anyone and everyone else were at fault. Both the anesthesia staff and the operating room nurses had reported him innumerable times. Despite multiple requests, the Urology department failed to handle the problem. Dr. Fairchild was both a curser and a thrower. The straw that broke the camel's back was an Allis clamp that he threw at a circulating nurse. It hit her in the eye, abrading the cornea. The Urology chairman gave a spirited defense of his black sheep faculty member. This latest misbehavior had really been an eye-opener. Rosemary laughed out loud at the unintended pun.

I shushed her, but too late. Every head in the room turned to look at Rosemary. "Nice work," I whispered under my breath.

The Urology chair continued after things settled down. "When Dr. Fairchild saw what happened to the nurse, and saw her crying, it was a transformative moment for him. He now knows that it's imperative he change his behavior. I would liken it to an alcoholic who's hit rock bottom. I would also like to mention that Dr. Fairchild is the Urology department's go-to guy for testicular cancer. It would be a real setback for both the department and the university to lose him."

"Did he just say that the medical university can't afford to lose its best ball man?" Rosemary asked a bit louder than necessary.

"Could you try to put a lid on it?"

"I'll try, but we're talking about possibly losing a top-notch ball man." Rosemary laughed out loud at her own satirical comment, causing heads to turn once again. I pretended I didn't know her.

The ball man did an excellent job of bootlicking; remarkable, because Urologists aren't known for their humility. They are the last of a macho breed of surgeons. When you can fix a broken ball, or make a penis larger and harder, you're pretty much at the top of the macho food chain. I didn't happen to know Fairchild, but to be picked from among all the other Urologists for this Peer Review honor could only mean that Fairchild must be insufferable. If I had a choice, I'd much rather be in an office next to the microbiology pervert than this, or any other, Urologist. After a few more questions and discussion, the Board voted to reinstate the Urologist with a letter of reprimand. The Board warned him that they'd have a zero-tolerance policy for any other unprofessional behavior, especially once they recruited another good ball man.

I thought that Rosemary might start hissing. Instead, she just frowned, and shook her head. She elbowed me hard in the side like it was somehow my fault.

Vincent Bellizia announced that the next disciplinary action involved Dr. Declan Murphy from the Ob-Gyn department. As he announced my turn, I looked around again for Dr. Petrus. His continued absence wasn't an accident. I was also the last "discipline" problem to be discussed. The order had not been alphabetical. In someone's view, the best had been saved for last. I stared at Vince Bellizia. I knew who my "someone" was. As opposed to the last time, when Laurence Nodeen rode in to my rescue, I held no expectation of a two-out ninth inning rally. Vince Bellizia was the other team's best closer.

Bellizia described the clinical events surrounding the Ramirez delivery with reasonable accuracy. He recounted in detail the conversations between me and Arthur Crumpler highlighting the various "threats" that I'd made. Bellizia left the outcome for Ms. Ramirez's baby a little fuzzier. Disingenuous, but I'd expected nothing less. I also wasn't surprised that no one asked for more clarity about the baby's status. They already knew.

Vince did me the honor of a Power Point slide show illustrating my post-operative note. That note caught the Board's attention. It also sealed my fate. Inflammatory was a modest adjective. He showed copies of various aggressive and accusatory e-mails I'd sent afterwards. He summarized the details of my meeting with Dean Shriver and Dr. Leslie, at which time we supposedly all agreed to cease and desist.

He followed with a Power Point slide of my letter of complaint regarding Arthur Crumpler. I'd sent that letter to the House Staff office. Moreover, I'd copied it to a long list of administrators including each member of the Board of Trustees. A slide depicting the chronology of events made it clear my letter to the House Staff office came after my meeting with the Dean. In all honesty, it didn't make me look like a very honorable person.

Bellizia continued with a summary of the sentinel event review. That report concluded that the outcome of the Ramirez delivery "was not anticipatable or preventable." Dr. Bokhanevich's absence was the result of an inexplicable failure of the paging system. Dr. Crumpler was appropriately following departmental policy when he determined that Ms. Ramirez was a high-risk intubation. Her safety would have been compromised by proceeding with intubation in the absence of Dr. Bokhanevich. While the outcome for the Ramirez baby was regrettable, the Sentinel Event Committee concluded that a maternal and fetal death would have been substantially worse. The report said virtually everything except "shit happens." Vince particularly relished adding that the committee gave specific recognition to Dr. Crumpler for maintaining his composure and high practice standards despite intense personal and unprofessional pressure from Dr. Murphy.

The findings of the Sentinel Event Committee resulted in the Dean referring the case to the Peer Review Committee. Vince brought up another Power Point slide that summarized that committee's findings.

Number one, Dr. Murphy had been abusive to an anesthesia resident appropriately following departmental policy.

Number two, given the airway concerns, Dr. Murphy's insistence that Ms. Ramirez be intubated in the absence of attending support placed her at considerable risk.

Number three, Dr. Murphy's record documentation inappropriately exposed the university to needless medico-legal liability with overly dramatic and inflammatory language .

Number four, Dr. Murphy lacked professionalism as evidenced by his bullying behavior in the operating room and his insubordinate behavior towards Dean Shriver.

Vincent Bellizia couldn't help but editorialize that Dr. Murphy was well known to the administration for being a headstrong clinician with a history of being resistant to policies which he didn't agree with. Dr. Murphy previously exposed the university to serious liability due to ungovernable behavior. I was a little surprised that he had the nerve to bring up Helene Eastland. Vince probably saw this as his last bite at the apple. Payback is best when served cold. Bellizia didn't bother to provide any clarification about Helene or my previous trip to this conference room.

Vince added that my departmental chairman, Dr. Petrus, couldn't be here today due to other clinical assignments, but wanted to express his support for Dr. Murphy. Dr. Petrus believed that Dr. Murphy was a talented Maternal-Fetal Medicine specialist, and important to the department's success. Dr. Petrus recognized that Dr. Murphy could be stubborn and temperamental, but, on balance, was still a valuable faculty member. Dr. Murphy would be hard to replace. Rosemary whispered something about damning with faint praise. I nodded my head without replying. I found myself wishing to be a good ball man.

Vincent Bellizia concluded his bravura performance by adding, that while I was currently suspended pending this appeal to the Board, the recommendation of the Peer Review Committee was termination. I could feel the wind escaping my sails.

Not a hand was raised, and no questions were asked. All eyes in the room turned towards me. For days, I'd been thinking about what I would say in response to that inevitable last sentence. I memorized a relatively mediocre and unrepentant speech. It didn't include any apologies. Now that the time had come, I didn't feel like saying anything. I wasn't afraid. I just didn't feel like humiliating myself any further. I was inside my own head when I heard them ask a second time if I'd like to address the Board. As I considered how to best decline, Rosemary passed me a note and stood up.

"In the absence of Dr. Petrus, I'd like to speak on Dr. Murphy's behalf."

I looked at Rosemary with an exasperated expression on my face, and then I looked at my note. It simply said, "Your metaphor is wrong."

"Ms. Winslow, this is not a legal proceeding," Vincent Bellizia replied.

"I understand that, Vince. I'm here as Dr. Murphy's friend, and as someone knowledgeable about these allegations. As you mentioned, Dr. Murphy is a singularly hard-headed man. I don't believe that he's capable of effectively speaking in his own defense. However, I feel that I have information which will be helpful to the Board and can illuminate this discussion."

Vince Bellizia looked around the table. None of the body language indicated a major objection to allowing Rosemary Winslow to speak. He didn't look at me.

"Please proceed, Ms. Winslow."

"My name is Rosemary Winslow, and I've known Dr. Murphy for the last couple of months. I'm a lawyer with the Holmes Law Firm. I was assigned to the recent Surrette versus MUSC lawsuit in which Dr. Murphy was a principal. In fact, I didn't know until today that the Surrettes' allegedly negligent care occurred on the same day as the Ramirez case being discussed by Mr. Bellizia. Unless you've been living on the moon, you've heard the name Surrette on the television or in the newspaper. The Surrettes are actually Hector and Paris Laveau from Louisiana. The media loves the Laveau story and I can promise you that it's only going to get better. Escaped fugitives, false identities, fraud and feticide are all headline grabbers, not to mention, incest. The Laveau case is a bestselling novel, a made- for- TV movie, if not a Hollywood blockbuster. When that movie is made, the hero is going to be Declan Murphy."

Rosemary paused to let that veiled threat sink in. "Declan Murphy is the 'hard headed man' who wouldn't give up on the search for the truth. Dr. Murphy is responsible for digging up the connection between the Surrettes and the Laveaus. He exposed them on his own dime and took a severe physical beating in the process. You would all be wise to visualize the week-long *Post and Courier* expose featuring the heroic doctor, Declan Murphy, who brought these baby murderers to justice. By the way, the same Declan Murphy recently dismissed from MUSC. Being the medical university's press secretary is getting ready to become one of the worst jobs in town." Rosemary had the rapt attention of every person in the room. Putting incest or feticide in any sentence will do that. Even more spellbinding, when you can put both in the same sentence.

With the Board now in the palm of her hand, Rosemary continued. "It won't take much digging for one of those reporters to uncover the Governor Eastland angle. I realize that our revered former governor is long gone, but politics are politics. Eastland still has numerous friends in the State House. Since you're all political appointees, it won't be hard for the newspaper to connect the dots. Once the stink of retribution is in the air, it's hard to put it back in the bottle."

Vincent Bellizia must be having flashbacks of well laid plans being derailed once again. He needed to break her momentum. "Ms. Winslow, that sounds a little bit like a threat. We're all aware of the Surrette litigation, and the role that Dr. Murphy played in getting the University, as well as himself, I might add, dismissed from that case. We absolutely appreciate what Dr. Murphy accomplished with this notorious case. However, these Peer Review complaints have nothing to do with the medico-legal case Dr. Murphy found himself entangled in. Beyond that, the notion that political influence is at play is preposterous. No one even remembers the abduction of Helene Eastland."

"Except for the fact that you just brought it up, and, if you thought that was a threat, then you really don't know me very well. Before you start throwing out terms like 'abusive', 'unprofessional' and 'insubordinate' you might want to make sure that you've done your due diligence."

At this point, Dean Shriver finally spoke up out of sheer frustration. " Ms. Winslow, I don't need a lot of due diligence to know when one of my faculty has willfully ignored my direct instruction. He just thinks he's right, when he's wrong, and he knows better than everyone else, when he doesn't."

"You're absolutely correct, Dr. Shriver. Dr. Murphy does believe that he's right. Most people in this room just seem to be concerned that Dr. Murphy is loud. What surprised me most about this case is that so little attention has been paid to whether Dr. Murphy is actually right."

Dean Shriver spoke up again. "The Sentinel Event Committee answered that question, Ms. Winslow."

"Did it?"

"Ms. Winslow, I think Mr. Bellizia mentioned at the beginning, this isn't a court of law. We're not here to re-litigate the facts of the case."

"That sounds awfully good, Dean, but before you take this Board somewhere they don't want to go, you may want to look at some of those facts one more time. They may surprise you."

Vincent Bellizia jumped in. "Rosemary, what surprises me, is that you've involved yourself so deeply in this issue. Does Henry Holmes know that you're here today? The Medical University has used the Holmes Law Firm almost exclusively for the past ten years for its medico-legal work."

Some of the Board member's heads were nodding. All eyes were now on Rosemary. Vince had just threatened her livelihood. You could've heard a pin drop. What Bellizia didn't know was that *sangfroid* was Rosemary's long suit. No blink of the eyes, no change in breathing, no shuffling of the feet or change in her perfect posture. It was impressive grace under fire. She smiled slightly and responded with no change in tone.

"Vince, that does sound a little bit like a threat. It also seems to strike a very negative note. To answer your question, yes, Henry knows that I'm here today. He understands that I'm here of my own volition, and as an individual citizen, to support Dr. Murphy. I'm not here representing the Holmes Law Firm. I'm also sure that Henry wouldn't expect my being here to adversely affect the business relationship he has with MUSC, if that's what you're implying."

"I'm not implying anything, Ms. Winslow."

Surprisingly, the Chair of the Board of Trustees spoke up and asked that Ms. Winslow to be allowed to speak her mind.

"Thank you, sir." Rosemary glanced down and gave me a wink. "When you strip everything else away, the crux of this entire matter is whether or not Dr. Murphy was right to insist that Dr. Crumpler proceed with the intubation of Ms. Ramirez. As a senior anesthesia resident, which he was, Crumpler can intubate as long as the patient is not at extraordinary risk. If Ms. Ramirez wasn't a high-risk intubation, then Dr. Murphy was correct in his opinion that Dr. Crumpler was performing beneath the expected anesthesia department standard of care. Crumpler negligently refused to intubate Ms. Ramirez. He insisted that she be operated on under local anesthesia. Really doctors, local anesthesia? We'll need to talk about that later."

"It's already been established that she was a high-risk airway," Vince Bellizia said.

"Don't worry, Vince, we'll get to that."

Rosemary continued, addressing the Chairman of the Board directly, "It's fair to accuse Dr. Murphy of being bullheaded and incendiary, but he's also smart. He anticipated that the Ramirez case and, particularly, his post- op note would be contentious. After writing his note, he copied the clinical records for himself. There's an interesting difference between the chart that Dr. Murphy copied immediately after the delivery and the copy that we paid medical records to obtain. The notation that Ms. Ramirez has a 'high risk airway' isn't found on the admission anesthesia records copied by Dr.

Murphy. On the medical records we received from the hospital, that notation is scrawled diagonally across the bottom corner of the anesthesia admission evaluation. It's in a different color ink than the pen that Dr. Bokhanevich used to fill out the remainder of the anesthesia admission note. It's also a curious coincidence that Dr. Bokhanevich's evaluation is the exact wording as the new Anesthesia department policy. Then again, maybe I'm just getting caught up in curious coincidences?"

Vincent Bellizia interrupted on behalf of the Board. "There could be any number of reasons for the 'curious' things that you're describing."

"You're right, so let's figure out what does explain them. It turns out that Sonia Bokhanevich feels more guilty about this case than many of the other people around this table."

"That's unfair, Ms. Winslow," the Chairman of the Board of Trustees said. "We all understand that this case had a tragic ending."

"We'll see if it's unfair or not."

Rosemary wasn't giving an inch. I thought about the Band's *Up on Cripple Creek.* Down in Louisiana, I'd sprung a leak, and Rosemary had mended me. Now, I didn't even have to speak, and she's defending me. Rosemary was a drunkard's dream if I ever did see one.

Rosemary looked slowly around the room, now in complete control. "I met with Sonia yesterday afternoon. I showed her the discrepancy between the two copies of the anesthesia admission record. Sonia unraveled like a pair of cheap Jamaican Espadrilles. Ms. Ramirez was a large woman, but Dr. Bokhanevich didn't believe that she had a difficult airway. She didn't make any note identifying her as a high-risk intubation when she admitted her. I want to say on Sonia's behalf, I have tremendous respect for her honesty. Before you try to roll her up, along with Dr. Murphy, you should know that her chairman, Dr. Kenny Leslie, instructed her to modify the medical records after the fact. Dr. Leslie, any comment?"

All heads turned to Dr. Leslie who was a back-bencher. At first glance, you could tell he was guilty as charged. Leslie did not have a brave heart and Rosemary could smell his fear. She took advantage of his reticence and kept the pressure on. "Kenny, feel free to pass the blame on up to the Dean, if that's how it went down."

Dr. Leslie finally stuttered out, "None of that is true."

"Are you calling Dr. Bokhanevich a liar?" Rosemary's mocking tone was unmistakable. I'd not heard it before. "I can't imagine what advantage Sonia would gain by lying about this."

"No, but it's not true. Sonia must have misunderstood my instructions."

"It was a pretty fortuitous misunderstanding now wasn't it, Kenny. The problem is, I don't think the Board will misunderstand."

"You're distorting what happened." Dr. Leslie now sounded far more plaintive than defiant.

"Well, I think we can leave it to someone else to figure out what you said, and what Sonia heard. Either way however, Ms. Ramirez was never identified as being a high-risk intubation before her cord prolapse. So, Dr. Crumpler had an obligation to do his duty, just as Dr. Murphy demanded. Crumpler's failure to do so represents a breach of anesthesia department policy, beneath the expected standard of care, unprofessional, unethical and, frankly, immoral. And, as bad as all those things are, none of them are as repulsive as the cover-up, and character assassination, that has gone on since that night."

Rosemary had thrown down a game winning slam dunk and almost everyone knew it.

The Dean was seething. "Ms. Winslow, you've clearly done a lot of homework regarding these allegations against Dr. Murphy. I hope that you haven't been billing any of those hours to the Medical University as part of the Surrette case. And, if not, I wonder if Henry Holmes knows you have been spending this amount of time on unbillable hours."

Once again, Rosemary looked down at me. I could see a sly smile cross her lips. "I don't think Henry cares about my hours. I resigned my associate's position at Holmes Law yesterday."

I looked up at Rosemary and mouthed the word "no." Rosemary gave me the safe sign with her hands. I don't think the gesture was meant to reassure me, but to warn me to back off and stay quiet. I followed instructions.

A still defiant Dean Shriver spoke again. “Ms. Winslow, I believe you’ll discover that you’ve made a terrible career decision. It’s hard to make it as an independent lawyer in Charleston. I don’t think many groups will be interested in you, if they hope to keep their MUSC business.”

A couple of Board member heads turned, surprised by the pettiness and vindictiveness of the last comment. Rosemary wasn’t rattled.

“I appreciate your concern, Dean Shriver, but I think I’ll be okay. I’ll be able to scrape together a few small cases and keep my head above water. It’ll be a struggle, but I believe that Dr. Murphy may have a strong civil suit involving a conspiracy to defame his reputation and deprive him of employment. He’s been subjected to Peer Review, suspended for more than a month, and as of a couple of minutes ago, the Medical University of South Carolina was planning to terminate him based on knowingly fabricated allegations. It won’t be hard to find people who’ll testify about the emotional distress Dr. Murphy has suffered over the past four months, as one university committee after another has criticized his practice and behavior. Sonia Bokhanevich will be one of them.”

Rosemary was now on a roll. Like a chess master, she could see the checkmate coming, a dozen moves in advance. Rosemary paused for affect. She inspected her nails and brushed her hair away from her face. She was preparing to deliver the *coup de grace.*

“I also met yesterday with Ms. Ramirez. It’s surprising how little contact the Medical University has had with her since delivery, even though her baby is still in the hospital. All she has is a pile of vaguely threatening letters emphasizing her responsibility for the escalating Neonatal Intensive Care Unit costs. It distraught her to learn that the Medical University of South Carolina mishandled her delivery by failing to respond to an obstetrical emergency. Due to her anesthesia coverage being beneath the standard of care, and the delay in starting her Cesarean, Ms. Ramirez must now care for a severely brain damaged baby. As you’re all aware, based on your multiple letters, Ms. Ramirez also faces enormous health care costs, not only right now, but also for her daughter’s entire lifetime. Ms. Ramirez expressed to me how much she’d love to have some help with this catastrophic financial burden. She expressed a good bit of anger that she'd been purposely drugged so that she couldn't remember the events surrounding her delivery. I didn't even bother to mention that her records had been falsified to cover it up. My suspicion is that these actions will anger a jury as well."

Once again, Rosemary paused to savor the moment. This time she straightened her Nehru jacket and smiled directly at Dean Shriver and Kenny Leslie before resuming.

"I believe that Mr. Bellizia can confirm for you that an angry jury often brings punitive damages into play. Those damages will be over and above what I anticipate will be an extensive and expensive life care plan. I'm honored to announce that Ms. Ramirez has chosen me to represent her and her child's interests in a complaint that'll be filed next week. So, Dr. Shriver, don't worry about me too much. I've got a couple of irons in the fire. My new little firm is off to a fine start. After sitting here today, I'm toying with the idea of having a boutique practice that specializes in cases involving the Medical University. I'm pretty sure that your operating room nurse, who got hit in the face with an Allis clamp, will be disappointed to find out that MUSC has lost interest in her humiliation and personal injury. Especially, since her assailant is the best ball man in the Low Country."

Rosemary was finished, and so were Vince, Kenny and Dean Shriver. The air was completely out of the balloon. Rosemary scanned the room for any rebuttal. No one raised their eyes to meet hers.

"If we're done, then I'll ask you to excuse us. I think it's time for me and Dr. Murphy to call it a day. It's been a long one, albeit, fascinating. Gentlemen, thank you for your time."

I stood to join her. Before we could turn and exit the room, the Chairman of the Board of Trustees spoke up. He advised us that the Board would continue to discuss my situation in executive session. However, he was confident that my continued employment at MUSC was secure. He expressed the university's appreciation for my efforts at exposing the Laveaus. He apologized for what was probably a misinformed Peer Review finding. He assured us that the Board was going to seriously investigate the charges that Ms. Winslow raised. He was concerned that I'd been misused, and the Board had been misled.

All the heads at the conference table kept bobbing up and down as he spoke.

"That would be nice, sir, but it's certainly insufficient," Rosemary responded for me. "Mr. Bellizia knows how to contact me."

We walked from the room hand in hand. Rosemary interlaced her fingers with mine. When we reached the horseshoe outside the Administration Building I gave Rosemary a huge hug.

"That was more fun than the Laveau deposition."

"I think you spoiled their party and saved my butt. Why didn't you tell me that you'd quit the Holmes Law Firm?"

"I don't know. I thought it might be a fun surprise. Plus, I wasn't sure that you were going to let me come with you to the Board meeting. I had to get in the door. I was afraid that you wouldn't fight back, even if I'd told you what I'd discovered about the medical records."

"Yeah, I would've. Maybe not as ruthlessly as you did, but I would've fought."

"Sure you would have, big guy."

"Whatever I would've said, it would not have been as good as the beat down you administered in there. I'm glad you're representing Ms. Ramirez. She needs everything that you can get for her. Her baby is in pitiful condition."

"We're going to get her a lot. By the way, I wasn't kidding about that operating room nurse with the eye injury. Is there any chance that you can find out her name?"

"I don't know. Maybe. I'll give it a shot."

"Thanks. I think we're going to make good partners. You keep finding me cases, and I'll be able to throw a few dollars your way."

"Sounds good to me. I'll make a great witness. I do have some concerns about working with a plaintiff's lawyer. I might lose my American College of Ob-Gyn membership card."

"Doesn't matter to me, I'll subpoena you. I'd enjoy treating you like a hostile witness."

"Don't worry. I'll cooperate. I don't want to be on the receiving end of what those guys just got. By the way, what did your note mean about my metaphor being wrong?"

"Remember, when we went to the fair, and you took me to that horrid boxing cage. You told me that you felt like the Citadel cadets being bounced around the ring. But, that metaphor is wrong. The correct metaphor is that I'm the bear. That conference room we just came out of is the cage. Those jokers around the table were a bunch of Citadel cadets without any hair on their balls. They're lucky that I had the big gloves on. Next time we meet over the Ramirez case, it'll be bare knuckles, and I'm going to beat them to bloody pulps. And, now that it's over, I want a beer."

"Okay, Roy Bean, I can make that happen. How'd you like to go to Carolina's for a celebratory dinner? I'll call and get us reservations for the Perdita room."

"I'd like that very much."

Chapter 6.
PERDITA'S

The only restaurant in Charleston south of Broad Street is Carolina's on the corner of Exchange Street and Prioleau, walking distance from Rosemary's place on Printer's Row. The seashell tabby building, which dated back to the 1700s, originally served as a cotton exchange. The intricate iron work balcony probably overlooked the waterfront before the eastside docks were reclaimed. Carolina's inherited the building following the closure of an iconic Charleston restaurant, Perdita's, in the mid-1980s.

Carolina's was a lively night spot for Charleston's young professionals. The bustling main room was fashioned into a bar-bistro with a black and white tile floor, a beautiful dark mahogany bar dominating the center space, and pecky cypress beams. Antique mirrors throughout the room satisfied everyone's need to see and be seen. When we arrived, I reminded the hostess that I'd requested the quieter Perdita Room.

Carolina's new owners respected the history and rich culinary tradition of the building. In addition to retaining several of the menu items that had made Perdita's famous, the owners also preserved an elegant Perdita Room which seated about eight tables. The Perdita Room had formal Queen Anne chairs, white tablecloths, imposing dark wood columns, and burgundy crushed- velvet walls. There were nights when the bar area was the place to be, but dining in the Perdita Room recaptured the sense of style, dedication to service, and intimacy that made the original Perdita's one of the best nights out in the world.

Gordon Bennett opened Perdita's in 1954. It soon became Charleston's epicurean jewel, and remained so, for almost forty years. While the culinary reputation of our sister city, New Orleans, flourished, Charleston drowsed its way through the first half of the twentieth century. After the war, Charleston's restaurateurs began to explore ways to commercialize the time-honored seafood traditions of the Low Country. In 1960, Perdita's received the prestigious Paris Medal of Honor. Only five other restaurants in the United States could boast such recognition.

Perdita's handwritten menu changed nightly. The techniques were high French and introduced Charlestonians to appetizers such as foie gras, escargots and truffles, and entrees such as Coquille St. Jacques, Tournedos Perigourdine and Chateaubriand. The French techniques, however, were never more exquisite than when married to Low Country ingredients, most of which were of West African origin. Perdita's mastered the art of culinary fusion long before it became trendy. Flounder, shrimp, oysters, scallops and crabmeat poured from the kitchen in savory sauces and fragrant papillotes.

Perdita's was elegance personified, but an expensive self-indulgence for a city still scuffling to recover from Reconstruction. There were separate waiters for the napkins, utensils, water, food, wine, and dishes. They re-folded your linen napkin every time you left the table. The waiters all wore tuxedos with service medals on their left lapel. The medal had an attachment for every five years of service. The waiter refilling our water glasses had, at least, ten years of service.

A maître d' stood about five feet behind the table. He directed every move the waiters made, anticipating our every need. His service medals represented thirty plus years. He stood motionless with his white gloves clasped behind his back while silently directing the entire orchestra with imperceptible nods of his head or instantaneous glances of his eyes. I couldn't imagine what might happen if one of the waiters with only five or ten years of service happened to spill a glass of wine.

Helene and I went to Perdita's on our first wedding anniversary, shortly before it closed its doors. I was bringing Rosemary Winslow to the exact same spot. My memory for a lot of sentimental things was poor. A failing I grew to regret more every passing day. However, I remembered every detail of the dinner Helene and I had shared on our first anniversary. Helene had the Fruit de Mer, a bouillabaisse-like seafood stew with shrimp, clams, mussels, scallops, salmon and yellow fingerling potatoes beckoning from a thyme-infused broth. Pale green celery leaves garnished the bowl which evoked an earlier era when celery was considered a minor delicacy. The best part of the Fruit de Mer were the grilled, butter-soaked crostini, essential for making sure that none of the rich, flavorful sauce made it back to the kitchen.

I ordered the Shrimp and Lobster en Papillotte Perdita. The shrimp and lobster meat were baked with lemon, butter, nutmeg, parsley and grated cheddar cheese, then smothered by a wine-infused mustard sauce. Perdita's served it wrapped in aluminum which the maître d' would hand-crimp into the shape of a swan. When the maître d' incised the aluminum clad papillotte at the table, the sealed aroma of the sweet seafood and savory sauce filled the room and your imagination.

The hostess took Rosemary and me to the Perdita Room. Anything close to the evening I'd shared with Helene would be a success. The hostess sat us directly across from a reproduction of Thomas Gainsborough's 1781 painting of the original Perdita which dominated the room. The original Perdita was an English actress, named Mary Robinson. She acquired the nickname Perdita after starring in London's 1779 season production of Shakespeare's *A Winter's Tale*. In December of 1779, Mary Robinson and company gave a Royal command performance of *A Winter's Tale* for their majesties, King George and Queen Charlotte, and their son H.R.H. George, the Prince of Wales. Young Prinny, smitten by the beautiful Perdita, began to obsessively court Mary Robinson. She finally succumbed to Prinny's royal charms and they began a brief, but scandalous, affair. The Prince and his Royal actress/mistress were relentlessly pursued by the English newspapers and scandal rags of the time, until an acrimonious break-up about one year later.

Mary Robinson appeared to be staring across the room at the reproduction of Joshua Reynolds' painting of Lieutenant-Colonel Banastre Tarleton which hung directly behind our backs. Tarleton, a British light cavalry officer, commanded the Green Dragoons during the Revolutionary War. After spending the early part of the war fighting in the North, Tarleton came to South Carolina in 1780. He served under the command of Sir Henry Clinton in the campaign that resulted in the capture of Charleston.

The British embarked on a "Southern strategy" believing there was more support for the crown in the Southern colonies. By controlling the South, they hoped to split the South away from the northern revolutionaries. Ultimately, the plan backfired. Despite his tactical successes, Tarleton's brutality turned formerly neutral Southern colonists against the English crown. Tarleton's lack of respect for the conventions of civilized warfare earned him the nicknames "Bloody Ban" and "Ban the Butcher." His Green Dragoon cavalrymen were referred to as "Tarleton's Raiders."

In May of 1780, Tarleton's cavalry came across 350 Virginia Continentals, led by Abraham Buford, at Waxhaw Creek, South Carolina. After sustaining heavy losses, Buford surrendered. Tarleton ignored the white flag and massacred Buford's men, stabbing the wounded where they lay. The incident quickly became known by the American patriots as the "Waxhaw Massacre" and "Tarleton's Quarter." The rallying cry, "Tarleton's Quarter" galvanized resistance to the British in the Southern colonies.

After Cornwallis' surrender at Yorktown, Tarleton returned to England, and became a politician in his hometown of Liverpool. Interestingly, on his return to England, he sought out and seduced the actress Mary Robinson with whom he had a fifteen-year relationship.

"So why did the owner name the restaurant after an English stage actress from the 1700s?" Rosemary asked, after we'd spent a few minutes considering our dinner companions.

"Actually, he didn't name his restaurant after her. He named it after a role she played."

"Which makes the question even more apropos."

"Mary Robinson's affair with the Prince of Wales was the talk of the continent, as well as the colonies. Her image was frequently engraved in newspapers that would've circulated in Charleston. At the time of the royal affair, the British were occupying Charleston, including 'Bloody Ban.' Legend has it, that this building was a favorite tavern and bordello, frequented by British officers who enjoyed the establishment's food, libations and ladies. The most beautiful of these ladies was the madam, who bore a strong physical resemblance to Mary Robinson. As a result, both she, and the establishment, came to be known as Perdita's after Mary Robinson's most notorious role. When Gordon Bennett opened the place in 1954, he named it after the original woman of the house. At least, that's how the story goes."

"Sounds like a lot of horse-shit to me. Let's order."

The new Carolina's had a very original menu, despite the homage it paid to the original Perdita's. The original Perdita's combined West African seafood traditions with classic French techniques. Carolina's new executive chef, Rose Durden, managed to infuse an Asian flair into traditional Charleston dishes. The thick walls of this small bistro on a cobblestone side street south of Broad had somehow managed to germinate culinary innovations that made the rest of the world stand up and take notice, not once, but twice. I ordered the Shrimp and Crab Wantons with a Lime Ginger Aioli for an appetizer, followed by Shrimp and Grits with Spicy Tasso Ham Gravy. Rosemary ordered the Carolina's Salad with Clemson Blue Cheese and then Jumbo Lump Crab Cakes with a mustard sauce and Spicy Chow Chow.

After tasting and accepting a delicious bottle of buttery 1986 Sonoma Cutrer Les Pierres Chardonnay, the waiter poured Rosemary a glass. Rosemary took a small sip and let it linger on her palate.

"It seems a bit tight. Let it relax for a few minutes and it'll open up beautifully," Rosemary said.

I nodded my head and lightly bit the inside of my lower lip. That might've been one of the sexiest things that I'd ever heard.

Rosemary sipped her Chardonnay and stared at the picture of Mary Robinson on the far wall. I decided not to mention the post card that I'd received from Paris. Talking about the Laveaus wouldn't accomplish anything other than putting us off a great meal.

We were honored when Rose Durden came out of the kitchen to ask after Rosemary. There's a sisterhood of accomplished women in downtown Charleston. Both Rose and Rosemary were members of that club. Rosemary introduced me, and I complimented her on our dinner. She thanked me, but I understood that she'd come out to our table to greet a fellow new-age Mason.

Chapter 7.
PARTNERSHIP

After Rose Durden returned to the kitchen I refilled Rosemary's wine glass. "Tonight, is a celebration. You were magnificent today. If it wasn't for you, I'd be out of a job right now. A toast, to the best barrister in Charleston. You saved my ass, not to mention putting those two sociopaths behind bars."

"Here, here," Rosemary said as she raised her glass. "Unfortunately, Paris Laveau has slipped the noose and is on the loose."

"I know. That bothers me a lot. Paris is a predator and has the survival instincts of a cockroach. I don't think either the Louisiana state police or the F.B.I. is going to catch her."

"She can't hide forever. The Laveaus are just glorified trailer trash. I don't know how she was able to get over on Marcellus, but she doesn't have the resources that are necessary to stay off the F.B.I.'s radar. Sooner or later, they're going to roll her up."

"I hope so, but I'm not so certain. Paris is an excellent chameleon, which actually makes her more reptilian than a cockroach. Sociopaths don't have an identity of their own, so they become great mimics. Paris doesn't have any internalized values to get in the way of her role playing. You've seen it yourself. One moment she's sniveling and trembling, and the next, she's chewing concrete and spitting nails. When I first met Paris Laveau, I read her totally wrong. I thought she was a battered spouse. Finding her isn't going to be easy. She's got a lot of tricks."

"I'm not as worried about her as you are. Somehow she got the better of Sheriff Greene, but I don't think there's any chance that she's coming back here. Right now, Paris needs a deep hidey hole. That hole is deepest in the bayous of southwest Louisiana. Coming back to Charleston only makes her more visible and vulnerable."

"You're probably right, but you should've seen the look in her eyes when you slapped her face. She hates you, and she hates me. Paris isn't the kind to forgive or forget a slight."

"When you're a lawyer, you meet despicable people like the Laveaus every day. With every trial, somebody new hates me. However, my experience with sociopaths is always the same. When they're exposed, their first instinct is to run away, and hide under whatever rock they emerged from. Sociopaths don't fixate on settling old scores because they don't have a conscience. They just move on to their next self-serving activity."

"You feel tainted just being around them, especially her. I'd be just fine if I never saw either of the Laveaus ever again."

"That's partly why they'd been so successful in bamboozling the legal system. Nobody wanted to deal with them. They counted on the fact that people would just prefer to pay them off and let them move on. You were the first one to sense that something wasn't right with the Laveaus. Moreover, you did something about it."

I shook my head and studied Rosemary's face. There wasn't a single line etched around her eyes. My mother told me that was a sign of an untroubled spirit. I knew my eyes did not return Rosemary's contented countenance. "Too much. You were right there with me. We found Dr. Gerrard together. You set up the deposition and drew them out."

"Don't be ridiculous. You got the snot beaten out of yourself. The fact that you were roached and steel-toed into a Dixie lullaby meant that you'd found the rat's nest. My private investigator hadn't found anything. None of us believed in your wild goose chase. To be frank, the narrative being peddled by the Medical University, and accepted by most, was that you were another over-inflated academic ego who couldn't admit that you'd made a mistake."

"Most?"

"I plead the fifth, and refuse to answer on the grounds that my answer may incriminate me."

"In the spirit of full disclosure, I'll admit that half the time I was looking for the Laveaus, I thought the same thing. I haven't been in a very good place in terms of my self-confidence. The apprehension that I was just too stubborn to accept that I'd screwed up was a constant companion. When you're angry all the time, you project those ugly thoughts onto other people. Not surprisingly, that doesn't make you either very believable or likeable. In case you didn't already know, that's the popular opinion of me over at the University."

"We all thought the Laveaus were a few bubbles off plumb, but that's a long way from believing the whole thing was pre-meditated. Maybe you had to be in a dark place to imagine that such a thing was possible. The suspicion that Paris Laveau instrumented herself to induce an abortion after setting you up with a scripted exam room visit is unimaginable."

"I don't know. Maybe. Nothing they did made sense to me. Their depositions were so perfectly deceitful. The sophistication of their lies didn't fit with the pitiable blue-collar personas they were trying so hard to sell. I expected that your investigator would find a trail of emergency room visits and minor skirmishes with local police. I believed that Hector had beaten Paris, after her visit to our Labor and Delivery unit, and she ruptured her membranes because of that."

Rosemary considered my theory. "What makes this so revolting is that would've been a happier ending to the story."

I grimaced at how hideous it was that Rosemary was right. "We need to stop talking about the Laveaus."

"Let's talk about happier things."

"Well, even though I wish it hadn't required my being stomped, I'm glad you came for me in Lake Charles. You were my angel of mercy."

"Morphine was your angel of mercy. You were working that pump pretty good for a couple of days. I'm surprised you remember much. I'd be having a conversation with you, then look up, and find you drooling on yourself. I'd heard about a drug-induced haze, but I'd never seen one."

"Those guys rattled my brain box pretty good. Some things are still a bit hazy, but I clearly remember being visited by an angel."

"I was there, and I didn't see one. It was probably a hallucination." We both laughed and took another drink of the Les Pierres Chardonnay.

I asked Rosemary if she was serious when she said that she'd resigned from the Holmes Law Firm.

"Of course, I was. What do you mean by that?"

"I didn't mean anything. I just hope that I'm not the reason you're no longer working at Holmes Law. I saw Henry Holmes come out of his office to congratulate you after the Laveaus had been taken away by the police. I thought that pretty soon, people might be talking about the Holmes and Winslow Law Firm." I was surprised when my compliment was met with a frown. "What's wrong? Did I touch a sore spot?"

"I've waited for the partnership invitation for two years. I was the senior associate but was passed over twice. I was more productive, and frankly, smarter than either of the other two guys who made partner. No brag, just fact. So, yes, it's a sore spot."

"What did they say to you?"

"Get this, they told me that Ashby had a law degree from Harvard which looked really good. I told them that your education isn't any better than what you understand. There was a bunch that Ashby didn't understand."

"That sounds like something I'd say. I suspect they didn't like that very much."

"They praised me for my hard work and effectiveness, but they had 'concerns' that I'm not a team player."

"What does that mean?" It was an odd question considering how many times I'd been accused of the same thing.

"What do you think, Declan? There are eight partners. All are male. You've been in a locker room before. There's stuff that gets said in the locker room that isn't meant to be discussed anywhere else. They're not comfortable with me a stool in their locker room. I'm not altogether sure that I fault them. They're right to have concerns. More than a few of them are unchaste. Single or married, it doesn't matter. All the degrees in the world can't wash the hound off some of those dogs."

Rosemary quieted and considered how far to go. "Henry Holmes is an accomplished man. He even has a generous heart. Unfortunately, his behavior is sometimes feral. I love to dress nicely, but I resent the fact that I receive more compliments on my appearance, than I do on my work. The last case that Henry and I had together, he told me at a break that a couple of jurors were checking me out during cross-examination. He told me that it'd be a good idea if I 'shook my moneymaker' a little more the next time I went up to the witness stand. I gave him a look that scorched. He didn't appreciate it."

"I'm sorry."

"It wasn't all big stuff, like the moneymaker thing, or the crude jokes. Little things bothered me just as much. I noticed the glances, the slight turns of the head and the momentary lapses in conversation that happened whenever I bent over or crossed my legs. Worse still, were the looks I got from the secretaries, for what they thought they knew. Hell, I would have loved to have gone to a Clemson or Carolina football game, tailgate in a luxury box or take a booze cruise around Charleston harbor with a bunch of clients. Instead, I always had to make an excuse. If I did any of those things, I would've created a situation that could've easily spun out of control. As a result," Rosemary paused for affect, "I'm not a team player."

There wasn't anything I could say. Both Rosemary and Rose Durden lived in, and understood, a reality that I could empathize with, but not fully appreciate. Despite besting the boys her entire life, Rosemary never received the appropriate recognition. When she finally committed herself to someone, he betrayed her. When it came to sexuality, Rosemary must have felt "damned if I do, and damned if don't." I wondered why women didn't give up on men altogether. We're a bad bargain. With the advent of infertility clinics, I was confident that our days were numbered. I knew there was something important I should say. I wished that I knew what it was.

"Telling Henry Holmes that I was resigning was one of the easiest things I ever had to do. He asked me to stay and said he was disappointed, but I could tell that he was a little relieved as well. I'll have some good memories from working at Holmes Law. The look on

Barry Banther's face when we exposed the Laveaus' ugly truth is a memory I'll treasure the rest of my life."

"The Laveau case has made you a rock star down at the courthouse. Are you sure that there isn't a way to work things out with Henry Holmes?"

"I don't want to. I'm looking forward to my own shop. I wasn't kidding this afternoon about a boutique practice focused on the Medical University. Your case, and the Ramirez lawsuit, are going to keep me busy, and well compensated, for the next five years. For the first time in a long time , I feel liberated."

I smiled and rubbed my hands through my hair. "Me too."

Rosemary lifted her glass of wine and we toasted again to our mutual liberation. Before sipping though, I felt the need to offer a *mea culpa.* "In the interest of full disclosure, I think you should know that I glance whenever you cross your legs, bend over or take off your panty hose in my car."

"You don't think I already know that."

"Are we okay?"

"We're okay."

Apparently, there are caveats that I'm genetically or hormonally incapable of understanding.

We finished the last of the wine. The waiter was disappointed that we were skipping dessert. Carolina's, and the Perdita Room, had come through with just the kind of evening that I'd hoped for.

Rosemary excused herself to the ladies' room. Banastre Tarleton and I watched her gorgeous backside as she walked from the room.

Chapter 8.
PELICAN WATCH

Rosemary and I walked back to her apartment on Printer's Row. When we reached her door, Rosemary asked if I'd mind using her toothbrush. I thought it might be a trick question, but I told her I didn't think so. She smiled and asked if I'd mind waiting a few minutes. Rosemary slipped into her apartment, leaving me excited, but confused. She returned in a couple minutes with a small travel bag.

"I've got a small condo out on Seabrook Island that I bought after my divorce. I was thinking about a long weekend. Can you drive? That is, if you're interested."

"I'm parked right over there."

Beyond the obvious reason, I thought a get-away to Seabrook for the weekend would be a perfect break from everything swirling around us. Even though I slipped the noose of a well-planned lynching, there were still significant decisions that needed to be made in the wake of my successful appeal. I hadn't ever considered the possibility that I wouldn't be terminated.

For Rosemary, the outcome of the Board of Trustees appeal was never in doubt. Every lawyer nerve in her body had to still be buzzing. Her confrontation with the Board of Trustees was personal, but the professional in her could still appreciate a dazzling cross-examination. She controlled the conversation, expertly set up the targets and then knocked them over.

Both Rosemary and I realized that after today, every tomorrow would be different. Rosemary wouldn't be going back to the Holmes Law Firm. There was a good chance that I'd never be going back to the Medical University. We were both going to face one of the rarest, and scariest, of all situations, namely, freedom of choice. A long discussion awaited us on the island. Our future together no longer seemed so abstract.

From Rosemary's apartment, I took Broad Street to Lockwood and turned south over the Ashley River Bridge. Traveling south on Highway 17, my thoughts drifted. It was years ago, but Helene and I had also slipped out of town on this same road. I fiddled with the radio to keep from having to talk. My emotions were on raw edge. My attraction to Rosemary was great. The thought of spending the weekend with her at Seabrook filled me with anticipation. When Helene died, I believed I'd never experience that kind of intimacy again. I'd underestimated the intolerability of living without love.

The trip to Seabrook gave me about thirty miles to figure out the depth of my feelings for Rosemary. I was no longer confident in my understanding of my own feelings. I'd felt empty since Helene's death. With Rosemary, I no longer felt that void. Was that the definition of love, or was I just a desperate soul? What I did know, was that my time with Rosemary wasn't perfunctory. I felt invested in another human being. If it wasn't love, it was still the most vital thing I'd experienced in years.

Could I be fortunate enough to feel this way about someone twice in one life? Can a second love ever achieve the full measure of the first? Did I have another piece of my heart, or part of my soul, to give to another person. What about the pieces that were already missing? Could Rosemary feel the same way about a wild card like me, after the disappointments she'd already experienced in her life? Those questions all needed answers, and they were assuredly getting ready to be prosecuted. Were my feeling for Rosemary love? I was ready to believe they were.

"What are you thinking?"

I couldn't tell Rosemary the truth. "Nothing, just concentrating on the road. Why'd you ask?"

"You left the radio on a country station. I didn't know that you were a Garth Brooks fan. You seem distracted."

I didn't answer.

I adjusted the radio to my favorite rhythm and blues station. The car was flooded with the plaintive resonance of Jimmy Ruffin's almost unbearable *What Becomes of the Brokenhearted.* Jimmy was the older brother of The Temptations front man David Ruffin. *What Becomes of the Brokenhearted* was Jimmy's only top ten hit. But it was unforgettable. Ruffin's anguished lyrics, and the mournful instrumentation provided by Motown's Funk Brothers, drove the heartbreak straight through you. My eyes filled when Ruffin asks what becomes of the man who's had love that's now departed. I had to turn away.

Rosemary silently understood and said no more. She rubbed the hair at the back of my neck. It had to be uncomfortable for Rosemary as well. Rosemary never asked a single question or made a single demand. Lawyers know to never ask a question if they don't already know the answer. Rosemary cared for me, defended me, and gambled on me without asking for anything in return.

We turned off Highway 17 onto Folly Road and crossed the Wappoo Cut before turning right onto Maybank Highway. Maybank lead to Bohicket Road which was the final leg out to Seabrook Island. Bohicket is a preserved historic road. We drove it under a moonless sky and a canopy of overhanging live oaks. The ancient oaks stood as immobile, impassive, unsentimental collectors of souls. Small white crosses and plastic flowers dotted Bohicket Road; mementoes of the price paid for not knowing when the deer are in rut, or that drinking and driving really don't mix. Live oaks have stood sentinel over Bohicket Road since it was only a trail used by the Kiawah Indians. They'd been undisturbed by some of the strongest hurricanes in history. A speeding Lexus did little more than skin a little bark off their knees.

Rosemary's condo was a modest one-bedroom place in the Pelican Watch Villas just off High Hammock Road, near Camp St. Christopher where the Medical University sometimes held faculty retreats. A piece of driftwood inscribed with "Sweet Magnolia Time" hung over the parking space beneath the elevated villa.

I looked at Rosemary, "Leon Russell?"

She smiled broadly, clearly pleased that I was familiar with one of the greatest, but most enigmatic, Rock and Roll superstars of the 1970s. "You betcha. Oklahoma's lonely cowboy and the master of space and time. My Walkman pumped out Leon's *Delta Lady* almost every day of my adolescence. I've wanted to be 'waiting wet and naked in the garden' for Leon since I was twelve years old. I didn't know what he was talking about, but it was the first time I ever felt sensual."

"Well, hummingbird, I'll be really impressed if you have a bottle of honeysuckle wine in the pantry."

"Nope, just bourbon and rum. We'll have to rough it this weekend. I like being called hummingbird though."

Our arrival disturbed the tranquility of the surrounding marsh. The bull frogs were now in full throat and were backed by popping from the fiddler crab holes. I didn't know if it was a welcome, or they were telling us to leave the way we came. Too late for that now.

Rosemary opened a bottle of Merlot and put *Will O' the Wisp* on the compact disc player. The first track was "Back to the Island." I nodded my approval of the perfect selection. Rosemary took my hand and suggested we take our wine to the bedroom. Rosemary excused herself. I stripped out of my clothes and climbed into the king-sized bed, making a point to stay on one side. I'd not been in bed with a woman since Helene died. There were a dozen reasons why, or at least, I told myself there were. The simple explanation, which I didn't want to acknowledge, was that I'd been crumbling into myself for some time.

When Rosemary came out of the bathroom she took my breath away. In Lake Charles, Rosemary slept on the couch in her blue jeans and an NYU tee-shirt. Not tonight. Rosemary wore an ivory satin nightgown that left little to the imagination. Her black hair cascaded down the right side of her face, highlighted by the creamy whiteness of the nightgown and her complexion. Stunning. Women always know their best side. Rosemary was no exception.

Rosemary left the bathroom door open a crack with the light on. She turned off the overhead before coming to the bed. She pulled back the covers and slid effortlessly into bed beside me. I couldn't take my eyes off her. She reached back to turn off the bedside lamp before turning back on her side to face me. The next CD track was the sensual "Bluebird." After an awkward silence, I finally found some words. "I'm not sure that I'm going to be very good. Don't get me wrong. You look incredible. It's just been a long time for me."

Rosemary searched my face for a moment, and then used her fingers to comb my hair away from my forehead. "I understand. It's been a long time for me as well. I only have one expectation."

"Which is?"

"If we're going to make this a regular thing, then I expect a goodnight kiss every time."

"You know about my wife, don't you?"

"I know."

"You're not afraid to kiss me?"

"No."

"Why not?"

"If there was anything to be afraid of, you'd tell me."

I'd been waiting for that answer since Helene's death. Rosemary lifted herself up and over me. Her breath was warm, and her lips were cool, as she gave me a gentle kiss which I returned. The kissing quickly became more passionate. I still had some lingering pain in my jaw and ribs from the beating I'd taken at Bebop's Ice House, but, right now, it didn't seem so bad. The heat emanating through Rosemary's satin nightgown was therapeutic. Even pain is better than the nothingness of being a ghost among the living.

Rosemary raised an eyebrow and gave me a questioning look. I nodded that I was okay. She straddled me and began to rock back and forth on me slowly. I feared I'd come too quickly given how long it'd been since I was last with a woman. That fear distracted me enough to not seriously shame myself. As my endorphins began to flow, my pain subsided, and I began to rise to meet her rocking motion.

I was ecstatic when Rosemary climaxed quickly. Her rhythm became erratic, her face flushed, and she moaned as she contracted around me. The physical and emotional stimulation of her orgasm was more than I could stand. I finished moments later. We lay together for several minutes enjoying every second of our intimacy. Eventually, Rosemary lifted herself off me and walked to the bathroom. She returned with a warmed, wet washrag. The sponge bath she gave me raised another erection.

Rosemary thumped my erection with her forefinger. Then she snapped it with the washrag.

"You're crazy if you think we're going again," Rosemary said, shaking her head, and threatening to snap my penis again with the washrag. "This is only our first time. I have no intention of setting a high bar."

"Hey, I'm not like that."

"Bullshit. I'm not going to hear your voice in my head saying 'Oh, only once?' every time we make love from this day forward. Not going to happen, my friend, so just lay that thing down and roll over. I will say for the record though, that I'm impressed by your enthusiasm."

Best blow-off I'd ever gotten.

"Goodnight, Rosemary." I leaned over and gave Rosemary the goodnight kiss that I'd promised.

The following morning, I awoke to find Rosemary lying against my side with her arm draped across my chest. Her Veronica Lake haircut fell across her face, like a game of pick-up sticks, the pattern rearranged from the last time I saw her. I delighted in studying Rosemary's face in the early morning light. She was a sound sleeper, which favored me with as much time as I wanted to memorize her every feature.

My sleep had been deep and active. My dreams were complex, comforting, and involved Rosemary. I planned to tell Rosemary all about them. However, as dreams do, before I could organize them for retelling, they blackened, crumpled and blew away with the breeze like a piece of burned cigarette paper. The effervescent memories abandoned me with only a feeling, but it was a good feeling. Morning sunshine sliced into the room through wooden Bermuda shutters while Rosemary slept at my side.

Before long, Rosemary's eyes fluttered to wakefulness. She rose on one elbow and brushed her hair back behind an ear. Her face glowed with untroubled thoughts. Rosemary gave me the unexpected gift of passion that I'd not expected to experience again. I could tell that she'd slept soundly and happily. I started to tell her about my dreams before realizing they'd completely evaporated. I could only return a dopey smile that I'm sure made me look simple. Rosemary laughed. "Yeah, you're fine."

As Rosemary walked from the bed to the bathroom, she stopped and slid open the glass doors to the screened porch. She stood there immodestly as the sea breeze billowed the voile curtains into the condo, enveloping her naked body. The sheer curtains encircling and highlighting Rosemary's beautiful body were dappled with golden sun beams. She reminded me of a sparkling Gustav Klimt painting. I immediately wanted to experience again the comfort her perfect body could provide.

I closed my eyes and etched the moment into my memory. I wouldn't lose this memory, like I'd lost my dreams of Rosemary.

Rosemary soon returned from the bathroom with a terrycloth robe. She tapped me on the forehead to rouse me from my day dreams.

"Let's go, lazy bones. Time to get up and get dressed."

I groaned and rolled over. "How about coming back to bed instead. We don't have a single thing we have to do today. Let's sleep in."

"That's what you think. Get moving."

"I thought we were both unemployed. How about another hour? What could we possibly have to do? Let's just open the blinds and enjoy this beautiful morning."

"You'll see. No more questions, and no more delay. Daylight is burning, and it's almost low tide."

Chapter 9.
CAPTAIN SAM'S SPIT

Rosemary waited for me on the screened porch with two cups of coffee. The condo porch had an expansive view of both the beachfront and the adjacent Kiawah River. I hadn't seen a clock, but the low placement of the sun over the Atlantic told me it was still early. The nearly horizontal sunbeams shimmered on the surface of the river. The day held a lot of promise.

Rosemary wore a black maillot bathing suit, cut high on each hip with a sheer fabric design on the left side. Over the suit she wore a white gauze beach cover-up. On top of her head she had a black New York Yankees baseball cap. I didn't have either Rosemary's fashion options or sensibilities, so I simply rolled up my pant legs and put back on yesterday's button-down shirt.

"Where are we going?"

"Over to Captain Sam's Spit. It's not far, only a couple hundred yards."

Captain Sam's Spit is a teardrop shaped strip of sand along Captain Sam's Inlet between Seabrook and Kiawah Island. The one-hundred-and-fifty-acre spit is a shape-shifter in the face of the wind and waves. The riverbank erodes the spit on one side, while the beachfront, on the other side, is accruing sand. It was a lush intersection of marshlands and tidelands that had been responding to the capricious whims of Mother Nature for innumerable years.

"Why are we going is maybe the better question."

"We're going to check out the Seabrook Island gang."

"Are they with the Bloods or the Cripps?"

"Don't be a smartass. Just shut up and follow me. You'll see."

We walked through the dunes and sea grass on the way over to the spit. The only other people we saw were a couple of women whose binoculars gave them away as birders. We nodded apologetically when they recognized our intrusion into their sanctuary. Rosemary explained that Captain Sam's Spit was a federally protected refuge for endangered migratory birds. Without federal protection, the grifters in state government would quietly sell the spit to heavily bankrolled, soulless developers. The Kiawah Island Company made no secret of their desire to "reimagine" the spit with "protective" sea walls and a string of mega-beach houses. As always, the conservationists were overmatched, but, so far, had been able to hold them off in South Carolina's regulatory courts.

The birders were probably looking for piping plovers. The piping plovers arrived annually from the Great Lakes region. For birders, the piping plover was considered a gem in their collection. There were fewer than one hundred breeding pairs left in the world. In the fall, they migrated south; stopping on Captain Sam's Spit to rest before continuing to their nesting grounds along the Florida coast.

"So, this is Can-Am week for the piping plovers?"

"Keep quiet. Those birders will slit your throat if you spook any of their feathery friends. They're on a mission."

"Thanks, important safety tip. I'll keep low and stay quiet."

"Seriously, though, there're some pretty cool birds that hang out on the spit. American oystercatchers, black skimmers, red knots and some royal terns. The loggerhead sea turtles also come ashore to lay their eggs."

"Are we going bird watching?"

"Do I look like a birder to you?"

"No ma'am. You certainly do not."

"Just keep up. We'll be there in a minute."

We crossed a marsh towards the Kiawah River which separated Captain Sam's Spit from Seabrook Island. Weather-beaten wooden walkways crossed the tidal marsh. The marsh buzzed with life. This morning, at low tide, the silver-grey pluff mud was pockmarked with crab holes in low places, and piled high in others, crowned by hostile-appearing oyster beds. Pluff mud is the ubiquitous black bottom of all Southern marshes, estuaries and creek beds. An oyster shell dropped from the walkway would disappear into the pluff, accompanied by a brief slurping sound, the intruding oyster shell enveloped by the pluff's soft slippery blackness.

The last rivulets of the tidal creek snaked its way through the lowest spots of the marsh. Dozens of snowy egrets stood eagerly by these tiny tidal streams, feasting on the exposed minnows. A scavenger vulture was at the marsh grass line, tugging at the bleached and bloated remains of a 4-foot-long gar that looked more dinosaur than fish. The marsh at low tide offered a stew of ceaseless life and death.

The marsh exuded its own unique smell. Mainlanders described the pluff as having a fetid, rotten egg odor. For those of us who'd grown up children of the marsh, the pluff was as far from rancid as was imaginable. It had an earthy aroma, as intoxicating as the scent of a woman. Being in the marsh only augmented the vital feelings that Rosemary had stirred in me the night before.

We emerged from the marsh at the edge of a pristine brown sand beach at the juncture of the Kiawah River and the Atlantic Ocean. Fifty to seventy-five yards away across the river inlet was Captain Sam's Spit. The narrow beach sloped steeply down to the shoreline. The tide was moving out and the current appeared fast. While it may be a birders paradise, it offered little for someone interested in shelling. Only the smallest shell fragments could be identified in the smooth sand.

"What are we looking for?"

"Find the pelicans," Rosemary said, scanning the beach.

Looking up and down, we identified a small flock of pelicans hanging out about one hundred yards back up the Kiawah River. While it was a lovely morning, I'd seen pelicans before. Rosemary ignored my lack of enthusiasm and again told me to keep quiet and watch. We closed the distance to the pelicans.

After a few minutes of waiting, we saw an Atlantic bottlenose dolphin raise its head from the river. Moments later, the river began to roil. A bow wave appeared which broke on the steep bank scattering mullet and other bait fish. The bow wave was immediately followed by an astonishingly synchronized rush of four 500-pound dolphins. The dolphins threw themselves on to the beach to feast on the helpless prey fish desperately flopping their way back to the water. It was one of the most spectacular things I'd ever seen. The cute, cuddly dolphins that I'd first learned about on Flipper were in reality cunning, ruthless, almost gleeful predators.

"Pretty cool, huh. Those guys are my Seabrook gang."

"You've seen this before?"

"Yeah, lots of times. Just wait. They'll regroup and make another run at the mullet. It's called "strand fishing" and only occurs along this part of the South Carolina coast. It happens the same way every time. The dolphins herd the fish together into a bait ball. One of the dolphins has the lookout job. He rises to check out the shore for a good place to strand. Once they've picked a spot, the dolphins form a line and rush the beach."

"The wave scatters the fish on the shore, then the big boys come after them."

"Exactly. What's cool, and no one knows why, but when the dolphins launch themselves onto the beach, they always end up lying on their right side. Wait till they come back. You'll see."

"Do they ever get stuck on the bank? If they get stuck, their feast has turned into a suicide mission."

"It must be a risk, but I've never seen it. They're incredibly strong. They thrash around to catch the fish in their mouths, and then they'll flop their way back to the river. Sometimes they'll make a mistake, and beach themselves on a bed of oyster shells. I'm told that the oyster shells can slice them up badly. I haven't seen that either. What I have seen, is a mother teaching her calves how to strand fish."

"How do you know that they're teaching? It might be innate behavior."

"Well, it wasn't the whole gang, and they didn't seem interested in the mullet. It was just one adult and several smaller calves. I assumed it was the mother. She was stranding on steeper banks than the ones preferred by the gang. I think she chose the steeper banks, so the calves would have an easier time getting back to the water."

"Here they come." The four massive bottlenose dolphins exploded again onto the shoreline. They all lay on their right sides as Rosemary predicted. They each snagged several doomed fish and then squiggled back into the river. The roiled water once again became still.

"They're more organized than we are. They develop a plan, communicate with each other and then act in perfect unison to get the job done right. How many committees have you been on that could pull off strand feeding?"

"I can't argue with you. I've always believed that the quality of any committee's work is inversely proportional to the number of committee members."

While I'd never seen strand fishing before, I wasn't surprised by the skillfulness of the bottlenose dolphin. "On Shem Creek once, I saw a dolphin lying on its side, using its fluke and pectoral fin to beat the marsh grass. The boat captain called it 'kerplunking.' The dolphin was flushing bait fish and shrimp out of hiding in the marsh grass. The startled fish flee the marsh grass into the waiting maw of the dolphin. But, kerplunking is nowhere near as cool as this. How many times will they beach themselves?"

"I've seen them come back a half dozen times. I guess they come back till they've eaten their fill, or they can't round up any more mullet. They'll also move on if too many people show up. They don't trust us to keep our distance."

"Like you said, smart."

The dolphins came back two more times before disappearing as quietly as they came. The only evidence of the dolphins' visit was a convention floor of squawking pelicans arguing over the bait fish blasted so far up the beach that they were safe from the dolphins.

"Why only here?" I asked.

"I've heard lots of things, but my favorite is that our Low Country dolphins are smarter than the Georgia or Florida dolphins. Other people have said that it has to do with the topography of the river bottom and shoreline."

"Any idea what that means?"

"Not a clue. I've also been told that it has to do with how rich the buffet is. In the sixties and early seventies, the Kiawah River was virtually dead due to agricultural run-off and industrial dumping up river. The Clean Water Act stopped all of that, and the river is now a moving seafood feast. My Seabrook gang might just be a bunch of old fat dolphins, who don't feel like chasing down their meals anymore."

After the dolphins left, we took a long walk on the beach scanning for shells that were nowhere to be found. As we walked, Rosemary took my hand in hers and again, interlaced her fingers with mine. By the time we got back to the condo, I couldn't get Rosemary out of her white gauze cover-up and bathing suit fast enough. We made love again, this time more eagerly. I was less of a passive partner. We made love together, well-coordinated, intimately communicative and mutually satisfying. The Seabrook gang would've been proud of us, if they'd been watching.

We spent the rest of the weekend either in the bedroom or on the porch. I kissed Rosemary goodnight without fail. I made a point of fixing breakfast each morning. I'd never been good in the kitchen, but Rosemary loved my Donald Duck sandwiches. It was Pop-Tart simple. Two slices of toasted white bread with a little mustard, ketchup and some grated Parmesan cheese. Between the pieces of toast, I put a couple of slices of crisp bacon and a fried egg over easy. Rosemary preferred grapefruit juice to orange, which I didn't understand, but to each their own. Rosemary had a great appetite, which I liked. She asked for a second Donald Duck each morning.

Sunday morning, we made another visit to Captain Sam's Spit. The Seabrook gang came back, every bit as awesome as it'd been the day before. Nature at its most elemental. The smart and strong will always devise a way to strand, and consume, the small and weak. Once you've been stranded, the only question that remains is whether the dolphins or the pelicans will get you. Like the mullet, I'd been stranded on the floor of the President's conference room. It was miraculous, but Rosemary saved me from the Dean on one side and the Board of Trustees on the other.

I'd spent more than a year ruminating about my disappointments and dark thoughts. Rosemary made it easy to ascend from those low places. She was vivacious, verbal and positive. We had conversations that ranged from medicine and law to politics and sports. Her interests were numerous, insights provocative and her opinions well crafted. I was careful about arguing with her. Her logic was impenetrable.

Rosemary refused to let me get down on myself. She'd been where I now was. If she could pull her life back together, then I should be able to bootstrap myself as well.

I understood that my attraction to Rosemary was, in part, a by-product of the intense situations that she and I had faced together. From exposing the Laveaus to my Board of Trustees appeal, our relationship had evolved under great tension. I considered and then rejected the notion that my feelings for Rosemary might only be a combination of relief and thankfulness. Instead, I believed that the immense pressure we'd been under served as a catalyst to an unexpected alchemy. Enough pressure applied to a lump of coal can produce a diamond. Although it had only been a short time, I believed that my feelings for Rosemary were both real and profound.

Sipping a crisp Chenin Blanc on the screened porch after dinner, Rosemary asked if I thought Seabrook was just an escape. I choose my words carefully knowing it was a charged question. I told Rosemary that, at least for me, Seabrook was transformative. If it was an escape, then I never wanted to stop running. Rosemary nodded. She didn't pursue it further.

I couldn't put Rosemary's question out of my mind. This weekend at Seabrook answered the question which troubled me on the drive out. Jimmy Ruffin wanted to know what became of the brokenhearted. On Friday, I didn't know. Now I did. You must allow yourself to heal, but once a heart has healed, it will soon want to again be filled. Seabrook, and Rosemary, proved to me that my heart had healed, at least enough, to know I'd be okay to share it with someone new. Every moment with Rosemary seemed precious. I couldn't imagine being away from Rosemary for even a minute. I was in love with Rosemary Winslow. I would need to tell her soon.

Two women now had a hold on me. It would always be that way. As wonderful as it was to again be in love, and be loved, I knew it would always be a shared affection. Both Helene and Rosemary would understand it too. It was astonishing I'd not figured it out sooner.

Chapter 10.
W.C. FIELDS

Rosemary woke me up with a crackling rump-roaster.

"Time to face the day, lazy bones."

The lulling rhythm of breaking waves and squawking gulls cued me to the arrival of another magnificent day. For the second night in a row , I'd slept untroubled, and awoke without cross thoughts. I sat up with my back against the headboard. Rosemary looked magnificent in only my white undershirt which made getting out of bed exceptionally difficult. Rosemary caught me looking her over.

"Forget it, Murphy. No time for shenanigans. You've got stuff to do."

"What's so important? I far as I know, I'm still under suspension. We left before they could return my identification card."

"Funny you should mention that. Your good friend, Tommy Petrus, called. He wants you to come in, so you two can discuss your coming back to work. You should know that he's very pleased with the outcome of the Board of Trustees hearing."

"Good God, I'm not ready for that conversation."

"As your lawyer, I would advise you to pass on that meeting. I seriously plan to file a civil suit on your behalf against the University. They trumped up Peer Review allegations based on knowingly falsified records. They dragged you before committee after committee, ruining your reputation at the university, and likely, in the community. We caught them red handed. They treated you like shit. I can make them pay."

"I'm not sure I had such a great reputation at MUSC before all this happened. This isn't the first time I've been told that I was more trouble than I was worth."

"Look Declan, what they did has nothing to do with whether you're popular or a pain in the ass. Kenny Leslie committed a crime.

Give me a shot at Leslie under oath, and I'll guarantee you that he gives up Dean Shriver as well. Either way, they ran with it, and suspended you. Regardless of any reinstatement, you'll be listing that, and explaining it, on every job application you fill out for the rest of your life. What kind of recommendation are you going to get from Dean Shriver when a prospective employer calls for a confidential opinion? Not to get on too high a horse, if they get away with this with you, what keeps them from doing it to the next person who comes along and causes a bit of trouble?"

"I don't see how prolonged *Post and Courier* coverage a nasty civil trial rehabilitates my reputation. How many women in Charleston will want to see the obstetrician that the university tried to fire?"

"I promise you that the suit will never see the inside of a courthouse. Hell, I'll never even get a shot at little Kenny in a deposition. MUSC will settle for whatever I tell them is necessary to make this go away quietly. Vincent Bellizia knows that all this shit is going to roll uphill. The Dean and the Board will never allow that to happen. You're going to end up being the heroic doctor who brought the Laveaus to justice. End of sentence. The Board of Trustees doesn't want to be on the wrong side of a story about the university trying to fuck you over."

"That all sounds great to me. I've got nothing against you making me rich. I hope that your percentage will be reasonable." I don't think Rosemary appreciated my smirk. "However, proceeding with the lawsuit isn't necessarily mutually exclusive with me going back to work."

"Again, as your lawyer, I'd advise you against it, at least for now. Going back to work, picking up the back pay they're going to throw at you, accepting a small raise, will all be used to mitigate my alleged damages. It's harder to argue that they created a hostile work environment when you go running back the day after they decide not to fire your ass. They'll probably make you the director of some new out of sight, out of mind office of something unimportant."

I laughed.

"Don't laugh, big boy. A week from now, you could be pushing papers around in the Student Health Office or as Director of Parking

Management. They did a terrible thing to you, and now they want to act like nothing ever happened. I plan to argue that they've ruined your personal and professional reputation, destroyed your practice and broken your heart. They're still going to settle with you, whether you go back to work or not. It will be for big bucks either way, but there'll be more Benjamins if you're unemployed, distressed and damaged." Rosemary smiled coyly. "Although, if I were forced to testify, last night you didn't seem like a shattered, shell of a man."

"Last night was therapy. I'm a broken man who needs rehabilitation. I was hoping for a little more rehab this morning."

"No more therapy for you today. We've got things to deal with. Speaking as your friend, not as your lawyer, I'd tell you to do whatever makes you happy. If you want to go back, then you should go back. But, do it on your terms. I promise you that they'll be amenable to anything that you want. If you want to oversee Parking Management, it's yours. If there is something else you want to do, that's on the table as well."

"What about the lawsuit?"

"Other than the size of the settlement, it won't change the lawsuit substantially. They're not in a position to negotiate. As your friend, I'd also add that those bastards don't deserve you. You stood up while everyone else in your department stuck their heads in the sand and covered their asses with both hands. Tommy Petrus folded up like a lawn chair. When it came down to a fight for your professional life, he didn't even show up. 'Other clinical duties.' What bullshit. Is he the fucking chairman of the department or what? The best he could come up with was that you'd be hard to replace. Pretty god-damned lame, if you ask me."

"Chairmen aren't usually hired for their bravery."

"Maybe they should be."

Chairmen are hired by the Dean. Chairmen all know where their bread is buttered. I knew I'd become a bit jaded, but my expectations aren't very high when it comes to chairmen standing up to the Dean.

Rosemary calmed herself a bit. "I know that you're attached to MUSC. I won't fault you if you choose to go meet with Petrus. Just make sure you remember that the Ob-Gyn department didn't have your back. I don't believe they'll have your back any better the next time. That is the definition of a hostile work environment. Believe me, I know. Also, don't think that Petrus is reaching out on his own. He's under orders to get you back into the fold. From the Board on down, they're trying to smooth this mess out."

"Solid advice, counselor. I know that MUSC planned to throw me to the wolves. Why I have loyalty to them is a question that continues to baffle me. I'm not very good at cutting ties. I was always prouder to tell people that I was a Professor, as opposed to telling them that I was a doctor. I'd hate to give up teaching. The residents and medical students are my favorite part of the job."

"I know that's important to you ."

"You met those two residents at the fair the other night. They had my back, even though I didn't really deserve it. I want to show them, and the new residents, the kind of attending I used to be. Not the sad imitation that's been grousing around for the past couple of years. I've still got some things that I'd like to prove to myself."

"I understand. I'm concerned that MUSC is never going to give you that chance."

"I know. You're right. Sooner or later, the piñata must figure out that the party isn't as much fun as it looked like when it started. I wish I knew for sure what the best move was." I gave Rosemary a sad sack face and patted the bed beside me.

"Focus boy. You've got some tough decisions to make in the next few days. My advice is to start thinking with your big head."

Rosemary didn't know that it wasn't going take a few more days. I'd been analyzing this decision up and down, and back and forth, for the past week. My interest in dragging it out any longer was nil. Tommy made it easy for me. When he didn't show up for the Board of Trustees meeting, I knew what I needed to do. No matter how I tried to spin it in my head, the medical university was a dead-end job for me. I didn't need to hear Tommy's jive. I'd have to find another way to teach, because I was planning to walk.

"Didn't W.C. Fields say, 'I don't want to belong to any club that would have someone like me as a member'?"

"No, lawyers are W.C. Fields experts. That's a Groucho Marx quote. However, that doesn't mean Groucho wasn't on point. W.C. Fields did say something appropriate to your situation though."

"What's that?"

"'If at first you don't succeed, try, and try again. Then quit. There's no point in being a damn fool about it.' MUSC has now seriously screwed with your life on two occasions. You need to think carefully about giving them another bite at the apple. They might get it right on the third try."

"Why do lawyers know so much about W. C. Fields?"

"We start with W.C. in the first year of law school, Litigation 101. 'If you can't dazzle them with brilliance, baffle them with bullshit.'"

"You must've done well in that course."

"Top of my class."

"I like the idea of being a kept man."

"Don't count on it. I filled that position once, and it didn't work out. That job description doesn't exist anymore."

"What would you say if I told you that I wasn't going back?"

"I'd be a little surprised, but really proud of you."

"I'm going to tell Tommy no thanks. Maybe, fuck you, no thanks."

"I'd be behind you one hundred percent."

"I've never practiced anywhere besides MUSC."

"It doesn't matter."

"I'm not sure what I'm going to do."

"It doesn't matter."

"I don't know where I'm going to go."

"It doesn't matter."

"Whatever I do, I don't think I can do it without you. I love you."

"That matters," Rosemary said, as she closed the distance between us. "Declan, I don't know what's going to happen either, but I'm willing to find out." She brushed the hair off my face and gave me a tender kiss. "I'm in," she whispered in my ear.

My heart swelled. Rosemary believed in me, probably more than I believed in myself. I didn't have the answer to very many of the pertinent questions, but I wasn't going to betray Rosemary's trust in me. "Starting over may not be as exciting as it sounds."

"It'll be romantic."

"I haven't felt romance in a long time."

"Neither have I."

Rosemary pulled me towards her and held me against her for what seemed like forever. For the first time in almost two years, I had a purpose; an unfamiliar, but affirming feeling.

Chapter 11.
HOMER LAHR

I drove down Folly Road keeping an eye out for the overgrown footpath leading to Bowen's Island. Nobody found Bowen's Island by accident or by following a map. You had to know where you were going to get there. The access from Folly Road was a tabby shell path, obscured by palm fronds and banana leaves. A small sign propped up against an overturned john boat with a hole in the bottom was the only marker.

Bowen's Island was Homer's favorite spot for lunch or a lost afternoon. The only structure on Bowen's Island was an aging cinderblock hot house on pilings. A rising pile of oyster shells dumped from the weathered veranda that surrounded the building threatened access to the restaurant. Calling it a restaurant was generous. Bowen's Island was more a state of mind; a state of mind that fit Homer Lahr perfectly.

I met Homer Lahr during my residency when assigned to a rotation at the Charleston Naval Hospital. We loved the rotation at the Naval Hospital. The first day, we read an oath, and were signed in as a Lieutenant Junior Grade in the Navy. We had very little responsibility for obstetrics which fell to their Family Medicine staff. Instead, we worked exclusively with the navy hospital's four-man Ob-Gyn staff. Most of the navy hospital Ob-Gyn staff were just out of residency training themselves and were accumulating gynecology cases as quickly as they could. They were all preparing for their ultimate release to a more lucrative private practice. We spent our clinic days treating the STD's and providing contraception to the enlisted men's wives. We spent our surgical days performing hysterectomies on the officer's wives, while their husbands were on nine-month submarine deployments underneath the polar ice caps.

When I arrived at the Charleston Naval Hospital in mid-October, the dismissal of the Ob-Gyn chief of staff, Dr. Ling, had thrown it into upheaval. Ling went before the Captain's Mast one time too many because of complaints from the nurses and female seamen assigned to the Labor and Delivery unit. The base Admiral decided to see if Dr. Ling could keep his Johnson appropriately stowed on a naval rock in the middle of the Indian Ocean called Diego Garcia. A new Ob-Gyn chief of staff was on his way from Michigan but was overdue and unreachable.

Homer Lahr received his transfer orders from Great Lakes Naval Hospital to Charleston. Great Lakes was relieved to see him go. He terrorized the base on the barely street-legal, souped-up Mustang he called "Lucy." When he got his orders to Charleston, he put "Lucy" in the government moving van and took off with a sonic-boom on his Harley-Davidson hog. On Homer's map, the road from Michigan to South Carolina ran through South Dakota. Homer wasn't going to miss the Sturgis Motorcycle Rally in the Black Hills. The Sturgis Rally had been over for almost two weeks.

Homer's arrival in Charleston occurred on the night of October 31st when he rolled up on a hospital Halloween party at the chief of anesthesia's house. Homer was wearing his full Hell's Angels colors, splattered with a month on the road. At six feet five inches, and almost 300 pounds, in black leather and chains, Homer easily took the door prize for scariest costume. No one knew who the hell he was or bothered to ask. The anesthesia chief called for back-up. Homer's official welcome to the Charleston Naval Base came courtesy of the military police. He didn't bother to produce his identification or orders until he got to the naval brig. It was classic Homer Lahr.

I took an instant liking to him. I loved his stories, although it was clear they had to be taken with a significant discount. Homer bragged about being an All-American football player at Oklahoma in the early 1960s, followed by a brief career in the National Football League with the Philadelphia Eagles. A blown-out knee put an end to that career. After the NFL, he joined the navy to help stop the falling dominoes in Southeast Asia. At the height of the Vietnam War, the various branches of the military weren't too concerned about a balky knee. Homer was a Petty Officer, First Class, and was made the captain of a PBR, or Patrol Boat River. He navigated up and down the Mekong

Delta, disrupting weapons shipments, and getting into firefights with the Viet Cong.

Homer didn't like talking about Vietnam. He'd just shake his head and say, "Tough little bastards. We were lucky to get out of those weeds alive." When pressed, he'd admit that they'd gotten into a few bad scrapes, and that he'd picked up a couple of medals. Like a true motor head, he enjoyed talking about his PBR. "That bugger had dual 180 horsepower Detroit Diesel engines, with Jacuzzi Brothers pump-jet drives. It could outrace anything on the river, stop on a dime and reverse direction at top speed in one boat length. Might've been the best boat ever built."

Homer took advantage of a special government program for returning Vietnam veterans, and started medical school at the University of California, San Francisco. After medical school, he re-joined the navy, and did his Ob-Gyn residency at the Oakland Naval Hospital. According to Homer, those were wild times. He lived in the upper Haight on Clayton Street, and worked at the Haight-Ashbury Free clinic. He treated Mama Michelle for an overdose, diagnosed Grace Slick's venereal disease, and did an abortion on Janis Joplin.

Homer told these stories at a series of naval base assignments over the years. No one ever believed him. The scuttlebutt was that Captain Lahr burnt out his wiring and confabulated his preposterous life story. While incredulous, the stories were spellbinding. The same scuttlebutt opined that his amazing surgical skill kept him from getting shit-canned.

I don't remember much of my naval base rotation other than operating with Dr. Lahr. His surgical schedule was full within two weeks of his arrival in Charleston. A few weeks after that I realized that the majority of his surgeries were waitresses from IHOP, Ryan's and Golden Corral, where Homer took most of his meals. I operated with Homer the first time he had a case with the anesthesia chief who'd called the cops on him.

Homer winked at him and said from behind his mask, "Good to see ya again, podna. Take extra special good care of Betsy. She always brings me the chocolate chip cookies when they're still warm and gooey. Good gal."

As we operated together more and more, I noticed that periodically, Homer's hands would go limp and he'd drop his instruments in the operative field. It was always momentary. I'd just tap his hands and he'd come around. When I looked in his eyes, sometimes there was an unrecognizing stare. Other times, his eyes were simply closed.

It wasn't long before the scrub nurses reported him to the anesthesia chair, and the anesthesia chair reported Homer to the hospital medical director. The order came to stop operating until he underwent testing for narcolepsy. I knew his goose was cooked. I'd made the same diagnosis weeks ago.

The following week I passed Dr. Lahr in the hallway. He grabbed me by the collar of my scrubs and pushed me up against the wall. "Better get saddled up, podna. We've got a case in an hour. Really nice girl who works at Breck's. They got the best blue cheese dressing at Breck's. They put it on your salad with an ice cream scoop. She's got bad dyspareunia. I think she has bilateral tubo-ovarian complexes from old PID. We gonna fix her up. Nobody should have pain with sex."

"Dr. Lahr, I thought your surgical privileges were suspended."

"Not any more, podna. Just got word. I aced my tests."

"Dr. Lahr, just between you and me, how'd you pass that EEG? You and I both know that you have narcolepsy. I've seen it."

Homer stuck out his tongue and winked. "Podna, I spent the summer of love in Golden Gate Park. I was hangin' with the Airplane when they wrote *White Rabbit.* Better living through chemistry, son. Whatever else I teach you, remember this, to be underestimated is an incredible gift." Homer's massive round face lit up like a jack-o-lantern.

"I got it, boss man." Homer liked to be called boss man. "Hey, and congratulations too, I guess."

"Don't crack wise with me boy. You better be in the OR in thirty minutes or boss man's gonna find somebody else to slow me down."

Homer laughed, shot me the bird, and took off down the hall. I couldn't do anything but smile. Asleep, or on bennies, there wasn't anyone better in the operating room than Homer Lahr.

Near the end of my naval hospital rotation, I went by Dr. Lahr's office to tell him thanks for a great experience. His stuff had just arrived from Michigan and his office was filled with boxes.

"What's up, Dr. Lahr? Finally decorating?"

"When the government's doing the moving, don't expect your possessions to arrive anytime near when you do. However, it'd been almost two months. I was getting a little worried that someone might've kidnapped Lucy."

"You packed a person in with your belongings, boss man?"

"Don't be stupid, son. Lucy's my mustang. I think she's been to San Diego, Portland, back to the Great Lakes and then finally to Charleston. No biggie. Lucy likes to travel."

As Homer told me about all the modification's he'd made on Lucy, I browsed around his office. On the credenza behind his desk was an open coffee-table book about the NFL's first fifty years. There was a full-page photograph with the caption, "Cleveland's Jim Brown slips the tackle of Philadelphia Eagle linebacker Homer Lahr in route to a long gain during the Brown's 1964 NFL Championship season."

A large framed picture of a bare-chested Homer Lahr in frayed bell-bottom jeans, stars and stripes embroidered down the outer seams, and a fringed brown leather vest had been hung above the cadenza. Only the face and the short military buzz-cut looked familiar. His huge, tattooed right arm was draped over a tiny, giggling Janis Joplin whose arm was wrapped around Homer's waist. In the corner of the picture was an inscription, "Homer, thanks for being there for me. All my love, Janis."

Dumbfounded, I turned and stared at Homer. He pretended to pay me no mind. I also noticed a half-filled cardboard box beside the credenza. I reached down and picked out a glass and mahogany display box. It contained Homer's military medals.

I held it out at him, like maybe, he'd never seen it before. "Is that the Medal of Honor?" Another dumb question because I knew that it was.

"Yeah, and that one is the Navy Cross and, of course, that's a Purple Heart."

"But, that's the Medal of Honor."

"Yeah, that was a nasty day." The subdued tone in Homer's voice was unfamiliar.

"What happened? You've got to tell me."

"A bunch of Navy SEALS got ambushed in the Rung Sat Special Zone. The Rung Sat is a 500 square mile tidal mangrove swamp that the VC used as a safe area and supply dump. It's inaccessible except by river. The SEALS went in periodically to clean the place out. This time the VC was waiting."

"You were a Navy SEAL?"

"Hell no, those boys are crazy. I was in my PBR working the Long Tau River. Long Tau is the main shipping channel between Saigon and Vung Tau. The Long Tau River runs next to the Sac Forest, so we got the call when the SEALS got their tit in a twist. The SEALS had been pushed back into the swamp. The Rung Sat swamp is shallow and weed-choked. The PBR only draws about 2 feet, which made us the only option to get them out. They were holding off the VC from behind mangrove stumps in waist deep water. They were badly outnumbered and getting flanked. They weren't going to last much longer. We went in hot and stuck our bow into the middle of it. At the front of the PBR we had twin 50 caliber machine guns, which we'd piggybacked on top of an 81 mm mortar. My gunner's mate deforested that swamp a helluva lot more effectively than Agent Orange ever did. We also kept the VC's heads down with some sawed-off shotguns. Me, and another one of my crew, got in the water and started loading what was left of the SEALS onto the back of the PBR."

"Is that when you got the Purple Heart?"

"Yeah, but it wasn't nothing. I only caught a slug in the shoulder. My crewman never made it out of the swamp water. My gunner lost an eye. My entire crew got the Navy Cross for what they did to save those SEALS."

"Why'd you get the Medal of Honor?"

"By the time we got the SEALS on board, we were too wedged into the mangroves to turn around, and the water level was too low for the engines to back us up in reverse. Waitin' on the tide to come back in wasn't an option, if you know what I mean."

"So, what did you do?"

"We'd done it before. We had a heavy rope on the back of the boat. I tied it around my shoulder, jumped in, and pulled the PBR back out into the current."

"Boss man, that sounds like Humphrey Bogart in *The African Queen*."

"All Bogie had to deal with were leeches and mosquitoes. I had about a fifty Viet Cong who believed they could get us all, if they could keep us fouled in the weeds. That's when I took the slug in the shoulder. A couple of V.C. jumped me while I was haulin' the PBR, but I surprised them. They didn't know that you can work a sawed-off shotgun with just one good arm. We got eight SEALS out alive. We left five behind along with my crewman."

I saw Homer look away with a thousand-yard stare. This time it wasn't a narcoleptic spell. "Sounds like the Medal was well-deserved, sir. You shouldn't leave it in a box. You need to put it on the wall."

"I like my picture with Janis better. She was a great gal. Great voice. I miss her every day. She had some demons, but if I could've had more time with her, she'd still be here."

I didn't doubt him. I'd never make the mistake of doubting Homer Lahr again. To be underestimated is an incredible gift.

Chapter 12.
BOWEN'S ISLAND

I looked for Homer's hog in the rutted pea gravel parking lot but didn't see it. At the far end of the lot, parked under a wind-bent Palmetto, sat a tricked out '69 Mustang that must be Lucy. The office said that Homer would be lunching at Bowen's Island, but it reassured me to have confirmation that he hadn't wandered off. I hadn't talked to Homer since Helene's death. He'd told me to give him a ring when I was ready to blow it out. I felt ashamed that I'd never called him back.

At MUSC, I heard about Homer often; always disparagingly. Homer left the Navy about two years after my rotation at the Charleston Navy Hospital. People said that he'd been a Section 8. Homer decided to stay in Charleston and opened a solo practice. What got everyone's goat was that he advertised himself as specializing in Reproductive Endocrinology and Infertility. He had no credentials as an REI specialist, but Homer never claimed he did. He just claimed that he specialized in Reproductive Endocrinology and Infertility. Homer's arrogance drove other physicians crazy with indignation and jealousy.

There was always a method to Homer's madness. His narcolepsy was the most poorly kept secret in the medical community. Homer would never get surgical privileges at any of the local hospitals. So instead, Homer bought a twenty-year-old three bedroom ranch house on Folly Road. He did most of the renovations himself; converting the back end of the house into exam rooms, a small, but sophisticated embryology laboratory and, most importantly, his own operating room where he could do minor surgical procedures. Homer established the perfect set-up for an independent in vitro fertilization program.

Instead of a waiting room, Homer left the living room virtually untouched.

Despite the snide comments and withering professional word of mouth, Dr. Lahr's Folly Road Fertility did nothing but succeed. Homer didn't know a thing about business, but he knew people. He also knew a business opportunity when he saw one. His fees were low, his pregnancy rates were high, and his patients loved him. Homer hustled the waitresses at the Med-Deli, DeLorces, the Crab House and a half dozen Bar B Que shacks along Folly Road. It never bothered Homer to do a little work off the books.

What Homer loved the most was not taking orders from anyone. He considered "lunch hour" a guideline rather than the rule. Within a year, Homer was kicking the shit out of the bona fide infertility specialists at MUSC. As I climbed the steps to the Bowen's Island veranda, I prepared myself for facing a force of nature. I reminded myself of the most critical rule of negotiation. To be underestimated is an incredible gift.

At Bowen's Island, you must pass through the kitchen to enter the dining area, with a separate room for roasted oysters beyond. The overseer of the kitchen was May Bowen, who owned the restaurant with her second husband, Jimmy. She ruled with an iron ladle. No one entered the dining area without first purchasing a basket of one fried seafood or another. May famously kicked Bjorn Borg and his entire tennis entourage out of the restaurant. He wanted to join friends in the oyster roasting room without having ordered the all-you-can eat oysters. Jeez, everyone knew better than that.

A basket of fried oysters was my ticket into the dining room. Dining room was a generous description. The rough-hewn picnic tables and cinderblock walls were covered with graffiti and obscene cartoons. It wasn't hard to find Homer among only a handful of customers. He was sitting at a back table with "Goat" Lafayette. "Goat" was nine years old when he began selling his crabs, oysters and shrimp to May Bowen.

Homer wore 2X blue surgical scrubs over his 3X body, a cloth surgical cap with sweat stains across the forehead and his size 16 white OR shoes with red, orange and black racing stripes drawn on the sides in magic marker. Homer capped off the look with his black leather, sleeveless jacket with his "Full Patch" Hell's Angels' colors indicating all-in club membership. The complete four-piece crest included the Sonny Barger "Death Head" logo, a top rocker "Hells Angels," a bottom rocker that said "Oakland, Ca." and the rectangular "MC" patch below the Death Head's wings.

Homer ate his fried shrimp three at a time from two baskets with one hand. His other hand was wrapped around a sweaty long neck Budweiser. Homer looked up as I approached his table.

"How ya doing, boss man? Hope I'm not interrupting anything."

"Declan, long time, no see. How the hell you doin,' podna? Sit down and take a load off. 'Goat' was just leaving. He's got to get out with the tide." Homer yelled for May to bring two more long necks. Only Homer got away with yelling for May. "Goat" nodded an unspeaking, simultaneous hello and goodbye as he stood to leave. I'd met "Goat" a couple of times and had never heard him speak, except to Homer. Other than Homer, "Goat" had never experienced a positive interaction with a white man his entire life.

"Homer, I hoped I might have a few minutes of your time."

"Always got time for an old friend. Surprised to see ya out here on the Island. Pull up a chair and grab a brewski." Homer handed me one of his beers. Homer rarely had a serious conversation that wasn't accompanied by a Bud.

I sat down and took a long swig. Pleased, Homer reached over with his greasy, over-sized shrimp-smellin' hand, and tasseled my hair like I was six years old.

"Been hearing a lot about you, podna. Congrats on taking down those two Cajun swamp trolls. You've been blowin' up my television. How you've managed to go from a wet behind the ears pissant to a God damn hero, I'll never know."

"That's all bullshit, boss man. You're the hero, not me. They were trying to shake me down. It was luck that we found out who they really were. I wish that you'd been riding shotgun with me. I got the crap beaten out of me down in Lake Charles. The guy, Hector, is locked up. Probably looking at life unless he can make a deal. His sister, Paris, poisoned the sheriff who was taking her to Louisiana and is on the run. They'll catch her soon, and when they do, I don't think she'll be getting any breaks. Once you peel back all the layers, you realize that you're dealing with a monster."

"You be careful. I worked down there on the gulf oil rigs when I was in college. The Cajuns aren't very bright, but they never forget a slight. They also take this Voodoo crap seriously. If this gal, Paris, is really a Voodoo priestess, like the paper says, then you need to keep your eyes wide open."

"I'm with you, boss man. The good news is that the Louisiana State Police aren't going to stop until they find her. She almost killed the Lake Charles sheriff. Finding Paris Laveau is their number one priority. I'm sure they're busting heads down in the bayou right now. One of her inbred Cajun cousins will give her up before too long."

"Maybe so, podna, but the law down there hasn't been updated since Napoleon. If she's got real Voodoo MoJo, then all her country cousins will be afraid of her. If they give her up, she'll put the root on 'em. Even if they catch her, there ain't no reason she can't still run her clan from behind bars. Either way, I'd put out some Claymores and keep your head on a swivel."

"Good advice, boss man, but that isn't what I came to talk to you about."

"If you came all the way out here to Bowen's Island, then you must have something big on your mind. Time to spill it, boy."

"I want to be your partner."

Over the next thirty minutes, I filled in Homer on my falling out with MUSC. I gave him my best pitch. As his partner, I'd share the expenses of his Folly Road office. He wouldn't have to pay me a cent. I'd build my own practice. I wouldn't be stepping on Homer's toes because we do different things. His practice is outpatient gynecology and infertility. Mine is prenatal diagnosis and high-risk obstetrics. It might even be a marketing opportunity. Homer's infertility successes can walk across the hall and see me for high risk care. We'd be keeping everything in house which had to be good for the bottom line.

I would contribute to the overhead at whatever percentage Homer felt was fair. As far as running the office, Homer would always be the boss man. I planned on being a sharecropper. Homer's word was law.

Homer scratched his chin with one hand, then rubbed his head through his surgical scrub cap. He took a draw on his Budweiser and digested what I'd said.

"My office runs on a pretty thin margin, Declan. I probably have a little more staff than I need. I can't bring myself to ever let anyone go unless the other office staff tells me their time is up. The embryology laboratory is really expensive. My Ph.D., Lou Guillette, costs a pretty penny, but he's a world class reproductive biologist and embryologist. And, to be fair, I give away too much care. I've been through a half-dozen business managers. Do you really think the downtown carriage trade is gonna drive down Folly Road to my little vintage bungalow?"

"Probably not many, but I'm not worried about the money, boss man."

I caught a fleeting smile before Homer wiped his lips with the back of his hand, still wrapped around his Budweiser. "That's something you don't hear every day. I don't meet too many people in our business that don't worry about the financials."

"I'm not, Homer. I'm really not. First, I'm confident that this will prove to be a successful practice model. I'm betting on myself, and I'm betting on your track record of success. Plus, I've got an ace up my sleeve."

I explained to Homer about Rosemary Winslow. She was already negotiating a settlement with the University over how they'd railroaded me. They'd damaged my reputation and shattered my practice. Rosemary believed those transgressions would translate into the high six figures at a minimum.

"Hell, if you take me on as a partner, Rosemary can use that as evidence of how far I've fallen. That'll kick the settlement up to seven figures."

"That supposed to be funny?" Homer asked, but we were both already smiling.

Rosemary also anticipated a multi-million-dollar settlement in the Ramirez case with her percentage set at one-third. If they don't settle, the verdict will be even higher. Homer liked the story about Rosemary taking the leadership apart at the Board of Trustees meeting.

He whistled softly. "Sounds like quite a gal. I'd like to meet her sometime."

"Slow down, Homer. Let's stay focused on why I'm here. You'll need to take me on as a partner before I'll let you try to hustle my girlfriend."

Homer laughed again. "So, you're old Charleston money now?"

"No, I'm not talking about High Battery money, but enough. Enough that I only need to work as much as I feel like working, and only do things I feel like doing. If things break right, I might even have enough cash to help upgrade the Folly Road digs. New carpet, pave the parking lot, some flowers, running water; you know, the luxuries. Come on Homer, we'd be great together."

Homer took another few moments, and then cracked his neck. He reached into his black vest pocket and pulled out a silver flask. After unscrewing the cap, he took a long slug, chasing it with a gulp of Budweiser. Homer leaned back with a satisfied smile on his face and extended his right arm with the silver flask.

"Fuckin' A."

I took a swig from the flask and chased it by draining my Bud as well . "Fuckin' A."

"Podna', this one's gonna be a stunner."

With another snort, the deal was done.

As if on cue, May's husband, Jimmy, started playing his saxophone from the worn out green couch on the opposite side of the dining room next to the oyster shucking room. Jimmy hailed from Savannah and had played with Count Basie. He'd been pissed off for thirty years over having to give up his music career to run a shrimp and oyster shack on the Folly River. When he couldn't stand it anymore, he'd go sit in the corner and play. It helped him remember better times, and better yet, it really pissed May off. I hoped his playing was a good omen.

"Homer, you're not really crazy, are you?" In retrospect, I should've asked that question 30 minutes ago. Not smart to anger your new partner after only one minute in business together. I might not want to know the answer.

“That’s a matter of opinion, podna. Navy thought I might be, but there aren’t enough sane people in the Navy to do a proper inquiry.”

“What happened, if you don’t mind me asking?”

“Do you remember Lucy?” Homer asked.

“I do. I saw your Mustang out in the parking lot when I drove up. She’s still lookin’ sharp.”

“Ain’t just a Mustang, tenderfoot. Lucy is a classic 1969 Ford Mustang Boss 429 Sportsroof with an 820-S NASCAR stock car racin’ engine.”

“They don’t make them like that anymore.”

“They never made them like that, bubba. I got Lucy back when I was a medical student in San Francisco. I’ve been working on her for more than twenty years. When I was stationed at Great Lakes Naval, Lucy and I went out late one night on a rat run to White Castle. I stopped at a bar I liked, called Corcoran’s, and had a few beers. It got late and I was worried that the base gates might lock up on me. It was snowing like hell when I came out of Corcoran’s. I figured I could shave some time off my trip back by cutting across the city park. It looked like a snow-covered soccer field. I didn’t remember the damn lake until I heard the cracking sounds, and the front end began to dip. The water rose over the hood to the front window. I scrambled out and sat on the roof.”

“How’d you get Lucy out?”

“I pounded on a few doors until someone finally answered and let me use their phone. I found an all-night towing service, but the jackleg wouldn’t come out unless I gave him a license tag number. I’d just gotten new Michigan plates and I didn’t have any idea what my license number was. I told him I didn’t know, but I was pretty damn sure that Lucy was the only car in the lake that night. The tow-guy hung up on me. When I went back to the lake, there were a half dozen cherry tops popping. The trooper in charge told me that he was sorry about the car. It looked sweet. I told him he had no idea. Huge acceleration and handled like a dream, but her flotation was for shit. That’s when I decided to name her Lucy, short for the Lusitania.”

I couldn’t help but laugh. I doubt the state trooper did, at two in the morning and four degrees.

"The cop was hot to find out who was driving. I told him it was Charlie. He wanted to know where Charlie was. I kept telling him that Charlie was still sitting behind the wheel. It eventually got ugly. The Navy sent me to see a psychiatrist."

"I bet he loved you."

Homer just smiled, and took another draw from his flask, chased by a gulp from his Budweiser.

"A clever little fucker for a Navy psychiatrist. He broke the ice by asking me if I'd like a cup of coffee, and whether Charlie might want something. I asked him what he meant. He responded with a question about whether I had an imaginary friend named Charlie. I jumped him for asking the most ridiculous question that I'd ever heard. Navy officers don't have imaginary friends. Admirals' maybe, but not line officers. Charlie was invisible. Big difference between invisible and imaginary and, as a psychiatrist, he should know that. I probably got us off on the wrong foot."

"You think?"

"Well, of course, he wanted to know if Charlie was with us. It disappointed him when I explained that Charlie was on vacation in Florida. Curious bastard though. He wanted to know why Charlie had chosen Florida. Again, I told him that was another stupid question. Charlie loves to ski when he goes on vacation. So the doc then asks me who's Charlie water skiing with. I told him that Charlie hates water skiing. Charlie only snow skis. Then the dummy asks why Charlie goes to Florida if he prefers snow skiing. So, I told him that Charlie prefers Florida because the lift lines are shorter. That seemed to bother my Navy headshrinker a great deal. We never really saw eye to eye after that."

Homer and I both smiled and tipped our Budweiser bottles together.

"After a couple of sessions, he got tired of me. Great Lakes decided that I might be the perfect man for the new opening in Charleston. The rest, as they say, is history." Homer raised his hands dramatically in a ta-da gesture, with a beautiful fried shrimp between the thumb and forefinger of each hand.

"Homer, I think this is going to be the greatest partnership in history."

"Fuckin' A." Homer handed me his flask again. "Let's take the rest of the day off and celebrate."

I staggered back to Rosemary's apartment about four hours later. I was embarrassed for her to see me in that condition. If I was going to partner with Homer Lahr, I'd need to up my game.

Chapter 13.
FOLLY FERTILITY

Homer picked the name for practice. I knew he chuckled every time he heard it. Building a new practice is a frustrating, painful and hand wringing experience. However, my first year at Folly Fertility couldn't have gone better. Several patients followed me from downtown, and Homer sent me a steady stream of his infertility successes.

Despite his lack of specialist training, Homer was a superb infertility doctor. His success rates were comparable to or better than most other highfalutin infertility centers. Homer tended to be heavy-handed with the number of embryos he'd replace. I'd already convinced him to limit himself to replacing no more than three embryos. Next year, I'd try to get him down to a maximum of two. I was awash with twins and triplets, but I enjoyed the challenge.

A lot of Homer's patients had been turned away from the other fertility practices. Most of the time they'd run out of money. That wasn't a problem for Homer. Sometimes, they had other co-morbidities that made them poor candidates for in vitro fertilization. Homer had a soft spot for the underdog. Homer's successes, even if they were a singleton, often became high risk obstetrical patients. Homer pronounced each baby as precious, and that they needed the best. The best just happened to be across the hall. Fertility patients are frequently older, and worried about chromosomal abnormalities. After years of trying to get pregnant, many didn't want to take any chances. I'd been trained in doing chorionic villus sampling and amniocentesis. Homer kept me busy doing both.

It didn't bother me at all when my schedule wasn't chock full. The pressure to pack dozens of patients into fifteen minute schedule blocks was the mortal sin of modern medicine. Scheduling templates didn't exist at Folly Fertility. I adopted Homer's practice of making my own schedule in a little notebook. If a patient needed an hour, that's what she got. If she needed five minutes tomorrow, that's what she got. If Homer needed to meet a patient at the Sand Dollar on Folly Beach during her break, that's what he'd do. If Homer needed an afternoon at Bowen's Island, that's what he took. Our scheduler had the easiest job on the planet. Patients would hand her a little torn off scrap of paper, with a note from Homer, describing when he wanted her back, and for how long.

At first, I thought this seemed a little loosey-goosie, but after a while, I came to love it. Institutional medicine only provides round holes and finds it difficult dealing with square pegs. It's impossible to eliminate all scheduling pressure, but doing it myself, got me closer than I'd ever been at the medical university. I found it thrilling to see women glancing at their watches wondering if I'd ever shut up.

Figuring out the convoluted billing arrangements that Homer worked out wasn't as easy. He offered fertility evaluations and IVF on lay-away, extended payment plans, no payment plans, and by bartering. IVF successes that Homer sent me for prenatal care that first year included a Filipino woman who brought a basket of deep-fried pork or shrimp filled lumpia every Friday at lunch. Another woman's husband traded lifetime mechanic services for Lucy and Homer's Harley for his wife's IVF expenses. When I asked Homer how to handle those things, he just advised me to keep things simple. The lumpia was outstanding.

Homer Lahr spent his entire adult life being a resistance fighter against conformity. Devoid of an agenda, Homer was a man in full who charted his own course on a day to day basis. I'd spent endless hours trying to figure out how to accomplish that feat. One evening after work, over a glass of Jack Daniel, Homer shared his secret.

"Son, never get religion of any kind. Never put anyone else's version of what's important ahead of your own. The minute you do, you're not making decisions for yourself anymore. You're dancin' to someone else's tune. Within two weeks of going in-country in Nam we figured out two things. First, no one gave a shit about you. We were the smallest cogs in a much bigger set of gears. Second, we all accepted that we were never going to get out of the shit alive. Once you gave up hope of ever getting back to anything you'd ever loved, it became easier to do what had to be done. Doing what had to be done often meant ignoring the bigger gears."

Homer paused and reflected on what he'd just said. "A word of warning, though. Once you decide that you're not going to be a small cog any longer, the real boss man who cranks the gears will try to strip you out. Not going along with the plan will always make you a target. The trick is to make sure there isn't anything so important to you that it hurts if they strip it away."

Homer leaned back and stared at the ceiling fan like its revolutions held the secrets of the universe. He refilled his highball glass with two fingers of liquid heat. "You know, nobody understands how I can do embryo transfers in the morning, and then pregnancy terminations on the same table in the afternoons. Civilians can't wrap their heads around it. The things we did in Nam didn't make any sense either. Civilians couldn't wrap their heads around it then. I think that's why we never get any abortion protestors."

"Homer, they're just terrified of you."

"Either way, I don't care. The point is, I don't ascribe to anybody else's orthodoxy. I decide for myself. Sometimes, it means helping a woman who wants to become pregnant, and sometimes, it means helping one who doesn't. Some might say there's too much moral flexibility in that, but I don't worry about what other people say. The only good thing that I learned in Vietnam was that you better think for yourself. Let the devil take the hindmost. If that means you need to be morally flexible, or work off the books or do things that others aren't willing to do, then that's just the way it has to be. It's a God-damn hard way to live. I need to make sure that you know the score."

"Boss man, you sound like a revolutionary."

"I'm an American, the original revolutionary." Homer drained his glass of Jack.

My respect for Homer grew every day. I aspired to be as single-minded, strong-willed and self-assured as Homer. It would be a long apprenticeship. In the meantime, I treasured the freedom Homer gave me to control my own time and set my own values. The practice of medicine I'd imagined when I got in the pre-med registration line in college. The illusion of independence had become harder and harder to find as governmental and business interests infiltrated and co-opted the doctor-patient relationship. Folly Fertility may be the last tattered remnant of the independent practice of medicine, and Homer Lahr refused to let it go.

Any good revolutionary needs a good lawyer. Rosemary Winslow also enjoyed a fantastic year. My settlement with MUSC was generous. Rosemary used the insult of my settlement, as well as a high demand, to goad Vincent Bellizia into taking the Ramirez case to trial. She outmaneuvered Vince at every turn. She made the University look worse than heartless. The jury got pissed. The verdict in favor of Ms. Ramirez's daughter made national news. The post-verdict settlement ended up being eight million dollars higher than Vincent could have gotten pre-trial. Rosemary also represented Sonia Bokhanevich who was fired by the Anesthesia Department in the wake of my leaving. By that time, MUSC was so terrified of Rosemary Winslow they agreed to her first settlement offer without any negotiation.

Rosemary opened a solo practice just over the Wappoo Cut Bridge on James Island on Wappoo Creek Drive. To anyone who asked, it was on Maybank Highway just after you turned off Folly Road. To those who were local, it was next to the Crab House.

Rosemary selected a modest office in a pre-fab row of white stucco commercial office space. The only thing that made her office stand out among the other business suites were the two large, glazed ceramic pots on either side of her door with narrow leaf Mexican sago palms. She didn't put her name on the door.

Inside, the office wasn't fancy, but it was exceptionally tasteful and noticeably feminine compared to other legal offices that I'd unfortunately been in. The walls were covered with French impressionist art reprints, plus one original, instead of the usual self-aggrandizing diplomas and awards. The carpets and curtains were a matched creamy-white hue. The office had comfortable settees instead of heavy mahogany and leather chairs. Tall, slender orchids with soft, variegated petals replaced plastic flowers in the waiting room. Rosemary's barrister bookcases were antique tiger-eye oak with their original wavy glass doors. The bathroom was a showplace.

While inviting and comfortable, Rosemary's office assiduously avoided any hint of ostentatious. Ostentatious made clients uncomfortable. Even the dimmest bulb could figure out that the office was being paid for by a cut of their money. The sizes of her fees were the last thing Rosemary wanted any new client to be thinking about during their first consultation.

Wappoo Creek Drive had several other advantages. Rosemary's divorce from the Holmes Law Firm had become ugly. She was happy to get out of downtown. The downtown legal Brahmin didn't intimidate Rosemary, but so much the better if she didn't have to bump into them at lunch. Her office on Maybank at Folly also put her five minutes from Folly Fertility, and thirty minutes closer to her condo on Seabrook Island. We went there each Friday afternoon before the traffic got unbearable.

The one luxury that Rosemary afforded herself was a broad picture window in her private office. The window allowed her to look down the Wappoo Cut to catch the afternoon setting sun. Rosemary picked me up from Folly Fertility on most days. I knew not to expect her until after she enjoyed a late afternoon drink, watching the splayed colors of the sunset dappled and blown across the tree line, marsh and currents at the western end of the Cut. A glass of fifteen-year-old port and the orchestral crescendo of Mother Nature, brought each day to a stunning end.

As I'd promised Homer, Rosemary and I invested some of our new money back into Folly Fertility. It was the first time the practice had ever been flush. Homer remained a cheapskate whether we were in the red or the black. We gave the staff long overdue bonuses, upgraded the office amenities and paved the parking lot. A contractor, with twin sons thanks to Homer, did the paving at cost. We also bought a nitrous oxide machine for our procedure room. Homer got really good with it. It proved vastly superior to the local anesthesia and intravenous analgesia regimen that we'd been using for most of our outpatient procedures. The staff couldn't remember anything that made Dr. Lahr as happy as that nitrous machine.

Chapter 14.
DIETHYLSTILBESTROL

Everyone's pride is hurt a little bit when they have to go ask for help. I didn't see a lot of Gynecology patients, and I knew my depth. I'd only been working at Folly Fertility a short time when I met Marley Clary. Marley was fifteen years old and had come in with vaginal bleeding and an unusual watery discharge. She'd put off telling her mother for almost a year. I added her on because my schedule was nearly empty. We talked for quite a while. I had an instructional flip chart that I used to walk her through what would be her first pelvic exam. Marley said she hoped to be a doctor someday.

Marley handled everything with great maturity. I used a pediatric Petersen speculum to make the exam easier. I worried that I wouldn't be able to see what was going on. Based on her symptoms, I worried about a foreign object. It wouldn't be the first toy that I'd removed from a vagina, but usually in younger children.

Marley's hymen wasn't intact, but I believed her when she said she was virginal. I wish I'd found a foreign object. Her cervix appeared malformed, and there was a diffuse abnormality of the upper vagina. I did a quick Pap smear and asked my nurse for biopsy forceps. I assured Marley that she wasn't going to feel the biopsy at all, and she didn't. I decided to defer a digital pelvic examination. I congratulated Marley on how brave she'd been. She smiled.

Embarrassed or not, I needed to talk with Homer about Marley's exam. I walked to the other end of the office. I found Homer in the laboratory talking with his embryologist.

"Homer, you got a minute for a curbside?"

"Damnation, son. You in trouble again? I didn't know that I was takin' ya to raise."

"I might be boss man. I just examined a fifteen-year-old. I'm scared about what I saw. I don't want it to be what I think it is."

"Fill me in hot shot. But first, let me introduce you to my partner, Dr. Louis Guillette. We all just call him Lou. He's the best embryologist south of the Jones Institute, and the smartest guy in the building. If you need anything, you come talk to Lou. Give him forty-eight hours, and his lab can do any assay you can think of."

"A pleasure to meet you, Lou. I've heard Homer rave about you several times. I'm excited to be working with you guys." I extended my hand. Lou shook it vigorously.

"Great to have you on board, Dr. Murphy. I can't tell you how tired I am of Homer's tall tales and balderdash. It's going to be refreshing to work with someone who isn't a legend in his own mind. Like Homer said, my lab door is always open."

I knew immediately that I was going to like this guy. I thanked Dr. Guillette for his welcome. I turned back to Dr. Lahr to discuss Marley's findings. "I've only seen one other case, but I think this girl has a vaginal clear cell adenocarcinoma."

"Not a chance, son. Almost never happens in pre-menopausal women. Rare as hen's teeth. Are you sure it isn't a severe inflammatory reaction? Did she forget to take a tampon out?"

"I don't think so. She doesn't even use tampons yet. I did a Pap and a biopsy. I sent the biopsy rush because I'm worried about what it's going to show."

Dr. Guillette interjected, "She's a DES daughter."

"No, she's only fifteen. No one has taken DES since the early 1970s." I instantaneously regretted being dismissive.

"Third generation," Guillette replied.

"Third generation? What does that mean?"

"Get an extended family history from her mother. I'll bet you dollars to doughnuts that the girl's grandmother received diethylstilbestrol when she was pregnant with Marley's mother. Marley is now a third generation DES granddaughter. If she has a vaginal clear cell adenocarcinoma, then I don't think there's any question."

"No, I think there's a huge question. I've never heard of third generation DES exposure."

"Actually, people have been looking out for these cases for quite a while. Before I was an embryologist, I was a reproductive biologist. All reproductive biologists are familiar with the Diethylstilbestrol tragedy. When grandma was given DES in the 1950s or 60s to prevent miscarriage, Marley's mom was exposed in utero. Biologically, the female conceptus, in utero, already has every egg that she'll ever release. Marley's vaginal adenocarcinoma, if that's what she has, is a consequence of her mother's eggs being exposed to diethylstilbestrol, when her mom was still a fetus."

Homer laughed and slapped me on the back. "I told you he was the smartest dude in the building."

I wasn't buying it. "Dr. Guillette, theoretically that sounds possible, but I've not seen anything that clinically supports it. If teenage vaginal adenocarcinomas were on the upswing, I think I would've heard about it."

Diethylstilbestrol (DES) is a synthetic estrogen prescribed to pregnant women between 1938 and 1971. Physicians believed that DES could prevent spontaneous miscarriages and maybe, recurrent preterm birth. In a few countries, diethylstilbestrol was even included in the prenatal vitamins. Women's magazines advertised DES with glowing young mothers holding angelic and perfectly formed newborn babies. Since it replaced a "natural hormone deficiency," physicians believed it to be perfectly safe. Between five and ten million women were exposed to DES in the U.S. alone, most during the first trimester when organ systems like the ovaries are developing.

In 1971, the FDA issued a Drug Bulletin Warning that DES caused a rare vaginal cancer in teenage girls, and children as young as eight years old, if their mother took the drug early in pregnancy. Vaginal clear cell adenocarcinoma only occurred in about one out of every one thousand DES exposed daughters, but it had otherwise been non-existent among pre-menopausal women. The drug disappeared from the market, and the magazines, almost overnight.

A huge group of DES exposed daughters were identified from pharmacy records. As these DES daughters were followed through their reproductive years, it became evident that vaginal clear cell cancer was only the tip of the iceberg. Almost a third of DES daughters had abnormalities of their uterus or Fallopian tubes that lead to infertility, and high rates of ectopic pregnancy or miscarriage.

Dr. Guillette responded confidently. "We see third generation affects in mice all the time. And, before you get on a high horse about it being mice, you should know that everything we now know to be true about DES exposure was predicted by the mouse model. The offspring of female mice exposed to DES in utero have increased rates of uterine cancers and ovarian tumors. Third generation male mice also have an increased frequency of reproductive tract tumors. The evidence in humans is just now beginning to accumulate. The Netherlands keeps much more detailed health records than we do. They've shown a twenty-fold higher incidence of hypospadias among the sons of DES daughters. We don't have data yet for third generation daughters, but there's no reason not to anticipate similar findings. It's just harder to assess for uterine and cervical abnormalities in females compared to hypospadias in males. Vaginal clear cell adenocarcinoma was infrequent in the original DES daughters, and it will be even rarer in the third generation. Unfortunately, I can promise you that they're coming."

"Son, if Lou says they're coming, then you better be ready. My partner in crime ain't wrong very often," Homer pointed at Lou and then walked away. Homer called back over his shoulder as he turned into a consultation room, "Let me know what the biopsy shows."

I turned back to Dr. Guillette struck by the calmness of his absolute certainty. "How could that be possible?"

"Twenty years ago, most scientists believed there was a gene for almost every disease. If that bad gene was present, you got sick. If it didn't, you stayed well. The idea behind mapping the human genome was to identify which bad genes were present in any given individual. With that knowledge it would be possible to predict what our future health would be. To the geneticist's surprise, instead of finding half a million genes, they found fewer than 30,000. Their assumptions had to be rethought. With so few actual genes, it became apparent that each one must play variable roles in multiple pathways associated with either health or disease. They discovered that the attachment of small proteins to the DNA sequence could create subtle alterations in how the DNA code is read."

"You're talking about epigenetic changes. Instead of being turned on or off like a power switch, the activity of genes could be turned up or down like a volume control."

Lou's face noticeably brightened.

"Exactly. Hormones are basically signals that tell the DNA what needs to be done next. If the DNA sequence has been modified by these epigenetic proteins, then the hormonal signal may not elicit the expected response, or the response may be inadequate. For you guys that might mean abnormally formed reproductive organs, delayed puberty, irregular ovulation, reduced sperm counts, infertility or even malignancies. There's no longer any doubt that exposure to the synthetic estrogen, diethylstilbestrol, during a critical period of fetal development, altered the functioning of estrogen responsive genes in the eggs of their unborn daughters. Those DES-induced epigenetic changes, and disrupted estrogen signaling, were then passed onto that woman's daughter twenty something years later when that egg was selected for conception. I hope to God that I'm wrong, but your young patient may die from a medication, marketed as safe, that her grandmother took to prevent miscarriage more than a quarter century ago."

"I need to go talk to Marley's mother."

"Be sure to keep me posted. Really interesting case."

Thirty minutes later, there wasn't much doubt. Neither Marley, nor her mother Mandy, had ever heard of diethylstilbestrol or DES. Mandy had been born in 1951. She'd always been considered a miracle because her mother suffered multiple miscarriages. Mandy experienced a ruptured ectopic pregnancy prior to conceiving Marley. The gynecologist who removed her ruptured Fallopian tube told her that her uterus was abnormally shaped. He was doubtful that she'd ever conceive normally. They were thrilled when Marley came along in 1978. After Marley, came several more miscarriages, and Mandy never had a second child.

I spent the rest of the day avoiding Homer's end of the office, and the inevitable, "I told you so."

Two days later I got a call from Gordon Hennigar, a pathologist at MUSC, and a friend from medical school. I sent the biopsy to his attention. Gordon Hennigar was the best pathologist I knew. He also had a special interest in gynecologic pathology.

"Declan, what was your clinical impression when you took this specimen?"

"I'm worried about a clear cell."

"It's a clear cell adenocarcinoma. A nasty one too. I hadn't seen one in a long time, so I showed it around to some of the other gray hairs. Not much doubt. I'm sorry."

"Thanks, Gordon. That was my impression as well. I'd hoped that it might come back as benign adenosis, but it looked far too angry for that."

"I did want to check one thing regarding your submission paperwork. What you sent over says that the patient is fifteen. Is that a typo?"

"I wish it were, Gordo."

"Holy shit, Declan. I'm sorry. What are you going to do?"

"Not sure but hold onto the slides. I'm sure that the oncologists are going to want to look at them. They're not going to believe the report."

"Will do, buddy. Hey, we miss you around here. Not as much fun to come to work without hearing stories about Declan Murphy's most recent shit storm."

"I'm doing just fine, thank you. Sorry that I'm not providing you with my usual entertainment value."

"Seriously, Declan, let's get together some evening for a few beers. I haven't seen you in an age."

"Thanks, Gordo. Let me get settled in my new place. I'll give you a call, and we'll catch up.

I contacted Mandy at lunch. She would bring Marley in after school. I dropped by Dr. Guillette's office to let him know that the diagnosis was confirmed. Surprisingly, he had the name of a Gynecologic Oncologist at Duke University internationally known for his treatment of vaginal clear cell carcinoma. Lou had already contacted him and set up an appointment for Marley at Duke for the first of next week. Lou asked if I minded him coming with me when I met with Marley and her mother. I couldn't say no.

It turned out to be a fortunate request. Lou held Marley's hand the whole time. He took over when I began to choke up. I tried to project hopefulness, but the meagerness of the prognosis kept clawing its way up the back of my throat.

Dr. Guillette captured Marley's gaze with his piercing clear-blue eyes. He explained the entire DES story as a fascinating medical mystery. He didn't sugar coat anything, yet his narrative was filled with compassion. He explained that Marley was incredibly unique. At the same time, she wasn't alone. Marley was now part of a medical tragedy that had affected millions of women. There were tears, of course, but Marley, and her mother, drew strength from Dr. Guillette's deep understanding of what had happened to her. They were reassured by his unblinking focus on Marley's well-being and future.

Dr. Guillette told them about their upcoming appointment with the Gyn Oncologist at Duke. There wasn't anybody in the country who knew more about her cancer, and his outcomes were the best. Lou understood that hope kept you putting one foot in front of the other when the going got tough. It didn't get any tougher than vaginal clear cell carcinoma.

Later that day, I passed Homer in the hallway. I congratulated him on hiring Lou to be his embryologist. "He's an amazing guy. You should have seen him with that patient of mine with the vaginal clear cell adenocarcinoma. It's a bit intimidating that your embryologist knows more medicine than I do."

"He knows more medicine than almost everyone. To be honest with you, he takes care of most of my fertility patients once they come around to IVF."

"We're lucky to have him. Plus, I like the guy. There's something about him that pulls you in. I don't know what it is, but you can see it in his eyes."

"Knew you'd see it too, Declan. People get captured by Lou's passion. Lou could've turned the Bataan Death March into a Shriner's parade."

Chapter 15.
LOUIS J. GUILLETTE, JR. PhD

I found myself spending more and more of my free time in Lou's laboratory. Homer found a kindred spirit in Lou Guillette. Lou grew up in a military family and spent most of his childhood in Spain. They returned stateside when Lou was in elementary school. Lou spoke English but thought in Spanish. After a school administered I.Q. test, Lou's parents were presented with the somber news that Lou might be able to make a living as a truck driver. What an incredible gift it was to be underestimated.

Lou had an eclectic breadth of enthusiasms and expansive interests beyond embryology. I'd worked at Folly Fertility for several months before finding out that Lou was the artist responsible for the amazing collection of wildlife photography that hung on our office walls. There were few places on earth that Lou hadn't visited. He shared his passionate love for wild places and the wild things that lived there

At fifty years old, Lou was in better shape than I at ten years his junior. During college, he'd worked as both a firefighter and a paramedic. He had the type of upper body development that you see in mountain climbers, which Lou had been in his Colorado Rocky Mountain youth. His face was magnetic and ageless , featuring an infectious smile, a full white beard, and longish hair, which he constantly brushed away from his face. You noticed the habit because flipping his hair revealed an unforgettable set of sparkling blue eyes.

Lou could endlessly entertain with impromptu tales of tracking African lions across the Serengeti, shivering in an ice cave waiting for a snow leopard to appear or probing the marsh grass with a cane pole searching for alligator nests. Once or twice a day, Homer dropped by Lou's laboratory to run the office staff back to their jobs. Lou came to work each day in cargo shorts, a crisp blue denim long sleeved shirt and well-worn hiking boots. He also went home for lunch every day. When I asked him why, he smiled and responded, "Declan, life's a three-legged stool. Family, work, and self, in that order. If one is missing, the stool falls over."

Lou taught Reproductive Biology and Endocrinology at the University of Florida before coming to Charleston. I once saw him jump up on a table in front of the office staff to demonstrate how to mount a surfboard. He possessed an adolescent sense of adventure, and the need for fun that is lost somewhere in each of us. I mentioned to Lou that he must've been the most popular professor at Florida. He reminisced for a moment, and then answered, "Teaching is like performance art. Don't let anyone tell you different. If you're not a performer, then you aren't doing it right."

Lou embraced being a scientist in the romantic sense of the word. To Lou, being a scientist was part adventurer, part detective, and part artist. He reveled in discovery, seeing things that no one else had seen, the small details, which may not be important now, but would matter later. New ideas were like a puzzle. All the pieces are there for anyone to see, but scientists take advantage of their curiosity and imagination to rearrange those pieces in an innovative way so that a new picture evolves.

The scientific ideas that Lou developed were every bit as beautiful to him as his wildlife photography. Lou dedicated himself to the search for new knowledge, and to teaching others the scientific method. Lou's academic contemporaries considered him a scientist's scientist. I did not question that assessment.

As a young professor of Zoology at the University of Florida in the early 1980s, Lou became interested in the health of the American alligator. Alligator meat and skin were in high demand. Florida wondered if their state mascot could become a renewable profit center and funded his research. His fieldwork took him to nearby Lake Apopka which was known to be heavily polluted. An astute biologist, he observed that the alligator population was declining, the egg clutches were smaller and the hatchlings had easily identifiable reproductive abnormalities. Many people made these same observations, but Lou saw something the others missed. A new way to put the puzzle pieces together.

He identified a link between the reproductive problems identified in the *Alligator mississippiensi* and the high levels of DDT found in Lake Apopka from surrounding agricultural run-off. The other major polluter of Lake Apopka was the Kennedy Space Center. Every now and then, NASA ignited a few million tons of rocket fuel flooding the surrounding swamps and lake with spent chemical compounds. Lou demonstrated that dozens of these chemicals had estrogen-like or anti-estrogenic capabilities. Lou asked an elegant new question, "Were endocrine disrupting environmental contaminants affecting the reproductive development and reproductive capability of the Apopka alligators?"

Lou also believed, when nobody else did, that the alligator was a superb sentinel species for human health. While alligators are reptilian, and most humans aren't, there are still many similarities. The alligator is an apex predator at the top of its food chain. Most of the endocrine disrupting chemical contaminants are stored in fat. As bigger fish eat smaller fish, the contaminants in their body fat are passed up the food chain. As a chubby apex predator, the alligator stores the highest level of these fat soluble, hormonally-active contaminants.

Alligators are also long-lived, with about the same life expectancy as humans. They'll stick around where they're born into adulthood, accumulating contaminants from its home environment over its entire lifetime. Like most humans, they also have a nasty disposition when unexpectedly disturbed.

More importantly, both alligators and humans have nearly identical reproductive hormones. Alligator estrogens and androgens generate the same developmental signals, at essentially the same developmental times, as they do in humans. Consequently, they can be disrupted the same way.

In his early studies, Lou compared the young juvenile males from Lake Apopka to other young males from the pristine Lake Woodruff. The juveniles from Lake Apopka were being exposed to substantially higher levels of multiple agricultural and industrial contaminants. The differences in exposure were strongly associated with reductions in both testosterone and dihydrotestosterone in the Lake Apopka alligators, the two androgens that play key roles in male genital development, just as they do in humans.

Compared to the alligators in Lake Woodruff, the male alligators in Lake Apopka suffered a twenty-five to thirty percent reduction in phallus size. Lou's hypothesized that estrogenic or anti-androgenic chemicals polluting Lake Apopka were interfering with the testosterone signal that should be directing penile development during fetal development, and later, during puberty.

Lou experienced his fifteen minutes of searing fame when he testified before Congress a few years later regarding endocrine disrupting contaminants in our waterways. He reviewed the national trends in male reproductive health. Trends that included increased rates of testicular cancer, increased rates of hypospadias, and a decline in sperm count of at least 50%, over the past two generations. Lou became infamous when he told the assembled Congressmen that every one of them was half the man his grandfather was. He challenged them to not let their grandsons be half the man that they are. No one could ever accuse Lou of not having a flair for the dramatic. After all, it's performance art, isn't it?

Following up on the publicity of his congressional appearance, Lou wrote the minority report regarding endocrine disrupting chemicals for a state-of-the-science paper by the National Academy of Science. His report was so beautifully elucidated and documented that the National Academy of Science did the unprecedented. They changed their mind, elevating the minority opinion to become its official NAS position on the significance of environmental endocrine disrupting compounds on human health.

Lou Guillette then discovered that when you get too close to the flame, you can get burned. Following his Congressional testimony and National Academy of Science report, Lou was pilloried by many of his colleagues. Accused of producing junk science, Lou received a "Cry-Babies Award" for his monograph on endocrine disruptors from one quasi-governmental, business supported organization. While Lou understood the science of endocrine disrupting compounds, he underestimated the far-reaching impact of his discoveries.

Endocrine disruption isn't just an environmental story. It's an industry story. An industry that doesn't bother to wrangle alligators to check hormone levels. Industry produces millions of tons of chemicals that fall into the category of being endocrine disruptors. Ubiquitous chemicals necessary for products we use every day. Pesticides, herbicides, plastic drink bottles, Tupperware, I.V. tubing, canned peas, Campbell's soup, printed receipts, cosmetics, perfumes, hair products and dozens of other "essential" consumer goods. That made endocrine disruption is a business story, and, in the United States, business stories became political stories. It's a story about big money. And, ultimately, a story that explains how Louis J. Guillette, Jr. Ph.D. ended up working for Homer Lahr.

First, the federal grants dried up. Endocrine disruption became sufficiently polarizing that no NIH study section could reach a consensus about funding further research. That left Lou dependent on the state or university if he wanted to continue his field research. In central Florida, the state University doesn't fund projects that irritate Florida's agricultural interests or NASA. The lack of any federal, state or institutional support for his research eventually drove Lou out of Gainesville.

Having to leave a university position due to lack of independent funding is a relatively common career detour. Ending up working in the office of Homer Lahr on Folly Road is an extraordinary career detour. What brought Lou to South Carolina was a longstanding friendship with another naturalist who worked at the Tom Yawkey Wildlife Preserve. With his friend's help, Louis J. Guillette, Jr. Ph.D. applied for, and received, a modest grant from the Yawkey Foundation to continue his environmental research on the health of the ample alligator population on their preserve. Working for Homer provided a steady paycheck, schedule flexibility and proximity to Yawkey. Lou was perfectly happy with the arrangement.

The Tom Yawkey Wildlife Preserve is approximately 24,000 acres of marshes, wetlands, forests and 16 miles of undeveloped beach north of Charleston in Georgetown County. William Yawkey was a turn of the century timber industrialist and owner of the Detroit Tigers. He purchased a share of the property as part of a hunting group. His son, Tom, inherited the property in the early twentieth century, when he was only 16 years old. Tom Yawkey later became the owner of the Boston Red Sox, and eventually bought the entire property.

Tom Yawkey maintained the property as an isolated hunting reserve, hosting baseball Hall of Famers like Ty Cobb and Ted Williams, along with other captains of industry. To this day, there's no way to get onto the property by land. Visitors must take a boat or a barge across the Intracoastal Waterway. On his death in 1976, Tom Yawkey gave the property to the South Carolina Department of Natural Resources in a perpetual trust.

The Tom Yawkey Wildlife Preserve is a habitat for more than 200 species of migratory birds, bald eagles, hawks, ospreys, falcons and other endangered species. The preserve beaches are some of the best nesting locations for the threatened loggerhead sea turtles. The habitat is also home to an unknown, but huge, number of great American alligators. As one of his deed restrictions, Tom Yawkey forbade the hunting of alligators. As a result, the Yawkey preserve boasted some of the oldest and most entitled alligators in the country.

Lou also craved the opportunity for collaboration with physician scientists. Lou approached MUSC, but not surprisingly, the medical university lacked both vision and available funds. Lou might have sought out Homer because of his involvement in gynecology and infertility. While Lou's findings on diminished penile size drew media attention, Lou found the abnormalities in the female alligator hatchlings more interesting. He discovered a uniquely abnormal pathology , which he called a multi-ototic follicle.

Female hatchlings from highly contaminated clutches, instead of having a single egg per ovarian follicle, had multiple eggs per follicle. Lou recognized that the multi-ootoic follicles he discovered in highly contaminated alligators looked almost identical to adult human polycystic ovarian disease. Polycystic ovarian disease just happened to be the leading cause of Homer's infertility referrals.

Lou could not have hoped for a better boss than Homer who didn't know what a punch clock was. Lou mastered embryology in short order and could set up any hormonal assay Homer wanted in less than 24 hours. The rest of Lou's time was his to use as he pleased. Homer enjoyed knowing that Lou did environmental research in his spare time, even if he didn't have a clue what it was all about. Whenever anyone asked Homer what Lou was up to, his standard response was, "My boy's goin' to cure PCOS someday. He's a god-damned alligator gynecologist."

Homer may well be right, but he wasn't curious about the details.

On the other hand, Lou's work fascinated me, Within three months of starting at Folly Fertility, I was going on field trips with Lou to help collect specimens. The nocturnal alligator hunts on the Tom Yawkey Wildlife Preserve were an eerie, once in a life-time experience. You could turn on a powerful flashlight, fan it across a lake and see dozens upon dozens of red alligator eyes shining back at you. Lou and I became research partners. Rosemary and I used a big chunk of my settlement money to upgrade Lou's embryology laboratory into a state of the art environmental research facility, buy several improved incubators, fund a laboratory assistant, and purchase an airboat, a fishing truck and other supplies necessary to support our field research.

I loved clinical work, but found myself anticipating and excited about upcoming weekend field work even more. I completely bought into the notion of alligators as sentinels of human health. Our work seemed as worthwhile as anything I'd ever done. My waders, work boots and mosquito repellant were always in the trunk of my car. I worried a lot about losing fingers or a hand and became highly disciplined. Lou was a fabulous field research mentor.

On our trips to Yawkey we'd assiduously collect water and sediment samples. At dusk, we'd hunt the juvenile and adult alligators. We'd collect their blood, urine, tissue samples and measure the size of the male alligator phalluses. It wasn't work for the squeamish or for those without duct tape. The last thing we did on each trip was locate the alligator nests. After making sure that mommy wasn't home, we'd raid them, and bring the egg clutches back to Lou's lab for incubation. Hatching season brought a new flurry of scientific activity.

Homer and the office staff liked coming by for the hatching. Lou and I carefully evaluated each hatchling's sexual development, and the hormonal and chemical environment in which the hatchling had gestated.

We weren't disappointed. The results were even more remarkable than they'd been from Lake Apopka.

Chapter 16.
SMELL OF MONEY

In July of 1976, a safety valve ruptured at a chemical manufacturing plant in Seveso, Italy. The chemical plant produced 2,3,5-trichlorophenol, an intermediate chemical in herbicide production. The industrial accident released more than thirty kilograms of 2,3,7,8-tetrachlorodibenzo-p-dioxin (TCDD) into the environment. The nearby population of Milan, along with multiple other Lombardian villages, were subsequently exposed to the highest ever recorded levels of dioxin, one of the most toxic of all man-made chemicals.

Despite being at, or near, the top of any list of the most dangerous environmental contaminants, TCDD is widespread in the environment. TCDD accumulates due to overtreatment with herbicides, as by-products of waste incineration, from bleaching processes used in making paper products, and the manufacturing of polyvinyl chloride plastics. Besides being ubiquitous, TCDD is also distressingly persistent. TCDD accumulates in body fat where it is protected from metabolism and excretion.

Dioxins, like TCDD, have been associated with multiple cancers, particularly kidney and bladder cancer, soft tissue sarcomas and breast cancer. Beyond cancer, high levels of TCDD exposure has also been linked to numerous immune disorders, skin problems, cataracts, intellectual and behavioral impairment.

The children of Seveso have been followed-up for decades. The reproductive potential of male children younger than age ten, living in, or near, Seveso at the time of the accidental TCDD spillage, was savaged by TCDD. Decades after their exposure, these men still carry high serum levels of TCDD and have remarkable reductions in sperm concentration and motility. Breastfeeding further increased their exposure. Breastfed males ultimately had even lower total sperm counts, sperm concentrations and number of motile sperm.

The United States Environmental Protection Agency has determined that TCDD contaminant levels below thirty parts per quintillion (ppq) are safe from an adult toxicity perspective. The EPA toxicity equations, however, don't consider the more difficult question of potential fetal toxicity. Could even miniscule fetal exposures to compounds, such as TCDD, affect the expression of hormonally responsive genes during in utero development, permanently altering the programming of primordial germ cells in the testicles and ovaries? These were the unanswered questions that interested Lou Guillette.

The first time he saw the multi-oototic ovarian follicles in his alligator hatchlings, Lou believed that he might be looking at the effects of a dioxin exposure. TCDD exerts its effects by binding to the aromatic hydrocarbon receptor. Interference with this receptor alters gene expression, resulting in a reduction in estrogen production.

Lou hypothesized that TCDD-induced suppression of estrogen signaling would have inevitable feedback effects on the pituitary production of Follicle Stimulating Hormone, essential to the normal development of ovarian follicles and an efficient ovulation process. In adult women, this abnormality, known as Polycystic Ovarian Syndrome, looks almost exactly like the multi-oototic follicles Lou was seeing in his newborn alligators.

Although not as well publicized, Lou also studied the reproductive problems experienced by women and female children exposed to TCDD following the 1976 Seveso disaster. In the year immediately following the TCDD release, there was an increase in the regional miscarriage rate. Lou also found a curious, but consistent, excess in the number of female births that strongly associated with paternal exposure to TCDD.

Twenty years after the fact, the Seveso Women's Health Study tracked the reproductive outcomes of almost one thousand women grouped according to what their individual TCDD level had been soon after the accident. For every ten-fold increase in the serum TCDD level, there was a 25% increase in the time required to achieve pregnancy, and a doubling of the odds for infertility. The Seveso Women's Health data also documented an earlier onset of natural menopause among women with higher levels of TCDD exposure.

Beyond the Seveso data, Lou's personal research experience also suggested that TCDD, or some other dioxin, was the cause of the reproductive abnormalities we were seeing in the alligator hatchlings from the Yawkey Wildlife Preserve.

Several years previously, while still on the faculty at the University of Florida, Lou was among several American scientists hired by the South African Department of Natural Resources to figure out why the Nile crocodile, *Crocodylus niloticus*, population was declining. The Crocodile River was being pressured by the combined effects of industrial, mining, agricultural and household pollution owing to its downstream proximity to South Africa's two largest cities, Johannesburg and Tshwane. For years, the deterioration of water quality resulted in massive algal blooms behind the Hartbeespoort and Roodekoppies Dams. Dead fish didn't affect tourism, but the absence of crocodiles in the lakes and on the river banks did.

Multiple factors were contributing to the decimation of the Nile crocodile population, but Lou, and the other American scientists, quickly established that diminished fertility was the major cause. Lou saw the same ovarian abnormalities in the Nile crocodiles, that he was now seeing in his American alligators. In South Africa, one of the major industrial polluters was a huge paper mill outside of Johannesburg dumping its effluents into the Crocodile River. First among the suspect chemicals were the dioxins that are essential to the paper bleaching process.

Lou's American alligators were inhabitants of the marshes and backwaters of the North and South Islands of the Tom Yawkey Wildlife Preserve. The North and South Islands stand at the mouth of Winyah Bay separating Georgetown, South Carolina from the Atlantic Ocean. Winyah Bay is formed by the confluence of the Sampit, Waccamaw and Great Pee Dee Rivers. A few miles north of Georgetown on the Great Pee Dee River stood the Taconic-Pacific paper and pulp mill. It didn't take Lou Guillette long to connect the dots.

Lou would point at the Georgetown county map, finding the Great Pee Dee River and the Yawkey Preserve with this first and middle fingers. "This map explains everything. It isn't an accident."

I nodded at the obvious geographical association.

"We have to prove it though. If the food and water isn't healthy for a baby alligator, it probably isn't very healthy for humans either."

The Taconic–Pacific paper plant is an older mill having been built in the 1940s. It's considered a Kraft mill, which is the dominate mill type in the industry, producing about seventy percent of the world's paper. Kraft mills primarily use chemicals to break down wood products. First the raw wood or recycled matter is put through a cleansing process. Chemically, the cleansing is innocuous, however, its waste water is high in dirt, wood fiber and other solid debris. In the second step, the "clean" matter is taken to a digester where the wood lignin fibers are broken down. The by-product of lignin breakdown is the generation of "black liquor." The "black liquor" waste water is of the greatest environmental concern because it contains potentially toxic chemicals such as acetone, various acids, alcohols and dioxins such as TCDD.

After digestion, the remaining wood matter is called pulp. The pulp is moved onto a third step where it's washed and bleached to further purify the paper fiber and create a crisp white finish. The waste water from this step contains mostly bleach. The finished product is produced when the paper fibers are mashed together and dried. The Taconic-Pacific mill in Georgetown primarily produces file folders, ReelCote, wallboard tape, specialty envelopes and pulp, which is then sent to other factories where it's used to produce diapers and cardboard packaging.

When tourists drive through Georgetown on their way to Myrtle Beach, they're assaulted by the pungent, acrid sulfuric odor of the pulp mill. They'll stop, and ask the locals, "What's that smell?" Native Georgetownians will always give you the same answer. "That, my friend, is the smell of money."

Chapter 17.
TACONIC-PACIFIC

The best part of a Yawkey trip was riding on the airboat. Airboats are flat-bottomed, driven by a giant propeller powered by an aircraft engine. They were effective in swamps or marshland where standard inboard or outboard engines with submerged propellers would be fouled by the shallow water vegetation. Airboats can skim across the marsh grass revealing alligator trails and nests.

The airplane propeller produces a rearward column of air that pushes the boat forward with a prop wash that averages 150-miles per hour. Steering is accomplished by diverting the rearward column of air either left or right with a rudder that the pilot controls. Airboats have no breaks and can neither stop quickly nor reverse direction; piloting one requires a huge amount of skill.

Lou Guillette was an expert airboat pilot. Lou commanded the elevated pilot's seat, allowing him to see over the swamp vegetation, and avoid floating objects, stumps and bull alligators, which could all flip the boat. Although maybe not his most notable invention, the first airboat was built in 1905 in Nova Scotia by Dr. Alexander Graham Bell. He called it the Ugly Duckling.

On each of our trips to the alligator nesting areas on the Yawkey Preserve, Lou would take his airboat up the Great Pee Dee River to collect water samples from the Taconic-Pacific waste water release canal. Lou scheduled his trips to the waste water canal to coincide with the tidal changes. Taconic-Pacific always released its waste water at the beginning of ebb tide. That way, the discharge flows back downriver , instead of lingering in the freshwater or travelling upstream.

The Great Pee Dee is a black water river system, but it becomes far darker and lifeless as you near the Taconic-Pacific waste water canal.

Approaching the canal, you first notice the deep brown to yellow color of the river, and the large amount of organic debris floating in the water. Next, you're assaulted by the rancid odor of decomposition. The "sulfur water" odor is a fermented combination of hydrogen sulfide, used in the wood pulping process, and the decay of the organic material clogging the spillage canal. The pungent smell in the canal was caustic to the eyes and set the nose hairs on fire.

Every time we traveled to the waste water canal Lou's expression was simply one of sadness. He'd been upriver too many times. His lips whitened against his teeth, his eyes hooded by a furrowed brow and the twinkle gone. He involuntarily shook his head with a mixture of anger and disappointment in his fellow man. The only words he would share was the observation that, "It gets worse."

The floating debris in the canal made navigation difficult despite eight to ten feet of depth. Without the airboat, it wouldn't have been passable because of the wood fibers, waste pulp and Spartina grasses fouling the propeller prop. The mud banks on each side were stained an other-worldly yellow and were lined by decaying trees and plants. The pluff mud lacked any fiddler crab holes or scrambling activity. There were no nesting birds or even buzzing mosquitoes. Every time up river I thought of Joseph Conrad's *Heart of Darkness.*

The canal was just as barren under the water's surface. All the dumped organic material creates a high biological and chemical oxygen demand which depleted the available oxygen dissolved in the water. The marine ecosystem is also destroyed by the eutrophication process. The organic nutrients, along with excess nitrogen and phosphorus from the pulp making process, fuel accelerated algal blooms that further consume available oxygen. The lack of dissolved oxygen in the water eventually kills the fish and other marine life in the area. The same thing Lou had seen on the Crocodile River in South Africa.

As we moved back down river away from the waste water canal towards the open bay, the black water mixed with inflow from the Black and Waccamaw Rivers. The river deepened, the water became less turbid and the odor disappeared. The river banks became richer in foliage and wildlife. While life returned above the water line, Lou wanted to know the health of things below the water line.

Lou carefully collected water and sediment samples at intervals down the river and across Winyah Bay towards the North and South Islands of the Yawkey Wildlife Preserve. We recorded environmental variables including weather, season, water type, water temperature, river shape, other industrial sites, and the presence of fish or other invertebrates in our cast net. At each collection site, we measured the salinity, chlorophyll content, nutrient levels, nitrogen, phosphate, and dissolved oxygen. Samples were collected in clean glass jars, and placed on ice, to slow biological activity for measurements of TCDD, other dioxins, and a variety of other nasty agricultural and industrial contaminants.

On one of the trips we took up the Great Pee Dee River to the waste water canal, Taconic-Pacific security officers met us. Via a bull-horn, they informed us that we were on private property. We needed to leave immediately. Lou was unperturbed. He yelled back that they were misinformed. The waste water canal was part of the inter-coastal waterway and, thus, public access.

Lou continued his sampling while the security guards huddled on the river bank. They re-played the intimidation card. They bull-horned again. We'd be arrested if we didn't vacate Taconic-Pacific property. Several of the security guards placed their hands on their holsters which caught my attention. However, the security guards didn't know who they were dealing with. Lou waved them off and ignored their threats. The guards got more animated.

Finally, Lou hollered back that they weren't going to arrest anyone. They were welcome to call the Coast Guard if they really believed we were trespassing. Lou was confident that the security officers were no more interested in calling the Coast Guard than they were in wading out into their own toxic black water. We both returned to collecting samples, while the security guards were left looking at each other.

Moments later, there was a distinctive sound of a shotgun blast, and the few birds left in the marsh grass took flight. Our heads jerked around. One of the security guards was standing at the edge of the canal with a smoking shotgun pointed towards the sky. I hunkered down against the floor of the airboat. Lou never flinched.

"What the fuck, Lou. Don't you think we ought to get out of here?"

"Nope, don't worry about those guys. As the pirates say, that was just a shot across the bow. They've come down here to hassle me before. They previously waved the shotgun around , but this is the first time they've fired. Once they brought down a video camera and filmed me. They're just trying to scare us."

"Well, they're doing a good job. They also seem pissed. Maybe we should call the cops and report them for firing at us."

"I don't think so. They're as certain that we aren't calling the cops, as I am that they aren't calling the Coast Guard. They sent me a cease and desist letter a couple of trips ago, but it was from their plant manager. It wasn't even from a lawyer. All they've got is bluster. They don't have any legal right to keep us from coming into this canal."

They ranted and raved at us for about ten more minutes while we completed our sample collection. Then Lou smiled his Santa Claus smile, and his eyed twinkled once again. "Time to buckle up. This is going to be fun."

Lou pushed the rudder flap all the way to the left and goosed the engine for just a second. The airboat began to rotate in the canal. When the airboat had turned one hundred and eighty degrees, and lined up with the canal's exit, Lou gunned the big airplane engine. The giant propeller sprayed a wash of black water and toxic muck backwards, drenching the Taconic-Pacific security officers. They scrambled away from the river bank like a scattered flock of seagulls. Lou raised his middle finger as the airboat roared away, just in case any of the security guards were still watching our exit.

Lou howled with inaudible laughter as he zoomed out of the canal. Lou knew how to pilot an airboat.

At the next sampling site, he ratcheted down the engine. We removed the headphones which protected us from the engine's roar.

"You're a dirty dog, Lou. You power washed those guys on purpose. Whatever's in this water can't be good for delicate fabrics if it's turning the mud yellow and killing the marsh grass. I hope the Taconic-Pacific security staff gets free uniform dry cleaning."

"It isn't my fault if they don't know that an airboat this size has a backwash. Plus, my momma told me a long time ago, what goes around, eventually comes around."

"What do you mean?"

"We don't know what's in this waste water, but they do. They don't have any reservations about pumping this crap into our water system. If they don't want their security guards being showered with toxic water then, maybe, they should stop dumping the toxins into the water. I know there's dioxin in this water from looking at the alligator ovaries. The question is the quantity. It's probably going to be in femtomolar amounts."

"Lou, don't use the word femtomolar. Nobody knows what you're talking about."

"Femtomolar means a lot. There's a lot of shit being pumped out of that plant. It's carcinogenic. It's disrupting reproductive function, and it's persistent. Pollutants like dioxin never go away. Did you know that the TCDD levels are still sky high in breast milk samples from Seveso? That spill occurred in 1976."

Lou was getting worked up. I tried to pump the brakes. "What do we know about this specific paper mill? I've read that most of the paper mills have put in secondary treatment processes that significantly reduce the effluents. The dioxin levels may not be what we think they're going to be."

"Not this mill. Taconic-Pacific built this one during World War II. Like the Savannah River Plant south of here, if it was good for the war effort, it was good for the country. The environmental consequences were not part of the equation. The older plants are harder, and more expensive, to upgrade. Compared to most other paper mills, the Taconic–Pacific plant in Georgetown is an outlier."

"Doesn't the state track health statistics by county?"

"Both the South Carolina Department of Health and Environmental Control and the Environmental Protection Agency know this place is a mess. Georgetown County has the highest cancer rate per 10,000 population of any other county in the state. The EPA says that people who eat just two, four-ounce servings per month of fish caught downstream from the Taconic-Pacific plant face a lifetime cancer risk of one in one hundred. Subsistence fishermen, who eat larger amounts, have a cancer risk as high as one in ten. The EPA says that the locals shouldn't eat the fish from around these plants anymore, but you know they do. There are people who live on the catfish and suckerfish that they pull out of this water. Those fish are the garbage trucks of the river bottom and are loaded with TCDD."

"If the EPA and South Carolina DHEC know all this, why don't they shut them down, or force them to install an upgraded bleaching process?"

"Don't be naïve. The EPA forced a paper plant in Maine to clean up its discharge. It took years, cost millions of dollars and considerable production time. The jobs disappeared, and the town died. It turned into a disaster, and worse, votes were lost. It became an intense political issue. The EPA lost political support and has been hesitant to be heavy handed ever since."

"So, the town is more worried about its jobs than its health?"

"Taconic-Pacific is the five-hundred-pound economic gorilla in the room at all City Council meetings. The company has a seventy-five-million-dollar annual payroll in Georgetown County. That payroll includes both current and retired employees, including those six security guards. Without that paper mill, the fabric of this community would unravel. South Carolina would lose about three hundred million in economic impact. You'd have to start piling up bodies on the county and state courthouse steps before anyone is going to force Taconic-Pacific to do anything."

"Sounds to me like the bodies are piling up already."

"True, but those are cancer deaths. It's the same story all over the world. Give people a choice between a modest increase in cancer mortality years down the road, and a good paying job right now that feeds, clothes and shelters their family, they'll take the latter every time."

"Sophie's choice."

"Yep. That's why we're here. Even though it sounds crazy, what we're finding on the reproductive damage caused by these dioxins is even more compelling than cancer. People don't worry so much about feeding, clothing and sheltering their family when they can't have one. Infertility and miscarriages are far more motivating than the risk of prostate cancer in thirty years."

"It'll take a lot to turn public opinion against Taconic-Pacific."

"Absolutely. Taconic-Pacific lobbyists will come out of the woodwork. They'll tell anyone who'll listen about the adverse economic impact of any upgrades. Constituents will be out of work for extended periods of time while upgrades are taking place. Proposed new water pollution regulations, will stir talk that Taconic-Pacific might have to shut down their Great Pee Dee River plant, and move somewhere else to build a newer, more cost-effective plant."

Lou looked away briefly. I think he was gathering his strength for a fight he knew was never-ending. It takes a tremendous amount of energy to always be pushing the boulder uphill. Lou continued with a more somber tone. "My experience is that even sympathetic Congressmen and Senators will fold under that kind of pressure. They'll talk about leaving a better world for the next generation, but the next generation doesn't vote, nor do they make campaign contributions."

I wasn't naïve. I understood exactly what Lou was saying. I wondered to myself how worthwhile our research actually was. I wondered if Lou ever entertained such doubts. As I watched him navigate the airboat back down river, I was convinced he never did. Maybe Lou might strike a nerve. Epidemics of infertility and polycystic ovarian disease could be a game changer.

Chapter 18.
DOGUE DE BORDEAUX

Neither Homer nor I were morning people, so the office didn't open until nine thirty. Homer usually took a mid-afternoon siesta, and we saw our last patient at six thirty in the evening. The office staff loved the "European" work hours. It kept them off Folly Road during the rush hours which saved everyone, at least, an hour per day. They felt more civilized than their friends in other office settings. Our clients loved it too. The after-work office visits were the most popular. Homer sent an unmistakable message to everyone in the office when he fired the last office manager. He'd bugged Homer one time too many about the "lost income opportunities" associated with opening the office so late in the morning.

The lack of a business manager would plunge most offices into anarchy. Instead, our staff spontaneously, and collectively, assumed responsibility for all office functions. They cross-trained themselves on all office functions. Homer's response to every new problem was, "Figure it out." And they did. Recognizing they'd assumed more job responsibilities than originally hired for, they structured and instituted appropriate pay raises. They never asked Homer's permission, and Homer never asked for details. It was exciting to be the first socialist infertility practice in the United States.

Given my partner's aversion to early morning work, I was surprised when my beeper went off just a few minutes after seven a.m. with a text from Homer. The L.E.D. light was blinking on and off signifying an urgent message. I rubbed the sleep out of my eyes to make sure I was reading it correctly. "Office ASAP. It's Dogue."

I leaned over on one elbow and brushed Rosemary's hair away from the nape of her neck. A gave her a gentle kiss and inhaled her scent. "Got to head to the office. No need to get up. It's still early."

“Okay,” she mumbled, without rolling over. “Have a good day.”

“Love ya, Rose.”

Dogue was Homer’s best friend. Homer picked him up as a rescue several years ago. Dogue’s age was a mystery. We suspected he was five or six based on the recent appearance of some white whiskers. From day one, Homer never called him anything other than Dogue. Their relationship was like father and dedicated, but strong-willed son. A curt monosyllabic “Dogue” meant get to work. Occasionally, Homer called him “The Dogue” which was like calling your teenager by both their first and middle name; a stern rebuke that meant straighten up and fly right. When Homer drew “Dogue” out with a guttural four to five second faux Southern drawl, it meant “wrasslin’ time.”

Dogue tended to get bored easily. Both Homer and Dogue had an inbred need to periodically get rambunctious. Homer was always willing to engage in some rowdiness when Dogue needed a diversion. Getting up off the floor, he’d look at the office staff, and turn his palms upward. “What? All work and no play makes Johnnie a dull boy.”

The staff never knew which one Johnnie was.

The kennel told Homer that he was a Dogue de Bordeaux and Labrador mix. The Labrador half was hard to find. Dogue looked like a classic Dogue de Bordeaux. He wasn’t particularly tall, but was thick, and broad-chested, with a characteristic pink nose, red mask, and light eye color. Dogue had a soft, fine coppery red coat with white markings on his chest and the tips of his toes. His body tapered down from his broad shoulders. The muscle definition in his shoulders and hips gave Dogue an intimidating athletic build. Dogue weighed about one hundred and ten pounds. There was no mistaking his power.

The Dogue de Bordeaux has the largest head in the dog world. Dogue had a head so massive, most of the time you wondered what could possibly be going on inside his colossal cranium. His jaw was powerful and undershot, which caused his upper lips to hang down thickly over his lower jaw. He had an impressive dewlap beneath his throat. At his best, Dogue appeared handsome, regal and proud.

Unfortunately, Dogue rarely was at his best. He never listened to anyone other than Homer. Initial positive impressions were usually dashed by troublesome problems with snoring, slobbering and flatulence. The office staff said that Dogue reminded them of Homer. Dogue had some deep scars on both forelegs. We didn't know where they'd come from. Homer had some tattoos on his forearms. He had no idea where they'd come from. They were two peas in a pod.

The Dogue de Bordeaux is a stubborn breed who, by nature, are inclined to do things their own way. Dogue had no idea how to be obsequious. He was also a slave to his ancestral DNA. His forefathers were trained as brave warriors, sworn to serve. Dogue responded to firm direction and dominance which Homer provided. Both Homer and Dogue were alpha males, but Homer was alpha-one and Dogue was alpha-two. They understood their relationship and loved each other.

The Dogue de Bordeaux is one of the most ancient of French breeds, dating back to the 1400s. The brawny breed originally worked pulling heavy carts. As their breed evolved, they were taught to be wolf-hounds to guard the flocks of sheep. Ultimately, they were used by the French elite to guard their castles. Dogue instinctually knew how to wolf-bait and was the only security system our office ever had or needed.

People invariably, and cautiously, asked about his temperament. Homer always gave the same response, "Dogue never started a fight, but he's finished lots of them." That made Dogue laugh. Whenever he heard it, he'd shake his head violently, slinging ropes of drool onto your clothes, furniture and walls.

Homer's presence kept Dogue relaxed. He usually found a comfortable spot with good sight lines and Homer to his back. Dogue made a point of greeting each member of the office staff as they arrived. He enjoyed interacting with the staff, but, have no doubt, each interaction served as a security check. He also understood the business aspects of our office, possibly better than Homer. He effusively greeted all the women who wanted to socialize. He merely brushed the leg and logged the scent of those who needed time to themselves. At closing time, the office was his. He protected it, just as his ancestors had protected the castle keep.

At night, Dogue patrolled the office with singular authority. Between his periodic rounds, he retired to the residence's former garage which Homer converted to a storage area. Homer usually came by early in the morning to let Dogue out before they went to IHOP together for breakfast.

When I arrived at our Folly Road office, the front door was still locked, but the side door to the garage was open. I walked inside and found Homer sitting on the floor, cradling Dogue's lifeless body.

Homer's reddened eyes rose to meet mine. "They killed Dogue, Declan." I'd never seen Homer cry. He told me once that Vietnam had taken all his tears.

"What happened?"

"I found him seizing and laying in a pool of vomit. He wasn't unconscious, but he couldn't lift his head. Then he couldn't breathe. He was wide-eyed lookin' at me, but his chest muscles were paralyzed. Then he died. I couldn't do anything. I just held him while he died."

"There wasn't anything you could do. Maybe Dogue was older than we thought."

Homer shook his head. The redness in his eyes changed from sorrow to fire. "He didn't get sick. He was poisoned. Somebody fuckin' poisoned my Dogue."

"What makes you say that?"

"After Dogue died, I looked around for something he might have gotten into. In the trash bin, I found a swollen stinkin' can of tuna fish that'd been cracked opened. Right next to it, I found a used syringe. Somebody grew *Clostridium botulinum* in that tuna can and used an insulin syringe to draw off the juice from on top of that spoiled fish. Dogue was paralyzed and suffocated. That's what botulism does. What kind of monster would inject botulism into my Dogue?"

"You can't be certain of that."

"The hell I can't. It's small, but I found an injection site in a fold at the back of his neck."

"Nobody would ever do something this low-down. Everybody loves you, and even if they don't, they love Dogue. He's never caused any trouble in the neighborhood."

"This isn't directed at me. This wasn't even directed at Dogue. Dogue's murder is a message to you."

"Why do you think that?"

"These were in the mailbox."

Homer reached into his jacket pocket and handed me two cards. I recognized them. The cards were from the New Orleans Voodoo Tarot. I also recognized both the message and messenger. A chill ran down my spine.

The four suits of the New Orleans tarot are based on the "four nations" of Voodoo tradition. Petro is taken from the "La Flambeau" rites practiced in Haiti and represents Fire. The Congo suit represents Water which wells up in the sacred places on Earth. The Rada suit arose from the rites practiced by the Dahomey of Africa and signifies Air. The Santeria suit is a sister religion to Voodoo, widespread in the New World, and corresponds to Earth.

The first card was number XIII of the Major Arcana which is called "Les Morts." Most people referred to it by its more common name, the Death card. On the Death card, the hands of the living are reaching down, trying to contact the souls of the departed. The Death card doesn't represent actual physical death, but rather, implies an end, usually of a relationship. In this case, I don't think the meaning was meant to be that subtle.

The second card was number II of the Major Arcana. Card number II depicted "Marie Laveau," the High Priestess of New Orleans Voodoo. In the mid-1800s, Marie Laveau mixed Catholicism, African spirituality, and magic into a Voodoo gumbo. She presided over a large New Orleans-based Voodoo culture from the Madam's office of her brothel.

It couldn't have been clearer if it had been a thank you card. Marie Laveau was the inspiration, and name-sake, of Paris Laveau's mother. Marie Laveau taught Paris all her Voodoo tricks, including the powders, potions and pendants that did her wicked bidding among the unwilling. Both Marie and Paris possessed extensive naturopathic knowledge, and an intimate understanding, of the beneficial and deadly capabilities of various herbs, flowers and grasses. The lethal effects of a *Clostridia botulinum* would be on any list of Voodoo black magic. Among Marie's uneducated backwoods apostles, being strangled with your eyes open, but no hands on your throat, sure looks like a Voodoo spell.

"I'm so sorry, Homer. This is my fault."

"That's bull shit. When you kill someone's dog, it's on you. This falls squarely on that black-hearted witch. She poisoned your sheriff friend from Lake Charles. Now, she's poisoned Dogue, and she's bragging about it. When I find her, I'm going to fuck her up."

"This isn't your fight, Homer. This message is directed at me. She might have thought that Dogue belonged to me. Maybe not. Either way, Paris is letting me know that she's back, and can take anything she wants away from me."

"You know that she didn't come all the way back to Charleston just to kill a dog. This isn't over. She's coming back for you. We've got to find her first."

"I agree, but this isn't something we can do on our own. I'm going to call the police. They've been looking for Paris Laveau since she poisoned Marcellus. They haven't had any leads in a long time. The police will find her."

Homer looked at me with a murderous calm. "The police can look for her if they want, but I'm gonna find her. When I do, your bitch Voodoo princess is going to find out that she's roped the wrong rhino. I'm going to put her ears on a God damn string around my neck."

With that statement, Homer dropped his head and fell asleep, still cradling Dogue in his arms.

I knew better than to disturb him. This would be the first of many bad days.

Chapter 19.
MARVELOUS MARCELLUS GREENE

Within two hours we were overrun. The initial response had been a single James Island patrolman, but the mention of Paris Laveau kicked over the ant hill. Charleston City detectives assisted the James Island police. They were soon followed by U.S. Marshals, F.B.I. field agents and crime scene specialists. Our entire Folly Fertility practice was encircled with yellow crime scene tape.

Thankfully, Rosemary arrived and took charge. She briefed law enforcement on the circumstances of my previous involvement with Paris Laveau, my partnership with Homer Lahr and Dogue. Attempts to interview Homer were futile. Homer was essentially incoherent with despair and anger but he was rapidly becoming agitated. An invaluable primal sense warned the detectives to back off. Everyone in the widening circle around Homer realized that something or someone was at risk of being broken. They were happy to have Rosemary as an informational go-between.

Following her escape from Sheriff Marcellus Greene outside Lake Charles, Paris Laveau had managed to elude a scorched earth search by a very pissed off Lake Charles Police Department and Louisiana State Police. The F.B.I. and the United States Marshal Service soon joined the search for a murderess on an interstate flight from justice. Setting a new family standard, Paris Laveau made the F.B.I. ten most wanted list. That was almost a year ago, and there hadn't been a ripple. The Bayou just opened and swallowed her up.

It's hard to take yourself completely off the grid. The "experts" believed that Paris fled the country, probably to Mexico. I knew they were wrong, but I had an advantage. I knew Paris Laveau and understood the genius required to conceal such profound wickedness. When your soul is irredeemable, the ability to hide it is an essential survival skill. I also understood Paris Laveau's ability to manipulate and command others. Her brother Dalton still did not understand how he'd been sacrificed. Paris would never leave the Louisiana oilfields, piney woods, swamps and bayous where she wielded invisible power, and enjoyed mindless loyalty.

It wasn't in Paris' nature to run. She was hiding in plain sight in the bosom of her Cajun kin. The F.B.I.'s modus operandi was to lean on family and friends for information on her whereabouts. They would never give her up. Cajun's have an antipathy towards the government that's hard wired in their genetic code. Beyond that, Paris was as feared as her mother, the Voodoo queen of western Louisiana. Betrayal would be paid for in blood; your blood, your family's blood and your dog's blood. Instead of a nationwide search, the F.B.I. would be more likely to find her by putting an agent in a wicker chair at the Sonoco station on the Beglis Parkway.

The police distributed pictures of Paris Laveau up and down Folly Road. An APB was broadcast to every mobile police computer in the state. Myself, I doubted that Paris personally stalked and killed Dogue. Paris formulated her plan for revenge but would not be the one to serve it. Far too risky to travel to Charleston just to send a hate-filled message in the black of the night. One of her inbred cousins or another cretinously imbecilic minion did the evil deed for her.

As the morning wore on, the more I considered Homer's warning. He was right. Poisoning Dogue wasn't a final act. It announced her return. An announcement that wasn't intended to be subtle. Killing Dogue would be the overture to a symphony of revenge that Paris had planned. Whether it was Paris herself, or a surrogate, there was more to come. As I looked up and down the street, and at the woods beyond, I knew it was only a question of when, not if. The early autumn breeze blowing across Folly Road gave me a chill.

I made the decision to close the office. After being interviewed by the police, the office staff went home, most of them in tears. Ginny, our office administrator, volunteered to stay behind to answer phones and reschedule patients. At some point, Rosemary got Homer off the garage floor and back to his office. She defused a tense confrontation between Homer and a Charleston County Animal Control officer. He wanted to take Dogue to the Coroner's office for an autopsy. I didn't know how Rosemary did it. By all rights, the Animal Control officer should be dead.

The last of the law enforcement people left at about six p.m. Ginny put a blanket over Homer who was sleeping at his desk. I hugged her, and thanked her, for all she had done. She started to cry for the first time all day.

"I'll be back in the morning."

"Don't worry about that. I think we'll stay closed."

"I'm still going to be here. Please keep an eye on Homer. I'm worried about him. He won't know what to do without Dogue."

"We'll be here for him. And I know you are too."

Rosemary and I both collapsed onto the couches in the waiting room. Sadness, exhaustion and fear weighed on us. We didn't speak for quite a while. Finally, Rosemary broke the silence and addressed the inescapable truth. "You know this isn't over."

"I know. This is just Paris saying hello. I think I knew this day was coming the moment I heard she escaped. I hoped that she'd disappear, but I never believed she would. Evil leaves a stain you can't wash out."

"What should we do?"

"I wish I knew. We need to stay alert. I want to talk with Marcellus."

The doctors couldn't believe that Sheriff Marcellus Greene survived the beating and poisoning that Paris Laveau and Big-foot had put on him. There's no antidote for cowbane. The only treatments are supportive and will. If Marcellus wasn't the biggest bad-ass in all of South Louisiana the beating alone would've killed him. He laid in the grass in the ravine beside the road for more than an hour, bleeding out from a ruptured spleen. Either the hemorrhage, or the seizures, caused him to have a stroke that partially paralyzed the left side of his body.

We'd talked many times since he'd gotten out of the hospital. His speech had improved remarkably but was still hard to understand at times. The Sheriff's office gave him an extended leave. Marcellus was pouring himself into rehab with the same fury he'd brought to summer football weight lifting in high school. He believed that if you could build stronger muscles, then you could build stronger nerves. I visited him once and talked to his physical therapist. Marcellus' will might prove him right once again. The therapist said that Marcellus was making amazing progress. However, he still had a way to go. With stroke recovery, small things can fall into the "amazing" category.

Rosemary asked me if I was sure about calling Marcellus. I wasn't, but I was going to call him anyway.

It took several rings for Marcellus to answer, which I thought was a bad sign. Once he'd picked up, I spoke loudly and slowly. I told Marcellus that this was Declan Murphy from Charleston, South Carolina.

"Declan, I've got a motor neuron injury, not a cognitive injury. If you ever talk to me again like I'm strapped to rubber sheets, I'll beat you to death with my good right arm, you douche bag."

"You're sounding better, Marcellus."

Marcellus updated me on his condition. He was getting around well with a walker. He'd tried a cane, but balance was still a problem. His left hand was functioning well, but his left upper arm and shoulder were going to require more rehab. I asked him if he had a timetable. When he answered no, I heard some resignation in his voice that I hadn't heard before.

"Man, we need you back in charge soon. Paris Laveau just paid us a visit. I don't think there's much chance that the F.B.I.'s going to catch her. They don't know the piney woods and backwaters the way that you do. We need you hunting her down."

"How do you know it's her?"

"She poisoned my partner's dog and left a New Orleans Voodoo tarot card with Marie Laveau's face in our mailbox. She also left a Death card. Killing the dog is just a taunt. She's back. Rosemary and I thought you might know something on your end."

Marcellus was quiet while he digested the information. "I don't know, Declan. There's a lot of heat on her right now. The guys on the force are actively looking. They keep me posted. Nobody here thinks she's in Mexico, like the F.B.I. says. She's out there, deep in the woods somewhere with her people. Keeping out of sight is a full-time job for her now. The Lake Charles police are rattling a lot of cages and busting a lot of heads. Something is going to shake loose sooner or later. Traveling all the way to Charleston to settle a relatively minor score doesn't make sense to me. Seems like an unnecessary risk, and she's a calculating bitch. No offense, but when you're on everyone's most wanted to shoot in the head list, it doesn't sound like a smart move to try to get even with an old mark who was rude to you. Paris always makes the smart move."

"I agree with all that, but who else would leave a Marie Laveau tarot card. Maybe Paris sent a surrogate."

"Paris has a lot of Renfields. However, it still seems risky for her to be obsessed with settling a score with someone so absolutely unimportant."

It was nice to hear Marcellus laugh again after insulting me. Marcellus was improving.

"Well, I wanted to make sure that you knew about this. I wanted to tell you personally before you heard it from your detectives."

"I appreciate that. I'm sure that the Charleston police have already talked to my boys. This will prove to be a good thing. It'll stir the pot and pay for another round of canvassing and rousting. Sooner or later, the day will come when Paris' going to piss somebody off that has a pair. Seven numbers and she'll be back in our hands. Paris better hope that happens before I get back on the job. It's a long ride from Portie Town to Lake Charles in the back of a police cruiser. A lot can happen on a long ride like that. I learned that lesson the hard way. She won't get over on me again."

"Good to hear, Marcellus. We need you back on the beat. We're not safe here, and all you're doing is going to the gym and drinking vegetable juice."

Marcellus laughed, but it didn't boom like it used to. "How's Rosemary doing?"

"She's doing great. We couldn't have gotten through the day without her directing traffic with the police." Rosemary blew Marcellus a kiss from across the room. "Have to be honest, though, we're both a little rattled. If Paris is back in town, she's got as big a bone to pick with Rosemary as she does with me."

" That's one girl who can take care of herself. She's much smarter than you are, probably tougher too. If I'd listened to her, I wouldn't be fuckin' around with rehab right now. She knew what Paris was capable of, when you and I thought she was just another piece of white trash."

"I believe you, but we're still worried."

"Look, just the possibility that Paris Laveau is up to new mischief is going to put everyone back out on the street. You're going to have an army of South Carolina, Louisiana and Federal police swarming all over you. I'm still skeptical that Paris would take such a big risk, but if she did, the only sane thing for her to do is get the hell out of there. Message sent. What do you think she's going to do? Kill you for catching her in the middle of a scam? She's got you wetting your pants. That's probably all she wanted. I can't see her hanging around."

"We put her brother in prison."

"No, she put her brother in prison. Then she skipped. Paris Laveau has never regretted anything she's ever done. She doesn't do anything unless there's something in it for her. Killing your dog, much less you, is an unnecessary risk with no upside for her."

"Hope you're right, Marcellus."

"Then again, maybe she's just a loony bitch."

"Great, Marcellus. That makes Rosemary and I feel a lot better."

"Don't fret. You're good, my man. But, you better keep that girl safe. She's a winner, and better than you deserve. If you slip up, I'm goin' come up there and put some of my best moves on her. I never lost blood supply to the stick shift. It's working better than ever. I'm on my third physical therapist."

This time, I laughed. "Sounds like you're on the mend for sure. Will do as instructed."

"Declan, before you go. There's something I need to tell you that I don't think I've told you before. I want to thank you and Rosemary for saving my life."

"We didn't do anything. Your still here because you're the toughest man I've ever known. Even the devil's scared of you."

"Nope. When I fell down that coulee and couldn't breathe, and Paris and her lap-dog where wailin' on me, the last thing I remember was reaching into my pocket looking for some keys or a knife. You know what I found? I found some pig bristles wrapped with a ribbon. I grabbed them and held on. That's why I'm not dead. I still have them. You and Rosemary need to get yourself some more. Do it tomorrow."

"We will Marcellus. You take care of yourself too. When we put this bitch back in a cage, Rosemary and I will come down and visit. We'll help you kill a bottle of Knob Creek."

"Sounds like a plan. Got to go now. My physical therapist wants to finish my leg lifts. I've got on some short-shorts with no drawers. She's been peekin'. It's making her steamin' hot."

The laugh I heard on the other end of the phone sounded more like the Marvelous Marcellus Greene that I knew.

Chapter 20.
THE GORDON CONFERENCE

As Marcellus predicted, the F.B.I., U.S. Marshalls and South Carolina Law Enforcement Division all came up empty in their search for Paris Laveau or any evidence of the woozy brutes that make up her clan. Potential leads went nowhere. Surveillance cameras caught nothing. No one recognized her picture or her seven-foot servile escort. If they'd seen him, they'd remember him. Interest evaporated as law enforcement became frustrated by one Paris Laveau dead-end after another. If Paris Laveau had been in Charleston, she was now gone.

The thought of Paris Laveau hiding in the azaleas initially generated fear. The exasperation of the fruitless search dulled our edge. Being hyper-alert was exhausting and hard to sustain. When you force yourself to be vigilant, everything seems out of place. There were signs everywhere, or maybe omens. They all proved illusory.

A pall hung over our office in the wake of Dogue's murder. Homer took two weeks off. The best thing was to leave him alone, which I did for a while. One night I decided to go over to his house with a bottle of Wild Turkey. Homer wasn't home. No forwarding number had been left with the office staff. No one knew where Homer was, and he didn't volunteer anything when he returned. I knew he'd been hunting Paris Laveau, but I didn't want to know where or any of the details.

Wherever he'd gone, he'd not found peace. Usually a tropical storm of activity, he kept to his office, uninterested in the day's schedule. His laugh disappeared , as well as his ubiquitous "Ooh Rah" that resonated throughout the building multiple times each day as Homer gave or received orders from his nurse.

"Ooh-Rah" is credited to John R. Massaro, former Sergeant Major of the Marine Corps. Massaro trained Homer prior to his assignment to Vietnam. After the Korean War, Massaro served as Gunnery Sergeant of the 1st Amphibious Reconnaissance Battalion and was transported on the USS Perch, a WWII-era diesel submarine. Whenever the submarine prepared to dive, a klaxon would sound the diving alarm: "AHUGA!" When reassigned to the Drill Instructor School at the Marine Corps Recruit Depot in San Diego, he took the dive horn sound "AHUGA!" with him. Massaro passed it onto his Drill Instructor students who, in turn, passed it on to their recruits. Eventually, "AHUGA" became incorporated into the Marine training lexicon, but morphed into the shorter, simpler "Ooh-Rah!"

While the staff missed Homer's "Ooh-Rah!" motivational greetings, they weren't as troubled by his expected somber mood as by the slippage of his practice. Gossip spread about his forgotten appointments and incomplete records. Homer started being short with patients, which no one could remember ever happening before. The office staff pledged to manage things until he could pull himself back together. If necessary, they'd take a bullet for him. What anguished them were the things they couldn't help him with. Homer continued to mourn Dogue's death, and his narcoleptic episodes now happened much more frequently.

The old Homer roamed the office whenever he wasn't seeing a patient. It came from his military reconnaissance training where he'd learned to walk the perimeter. Both Dr. Guillette and I would have several unscheduled status reports with Homer each day. Never anything important. Homer was just an expansive man who loved to know what was going on around him. He didn't necessarily want to be involved. He was just interested in us. Homer hadn't come by my office in days.

Although Homer was engaging, his relationships were superficial. I suspected that also came from being a commander of men in the meat grinder of Vietnam. Know what everyone is doing, what their capabilities are, but don't get too close. Other than Dogue, Homer didn't have a deep emotional connection with anyone. As far as I knew, Homer's closest relationships were with a waitress friend at the International House of Pancakes and the bartender at the Blind Tiger. I worried whether Homer would ever recover from the loss of Dogue.

Rosemary helped immensely by continuing to run interference with the police. They maintained surveillance of our Folly Road office, Rosemary's office and our home. They offered Homer police protection as well. The look in his eyes told them that was a non-starter, so they decided to utilize their resources elsewhere. I'm sure Homer hoped someone would creep his house. Knowing Homer as I did, I worried that he didn't have the capacity to ease his pain other than through violence.

While I was convinced that Paris Laveau was responsible for the killing of Dogue, with the passage of time, I also came to believe that she was now long gone. She eluded multiple law enforcement agencies, and the extremely dangerous man in the other office. The police told me in confidence that Homer came by the office late at night and waited inside with the lights off. I knew exactly what he was up to. If Homer found her, it'd be terrible for both of them. Having the F.B.I. looking for you is one thing, but Homer Lahr was another. The smart move for Paris was to find the darkest hole she could find, as far away as she could, and climb in.

After three weeks, we all agreed to let the patrolmen go home at night to their families. Rosemary was anxious to get back to her new practice and was relieved when our police surveillance ended. Beyond the two big MUSC cases, Rosemary had also gotten a substantial settlement for Sonia Bokhanevich. Sonia falsified the records in the Ramirez case. When Rosemary interviewed her, she confessed that she'd been instructed to alter the medical records by her chair, Dr. Leslie. So, what did the dumb-fucks do? They fired her. Rosemary slapped them with a wrongful termination lawsuit. The university never had a chance. Sonia and her husband, a Russian ex-patriot named Demitri, moved to Seattle. Sonia now worked in the anesthesia department at Swedish Hospital.

The icing on the cake was that MUSC terminated its Chief Counsel, Vincent Bellizia, after the Bokhanevich settlement. Having whiffed on three straight fastballs from Rosemary, she wondered if Vincent might reach out to her for representation. My settlement and Rosemary's courtroom successes had suddenly made us both financially independent. Other than supporting Dr. Guillette's research laboratory, we still hadn't figured out what our new wealth would mean for our future. Money could be confusing.

Rosemary's dramatic success garnered a lot of attention, especially in a city the size of Charleston. Holmes Law offered her a partnership if she'd come back. She received some inquiries from some mega-law firms in Washington and New York. Everything was happening too fast, and Rosemary declined all offers. She sensed that when your life was accelerating as fast as ours, the smartest move was to probably tap the brakes. Her thoughts on adding an associate were put on hold. Without specifically discussing it, we decided to delay any major decisions until the Paris Laveau problem resolved.

With Homer's emotional retreat, I found myself spending more of my time with Dr. Guillette. We worked to prepare our alligator data for presentation. Our findings on ovarian development in the fetal alligator got selected for presentation at the Gordon Research Conference at Woods Hole, Massachusetts. Our hypothesis that in utero endocrine disruption may be playing a role in the epidemics of both obesity and polycystic ovarian disease in the human female population intrigued them.

Oral presentations at the Gordon Conference are a prestigious honor in the world of environmental science. Many of the premiere Gordon Conference presentations end up as highlighted papers in *Science*. The Gordon Conferences are international scientific roundtables limited to 200 attendees and are dedicated to advancing the frontiers of environmental preservation and human health. Having begun in 1931, they proudly note that the discovery of the triple helix structure of DNA was first described in a Gordon Research Conference oral presentation. Beyond the scientific presentations, the Gordon Conferences are also known as a crucible of intense debate and dynamic intellectual exchange.

Although he'd attended many times, this would be Louis' first plenary session presentation. He looked forward to the interactive exchange of ideas. In preparation, Lou was going to double and triple check the data. We spent most afternoons after work reviewing the laboratory techniques, the accuracy of our data analysis and brainstorming other possible interpretations. Lou probably practiced his presentation a hundred times. The more comfortable he became with the presentation, the more worried he became that we might have overlooked something.

Lou wanted me to ask questions. The more the better. The more off-the-wall the better. We'd been at it so long I was running out of questions. Eventually, Lou convinced himself that we had all the angles covered. Only then did he allow himself to become excited. The findings were robust and the implications huge. The only thing that caused him any residual concern was the reproducibility of the findings. Of course, with any ground-breaking research, that question will always linger until someone else can duplicate the results.

Lou's solution? Collect a couple more alligator egg clutches to make sure the findings held, even though he knew they would. We planned another field trip to the Yawkey Wildlife Preserve the following weekend. Nothing energized Lou like a trip to the field.

By the following Friday, things were beginning to get back to some semblance of normalcy. We often closed the office on Friday afternoon, but today we were working late. Catching up with all the work we'd missed during the few weeks that Homer was missing would take a while. Homer was gradually getting back in the groove having done several in vitro fertilization embryo transfers this week. While the work ethic was returning, a gloom still surrounded him, and permeated the fabric of the office.

Homer never did egg retrievals or embryo transfers on Friday. That freed up Lou to prepare for his field work at Yawkey. I'd bought him a beat up old fishing truck when I joined the practice, and we tricked it out with oversized mud tires and a shiny silver toolbox. Lou loaded the back of the truck with his alligator wrangling equipment, swamp waders and portable incubators for the anticipated egg clutches. Lou finished triple checking everything before cinching a tarp down over the truck bed. Before taking off, Lou dropped by my office to confirm our plans.

"You still good for an egg hunt up at Yawkey tomorrow?"

"Yeah. Do you want to swing by and pick me up at Wappoo Heights, or should I follow you?"

"No need for you to drive. There'll be room in the truck. Margaret McGinley, who's in the Marine Biology program at the College of Charleston, will be going with us. We've got nice bench seats. It'll be cozy."

"Sounds good to me. It'll be good to have Margaret with us. Otherwise people will think that we're just a couple of guys sneaking off for a weekend at the Sunset Lodge."

Everyone is South Carolina, and many up and down the east coast, knew about the high-class men's "sporting club" south of Georgetown. In the religiously tightly-wound south, the name "sporting club" is preferred to whore house. Tom Yawkey enjoyed his hunting, fishing, drinking and carousing with buddies in Georgetown more than the stuffy social events of Manhattan or Boston.

The Sunset Lodge was locally infamous for its cultured, beautiful girls in long elegant dresses, hand-picked by the gracious "Miss Hazel." Tom Yawkey recruited Miss Hazel from Florence to operate the brothel. Yawkey's plantation, and other amenities, became a popular spot for Yawkey's Boston Red Sox players who would stop over when traveling to and from Florida for spring training.

By day they would hunt, fish and play baseball. Yawkey built a ball field on Cat Island. You can still see where home plate had been located. He also built a 550-acre pond in the needle rush marsh to attract the Canadian geese migrating south. In the evening, the players would eat and smoke beneath pictures of Ty Cobb, Ted Williams and massive Elk trophies in the magnificent hunting lodge that Yawkey built on South Island. The lodge featured heart pine floors, pecky cypress wood panels under arching boat hull ceiling beams. Late night, after well-aged Scotch, many would meander over to the Sunset Lodge.

"What time do you want to head out?" I asked.

"Takes about an hour and a half to get there, so I'd like to be rolling by seven-thirty at the latest. You can slather on the bug repellant along the way. They'll have the air boat gassed up and ready to go by the time we get there."

"No problem. If I'm not waiting outside when you pull up, just hit the horn. Rosemary will make us some tomato sandwiches. I'll also pack some cold fried chicken in a cooler along with a half-gallon of iced tea."

"Make sure she uses Duke's mayonnaise. It's not a tomato sandwich without Duke's mayonnaise."

I walked Lou out to the parking lot. Every head turned within a hundred yards when he pulled out and accelerated down Folly Road. Smoke billowed out of a toasted tail pipe and the engine noise of the old fishing truck rumbled out of a whipped muffler. Lou hated being late for dinner at home.

I returned to the office to complete some chart work. On the way, I stuck my head in on Homer. His size 16 shoes were up on the desk. He was leaning back in his chair with his head thrown back, and eyes closed. I thought for a second that Homer might be asleep, until he yelled, "I'm fine. See you Monday."

"Okay, Homer. I wanted to let you know that I'm going with Lou to Yawkey tomorrow to collect some more alligator eggs for our research. We'll be back late Saturday night. Have a good weekend. Give me a call if you'd like to watch some football on Sunday."

I thought I heard him grunt and say, "Yeah, maybe."

I waited in my office for Rosemary to pick me up. I had charts in front of me, but mostly, I worried about Homer.

Rosemary didn't work on Friday afternoons either, but she told me that morning she had errands to run. About four o'clock Rosemary called. She'd be there in a few minutes. She asked if Homer was still in the office.

Ten minutes later, when Rosemary came in the front door, she had a boxer puppy on a leash. He immediately squatted and peed on the waiting room rug. Rosemary had a huge grin on her face, proud of her most recent find. "He is a fancy brindle with white on his chest and all four feet. Homer is going to love him."

"I'm not so sure. If it's a male and squats to pee, Homer isn't going to tolerate that."

"Don't be a dummy. All little puppies squat until they learn to lift a leg."

“Well, he’s quite handsome, and this is really sweet of you. I don’t know how Homer’s going to respond to a new pup. He’s still pretty broken up about Dogue.”

The pup yelped his disapproval of my negativity. Moments later, Homer Lahr appeared at the door to his office. The boxer pup unhesitatingly rushed him. The pup rose up on his hind legs to left/right/left punch him, affirming his blood line. Homer reached down and picked up the pup in his giant hands. It looked like a scene from Jack in the Beanstalk. The pup continued to yelp while kicking his back legs and punching the air with his forelegs.

“The little guy has some brass balls. Whose dog is he?”

“He’s yours, if you’re up for it,” Rosemary said. “He needs a good home. I’ve got all his papers. He’s had all his shots. He’s a gift from Declan and me, if you like him.”

Homer tucked the pup into the crook of his left elbow like a football and gave Rosemary a one-armed hug that I thought might snap her spine.

“He’s got a wicked left hook. I’m going to call him Smokin’ Joe.”

Chapter 21.
LIAM GLASHEEN

My beeper went off a few minutes after five a.m. with a number I didn't recognize. I thought it might be Lou calling to cancel our field work for one reason or another. I wondered if it might be raining but didn't hear anything on the roof or the windows. When I called the number back, an unexpected voice answered the phone. A familiar voice, but at five a.m., I wasn't going to come up with a name. He identified himself as Clarke Peyton Floyd, husband of Tracey Floyd. It took a moment for the early morning mist to clear, but eventually I placed the names. Tracey was a new OB patient I'd seen about two weeks ago. Homer helped Tracey get pregnant with in-vitro fertilization.

Tracey's husband was several years older than she, but they seemed like a happy and energetic couple. I remembered talking to them about a trip they'd recently taken to Arizona for a hot-air balloon festival. Clarke owned a company that supplied containers to the port authority. In Charleston, that meant big money. I remembered Clarke Peyton Floyd's voice because its deep, rolling stentorian tone. A child was the only missing puzzle piece to their life. They'd been over the top excited with Homer's success when I saw them for their new obstetrical visit.

He apologized for waking me so early. I could hear fear in his voice. He explained that they were in the Emergency Room at MUSC. Tracey awoke with severe abdominal pain about two hours ago and fainted twice as he drove her to the hospital. The E.R. doctors told Tracey that she needed surgery for a ruptured appendix. He asked them how the baby would do if she needed surgery but they didn't know.

Clarke asked if I might be available to offer a second opinion and be there for the baby if Tracey needed surgery. Clarke didn't know, and didn't care, that I no longer enjoyed faculty status at MUSC. He was terrified for Tracey and their long hoped-for pregnancy. I knew the chaos and anarchy of the emergency department. If I could run interference for them with the E.R. and Surgery staff, then I would. The emergency department people wouldn't know I wasn't on the faculty any longer. I also still had my MUSC identification badge.

I told Clarke I lived just over the Ashley River in Wappoo Heights. I could be there in fifteen minutes. I told him to make certain they didn't do anything with Tracey until I got there.

Our conversation woke up Rosemary. She returned from the bathroom as I hung up the phone. She wore her ivory satin nightgown with the off-set slit to mid-thigh. The back lighting from the bathroom created an alluring translucency. I wished I'd told Mr. Floyd thirty minutes instead of fifteen. The better part of me regained control of the wheel.

"What was that?"

"One of my new OB patients is over in the E.R. at MUSC. She may need surgery for a ruptured appendix. They're petrified and want me to be there. I think she's thirteen or fourteen weeks pregnant. This is her first success after 4 IVF attempts. Her husband sounded shaken. If she develops a bad peritonitis, she'll probably lose the pregnancy."

"I thought you were going to Yawkey with Lou to piss off the gators?"

"I was. Would you mind calling him around six and let him know that I'm tied up with a patient. I won't be able to make this trip."

"Will he still be able to go without you?"

"I think so. A College of Charleston graduate student is going with him. She'll be able to help him with the egg collection."

"All right, I'll let him know. Good luck. Go piss off the people at MUSC instead. See if you can drum me up some more business."

"Your lips, to God's ears. I probably will."

Rosemary reset the alarm for another hour and crawled back into bed. I shook my head, appreciating the magnitude of the missed opportunity. I didn't mean a trip to a bug infested alligator swamp either. I imagined sliding my hand over that satin gown. I pulled on some surgical scrubs, brushed my teeth and combed my hair. I found my old MUSC ID badge in the top drawer of my highboy dresser and headed out to my car.

I crossed the Ashley River Bridge in the pre-dawn quiet. A full moon hung low in the sky over the Charleston Harbor. I rolled my windows down to enjoy the bracing early autumn chill and turned on the radio to hear Gregg Allman reminding me about living a life I love.

On the best of days, the MUSC emergency room is a maze. Early Saturday morning is not the best of days. The Charleston Knife and Gun Club usually holds its meetings late on Friday nights. I anticipated that the E.R. would be a zoo. Coming in through the automatic sliding glass doors I encountered a familiar scene. A tall, burly, sleep-deprived Irish trauma surgeon was screaming at a couple of Charleston City police officers. The cops clearly had no idea what the Irishman was ranting about. Nor did they understand his references to "gobshyte." They started to get the picture when he demanded they get off their "arse" and do their "fecking" job. Eventually, the police officers decided they were no longer enjoying their cross-cultural experience.

I'd heard Dr. Liam Glasheen go on this rant before. He'd never seen a shooting victim in the E.R. who hadn't caught a bullet from "some dude." Every beating victim had been sucker punched by "a couple of dudes." Every stabbing victim had been knifed by "that bitch." Glasheen believed that you could empty all the riff-raff out of his E.R. if the police would just quit "arsing around" and catch four people; "some dude, a couple of dudes, and that bitch." Every new page to the E.R., only made Liam angrier that these arrests hadn't yet been made.

I walked up behind Liam as he stuck his finger in one patrolman's chest and continued to dress him down. "Get up the yard ya Bombay shitehawks. I don't need ya sitting around my emergency room eating our doughnuts and passing air biscuits. Why don't you go out and find a clue? May the cat eat you, and the Devil eat the cat." The two patrolmen turned and left, without any idea what the Irish madman was saying.

Instead of doing the smart thing and walking on past, I decided to stop and poke the bear. I also wanted to make sure that Dr. Glasheen didn't throw anything at the retreating members of Charleston's finest.

"How's it going Liam. Glad to see that you are still in charge of community relations."

"Don't feck with me right now, Murphy. Those two mongo saps are the king and the archduke of the eejits. How they got on the police force is beyond me. They're both probably on the short list for the Chief of Police position."

"No doubt. I'm sure they appreciated your career advice."

"Aw, those two muckshits aren't worth my time. They'd be scundered if they weren't such neddies."

I'd know Liam for years, but I didn't have any idea what he was saying.

"What are you doing here? I thought they eighty-sixed your arse."

"Naw, just a nasty rumor that anesthesia started. I've got a patient in the E.R. named Floyd that might have an appy. Any idea where she is?"

"I saw her name on the board, but I don't know which cubicle she's in. It's a mess in there. One of the scanners is down, and everything's backed up. We've got a handful of steamboats and a couple of Citadel boys with terrible doses of knob rot from skimming the trolls at the south end of Market Street."

"Sounds like you're doing God's work tonight. Sorry for keeping you from your people."

"I got no more time for you, Murphy. Go take care of your giblets. I've got to go pick dingle berries off some flaming dirtball."

"Sounds romantic. Sorry, it's been a bad night. I'll find Ms. Floyd. I'm glad that she's still down here. Might be a good idea for you to clock out before those patrolmen figure out what you said to them. Remember, they are duly sworn representatives of the City of Charleston."

Liam only grunted.

Liam called after me as I walked away towards the E.R. desk. "You're not fooling me, Murphy. Get a job, ya fecking pikey!"

Checking the board at the E.R. desk, I found out which cubicle housed Tracey. Clarke greeted me with relief. He informed me that they'd not seen anyone since we talked on the phone.

Tracey didn't look well. She was pale and diaphoretic. She acknowledged my arrival, but her eyes quickly closed again. She was in significant pain and looked ready to pass out. Clarke said that the abdominal pain woke her up a little after two in the morning. He brought her to the emergency room straightway. She passed out in the waiting room, and again while she was going for an ultrasound. To him, she looked as white as a sheet.

The monitor above her bed showed a heart rate of one hundred and thirty beats per minute, and a blood pressure of ninety over fifty. Her respiratory rate was a bit fast, but her pulse oximetry was normal. Her intravenous fluids were running wide open. Antibiotics in a separate bag were also infusing. I couldn't hear any bowel sounds. Even the pressure of the stethoscope elicited tremendous pain. It was an acute abdomen, but she didn't feel warm to my touch.

Clarke told me they had spaghetti with meatballs for dinner, and Tracey ate well. Tracey experienced some intermittent morning sickness, but he was unaware of any recent nausea or vomiting. Tracey hadn't complained of any abdominal discomfort until she woke up this morning.

I pulled Tracey's medical file from the plastic wall basket outside her cubby. Her pregnancy test was positive. A totally unnecessary test with a uterus several fingerbreadths above her pubic symphysis. Her CBC revealed a low hemoglobin of 9.0 gm/dl and a hematocrit of 27.9%. I couldn't remember the prenatal blood work from her first visit, but I didn't remember her being anemic. Her white blood cell count was mildly elevated at 16,000. However, the differential of the elevated white count didn't show any immature bands. With a ruptured appendix there should be a high percentage of bands.

Her chart confirmed what my hand told me. Her maximum temperature had only reached 99.2 degrees. An obstetrical resident I didn't particularly care for, Christie Lowe-Atkinson, left a consult that was essentially an ultrasound report. She confirmed a viable intrauterine pregnancy at thirteen weeks. She saw free fluid in the cul-de sac of the pelvis. Lowe-Atkinson recommended a surgery consult and a spiral computed tomography (CT) scan to evaluate her for a ruptured appendix. Her assumption was that the fluid in her pelvis was pus. The surgery team called in the antibiotics. They planned to come down and see Tracey once the spiral CT scan was completed. The CT scan order had been put in more than an hour ago and it still hadn't been done.

I hit the call button for Tracey's nurse. When she arrived, I asked her what she knew about the CT scan. She wasn't sure. The E.R. scanner was down, and they were sending people up to Radiology. However, traumas got priority, and the Radiology Department was much slower when it came to turnover compared to the Emergency Department. I asked her to page the OB attending. I suspected, but wasn't yet positive, what Tracey had. However, I knew it wasn't appendicitis.

I hoped the OB-GYN attending was someone I knew. Of course, it wasn't. About 15 minutes later, Dr. Becca Cathcart arrived at Tracey's bedside, accompanied by Christie Lowe-Atkinson. I wondered if this woman had been my replacement. Lowe-Atkinson was surprised to see me, but said hello, and introduced me to Dr. Cathcart. Cathcart made no effort to hide her displeasure with being called down to the E.R. to see a patient she'd already directed to General Surgery. Dr. Cathcart was probably ninety pounds soaking wet with a perpetual "I smell shit" expression on her face. She had plucked her eyebrows so much they looked like semi-colons around her nose. I anticipated that this was going to be a chore.

Dr. Cathcart said that Dr. Lowe-Atkinson told her I was formerly on the faculty, but no longer with the university. I ignored the smug superiority in her voice. I calmly explained that Ms. Floyd was my patient and that I saw her as a new OB just a couple of weeks ago. That didn't seem to make much difference to Dr. Cathcart who asked me a second time why I was there. It was time to stop dancing.

"Two reasons actually. First, they called me, and I come to see my patients when they're in trouble. Second, I need to correct the misdiagnosis of a ruptured appendix. This is a ruptured ectopic. We need to take her to the operating room immediately."

"I'm sorry, Dr. Murphy, but we've already documented a normal intrauterine pregnancy. We're waiting on a spiral CT but feel certain enough about appendicitis to have started her on antibiotics. I see that her temperature is already down."

"It was never up."

"Not a lot, but her exam is consistent, her white count is elevated, and we saw pus in the cul-de sac on ultrasound. The spiral CT will confirm a ruptured appendix."

"That's not pus, it's blood. It's a ruptured tubal pregnancy. More importantly, we don't have time to debate it, much less wait for an unnecessary CT scan." I could feel the color raising on my neck. I realized that losing my composure wouldn't help things.

Dr. Cathcart crossed her arms across her chest, lowered her eyes to the floor and shook he head negatively in a way, I knew, had angered and exasperated hundreds of people before me. "We know from the ultrasound that this isn't an ectopic pregnancy. Our judgment is that Surgery needs to see her."

"Listen Dr. Cathcart, it's a heterotopic pregnancy. She has one pregnancy in the uterus and one pregnancy in the tube. The one in the tube has ruptured. It's time to saddle up. I'll scrub with you and assist."

"Heterotopic pregnancies are extremely rare. I've never seen one."

I resisted the urge to point out that there were probably a lot of things she'd never seen. Instead, I said, "Heterotopics aren't that rare following IVF with multiple embryos replaced."

Dr. Cathcart turned and gave Lowe-Atkinson the stink eye. She obviously hadn't been told that Ms. Floyd was an IVF pregnancy. Cathcart composed herself but gave no indication that she was prepared to yield.

"Heterotopics are more common with multiple embryo transfers, but they're still unusual. The CT scan will sort this all out. In the meantime, I need to talk with my division chief. I can't imagine that you're allowed to be here, or that you could assist with surgery. If you'll excuse me, Dr. Murphy, I'll be back when the CT is completed." With that, she turned on her heel and walked out.

The room was oddly quiet for a moment. Finally, Clarke Peyton Floyd looked at me, and simply asked, "Dr. Murphy?"

I looked at Christie Lowe-Atkinson and captured her attention. "Go out to the desk and order four units of blood stat, then call the O.R. and tell them we're coming." When she hesitated, I added, "Now! Get going." The tone of my voice didn't leave any room for uncertainty.

I turned to the nurse. "Get me a speculum, an 18-guage spinal needle and a twenty-cc syringe."

When Christie Lowe-Atkinson returned from the E.R. desk, the nurse and I had placed Ms. Floyd's bottom on an inverted bedpan, raised the head of her bed, and I had inserted a speculum. "What are you doing?" Lowe-Atkinson asked.

"A culdocentesis. We'll have an answer in two minutes instead of two hours." The Pouch of Douglass is the lowest point of the abdominal cavity. It extends down as a cul-de sac deep into the pelvis behind the uterus and over the rectum. When people sit up, any free fluid in the abdominal cavity runs down into the Pouch of Douglass. In the semi-sitting position that Tracey was now in, the posterior cul-de sac bulges into the vagina just below the cervix.

With the speculum in place, I attached a spinal needle to the syringe, and identified the bulging vaginal mucosa. There's less than a quarter inch of tissue between the vagina and the abdominal cavity. The needle was inserted without a flinch, given the pain that Tracey was already experiencing. I immediately aspirated back a syringe full of dark red non-clotting blood.

"Does that look like pus to you? It's time to roll."

Christie Lowe-Atkinson immediately picked up the phone and called the operating room. "We're on the way up. We'll need a laparotomy set up. Call the blood bank and have them send her blood down to you. She's going to need it intra-op."

Lowe –Atkinson turned back to me and asked about Dr. Cathcart.

"You can call her if you want. But we're not waiting. She's bleeding to death and needs surgery, not pussyfooting around."

Generally, residents are fairly dull creatures of survival. But when motivated by the true consequences of their lassitude, they can become a whirlwind. Christie had us in the O.R. in less than ten minutes. Tracey's abdomen was open in fifteen. There was about three liters of blood in the abdomen. Tracey's blood pressure collapsed as soon as we sucked out the blood. Fortunately, type specific blood had just arrived from the blood bank. Anesthesia ran the blood in rapidly through two large bore intravenous lines. Initially, Tracey had no urine output, but with fluid and blood resuscitation, a golden trickle returned by the end of the case.

Just as expected, Tracey had ruptured a right sided cornual ectopic. Cornual ectopic pregnancies are stuck in the portion of the tube that transverses the muscular corner of the uterus between the external fallopian tube and the intrauterine cavity. Because of the thicker muscular wall surrounding this portion of the tube, a cornual ectopic can grow larger before they rupture. The amount of hemorrhage with a cornual ectopic can be dramatic, and it was.

After removing the ectopic pregnancy, we carefully over-sewed the ruptured cornual portion of the uterus. Lowe-Atkinson had more surgical skill than I'd given her credit for. We were able to quickly get the hemorrhaging under control. Fortunately, the ectopic had been closer to the external fallopian tube than it was to the uterine cavity which was why we were able to preserve Tracey's intrauterine pregnancy. About thirty minutes into the case, Dr. Cathcart arrived in the O.R. with the news that I had no privileges to be operating at MUSC.

The O.R. nurses who'd been scrubbing with me for years looked at the newbie like she was crazy. The O.R. Charge nurse, Pamela G. Smith, took Dr. Cathcart by the elbow and escorted her out of the operating room. Pam started her career as a nurse on the Labor and Delivery unit. I'd delivered her twin girls several years ago. It had been a complicated delivery, but everything turned out well. Her twins were both beautiful and talented. Pam sent me a Christmas card every year with their picture.

I didn't know what Pam told Dr. Cathcart outside the O.R. doors, but I doubted it was subtle. When they returned, Cathcart looked chasten. She stood quietly by the door, which is where I assumed Pam told her would be an allowable point from which to observe the case.

Once the uterine rupture had been closed, I told Dr. Cathcart that she could take over the case if she wanted to. At this point in the case, the only thing left to do was close. From the expression on her face, I could tell that Dr. Cathcart didn't appreciate my sarcasm or being asked to clean up. She peeked over Lowe-Atkinson's shoulder and looked in the belly. Cathcart opined that I seemed to be doing fine and could finish up on my own. She didn't speak again during the case. More importantly, no security officers showed up in the operating theater.

After 4 units of packed red blood cells, and about two hours of surgery, we closed the abdomen. I high-fived with the scrub nurse and head bumped Pam Smith to express my appreciation. She nodded back and smiled. On the way out of the O.R. I couldn't help myself, and took one more shot at Cathcart. "Why don't you go ahead and bill for this. God knows, I couldn't have done it without your assistance." She was fuming as we rolled away down the corridor.

I spoke with Tracey after she awoke from anesthesia in the Recovery Room. I reassured her that her vital signs were stable, and that she was going to be fine. Christie Lowe-Atkinson got a portable ultrasound machine from Labor and Delivery. We checked the remaining fetus and the heart beat was strong. We'd have to keep a close eye on her for the next several days, but I thought that the baby was going to be okay. The biggest risk was the pre-op and intra-operative blood loss which she'd already gotten past.

I gave Christie detailed instructions for Tracey's post-operative care, knowing I probably wasn't going to be allowed back in the building. I gave her my beeper number and told her to let me know if she took any heat for operating with me.

"Tell them I threatened to kill you if you didn't. They'll believe it."

"You aren't concerned that you just operated at a hospital where you don't have any privileges?"

"Trust me, the hospital and I have been around the block more than a few times. They always end up embarrassed and a few dollars poorer. What's the crime? All we did was save a woman's life and her pregnancy. The university's plan had been to let Tracey bleed to death in a broken CT tube. Nobody's going to the woodshed over this."

"I hope you're right, Dr. Murphy."

"If I'm not, tell them I said to pick on somebody their own size, and that I'm waiting. I promise you, they'll lose interest."

Next I went to the Surgery Waiting Room. I filled Clarke in on Tracey's condition and that of the baby. We weren't totally in the clear, but we should be optimistic that both mom and baby were going to do well. I advised Clarke that I probably wouldn't be allowed back into the building for the rest of her stay. Dr. Lowe-Atkinson and her colleagues would take good care of Tracey. She might be in the hospital three or four days. Clarke thanked me for everything. He told me to let him know if I had any problems with the hospital. He understood what was going on.

"I'm pretty tight with a number of guys who work on the Ports Authority Commission. The port is the only bigger fish in this town than MUSC. They don't like to throw their influence around, but they will when they must. They'll help if I ask them to. You know where the five-hundred-pound gorilla sleeps?"

"Where ever the hell he wants."

"Exactly."

I told Clarke that I didn't think I was going to need his help, but I thanked him for it. As I headed home, I couldn't help but hope that Rosemary might still be in that ivory satin nightgown.

Chapter 22.
CARNIVAL GLASS

Rosemary grudgingly approved my vegetating in front of the television the rest of the day on Saturdays but Sunday we'd be following her plan. The constantly rebuilding South Carolina Gamecocks took it on the chin once again from the Georgia Bulldogs. The University of South Carolina faithful were as fervent as any Pentecostal preacher, certain of victories, which no one else believed possible. Every loss a fluke, easily turned around by one big play, a better spot of the ball or a yellow flag that should or shouldn't have been thrown. The next Gamecock game always the start of a championship run.

I didn't go to the University of South Carolina, but I did grow up in Columbia. I selected the Gamecocks as "my team" at some formative point during adolescence. As kids, we played football on Saturday mornings on a large field behind the North Trenholm Baptist Church. The church was an intersection of multiple neighborhoods and sat on the dividing line between Richland County School District number one and District number two. More than enough territorial pride on that field to make for some manhood defining sandlot games.

I was big for my age, and usually played fullback. My friend, Lane Felty, was faster and played tailback. We called ourselves the "Benny boys" after our Gamecock football heroes. I was Benny Galloway, the USC fullback, and Lane was Ben Garnto, the USC tailback. We were a legendary school yard tandem.

Ultimately, all South Carolinians must choose sides. Although the Clemson Tigers were generally more successful, the Gamecocks had been my childhood team. While I watched their games, and enjoyed their victories, I didn't live or die on every possession. College football fandom in the Deep South came closer to its root word than any other sport passion.

While Rosemary indulged me on Saturday, there wasn't any chance I'd be able to glue myself to the pros on Sunday. Rosemary's scouring of the newspapers resulted in a militarily precise battle plan for Sunday. For her tactical design to be a success, we'd have to be out of the door early and keep a tight schedule. Rosemary loved yard sales and swap meets. For promising ones, she'd cruise by the night before to scope it out. I knew she was excited about the prospects for today's targets.

Rosemary was highly selective, while I was an impulse buyer. It made Rosemary livid when I complained about going to the yard sales and ended up bringing home a half dozen shiny treasures. The last time we went out for yard bargains, I brought home a beautiful bag of brand new PING golf clubs. I don't even play golf, but the savvy scavenger never misses the opportunity to take advantage of others misfortune. The man of the house had cheated on her, and now it was payback time. The entire club set was mine for only ten dollars, if I took them away before her future ex-husband returned from his paramour's house. Rosemary encouraged the purchase, which surprised me, because she detested golf. I wondered if she just couldn't walk away from such a great steal, or whether she was sympathetic to the wife's planned revenge. I didn't ask.

Rosemary's eye for furniture was very modern. She ignored the ubiquitous "antique Victorian pieces" moved out to the driveway. She also turned up her nose at "vintage clothes" hanging in the garage on makeshift garment racks. I constantly found things I thought she would look fabulous in. She didn't have many quirks, but one was other people's clothes. She believed in microscopic body odor flakes that couldn't ever be washed or bleached away. I started pointing out yard sale lingerie, and bathing suits, just to see her get fired up.

What Rosemary did hunt was glass. She was a regular at Roumillat's, Pages Thieves Market, Birlant and Company and other antique shops throughout the Low Country. While yard sales weren't usually high yield when it came to glass, Rosemary wasn't going to take any chances. She knew an unnatural amount of glass history. She could glance at a piece of glass and instantly know its era, designer, manufacturer, and rarity. As opposed to many other collectibles, most people didn't know the value of their glassware. The average yard seller would know that their pristine Beanie Baby was worth exactly twenty-five dollars. They had no idea that their turn of the century, small, opalescent Vaseline glass bowl was worth at least one hundred dollars.

Among her legal peers, Rosemary was considered the straightest of arrows. Professionally, no one would ever have a reservation about writing her a letter of recommendation that contained the phrase "highest moral and ethical standards." However, none of those people ever witnessed Rosemary cruising between coffee tables, book shelves and folding card tables on the hunt for unappreciated pieces of carnival glass, Depression glass or milk glass serving pieces. When it came to taking advantage of an uninformed glass owner, Rosemary never flinched. As she made the kill, her eyes would roll back in her head like a shark.

The first yard sale we visited was almost exclusively clothes. Rosemary was disappointed and we left after ten minutes. Nothing caught her attention at our second stop either. I could sense her frustration building. We didn't come away empty handed though. I found a copy of the Allman Brothers Live at the Fillmore East double album in good condition for only two dollars. I suggested to Rosemary that we head home for twenty-six minutes of Whipping Post. She gave me a look which made that seem unlikely.

The trajectory of our day changed dramatically at our third stop. Rosemary found a giant, emerald green carnival glass rose bowl that dated to the early 1900s. She worked the unknowing South of Broad trophy wife like a Moroccan rug merchant, walking away three times from the two-hundred- dollar price tag. On the fourth fly-by, she finally sealed the deal for one hundred and fifty. She begged the woman not to mention the scandalous price to me. She agreed, with a fatuous grin on her face, as Rosemary counted out the money.

It was pretty, but it seemed like a lot to me. "Are you sure it's worth a hundred and fifty dollars?"

"No. I'm sure it's not."

"Then why did you buy it?"

Rosemary cut her eyes at me, and whispered, "Because, it's worth more like fifteen thousand."

"That's my girl."

On the way home with our prize, we stopped at the Med Deli for what was becoming a regular Sunday brunch. Crab cake eggs benedict for Rosemary, and a Monte Cristo with a bowl of gazpacho for me. We celebrated our "steal" with a bottle of Gundlach Bundschu Gewurztraminer. Rosemary explained the market for collectible glass to me again for the umpteenth time. The carnival glass rose bowl was the Hope Diamond of glass collectibles. She then explained the history of the bowl, and how it had probably ended up on the shelf of that mansion on South Battery.

Although a Yankee by birth, Rosemary was rapidly assimilating South Carolina's piratical nature. I thought back to the Jackpot smugglers, Steed Bonnet, Blackbeard and Anne Bonney, all before her. Rosemary would correct me, that she's really more of a privateer. Despite the value of the rose bowl, I knew it was a trophy we'd never sell. In fact, it might even cost us a new back-lit curio cabinet.

Returning to our Wappoo Heights home on Palmetto Road after brunch, we were surprised to find Lucy parked in front of our house and Homer Lahr sitting on our front porch steps, with Smokin' Joe on a long leash. Smokin' Joe was chasing and retrieving a small squeaky ball. The look on Homer's face didn't match the boxer's joyfulness.

Homer greeted us both. Rosemary gave Homer a hug and scratched Smokin' Joe behind the ears. Rosemary showed him our new carnival glass rose bowl and described how badly she outplayed the seller. Homer called it lovely, but I knew he wouldn't have paid a buck fifty for it, much less, one hundred and fifty. Nothing personal, just his life view. He lived a life that was perpetually moving forward. Some might say hurtling forward. Tomorrow mattered to Homer. Yesterday was old news, and best forgotten. Other than baseball cards, I doubted that Homer had ever been interested in collecting anything.

"Declan, you got a minute to take a walk with me and Smokin' Joe?"

"Sure, boss man." Rosemary and I gave each other a look of concern. She gave Homer a kiss and excused herself. "I'll make some lemonade for when you guys get back."

We walked in silence down to the Wappoo Cut, and then over to the public dock. We only stopped to allow Smokin' Joe to mark his new expanded territory. Homer seemed to be struggling with how to address whatever it was he needed to tell me.

"What's on your mind, boss man?"

"I just found out that you didn't go gator egg huntin' with Lou yesterday."

"No. I cancelled. One of your IVF patients, Ms. Floyd, came into MUSC with a ruptured cornual heterotopic pregnancy. She almost bled to death, but we got her to surgery in time. I checked in with the obstetrical staff this morning. Ms. Floyd's doing well, and the pregnancy is hanging in."

"Good fortune for her that you stepped in. I spoke with Clarke Floyd earlier this morning. He's highly appreciative of everything you did."

"He's a good man. I was glad to be there for them. I might get a little static from MUSC, but in the end, they'll let it slide. You'd done the same thing."

"Fuckin' A, podna. A ruptured cornual heterotopic with that much blood loss, it's a blessing that both mother and fetus survived."

"Thank you, boss man. We gave her four units of type-specific blood. I think it was just in time. But, I don't think you came over just to tell me I did a good job. I don't think you've ever been over to our house before."

"Sorry about that. I should've been over sooner. But, to answer your question, I didn't come over to socialize. There's a problem."

"What can I do to help, boss man?"

"Lou's airboat didn't come back from the swamp last night. He hasn't responded to his beeper, and no one's heard from him."

"My God. I didn't know. He might have flipped the airboat."

"We don't know. Both the Department of Natural Resources and the police are out there looking for him. Primal swamp, murky water and darkness made any rescue effort last night impossible. They went out early this morning. They haven't found anything yet."

"I'm sure they'll find him. I've been on the airboat with Lou several times. He's a great pilot. He never hot dogs like most do on an airboat. He takes it slow and is always watching for floating logs or big gators in his path. I also know that he's flipped an airboat before. He knows how to handle it."

"Well, if he flipped the boat, he would need to survive the night in the swamp."

"That's not a worry, boss man. Give Lou a pair of boots, a few yards of rope and a Swiss Army knife, and he is the most dangerous predator out there. As long as he's okay, then he's okay, if you know what I mean."

"Who knew that you were going with him?"

"Not many. Rosemary, you, some of the office staff, Lou and whoever he might have told. I think I told the guy at the Sportsman Shop when I went by Friday night to get some gear for the trip. Why?"

"Who knew that you didn't go?"

"Just Rosemary and Lou, and I guess, Lou's graduate student."

"What graduate student?"

"A marine biology master's student from the College of Charleston was going with us. I think her name is McGinley. I guess she knew I was going, and then found out Saturday morning that I wasn't."

"I need to notify the police. They don't know that Lou had a student with him."

"What is going on, Homer? Why are the police involved, and not just the Department of Natural Resources? What's going on that I don't know about?"

"At first, I just expected a call that they've found Lou sitting on the back of a flipped airboat or paddling around with a broken prop, waitin' on a rescue. But now the fear was deepening that the call would be something different."

"What's got you thinkin' so negative?"

"I found another Le Mort Tarot card in our office mailbox this morning. As far as anyone knew, you were supposed to be with Lou yesterday."

Chapter 23.
GEORGES DEMOSTHENES

The office mood vacillated between somber and edgy on Monday. With each passing hour, darkness clawed at our longing. Every ring of the phone snapped heads. Fear of hearing the next shoe drop fed the growing dread. Moods darkened as the day dragged on. Homer and I decided that we wouldn't mention the new Tarot card to the office staff. As of now, it meant nothing, and would only turn things uglier, and more fearful. Personally, it was all just unimaginable, except that it wasn't.

The next shoe dropped with a telephone call to Homer at about four o'clock. Homer listened quietly for several minutes. The bodies of both Lou Guillette and Margaret McGinley had been recovered. There had been a "massive mechanical failure" of the airboat, and both bodies experienced "significant trauma." Neither had suffered.

"What do they mean by significant trauma?"

"They were torn apart, podna. Real bad."

Homer looked away. He'd seen such things before. It was hard for him to revisit those blood slicked memories. A loner, he'd never married, and his liaisons seldom lasted longer than a few months. He regularly invoked Jimmy Buffett and joked that it was best to end things when they both could still manage a smile. Homer's reticence to get too close with people was a survival tactic he'd learned on the stagnant, unforgiving tributaries of the Mekong River. That said, I knew he had grown close to Lou Guillette.

Louis was everything that Homer wished he could've been. Lou was a pacifist, who'd marched against the Vietnam War. Homer learned to be a pacifist the hard way. Louis asked questions of importance to the reproductive survival of humanity. Homer practiced medicine to make a buck. Homer read Ob-Gyn journals to keep up with the newest clinical procedures, to maintain his competitive edge. Louis read *Science* and *Nature* to understand the interface of human health and the world we lived in. Homer went to Reproductive Endocrinology and Infertility meetings in Las Vegas, and spent his time picking up freebies in the Exhibitor Hall, burning cash at the craps table and picking up not so freebies on the Strip. Louis went to Gordon Conferences in Woods Hole and spent his time presenting paradigm changing research. Louis spent his weekends collecting research samples in the marsh and swamps of the Yawkey Preserve. Homer spent his weekends chasing the scent of Folly Road waitresses. Homer understood that the doctor in front of their names were not equivalent. He was a tradesman, Louis was a scientist.

Louis dying in the shallow water and spartina grass of the Yawkey Preserve was a colossal inequity. Homer had now lost his dog, and best friend, within a short period of time. For him, it was further evidence of the myth of a wise and benevolent God. A God he'd given up on long ago, lying in the bloody muck of a riverbank ditch feeling the vibration of high velocity slugs slamming into the lifeless body of a buddy, Homer was now using for cover. Louis' death would cause Homer to again question what he'd done to deserve his life. Despite his immense personality, Homer's belief in his own self-worth had long been compromised. Lou's death would not sit well with him.

"Do they think the alligators got to them?"

Homer's head was down, already pained by the conversation. "I don't know. I don't think so. They think something big came into contact with the propeller. The propeller then turns into a Gatling gun, and spews out projectiles that'll rip a body up. It's a God-damned airplane engine after all."

"Did they say if it was the propeller that broke up, or a tree branch?"

"I think the propeller from what he said about the airboat."

"That doesn't make a lot of sense to me. The engine and propeller are enclosed in a protective metal gage. It's designed to keep out the big stuff that could disrupt the engine. Small branches, birds or vines might get in, but those would only be pulverized into a mist. Plus, any spray would be out the back with the propeller wash. Are they sure there weren't alligators involved?"

"I don't know, Declan. Maybe. The bodies are in the morgue down at the Medical University."

"Did they find a Tarot card at the scene?"

"They barely found the airboat. Whether they did or didn't, this isn't a coincidence. They can call it a "mechanical failure" if they want, but this wasn't an accident. Paris Laveau is behind this."

"I don't know, boss man. Paris likes to do her business up close and personal with poisons and potions. What the hell did she have against Lou?"

"She didn't give a shit about Lou. It's you that she's after, and, as far as anyone knew, you were on that boat with him. I don't think there's anything that's outside the realm of possibility when you're dealing with Paris Laveau."

"God, I hope you're wrong."

"I don't think I am. Maybe. I don't know any more. Maybe it was just a wrong place at the wrong time accident. Another shitty thing, to join all the other shitty things, which happen every day."

"Homer, I want you to know I'm very sorry about Lou. I really liked him, and I loved working with him. I know you guys were close. If Paris Laveau is responsible for this, I'll never be able to forgive myself, or deserve your pardon, for bringing her into our practice."

"That's nonsense. No body picks and chooses their brushes with evil. Evil's never expected, and shows up out of nowhere, like the V.C. popping up out of their God-damned rat holes. If Paris Laveau caused Lou's death, then I'll see to it that she pays for her actions. And, Declan, I don't want there to be any confusion, I'm an eye for an eye kind of guy."

"I appreciate that Homer, but I know who's answerable for Paris Laveau. Lou was a great man. I don't know very many of those. We need to let the police know about the Tarot card. This will stir the Paris Laveau pot again."

Homer called a meeting to inform the office staff. There were lots of tears. Homer closed the office again and told everyone to go home.

Homer left to go over to Lou's house to be with his wife and children. I was going downtown.

The morgue is hidden among a catacomb of administrative hallways in a building forgotten by the custodial staff between Sabin Street and Baruch Auditorium. The entrance was an archaic, wood-paneled door, with an odd gold plaque announcing "Decedent Affairs Office." Every morgue looks and feels the same. On the other side of the dungeon door, the air turned thick and musty. The hallway was narrowed by parked steel gurneys. Bodies covered by white sheets, stained with various bodily fluids, and unnatural in appearance due to the endotracheal tubes, plastic IV lines and EKG leads; remnants of failed medical efforts.

The autopsy room itself has a depressing stainless steel and ceramic tile industrial character, even more striking for how out of place it seemed in a hospital setting. The tile had originally been a vibrant royal blue, but now had faded to an ecchymotic blue-brown stain. Across the room, was the infamous wall of ammo. A huge cork board lined with hundreds of mangled rounds of ammunition, from the smallest pea shot to gigantic ten-gauge slugs. The dominate and constant sound was that of sluicing water reverberating off metal surfaces, gurgling down dozens of drains, rinsing blood from the sinks, and off the tables and floors.

The morgue comes to life afterhours, which is aesthetically preferable, and a better match for the demented staff who make mortuary science their life. Despite the need to feel reverent, church appropriate whispers were drowned out by the whirring of bone saws, dispatching rib cages and craniums. Detached organs overflowed steel basins, suspended from the ceiling on large produce department scales, while a fearsome, bearded African American man in a bloody white smock sliced through them with the skill of the finest kosher butcher.

I didn't need to call ahead. I knew the entire autopsy staff would be there. Lou Guillette and Margaret McGinley would be at the top of their work list.

The Medical University fought to establish a professional Medical Examiner system more than two decades ago. The county still elected a retired biology teacher as coroner every four years. The coroner had the legal responsibility to sign off on all deaths. However, anything with the slightest hint of suspicion came to the Medical Examiner's office. The Charleston County M.E. didn't crack cases with the regularity of Quincy, but having a M.E. made a difference.

The current Charleston County M.E. was Dr. Georges Demosthenes, who was everything you'd imagine him to be. Georges and I knew each other since medical school when he taught us Forensic Pathology. His lectures were some of the most interesting and funniest of my basic science years. Quincy had nothing on Georges Demosthenes. Georges knew his business when it came to a forensic investigation. You wouldn't know it to look at him.

Georges was a short, overweight, balding second-generation Greek. He performed his autopsies with a pair of half-glasses teetering on the tip of his ancestral Greek nose, and the stub of a cigar clenched between his teeth. He'd been warned repeatedly by a revolving door of Pathology Department Business Managers about his slovenly appearance, but he always responded with the same quip, "My patients never complain."

Georges was there, directing a myriad of simultaneous activities, just as I knew he would be. He looked the same as he always did. A rumpled, dingy white shirt inadequately covered by a blood smeared surgical scrub top. His pants were made of a grey-green quilted fabric that I'd never seen on anyone else other than a refugee or a gypsy. His pants had lost the battle against his beer gut but were supported by a pair of maroon suspenders that I'd never seen him without.

It's disconcerting to spend any time in the autopsy suite. It wasn't a discomfort with the concept of death. I had more than enough familiarity with the grim reaper. The volume of death in Ob-Gyn was nothing compared to that experienced by medical internists, trauma specialists, oncologists or others who worked solely in the Intensive Care Units. However, while maternal death is a rare event, stillbirth is a constant threat for the Obstetrician, always lurking, and always requiring consideration.

The young and vigorous hold an expectation of perfection that leaves them stunned when death decides to mark their door with goat's blood. The thirty-eight week perfectly formed stillborn who'd entangled itself in its own umbilical cord. The twenty-something married couple holding their twins in the delivery room, just now realizing their life's purpose. Then the new mom coughs up some bloody spittle and tells anyone who'll listen that she thinks she's about to die. Minutes later, she's prophetic, victim of a massive cardiovascular collapse , triggered by a fickle embolism of amniotic fluid. The young father, left alone, holding two newborns in his arms, with no ability to fathom his future. The forty-year-old successful businesswoman with inoperable cervical cancer. She'd put off a family, as well as her regular gynecological appointments, for years. She didn't know that a college homecoming weekend boyfriend had given her a virus that would enflame oncogenic genes capable of producing a pelvic tumor large enough to block both ureters. She would drift off into an endless uremic sleep, wondering what had become of her deferred dreams. The stupefying magnitude of these tragedies is unimaginable, especially in the "joyous" practice of Ob-Gyn. When they did happen, they left deep scars which never faded.

The haunting peculiarity of the autopsy room wasn't its dedication to the exploration of death. It was its stark utilitarianism. The maternity floor evolved into a sleek, concierge served, home-like, mother and baby friendly facility. The non-patient care areas gleamed, resplendent with metallic, anti-septic white-tiled beauty. In unsettling contrast, the autopsy suite resembled an industrial work space, reflecting the fact it never received a patient complaint. Entering the room, you might be coming to observe an autopsy, or possibly to watch a stolen Jaguar being stripped down for parts.

The metal autopsy tables had long since stopped shinning. The scattered equipment didn't appear appropriate to any part of a hospital. The sophisticated Stryker lights of the Labor room were nowhere to be found. The autopsy tables were illuminated by 150-Watt bulbs hanging from the ceiling on frayed black cords and enclosed in a wire mesh basket. Dr. Georges Demosthenes was hosing off a body with an orange garden hose, running through rings dangling from the ceiling, with an adjustable spray nozzle that looked exactly like the last one I'd bought at Lowe's Home Improvement. I stepped over a stream of dark, bloody fluid running to a drain located in the center of the tiled beige floor. At least half the metal slots in the large drain were occluded by indescribable and unidentifiable human matter. I momentarily considered, and then dismissed, contemplation of where that hole in the floor might possibly drain.

Georges greeted me with a wave, and an undiscernible insult. Between his thick Greek accent, obstructive cigar butt and professional ambivalence over whether anyone understood him or not, most people missed about half of what Georges Demosthenes said. An ancient dictation system was rolled around on a metal cart. There couldn't be any available replacement parts. The Pathology Department must've hired Georges' sister or cousin to type his dictated autopsy reports.

Georges didn't like to be disturbed when working. I fully anticipated getting an old fashioned Greek butt-reaming for coming into his sanctuary unannounced.

"Murphy? What's your sorry Irish ass doing interrupting me while I'm taking care of my patients?" At least, that's what I think he said.

"I'm really sorry Georges. Dr. Guillette is a friend of mine. The police say he was killed in an air boat accident. I need to know for sure."

Georges said something unintelligible. He waved me over to the autopsy table and drew back a plastic tarp that covered Lou's body.

"What's your diagnosis? Boating accident?"

At their best, forensic autopsies are gruesome. At their worst, they're traumatic. As medical students, Demosthenes enjoyed bringing us into this room to observe an autopsy on a floater from the Stono River. He smiled when half the class excused themselves because of the smell alone. Once an incision pierced the methane bloated corpse, the other half, including myself, beat a hasty retreat as well. Georges didn't offer any of the students the oil of Wintergreen he'd applied liberally to his upper lip.

Lou experienced catastrophic trauma to his face, scalp, torso and presumably his legs, although they had been traumatically amputated. This was as bad as I'd ever seen. I don't think Georges ever saw any worse, either.

"No, this doesn't look like a boating accident to me."

"Well, look at you with the big brain. Maybe you're not as stupid as your mongrel Irish potato farmer ancestors."

"How about a boating accident followed by gators?"

"Not a chance. No teeth marks anywhere. The girl either. Plus, when a gator takes you, you don't find the body."

"What did this then?"

"They were blown up."

"An exploding boat engine did all of this?"

"Nope, I mean somebody blew them up. This wasn't an accident. It was murder."

"How can you be so certain, so fast?"

"Simple. There are two broad categories of explosions; low-order and high-order. If the boat engine gas tank explodes, that's a low-order explosion. What happened here was high-order."

"What kind?"

"I don't know for sure. TNT, dynamite, nitroglycerine, maybe military stuff like C-4 or Semtex. The lab will figure that out from trace."

"So, what tells you that this was a high-order explosion?"

"High-order explosives create a blast wave. The over-pressurized blast wave causes specific anatomical and physiological changes when it impacts the body's surface. The changes are unique to high-order explosives. The compression wave spreads concentrically from the blast's epicenter. The high-pressure compression wave is followed by a weak wave of negative pressure. Anyone in the path of the blast wave is assaulted by rapidly fluctuating changes in pressure. Obviously, the magnitude of the blast varies with the energy released by the explosive, and with the distance from the epicenter. However, in this case, your friend was basically sitting right on top of the bomb. Based on both the blunt and baro-trauma, I would estimate they were exposed to well over eighty psi blast pressure."

"Come on Georges, quit with the mumbo jumbo. How do you know they didn't simply crash?"

"Jesus, Declan. Try to keep up. The blast pressure associated with a high-order explosive produces a characteristic pattern of injuries. At greater than ten psi, eardrums rupture. Your friend's eardrums were both ruptured. Between twenty and thirty psi, gastrointestinal injuries occur. Your friend had a ruptured liver and evulsion of the superior mesenteric artery from the small bowel."

"What did the chest radiograph show?"

"Classic 'blast lung.' You see that at forty to fifty psi. That's his chest X-ray over there on the wall. The shock wave penetrates solid tissues like muscle and rib with minimal or no damage. But in the lungs, the variation in tissue density between the alveolar walls and the air sacs causes a vibratory affect as the shock wave passes through the lungs. The shock wave tears the alveolar septa causing diffuse hemorrhage. 'Blast lung' creates the typical 'butterfly' pattern that's obvious on your friend's chest X-ray."

Georges walked over and used his finger to outline a white butterfly on the chest X-ray. "Nothing else causes a picture like that except a high-order explosive. People die when the blast pressure exceeds thirty-five or forty psi. Everyone dies when the blast pressure exceeds sixty-five psi. I think you friend was subjected to an explosion far above that."

"You know a lot of arcane stuff."

"You forget that I'm a board –certified forensic pathologist. That means I'm at the top of the medical pyramid. Forensic pathologists know everything there is to know. That's why we're the ones you call when you need to catch the bad guys."

Then Georges said something I didn't understand, but I don't think was very complimentary of the Charleston City Police. I'd learned what I needed to know. This wasn't accidental, and the wrong people were dead. In the pit of my stomach, I knew that the bomb was meant for me.

"Georges, thanks for your time and for your unparalleled expertise."

"No problem. When it's the truth you seek…" I finished the sentence for him, "come see the Greek."

"Correct as always, you Irish thug. I thought you'd been fired."

"News of my demise has been greatly exaggerated."

He responded with another unintelligible utterance. I think it translated as good.

" I do have one more question for you. I've been wondering about it since you tortured us with that floater back in medical school. How on God's green earth do you stand doing this kind of work?"

A big smile lit up Georges face. "You know, Declan, sometimes my spirits do get down. I worry about whether I'm doing anything worthwhile with my life. And then, when I feel like I'm at my lowest, do you know what happens? Another dead body shows up, and my spirits perk right back up."

Dr. Demosthenes laughed so hard at his own joke that he started coughing and had to spit his cigar butt in a waste bucket. He fished the butt out of the can and stuck it right back into his mouth. "You are one unhealthy specimen, Georges, and I mean that in every way possible."

"I know," Georges said, still coughing and laughing at the same time.

"How many times have you used that line?"

"Been saving it for you. Been waiting almost twenty years, but it was worth it. Seriously, though, I am sorry about your friend. We'll do some chemical analyses on the bomb residue. It might help figure out the son-of-a-bitch who did this."

"I already know who the son-of-a-bitch is , and my friend's name was Lou. I promise you, there'll be a reckoning."

Chapter 24.
FOUR IRON

Law enforcement eventually caught up and figured out that Lou Guillette and Margaret McGinley had been murdered. The airboat forensics were conclusive. A large amount of TNT had been hidden in the engine. Enough TNT to be certain. They couldn't find a timer, and the trigger was unknown. It looked like they'd been going for about an hour out into the backwaters. Even so, with the amount of TNT, it was surprising that no one heard the explosion.

Marina security was provided by an alcoholic who'd been fired from his last job as a long-haul trucker. He'd gone on a bender and left an eighteen-wheeler filled with frozen turkeys to rot in a Wal-Mart parking lot in South Bend, Indiana. He hadn't seen or heard anything the night before Lou took out the airboat. Given the number of empty Smirnoff Vodka bottles in his office, it's unlikely he would've seen or heard anything if the airboat had blown up in the middle of the marina. Other than the Le Mort Tarot card, there were no clues as to their murderer.

Over the ensuing days, an even larger parade of law enforcement agencies marched through our Folly Road office. Both Charleston and Georgetown County police, the South Carolina Law Enforcement (SLED) Division, the Federal Bureau of Investigation (FBI), the Bureau of Alcohol, Tobacco and Firearms (ATF) and the United States Marshall's Service all wanted a few minutes of my time. They were much more serious about a double homicide than they'd been about Dogue.

None of them had much to add to what I'd already learned from Georges Demosthenes. Embedded war correspondents talk about their distorted view of battle because of the narrow straw through which they observe the conflict. Similarly, each set of law enforcement personnel looked at the bombing through their own narrow straw of self-interest and expertise. They talked incessantly about inter-agency cooperation, but I saw no evidence of it. I told all of them the same story. What each of them heard was distinctly different. They all walked away with their own individual takes on what had happened, and what needed to be done.

The county police just wanted to hunker down and defend home court. They'd keep their eyes out for Paris Laveau. If she showed up, they'd be ready. SLED and the U.S. Marshalls were always up for a manhunt, albeit, on different scales. The F.B.I. wanted to start twisting arms back in Louisiana, always confident of their ability to intimidate the truth out of some simpleton backcountry cousin. The ATF was going to track down the bomb materials and identify the bomb maker. The only thing they all agreed on was that I'd been the bomb's primary target, not Lou, and certainly not Margaret.

Once again, the search for Paris Laveau was proving fruitless. Other than the Tarot card, Paris hadn't left any evidence of her malevolence. The F.B.I. arm twisters underestimated before, and would underestimate again, the rock-solidarity of the inbred Laveau clan, or the fear that Paris could engender. No one had seen Paris since her arrest in Charleston. Maybe they were telling the truth. Maybe not. The F.B.I. would never know. Paris Laveau held far more sway over her kit and kin than any F.B.I. threat to crawl up their ass with a microscope.

The TNT used was commercially generic. No unusual purchases or thefts could be found. The detonator was unknown. The explosive pattern offered no unique identifiers. The Laveau's brand of criminality lacked complexity, a banality of evil. It came straight at you, plain and direct, and used whatever blunt instrument was available. Its lack of precision planning made it hard to track. Its willingness to do whatever was needed, whenever needed, made it hard to predict. Just like after Dogue's poisoning, Paris left nothing but a cold trail.

At the end of the day, law enforcement decided that the only strategy left was sitting on me to see what might happen next. It was a strategy that always worked on television. In real time , it didn't feel good to be the cheese left out for the rat. Charleston County and City police, along with SLED, took turns watching our Wappoo Heights house, cruising our Folly Road office and following us around town.

Rosemary and I were not reassured. Whoever poisoned Dogue, blew up Lou and Margaret McGinley, and left Tarot cards to sign their work, did so without leaving a trace. They moved among us unseen and unhurried. Weeks passed between poisoning Dogue and blowing up Lou. They were deliberate, and careful. Rosemary and I appreciated, more than the police, how much observation and information gathering had gone into each attack.

Paris, or whoever she sent, knew which dog belonged to Homer. They knew that Homer kept him at the office at night. They knew Dogue would never give up on a fight and would have to be incapacitated. They knew Lou's plan to go to Yawkey to search for alligator nests and egg clutches. Moreover, they knew he used an airboat, and which one he used. If it weren't for a middle of the night emergency phone call, they knew that I'd be on the airboat with Lou. Without the unanticipated phone call from Tracey Floyd's husband, I'd also be on Georges Demosthenes' autopsy room table.

We also thought that the pattern of the attacks was revealing. If Rosemary or I were Paris' targets, she could have taken either, or both, of us out, at almost any time, when we were completely unaware. Killing Homer's dog and leaving the Tarot cards behind only served to warn us. I thought back to the post card she'd sent to my office. She wanted to warn us. Her revenge wouldn't be sweet enough unless she sprinkled the beignets with some visceral fear. Paris enjoyed manipulating others to her will. It is what she'd done with her brother Hector, and all the other physicians she sued, Paris enjoyed the hideous game. It wasn't satisfying enough to just take pieces off the game board. Paris savored the opportunity to move them around the game board first.

It helped that we both recognized what Paris was doing. She was more than a murderer. She was a terrorist. Rosemary and I didn't consider ourselves particularly brave, but we weren't going to be terrorized. Bravery is not the absence of fear, but rather, acting despite fear. We would not allow Paris Laveau the satisfaction of moving us around like pawns.

That isn't to say we weren't on alert. We viewed all strangers in the neighborhood with suspicion. We spent more time looking in the rear-view mirror. We asked more pointed background questions to any new patients in our office. It isn't paranoia, if they're really after you. Suspicion is a heavy blanket to carry around with you wherever you went.

Law enforcement's failure to find even a hint of Paris Laveau convinced them that the murders were likely a hired hit-and-run attack. They continued to believe that the Bayou was where Paris Laveau would ultimately turn up. Rosemary and I felt differently. We were being stalked. Our stalker was quiet, careful and cunning. Our bet was that we were still being watched. Paris enjoyed this game of cat and mouse too much.

The police did not have infinite resources. Sooner or later, they'd lose interest in a trail that was cold. They would eventually accept the false narrative that their search and surveillance had spooked the perpetrator, and that they'd moved on. There was absolutely nothing about Paris Laveau that suggested she could be spooked. Rosemary reminded me that wolf packs would wait all night for the shepherds to fall asleep.

We maintained a red alert for weeks. We changed the door locks and added window locks. We started locking our cars overnight in the garage. I checked underneath the cars each morning. On the advice of SLED, we installed a high-end security system with motion activated lights for the front and back yards. The police screened our mail and incoming phone calls. A SLED agent recommended that we purchase handguns, but neither Rosemary nor I believed in guns. I kept a Louisville Slugger by the door. Rosemary preferred the four iron from the set of PING golf clubs I stole at a yard sale.

Eventually the weeks turned into months, and anxiety dissolved into apathy. By the time the various law enforcement agencies told us they were suspending their active investigation into Lou's murder, we were relieved. I confirmed with Rosemary that she was okay with losing our protective surveillance.

"I don't give a rat's ass if I never see another police cruiser parked across the street from our house. I'm sick and tired of watching them eating Krispy Kremes and a sac full of McDonalds every morning, noon and night."

I took that as an unequivocal response.

Our unease gradually slipped away and work forces you back to a normal routine. After putting it off as long as he could, Homer finally hired another embryologist to support the in vitro fertilization program. He wanted to just get somebody part time, but I convinced him that he was only putting off a hard, but inevitable decision. Homer agreed but dragged his feet. The poor guy he hired didn't understand that he was going to be an unpleasant reminder for a year, if not longer.

I greatly missed my scientific discussions with Lou. He always had unique perspectives on whatever was the topic of the day. Few people were better than Lou in tweaking me to think about things differently. I notified the Gordon Conference of Lou's death. I would be speaking in his place. I knew things were getting back to normal when Rosemary woke me early on a Saturday morning with a list of yard sales. She outlined a strict schedule to make sure we caught them all before noon.

I refused to believe that we'd be blown up or a victim of a drive by shooting at a James Island swap meet. I just didn't want to get out of bed. However, after two months of limited activities, Rosemary was not going to be dissuaded.

"All right, I'll go, but I won't haggle. Just let me take a quick shower."

"Good deal. I'll brew some coffee and make a couple Donald Duck sandwiches. I'll put them in Saran Wrap for the road."

I told Rosemary it'd be a quick shower. I knew it was a lie when I said it. I'd stayed up too late watching *Alien* again for the hundredth time. I hadn't figured on Rosemary getting me up so early. I stood with my hands against the back wall of the shower while the steaming hot water beat down on my neck. I was going to enjoy this for a while.

I didn't turn, but smiled, when I heard the shower door open. I smiled again when I felt Rosemary press herself against my back, butt and upper thighs. She reached around with a soapy hand and began to stroke me. I responded immediately and tried to turn around to face her. Instead, Rosemary leaned more heavily against my back, grabbed me tightly with her hand, and told me to stay where I was.

She resumed stroking me with her soapy hand. Slow at first, then faster. My excitement rose quickly as well. Rosemary giggled when she brought me to an embarrassingly rapid climax. I exhaled, turned and opened my eyes just in time to see Rosemary's cute ass exiting the shower.

"Hey, wait up."

Rosemary turned and reopened the fogged glass shower door. "What? We've got a yard sale in Creekside Park to get to. I couldn't wait for you to finish on your own."

Rosemary had the mischievous grin on her face of a child who had done something bad and knew it. She struck the pose of a victor. She looked gorgeous, and more desirable than any woman I'd ever seen. I pointed at the shower drain.

"There's somewhere else I would've preferred to put those ten million willing warriors."

"No need, big guy."

"What do you mean?"

"I'm pregnant. Now get your butt moving. I want to be in Creekside by nine."

Rosemary smiled again, did a sexy naked curtsey and a playful two-finger salute that reminded me of Shirley Temple.

I'm sure that the sappy smile on my face wasn't attractive. I returned a snappy military salute that would have made Homer Lahr proud. "Ooh Rah."

Rosemary giggled again and closed the shower door.

Chapter 25.
ANGEL OAK

"I'm pregnant."

No other two words can stop time in quite the same way. They're words without fuzzy edges. They have the blue steel hardness of unambiguous reality. The first thoughts that follow these words are the sound of an explosion. You either run towards it or run away.

"I'm pregnant," demands a perfect response. You only get one chance at responding to those two words. Anything short of perfect will haunt you for the rest of your life. There may be a million reasons why, but short is short. You'll never have another shot at perfect.

Rosemary would make a fabulous poker player. She pushed her chips all-in with "I'm pregnant," without a hint if she was holding or bluffing. If Rosemary had a tell, I hadn't found it yet. I didn't know what was going to happen next, but it wasn't going to be a yard sale. Fortunately, my response did not require words. Joy involuntarily filled my heart and radiated from my eyes. Wordlessly, I provided the perfect response. Rosemary and I embraced. I tightened my embrace of Rosemary, then I looked her in the eyes.

"Rose, I'm all in. I haven't been much of a man for the last couple of years. Until you threw me a lifeline, and I grabbed it. I'm not talking about what you did for me as my lawyer. I'm talking about what you did for me as a woman. You made me want to be a better man again and I want to be a good father to this child. This past year, you gave me the chance to try again which was something I didn't think I'd ever deserve."

"I didn't save you. You saved yourself. You rebuilt your practice. You rebuilt your life. I know how hard that was for you. You saw the potential of partnering with Homer, you made that work, and your patients love you. Ask Ms. Floyd who saved who. And, you've made me happier than I've ever been. These, baby, are the salad days."

"You know better than most that I come with baggage. Paris Laveau is still out there somewhere with a red-hot chili pepper up her ass for me. She's not going to stop until she has her revenge. You know that she won't hesitate to go through you, to get to me."

"Get over yourself. Don't try to scare me with your boogie-woman. She has as much reason to wish revenge on me, as she does on you. I'm not afraid of that Cajun bitch. We're going to put her down, like the rabid dog she is."

"Well, now. I've heard that some women can become short-tempered early in pregnancy."

"You better button that up, Jack. I'm not some women."

I had to laugh. "Oh, that I know. I hope that you've got some more of those pig bristles. Nobody else seems to have a solution for Paris Laveau."

"You leave Paris Laveau to me. I've got plenty of pig bristles. When I find Paris, I'll shove'm were the sun don't shine."

"Okay. No issues with early pregnancy emotional liability here. Paris is smart to have retreated back to whatever rotten cypress log she hides under."

"Damn straight, she's dealing with a momma bear now."

"I can see that, but back to my point, I've let people down. I've hurt people. I don't ever want to do that to you. It's not unfair to be unsure of me."

"No, you're just a big dummy. You're no more damaged than anyone else. Helene caught a disease, which you didn't give her, and she died. It's a terribly sad thing, but it doesn't make you guilty, and it doesn't make you special. My husband played me for a fool. He tricked me into giving up my dreams. Then he cheated on me with every piece of white trash he could lay his grubby hands on. When I kicked his ass out, the only things that bastard left me were shame, a profound sense of worthlessness and a shattered self-confidence. Now, you tell me who's damaged goods."

"Ain't we a pair?" I grinned, but quickly realized this wasn't the time for levity. Rosemary had a serious expression on her face and was searching my face. Believing that she'd found a man she could trust, and once again, put her faith in, was a big step for Rosemary. The ante on that question had now been upped by the presence of a baby."

"Your husband was a fool. Dummy or damaged, I'm smart enough to not let him ruin what we have. I promise that I'll never treat you the way that he did. I love you, Rosemary, and I want to build a life together with you, and with our child."

Rosemary smiled. "That's what I want as well. Are you sure that the baby doesn't make that harder? If it's going to make it too hard, then we need to figure that out right away."

"I've already figured it out. I figured it out the moment that you told me you were pregnant. Our life won't be complete without strapping young Hobart."

"Don't you mean Phoebe?"

"Hobart, Phoebe, it doesn't matter to me. Like I said, I'm all-in."

"Then I'm in too."

"You know this is bigger than a yard sale."

"What do you have in mind?"

We looked at each other for a few seconds, then simultaneously answered, "Road trip."

We stopped at the Med Deli in South Windermere and bought some hard salami, a block of Havarti with dill and a nice baguette. I also picked up a light Chenin Blanc, because I'm stupid. Rosemary gave me an incredulous look. I added a second bottle of sparkling grape juice and got a nod of approval. It was a cool November Saturday, nice enough for a picnic. I knew the perfect place.

The Angel Oak is the oldest living thing east of the Mississippi River, estimated to be between five hundred and fifteen hundred years old. The Angel Oak stands over sixty-five feet tall with a trunk circumference of twenty-eight feet, and a canopy which shades an area greater than 17,000 square feet. Shafts of light sliced through the upper branches. Rosemary and I felt like we were standing in the nave of a gothic Catholic Church. The Angel Oak had been standing majestically over a small piece of John's Island since well before the Kiawah Indians ever encountered a white man.

We spread a blanket under the boughs of the live oak and opened both the bottle of wine and the sparkling grape juice to toast our unborn child. We were in the right place. There were a few other families also picnicking under the shade of the magnificent Angel Oak. A handful of children scurried around under the massive branches. Branches which stretched out to ninety feet in length, and so heavy they rested on the ground in places. We experienced ourselves as a family for the first time.

Rosemary said that the oak's spreading limbs reminded her of angel's wings and asked if that's how Angel Oak got its name. I told her the real story. The land on which the oak stood was granted by the King of England in the early 1700s to colonist Abraham Waight. Waight's daughter, Martha, married Justus Angel in 1810. The land and the tree passed to them. The descendants of Justus and Martha Angel owned the land until the mid-1900s when the City of Charleston bought the site to protect it.

"Well, I like my story better."

"Okay, we'll go with your story. However, given what we've been through, the story of the ferns is even better."

"What fern story?"

I pointed up to the ferns growing in the bifurcation of the branches, and along the tops of the large muscular arms of the oak. "Those are resurrection ferns. They're epiphytes, like Spanish moss. Instead of hanging down, they grow upwards off the branch. They live symbiotically with the tree."

"So, what makes them resurrection ferns?"

"The fern can live for years without any water. They go dormant during long periods of drought, but then spring back with just a little bit of rain."

"Do you feel like you're in the middle of a drought? I have evidence to the contrary."

"No, not that. I feel like we're both coming back from something. We're both waking up to a new start. A resurrection, if you don't mind the religious reference. At least, that's how I feel about it."

"I love you, big dummy."

After our picnic, we decided to spend the rest of the weekend at Rosemary's place on Seabrook Island. It'd been a few months since we'd been out to Pelican Watch. When Rosemary suggested it, I immediately agreed. Sea breezes clear the mind. It would only be one night, but we both looked forward to some "Sweet Magnolia Time."

Despite being early pregnant, Rosemary was feeling good. The romantic picnic, or the knowledge that she was already pregnant, made Rosemary particularly amorous. By the time we pulled the car in beneath her beach condo, it was clear that we weren't going to make it upstairs. In a tangled embrace, we knocked over folded beach chairs, and almost slipped on a lacquered skim board. Rosemary yanked me into the downstairs, outdoor shower and we made love on the wooden shower bench.

Seabrook was the perfect spot to decompress. We threw some couch pillows on the floor and laid on her sea grass rug. We ate delivered pizza and watched an old movie on television. Eventually, I began to fidget.

"Doesn't this sisal make you itch?"

"No, but then again, I'm not a delicate flower like you are."

"Seriously, this rug stuff doesn't make you itch?"

"Not me, but maybe I'm immune to it. I love its musky smell. If you're itchy, though, we can go into the bedroom. I think the sheets are Egyptian cotton. Seems to me that you might be better suited to Egyptian cotton."

I thought that was a jab, but I didn't make her have to ask me twice.

The following morning, we had a quick breakfast of leftover salami and cheese. I retrieved an unused shrimp net and a plastic bucket from the downstairs storage closet. We decided to head over to the public dock. To properly throw a shrimp net, you had to be Low Country born and raised. Rosemary wouldn't take the lead-weighted edge of the shrimp net in her mouth, essential if you wanted to get the perfect swirl of the open net on the fling. Appreciation for the briny taste and scent of creek water was imprinted, not acquired.

Early and cold, the dock was empty, so we had our private kingdom. Unfortunately, we mistimed the tides, and arrived at dead low. The shrimp would come in with the tide. We laid on our backs on the weathered boards of the dock with Rosemary resting her head on my chest. We watched the osprey and blue herons flying back to Captain Sam's spit to roost. We inhaled the complicated aroma of honeysuckle, salt and the primordial smells of the tidal creek.

We rolled over on our bellies to watch the teaming world of the marsh through the window between the boards. The pluff mud was pocked with thousands of tiny mysterious caverns. Armies of skittish fiddler crabs emerged, explored and retreated to their respective holes. At least, we thought, they were retreating to their respective homes. Other than the single big claw on the males, the fiddler crabs didn't have a lot of other distinctive features. I wondered what kept the small crab holes from collapsing. Every Low Country boy had lost a shoe to the thick as chowder pluff at the bottom of the creek bed.

The fiddlers chased invisible prey around scattered clusters of oysters that would slice a pair of bare feet to pieces. They chased periwinkle snails up stalks of the spartina grass. Gradually, the tide returns, flooding the tiny holes. Crabby activities cease, and a sunlight shimmer returns to the creek bed. The breeze ran its hand across the tops of the marsh grass, the tips sparkling like gold. I rolled onto my back again and looked at the sky. I thanked God for the warm blueness above me, and for the cold green-brown water rising beneath me. I heard God's answer in a gust of wind rattling through the palmetto fronds and in the splash of a flying fish in the creek.

In time, the creek rose high enough for casting. Like feral box car children, we began to cast, as if failure meant we'd starve. Eventually we realized there aren't any shrimp in November. I wasn't sure what I was thinking. We were lucky, however, and netted a good sized flounder. We also netted two large blue crabs that Rosemary extricated from the shrimp net. She threw then unceremoniously in the stained plastic bucket with the flounder. It was one of the finest mornings of my life. Shortly after noon, we returned to Pelican Watch with both lunch and dinner.

Hating the thought of ending our weekend, we put off our return to Charleston until late. It took about thirty minutes to get from Seabrook back to the Wappoo Cut. The first fifteen miles were on Bohicket

Road. Bohicket Road is a national historic highway following the old Indian trails to Kiawah and Seabrook Islands. A two lane black top enveloped by overhanging live oak trees, shrouded with thick Spanish moss. Neither moonlight nor starlight penetrated the live oak canopy. The road itself was devoid of a single house or light.

Always a spooky drive, Rosemary and I didn't expect there to be another sole on the road at almost midnight. I took little note of the headlights behind us except to be pleased by the extra illumination on the inky black roadway. The height of the headlights suggested a pick-up truck, which soon was right on our tail. Their brights in the rearview mirror blinded me so I slowed to let them pass.

Instead of passing, the vehicle smacked us a good one from behind.

"What the fuck!" I pulled over to look at the damage. The shoulder was narrow, but there was no traffic. The pick-up pulled over as well. It looked like there were two people in the front seat, but the bright lights made it hard to be certain. I hesitated, expecting them to get out first considering they'd hit us. As I waited, the pick-up honked its horn and flashed its headlights.

I looked in the rearview again, and Rosemary grabbed my arm. "Get out of here. Get out of here now. This isn't right."

I gunned the engine on my Lexus LS400 and fishtailed back onto Bohicket Road, accelerating away. The pick-up took off after us. It stayed right on our tail for about a mile. Rosemary peered out the back window and urged me to drive faster, until I could yank her back down into her seat with my free hand. Ultimately, the pickup was no match for the engine power of the Lexus. We beat them to the intersection of Bohicket and Main Road by good half minute. We turned right onto the busier Main Road toward Charleston. With no taste for a high-speed chase on a crowded, more commercial road, the truck left turned and disappeared toward Wadmalaw Island.

"Do you think we just fled the scene of an accident?"

"Not a chance. That was Paris Laveau, or someone she sent. I could feel the chill in the air. If we'd gotten out of this car, we'd be dead. Might've been dead even if we stayed in the car. That bitch just isn't going to quit."

“How could she have known where we were. No one knew we went to Seabrook. We didn’t even know we were going until we finished our picnic. We didn’t talk to anyone while we were there. How the hell did she know? How is it that we never see anybody watching or following us? Maybe we just swapped paint with some drunken John’s Island cooter.”

“I hope you’re right baby, but I didn’t like the feel of things. We couldn’t take that chance out there on that empty blacktop.”

I’m with you. Nothing good happens on Bohicket Road after midnight.”

We drove the rest of the way home below the speed limit. As my lawyer, I asked Rosemary what we should say if the police came by tomorrow with our license plate number. They’ll want to know why we left the scene of an accident. Rosemary said we would report it ourselves. “Every law enforcement officer in the tri-county region is supposed to be looking for Paris Laveau. We won’t take any heat.”

When we reached Wappoo Heights, I pulled into the driveway which activated the motion sensor security system. The first time I found it reassuring, instead of aggravating. I felt bad that it was going to wake the neighbors. We hustled to get inside, to turn the system off, before every law enforcement agency in the area was mobilized.

The porch light was out, and we fumbled for our house keys in the dark.

We almost missed the Les Morts Tarot card propped up against the base of our front door.

The house no longer felt like a sanctuary.

Chapter 26.
AMADO GARRILLO FUENTES

The police response to our hit and run was quantitatively and qualitatively different than it had been after either Dogue's poisoning or Lou's murder. The local police responded, but not the big cheese. There was no sign of either the F.B.I. or the U.S. Marshalls. Surprising since Paris Laveau's face was still on prominent display down at the post office. Charleston's finest assured us they'd keep the Federals notified.

Besides the diminished numerical response, there was also a noticeable lack of urgency. After finding the Tarot card, Rosemary called the detective assigned to the Guillette murder. He told us they'd be out to see us in the morning. Rosemary hung up the phone and stared at me incredulously. When they did show up, their questions were, at best, perfunctory. They had the enthusiasm of someone completing "required forms."

We had no answer to the question of how anyone could've known we'd gone to Seabrook for the weekend. It was an unplanned getaway. The detective suggested that we'd probably been followed. Rosemary and I both thought that unlikely. The Angel Oak is a secluded spot, and there weren't many other visitors. We were there several hours and couldn't remember a soul that seems out of place. If there were any would be assassins stalking our picnic, they were well disguised by a handful of children under the age of twelve. Asked if we were sure, Rosemary responded , "After someone tries to blow you up, you tend to be vigilant."

I added that the road from the Angel Oak out to Seabrook is about ten miles and it isn't busy. We didn't remember anyone behind us after we left our picnic. The police checked our car for an electronic tracker but found nothing. While we didn't understand how anyone could've known that we were at Seabrook, Rosemary and I were both convinced that someone had. Maybe we'd been tracked, and the tracker removed while we were at the beach. The detective's dull-witted indifference did nothing for our equanimity.

Our car had a dent in the rear bumper and some swapped paint. Samples were collected in case a possible pick-up truck donor was identified. No suspect vehicles had been found along Bohicket or Main Roads. No police reports came across any law enforcement agency's desk from Sunday night. Unless we could remember a make, model or license plate number there wasn't going to be anything the police could do. Of course, they were very sorry.

I asked the detective how somebody could have placed a Tarot card on our doorstep without triggering the motion sensor. They didn't have an answer. They opined that whoever placed it, must have come by during the day, before the security system kicked in.

The detective asked if I knew where this kind of Tarot card could be found commercially. The detective was obviously uninformed about the background of the Paris Laveau case. He carefully recorded my annoyed observation that they could be found in almost any of the Voodoo shops along Bourbon Street in New Orleans.

Rosemary read more into the question than I had. I assumed that our detectives were simply dolts, slow on the uptake. Rosemary leaped to her feet and got directly in the detective's face. "You think we put that Tarot card out on our front porch?"

"No, not at all. I was just wondering how available they might be. How hard would it be to find these cards if you wanted them?"

"That's bullshit, detective." Rosemary's finger was now jabbing the detective in his chest. "What reason would we have to keep you chasing after a phantom Paris Laveau? What reason would we have to poison an innocent dog? Why would Declan kill his best friend? Why would Declan plan to blow up an airboat that he would've been on had it not been for a hospital emergency that no one anticipated? Who doubts that Paris Laveau is an amoral, vicious beast? A woman who, by the way, has vowed revenge against us, and, in case you've forgotten, escaped police custody by almost killing one of your own. Unless we are unaware of something hot off the press, Paris Laveau is still on the loose. She's the one, and only, suspect. Not Declan, and not me."

"You misunderstood my question."

"Did I? Could it be that one of the country's ten most wanted fugitives is cruising around John's Island in a dented pick-up truck, and neither you, nor any of your Federal colleagues, can even get a whiff of her foul breath? Maybe it lightens your load to pin this on us, so you don't have to explain anymore your failure to find Paris Laveau?"

"Believe me Ms. Winslow, we are as frustrated by our inability to find Ms. Laveau as you are."

"Oh, you are! I guess that means that Paris Laveau has tried to blow you up and run you down."

Before this went too far, I stepped in. "Rosemary, I don't think the detective believes we placed the Tarot cards ourselves to re-engage them in this investigation."

"You don't, huh! I believe that's exactly what they think."

"Time for you to jump in detective."

"Dr. Murphy is right. We still have an active investigation ongoing, targeting whoever has done these things. The Charleston Police Department continues to believe that Paris Laveau, or someone acting on her behalf, is the primary suspect. We have lost some of our support from the F.B.I. and the U.S. Marshalls. They have reason to believe that Paris Laveau is no longer in the area. However, the events of last night may change their minds."

"What do you mean 'reason to believe' that Paris Laveau is no longer in the area?"

"I can't say, Dr. Murphy. The Feds don't share that kind of information with us. They treat us like mushrooms. They believe that we flourish when we're kept in the dark and fed a steady diet of bullshit."

"Well, if you're still looking for her, what've you done?"

"Since the card was probably placed during daylight hours, we've canvassed the neighborhood to see if anyone might have seen anything unusual."

"And?" Rosemary interjected.

"Not much. Your neighbor to the left, Ms. Mikell, thinks she saw someone, but I'm skeptical. She heard a metallic thwap of a screen door slamming and went outside on her porch to investigate. Ms. Mikell saw a man in black jeans, a long-sleeved plaid shirt and a red do-rag on his head. She thinks he was Mexican. He was walking down the dirt path towards Folly Road and was in a hurry."

"And why are you skeptical?"

"First of all, you don't have a screen door. Second, this is the fourth time in the last six months that Ms. Mikell has called the city police about suspicious Mexicans wandering through Wappoo Heights. The last time she called, there was a short Mexican throwing rocks at her windows. When we came out, we found a 10-year-old boy in clam diggers and a white tee-shirt hitting a tennis ball against the side of her house. Mexicans are uncommon in Wappoo Heights. She's probably watching too many episodes of Cops."

The police left about an hour later. Rosemary was steaming. "What the hell was that all about? They've signed off on finding Paris Laveau. If something happens, I promise you, I'll sue the police department for professional misconduct. I'll rip them a new one."

"Pump the breaks, Rose. We need to find out what he meant by the F.B. I. and the U.S. Marshalls not believing that she's in the Low Country."

"How do you plan to do that?"

"Laurence Nodeen."

I hadn't talked to Laurence in quite a while. No matter how long it'd been, I knew Laurence would help us. Laurence Nodeen had busted Helene's pedophile father. He picked apart MUSC's collusion to violate Helene's civil rights. He'd helped me figure out the true identities of the suspicious Dalton and Magdalene Surrette. Laurence picked up on the third ring.

"Clarence, my man. It's been a while. What's going on?" We bonded over basketball, as well as my constant need for his help. His friendship was far more than I'd earned. He called me Clarence after the sponsor of our city league basketball team, Clarence "Don't Turn Nobody Down" McCants. What really bonded us, however, was that I was so good at starting fights, and he was so good at finishing them.

"How did you know it was me?"

"Don't be so thick. I work at the Justice Department, and I sit in a big chair. I've been expecting your call. I'm a little put out that you waited so long."

"So, you know what's going on with Paris Laveau?"

"Sometimes your intellectual limitations surprise even me. Paris Laveau is the F.B.I.'s wet dream. She's an escaped fugitive wanted for feticide or infanticide depending on the particular state involved, multiple counts of interstate fraud, attempted murder of a police officer and being a hideous human being. Since you obviously haven't figured out all these complicated details, you should know that part of my year end evaluation is my ability to keep up with the nation's ten most wanted fugitives."

"All right, I hear you. The sarcasm is dripping out of my end of the phone. Any chance we can put that on hold for a minute, because I could really use your help."

"No problem. What can I do for you? You know we don't have Paris Laveau in custody."

"Sure, but where do you guys think she is? Rosemary and I were driving back from Seabrook Island last night, and a pick-up truck tried to run us off the road. We didn't stick around to find out what else the driver had in mind. When we got home, we found another of Paris' Les Morts Tarot cards on our front door."

"You have to respect someone that's proud of their work," Nodeen said with a chuckle. "That sounds like our girl."

"I thought so too, but when the locals came to investigate, they did a great impression of going through the motions. When we asked where the F.B.I. agents were, the locals said they no longer believed that Paris Laveau was in the area. Of course, he couldn't elaborate. I thought you might be more forthcoming."

"I'll pass on this new development to the investigators. However, somebody may be jacking you around with the Tarot cards. We have some pretty good evidence that Paris Laveau, and her man-mountain bodyguard, have crossed over into Juarez, Mexico from El Paso. The images of them crossing the border are poor quality, but her man is hard to miss. We also have some audiotape which puts Paris Laveau with Amado Carrillo Fuentes. Fuentes is now on top of the Juarez cartel. That's a nasty pair to team up."

"Can you get to her?"

"Wish we could, but no. The Juarez cartel is pulling in more than 200 million dollars per week from the sale of coke, heroin and meth. They've used that money to bribe or intimidate almost all high-ranking governmental officials in Juarez. The cartel knows about every planned law enforcement operation. They have unimaginable police and judicial protection. They also use the money to fund La Linea, a group of corrupt former and current Chihuahua police officers. La Linea is street level muscle. They'll assassinate anyone Fuentes wants to get out of the way. Bottom line, if Paris is under Fuentes' protection, we can't touch her."

"What's she up to?"

"We're not certain, but she's playing a very dangerous game. The Juarez Cartel controls some of the most effective drug transportation routes from Mexico into the United States; billions of dollars' worth of illegal drugs. Once the drugs enter the U.S., they generally head west and north, and are distributed from Los Angeles, San Diego and Chicago. I'm sure that you've heard of the Sinaloa Cowboys in the California Central Valley. We think that Paris is trying to sell Fuentes on a distribution route that goes east through New Orleans, then swings along the Southern Crescent. We don't know if she's capable of pulling that off or not. However, she better not promise more than she can deliver. Nobody fucks with Amado Garrillo Fuentes more than once."

"Maybe she's just trying to find sanctuary."

"Maybe, but, if she doesn't have anything to offer, then your problems with Paris Laveau may be solved. The Mexican cartels have turned murder into an art form. These guys are as far from your Jackpot gentleman smugglers as Paris Laveau is from June Cleaver. If Paris crosses, or even disappoints, the cartel, they'll hang her from the Bridge of the Americas."

"Couldn't happen to a nicer girl. Not that I care, but somebody better be watching Fuentes back. I'm sure Fuentes is a bad guy, but Paris emanates a nameless, ineffable depravity."

"I hear you, Clarence. Mexico is filled with a cavalcade of two-bit caudillos, but Amado Fuentes is the real deal. I've seen the videos of blood, brains and skull fragments being hosed out of the House of Death."

"It sounds like you're pretty sure that she's in Mexico. Could she have left somebody behind to settle old grudges?"

"I can't guarantee it, but we've got several strong pieces of evidence that she crossed the bridge from El Paso into Juarez, and found her way to the heart of the Juarez Cartel. Could she have sent someone to Charleston? It's conceivable, but I'm doubtful. She has some resources, but they're not unlimited. Setting up a drug smuggling operation with the Juarez Cartel is a full-time gig. The downside of making a mistake is terminally steep. She's also a sociopath. Sociopaths don't make attachments, and by extension, they don't develop grudges. I hate to disappoint you, but our behavioral psych people think that once you are out of Paris' sight, you're out of her mind."

"You don't think Paris cares about me anymore?"

"Hate to disappoint you buddy. You're just a mosquito smashed against the headlight of her motorcycle."

"I hope you're right, Laurence, but things are off down here. If your suspicion is true, then I need to figure out who's been fucking with me."

"I can't answer that one Clarence, but, you know, you have that effect on people."

Laurence promised to keep me posted on whatever new information came along. He swore me to secrecy about the F.B.I. information on Paris Laveau. He knew that promise wouldn't apply to Rosemary Winslow. The lack of clarity was troubling, but, I trusted Laurence, and hoped that we might be close to putting Paris Laveau behind us. The overwhelming desire to let Paris Laveau slip out of my consciousness was highly seductive.

Unfortunately, a soft voice in the back of my mind kept saying, "not so fast." I'd be wonderful to let the Juarez Cartel deal with Paris. Soon enough, they'd discover that the phrase "honor among thieves" didn't apply to their sociopathic Americano bitch. It wouldn't be long before they necklaced her with petrol-filled tires. Paris' blackened body would match her blackened heart. That soft voice reminded me that it was a gift to be underestimated. Paris feasted on people who underestimated her.

I couldn't think of a single time that Laurence's counsel had not been on point. He'd saved my bacon on several occasions. But even Laurence admitted that he wasn't one hundred percent sure about Paris crossing the Rio Bravo. Rosemary and I, and especially Marcellus Greene, had already learned a hard lesson. As soon as you think that Paris Laveau is no longer a problem, that's when you're the most vulnerable. Even if the local police and the F.B.I. believed that Paris now resided south of the border, I wasn't yet comfortable with making that assumption.

Chapter 27.
LIEBER CORRECTIONAL

Rosemary listened carefully as I recounted my conversation with Laurence Nodeen. Despite Laurence's intelligence sources, I expressed my hesitancy to assume that Paris Laveau was no longer a player in our local drama. By nature, and professional training, Rosemary was cautious as well. She reminded me that to assume, was most likely to make an "ass" out of "u" and "me."

Rosemary remained unsettled by the police stepping off. "What do you think we should we do? The police don't think Paris is behind this. Hell, they might even think that we are. We can't just sit back because the F.B.I. thinks she's in Mexico. Declan, I think we're on our own if we want to stay safe."

"We've been in this spot before. We beat Paris Laveau then, and we'll beat her this time too. You're right, though, we need our own plan."

"I hope it's a better plan than the one you took to the parking lot at BeBops Ice House."

"Definitely, my BeBops plan needed a few tweaks. What we need to do is ask someone who knows for sure."

"Who's that? If Nodeen isn't sure, who has better information than him?"

"Hector."

The next day, Rosemary and I took the forty-five-minute drive up I-26 to Lieber Correctional Institute in Ridgeville, South Carolina. Lieber was one of South Carolina's maximum-security prisons, and widely known as the state's most dangerous. It was also going to be home to Hector Laveau (a.k.a. Dalton Surrette) for at least the next thirty years.

Hector was Paris Laveau's brother, father of her aborted babies, and the guy who Paris left holding the bag. Her elocution to the judge, when he granted her extradition back to Louisiana, was the nail in Hector's legal coffin. He broke the hearts of the local prosecutors when he decided to plead guilty to a string of nasty charges, in exchange for pre-meditated murder being taken off the table. Truth be known, Hector probably did the prosecutors a favor. Under South Carolina law, the Laveau baby was only borderline viable. His lawyers still had my alleged malpractice as a defense, even though the civil suit was dismissed. Most importantly, while the prosecutors had Paris' elocution testimony, the person accusing Hector of being the abusive mastermind of their abominable acts was nowhere to be found. What Paris did to Sheriff Greene didn't advance the argument that she'd been a passive vessel for Hector's obstetrical crimes.

The Charleston County Solicitor believed he could stock the jury with enough fundamentalist Southern Baptists, evangelical Pentecostals and high-born Charlestonians to ensure a murder conviction. Hector's defense lawyers might've believed it too. More likely, they were motivated by the desire to extricate themselves from any association with Hector Laveau and his degeneracy. To his credit, the presiding judge didn't let the defense get away with pleading down. The judge maxed Hector out on all counts and ordered that the sentences be served consecutively rather than concurrently. Hector would be eligible for social security before he was eligible for parole.

As we drove, Rosemary and I discussed the best approach to take with Hector. She had better instincts for this than I did. Only one of us would be allowed to meet with Hector. Rosemary believed that he'd be more likely to talk with me. Hector was too hard to try sympathy and too simple for subtlety. He'd also be hard to trick. We'd fooled him once already, so he'd be wary of any overtures. Ultimately, we decided to take the same tack that Rosemary used in his deposition. I was going to piss him off. Then we'd see what was really on his mind.

While I talked with Hector, Rosemary would go by the administrative office. She'd find out what she could about Hector's visitors.

Like most correctional facilities, Lieber was located several miles past nowhere. At first glance, it looked a little bit like a small college campus. The major buildings all shared the same fancy brick façade. The open spaces surrounding the core buildings were crisscrossed with wide sidewalks. The outdoor athletic facilities looked to be first rate. There weren't any ominous gates or foreboding walls. Only on second look did the surrounding fences became obvious. Fences topped with razor wire, designed to cut and kill.

Entering the facility, any confusion with a college campus was quickly dispelled. Rosemary and I had to remove our shoes, go through a metal detector and be patted down by a corrections officer. As we moved further inside we noticed the incessant disorganized noise, followed closely by the smell. The smell of 1500 men in a confined space who no longer gave a damn. Lastly, you could feel the vibration of the heavy steel doors slamming behind you.

Rosemary waited in an unreceptive reception area. A corrections officer took me to the visitation room. He sat me at a cubicle, facing thick Plexiglas with a telephone handset. I waited a long time for Hector to appear. With a thirty-year sentence, promptness was not valued as a major virtue.

He finally arrived wearing a beige jumpsuit with SCDC stenciled on the back. There were black stripes down the outside of each leg. His hair was long and unkempt. He sported a raggedy, patchy beard that reminded me of how he'd looked when I first met him. Facial hair wouldn't grow in his cystic acne scars. He stood behind his chair with mouth agape. I wasn't the visitor he'd expected. He was considering shooting me the bird and heading back to his cell, but his curiosity got the better of him. He pulled up a chair and sat down.

"What the fuck do you want, doc?"

"Just felt sorry for you, Hector. I thought you might be lonely after Paris sold you down the river. I'm sure that you haven't made any friends in here."

"I've got friends."

"Sure you do. You're white, you're an ignorant hillbilly, you fuck your sister, and you kill babies. I'm sure you're on everyone's A-list when the party invites go out. Maybe the Aryans will take you in, but you'll need to shave your head, get a swastika tattoo, and learn to live with constant anal leakage."

"Fuck you."

"No, it's the other way around. You're the one who's fucked. But hey, don't get mad at me. It's your sister who put you in here."

"And she's going to get me out of here too."

"You sure about that? I hear Paris is sunning herself on the beautiful beaches of Acapulco. Layin' out on the golden sand with a hairless, twenty–something Latin lover with light brown skin slathered with baby oil."

For the first time, I saw a glint in Hector's eyes that hinted at an understanding of what I might be doing. A slight smile curled its way around his dry scaly lips.

"I don't have any idea where Paris might be. Wherever she is though, she thinkin' about me. She'll figure out a way to get me out of here. She makes sure I have everything I need."

"That's sweet. Does she visit often? Do they allow brother-sister conjugal visits? That's far more progressive than I thought Lieber might be."

"You know damn good and well that Paris ain't been to visit me. But that don't mean I don't hear from her. Paris is a helluva lot smarter than you are, doc, or the high school drop-outs they got running this joint. But, like I said, I ain't got any idea where Paris is."

"Maybe you don't, but I do. The F.B.I. does, and the U.S. Marshalls do as well. It won't be long until she's also looking at the world though bars."

"Where is she then?"

"Well, you know, I'm not at liberty to say. What's important though, is that she's bugged out of South Carolina. I think it's interesting that you don't know for sure where she is. I guess you haven't gotten a recent postcard. More importantly, I'll bet she doesn't have any clue where you are."

"Yeah, says you. Paris has my back wherever she's at."

"Like I said, that's sweet. If she isn't beaching it in Acapulco, then where do you think she's getting her lovin' these days? Younger brothers, a cousin? I know she likes to keep it in the family."

Hector exploded from his chair and punched the Plexiglas. He had the same murderous look in his eyes that I'd seen in Rosemary's office when she was rolling them up. He slapped both of his hands against the glass, and then sat back down when the visitation room guard yelled at him. To my surprise, Hector quickly regained his composure. He smiled again and ran his fingers through his greasy hair.

"Hector, I didn't mean to upset you. You've got to face reality. By the time you get out of here, your dick will be as flaccid as your rectal sphincter. Paris is a vital woman who needs a steady diet of thick man meat. She's bound to move on, likely sooner than later. You need to prepare yourself for that eventuality."

"You don't need to be worrying about my love life, doc. What I hear, is that you're shacking up with that lawyer bitch."

"Where did you hear that?" As soon as I said it, I realized I'd given myself away. Hector smiled again, knowing he struck a nerve. I didn't see the point of trying to keep up pretenses any longer.

"Listen, you perverted imbecile, where ever Paris has run off to, you let her know that she needs to keep on running. If she does anything else to mess with me or Ms. Winslow, I'll not rest until she's dead, or wishes she were."

Hector just laughed. "Oooh, I'm scared. What you need to know, doc, is that Paris can reach out and touch anybody she wants, anytime she wants, from anywhere she wants. Put that in your pipe and smoke it."

"Tell Paris to back off. If I see you again, it'll be to deliver some really bad news." I hung up the phone and walked away. I could hear Hector laughing through the Plexiglas.

I met Rosemary back in the reception room where we'd passed through the metal detector. We gathered our stuff and headed back to the car.

"How'd it go?" Rosemary asked.

"Not like I thought it would. Hector didn't rattle. He rattled me a bit when he mentioned that you and I were living together. Somehow, he's communicating with Paris. He also meant it as a threat. He's convinced that she is going to get him out."

"Did he give you any idea if she was in the area?"

"He was cagey about that. I said twice that we knew Paris was no longer in South Carolina. He didn't deny it, either time. What did you find out?"

"The warden's people were helpful. Hector's not very popular. No big surprise. Other than a couple of visits from his lawyer, he hasn't had any visitors until we showed up today. As far as anybody knows, he's never had a phone call. His mail is sparse, and everything is screened before he sees it. He's had a couple of letters from his lawyers with periodic updates, but nothing from Paris, or any other family."

"So, how's he hearing from Paris? I dug at him about her abandoning him. It didn't push any buttons at all."

"Maybe I know. The most interesting thing they told me in the administrative office was that Hector spends most of his time hanging out with the Mexicans. Lieber has some associates of La eMe. Although La eMe started out in the Southern California prison system, it's nationwide now. La eMe is an extension of the Mexican cartels and is responsible for most of the drug distribution within the U.S. prison system. It has a loose alliance with the Aryan Brotherhood, but only because the black gangs are their common enemy. Even with that alliance, it's very unusual for the Mexicans to let a Caucasian inside. Especially, when the dude's a deviant. I think Paris has worked out a deal with the Juarez Cartel. Protect Hector in exchange for whatever she's doing for them."

"They might also be Hector's source of information. It matches with what Nodeen told us about Paris being in Juarez under the protection of Amado Fuentes."

"That's better than Paris being around here."

"Maybe yes, maybe no. Hector told me twice that Paris was going to bust him out. I thought it was just big talk, but if Hector has the Latin gangs backing his play, then it might not be so far-fetched. As I left, Hector also warned me that Paris could reach out from anywhere to lay hands on us."

"Well, if she touches me, I'll touch her back."

"Let's get out of this pig sty. I've got a life to get back to."

Chapter 28.
ACCLIMATION

It's a normal human trait to acclimate. Acclimation is evolution's self-protective algorithm. I have no idea how it's programmed, but I'm sure it is near the heart of the motherboard. There is a fight or flight center somewhere that is archetypal and deeply hardwired as part of our innate survival instincts. However, that autonomous survival function must be subject to regulatory feedback. No human system can continuously run with the dial turned all the way to the right. Sooner or later, every system demands time to stand down, or else it will break down. Rosemary and I had been keeping ourselves at a heightened state of alert for too long. Like heroin addicts, we were becoming desensitized to the fear that Paris could inject into our veins. If we kept upping the dosage, we would certainly do ourselves in. We couldn't allow Paris Laveau to dominate our daily lives any longer.

We both decided to withdrawal ourselves from our daily fix of Paris Laveau by returning to our respective offices full time, with complete focus. Rosemary began accepting new clients. I started booking new obstetrical patients. It doesn't take long for the problems of other people to push aside your own. Homer was glad to see me getting back into the swing of things. "Do what you know how to do and put yesterday behind you. Take back control of your life, rather than wasting your time on a piece of trash you can't control." Homer was prophetic. Energy and enthusiasm returned to our office.

Except for depressing daylight savings time, November is my favorite month of the year. The weather in Charleston finally, and reliably, turns crisp and cooler. Charleston's oak trees drop their leaves onto the sidewalk where they're stirred around in circles by the harbor winds. The dried, brown Palmetto fronds rattle in the breeze.

The full arrival of November renews sun-sapped energy. Young boys play football to assert their manhood, one of the oldest southern rituals. Young men daydream about romance, the oldest of all rituals. For the first time in a long time. Paris Laveau was no longer hiding in our bedroom closet. Rosemary and I reclaimed our bedroom for the rituals we enjoyed the most.

Each evening, Rosemary would discuss her interesting new cases. Each case came with an aggrieved victim, a dastardly villain and monumental implications. I liked to guess what strategy Rosemary was planning to pursue. I repeatedly proved myself to not be a lawyer. Rosemary's devilish plans, and clever ruses, startled me. I knew how formidable a partner I had in Rosemary. I also realized how formidable an opponent she could be.

Sometimes I'd talk about my complicated OB cases, but they always lost something in translation. Doctor's seldom realized how boring their cases are to non-medical people. We never discussed either of the Laveaus. We enjoyed our evenings and our weekends, with yard sales in the morning, and football in the afternoon. On this particular Sunday morning, I was savoring a thick waffle, with pecans and maple syrup, courtesy of a new industrial-sized waffle iron purchased on James Island for three dollars, when the phone rang.

Laurence Nodeen's voice on the other end was a pleasant surprise. Quickly, he assured me that he was calling with good news. The F.B.I. had obtained another photo of a woman they were certain to be Paris Laveau taken at a Santeria shop in Juarez. We still don't know exactly what she is up to or why. However, Paris is in Juarez, and hasn't made any effort to contact family or friends in Louisiana or South Carolina. She's been in Mexico for at least a month, if not longer. Laurence gave us the direct number for the local F.B.I. field chief. Laurence didn't think that we were going to need it, but if we did, the field chief would be there for us.

"Declan, if anything comes up, call the pros. The local cops have a hard time thinning out traffic after a Citadel football game. Remind them who gave you their number. They're smart guys. They know where their bread is buttered."

As always, we ended up expressing our gratitude. We added another entry to the ledger of debts owed to Laurence Nodeen.

I'd put off completing the research presentation for the Gordon Conference. Lou had pulled together all our data and completed the analysis, but didn't get a chance to put together the slide presentation. He was so familiar with the subject matter, he might not have organized his actual talk until a day or two prior to the conference. I didn't enjoy that luxury.

I understood our research findings and their significance but I lacked the depth of Lou's background knowledge. My biggest challenge was to relate our findings to research that had been previously published. I burned the midnight oil reading through the *Journal of Environmental Health and Toxicology*, with which I had little familiarity. A voice in my head, which sounded a lot like Lou, reminded me that it wasn't just about the science. The presentation of good science required showmanship if you wanted it to have an impact. I wondered what the attendees would think if I jumped up on a table, like mounting a surf board.

I didn't want to short change our research and, more importantly, I didn't want to disappoint Lou. Dr. Guillette joined Homer Lahr as an Embryologist in order to do his alligator research. He collected data for two years before I started working with him. I didn't want to fumble the ball so close to the goal line. After two weeks of working on the presentation, I felt like it was close to where it needed to be.

The organizers of the Gordon Conference thought so too. My presentation would be part of their opening session. They also asked if I'd make myself available to the media at a press conference after the plenary session. That would be a first for me. The press made me more nervous than the presentation. I could feel the first tingles of a circular rash on my right outer thigh. A stigma of internalized anxiety ever since I was a teenager. I scratched it through my pants pocket.

Rosemary was doing great with her pregnancy. She had the constitution of a Clydesdale. She never experienced any nausea, and her only craving was for cantaloupe. Turns out that cantaloupe is good with waffles. Pregnancy had not affected her healthy sex drive, although breast tenderness had created a limited no-fly zone.

Rose struggled with her pregnancy dating. She decided that all of obstetrics was based on a fraud. The omnipresent pregnancy wheel calculates the estimated date of delivery from the first day of the last menstrual period. Delivery could be anticipated forty weeks following the beginning of the last menstrual period. Rosemary figured out that ovulation and fertilization occurred about two weeks after the onset of menses. Consequently, she figured that the actual length of pregnancy was only thirty-eight weeks. When Rosemary was told that she was in her tenth week of pregnancy, she calculated that she was only carrying an eight-week-old baby. She struggled to get her head wrapped around what she considered a craven deception.

She declared this an intentional duplicity designed to keep women uninformed and off balance and railed against it every time we talked about her gestational age. She'd already been through my obstetrical textbooks, like preparing for trial. Rosemary was going to be a handful. The pragmatism of obstetrics was not going to sit well with a woman dedicated to exactitude.

I encouraged Rosemary to go to one of my former colleagues at the university. Despite now being deeply entrenched in private practice , I kept my academic bias. My new private practice colleagues had the same training, and were as smart, as my former partners at the university. I preferred the university primarily because of the resident physicians. With a small army of Ob-Gyn residents rotating call responsibility, there was always the safety net of a sharp and eager young physician anxious to prove themselves.

Labor and delivery is a twenty-four hour, seven days a week responsibility. The most grievous mistakes in obstetrics had nothing to do with education or training. They had everything to do with the weakness of will, and lapses in judgment, that occur when men or women are asked to perform beyond their physical and emotional limitations. As the military has long understood, exhaustion makes cowards of us all.

After a long day, it's the phone call at three a.m. that does you in. You desperately listen for a skinny reason to put off evaluating your patient until the morning, rather than meeting her at the hospital. A self-deception that has its roots deep in your fatigue. You never believe that your number is going to come up, but with four million deliveries each year in the United States, it will. It would've been easy to tell Tracey Floyd's husband that she was safe with the emergency department staff.

Rosemary, unfortunately, had seen too much of the Medical University. My peer review experience, the Ramirez case and the other cases she'd picked up involving the medical school irretrievably soured her. She referred to my former employers as "a two-bit, fly-by-night organization."

She came home one evening after a mediation at MUSC with Vincent Bellizia. As soon as I met her at the door, she slapped my face.

"What's that for? What did Bellizia say to you?"

"You doctors are insufferable. What a bunch of douche bags. The lot of you."

Careful to not get too indignant, given my affiliation with a known terrorist group, I decided to proceed carefully.

"You are very intuitive. What did one of my clueless brothers or sisters do to offend you? Whatever it was, let me apologize unreservedly."

"Don't patronize me. You're a douche bag too."

"Yes, I am. Just tell me what happened."

"I rode down the elevator with two surgeons who thought they were all that, and a bag of chips. Have you ever noticed that surgeons wear their I.D. badges attached to their scrub pants? If you want to know who they are, you have to look at their junk. Also, where do they get their scrub tops? The V-neck on surgeon scrubs plunges down about three or four extra inches compared to everyone else. They were talking about the girls they picked up at the Blind Tiger last night. He called one of them a freak. One asked the other when his next case was. You know what the douche bag said?"

"No telling, but I bet it's bad."

"Whenever I get back from lunch."

"Horrid."

"What is the matter with you people? You know don't you, that the earth still revolves around the sun. At what point in medical school do they teach you that the sun revolves around you."

"You've never been more right. Those surgeons are royal ass wipes. They can't help it. It's part of their selection criteria. The operating room staff won't mind waiting till after the surgeon's midday repast. Can you imagine how unbearable the surgeon would be if forced to operate with a growling tummy? Best all-around really." I knew I was treading on thin ice to introduce a bit of levity. Rosemary was either going to grin or slap me again.

"Don't fool yourself. You're no better than the rest of them. I'm not going to forget that either." I heard Rosemary mumble "douche rocket" under her breath as she walked away.

Situation defused.

For her pregnancy, Rosemary had decided to stick with her gynecologist, Bobby Richmond. Bobby and I went way back. When I was a medical student on the Ob-Gyn rotation, Bobby was my Chief Resident. He always treated me square. Dr. Richmond never hesitated to involve us in patient care. He'd hand us a pair of gloves, and announce, "Young Dr. Murphy is the ultimate obstetrical authority on this case." We knew it wasn't true, but it engaged us to participate as best we could. We also learned quickly, how easy it was to get in over your head.

Dr. Bobby Richmond played free safety at Southern Mississippi back when tough-as-nails, working class white guys still played that position at southern colleges. During his residency, he had the swagger of an ex-athlete, and a reputation as a lady's man. Once in clinic, a nurse was yanking his chain about the inevitable weight gain that happens during residency. She mentioned that it looked like he was building a "shed in the back yard," a southern euphemism for having a big butt. Bobby didn't miss a beat. He turned his head, his eyes twinkled, and he responded, "Darlin', you can't drive a railroad spike with a tack hammer."

Dr. Richmond had settled down since going into practice. He married a female lawyer who Rosemary liked. By all indications, it was a great marriage. Rosemary held that credential in high regard.

Bobby was also a good doctor. He joined a successful practice downtown and became its principal as the older partners retired. He hired three new partners. Within a few years they'd forced him out in a palace coup. Now he is in solo practice and enjoying himself for the first time in years. Bobby learned to be a southern gentleman, but never lost the cockiness and bawdy sense of humor that he'd learned on the wrong side of the Starkville, Mississippi tracks. Rosemary loved the latter two traits of Bobby Richmond best.

She wasn't going to hear about seeing anyone else. Even though she never had any significant gynecological issues, she trusted Dr. Richmond's care. When she discovered her husband's infidelity she came to Bobby to be tested for sexually transmitted diseases. Nothing was found, but Rosemary suffered an uncharacteristic breakdown. Bobby handled it with compassion, empathy and the needed amount of time. He helped her through a hard time, which Rosemary would never forget.

Any hesitancy that I had was dispelled in Rosemary's twelfth week. She woke up in the middle of the night with a small amount of vaginal bleeding. Bobby didn't give her any false reassurance or suggest that she wait to see what happens next. He immediately told her to come to the hospital for an evaluation. While the ultrasound technologist performed her scan, he held her hand. It left me feeling oddly third-wheelish, but I could see how appreciative Rosemary was.

After years of doing obstetrics, it was the first time I ever completely understood the anxiety associated with those fuzzy first trimester ultrasound images. As the machine warmed up, I saw tears welling up in Rosemary's eyes. Every woman having an early obstetrical ultrasound must be quietly terrified. Will we be able to find that little flicker of a heartbeat? The tears of joy that we regularly see in the ultrasound suite, are actually the release of the sorrowful tears prepared in anticipation of the most elemental disappointment there is. The depth of pain experienced by women with repetitive miscarriages is hugely underestimated, too often discounted by the thoughtless, "Well, we can always try again."

Rosemary looked at Dr. Richmond instead of the ultrasound screen. The big smile on Bobby Richmond's face was all that

Rosemary needed. The tears began to flow. Given Rosemary's trim figure, the ultrasound images were clear. A strong, regular heartbeat was obvious. The baby looked perfect for a fetus at twelve weeks. Really only ten weeks, Rosemary would correct me later. I watched over the sonographers shoulder until I was satisfied there was only one.

Everything looked reassuring, but bleeding was still bleeding. Bobby made a point of letting Rosemary know that these sorts of bleeding episodes were relatively common. Nothing usually came of it. Exactly what I'd told her. When Dr. Richmond told her, it was reassuring.

Rosemary asked about work. Bobby advised her to take it easy for a few days, or until the bleeding stopped. She asked about sex. Bobby told her it was probably fine if it was just with me, then he winked at Rosemary. Rosemary laughed for the first time that morning. I decided to let it pass. Bobby made an appointment to follow up with Rosemary in about two weeks.

On the way home, we turned on the radio and were treated to Freddie Mercury and David Bowie singing "Under Pressure." We both smiled recognizing the irony of the lyrics. We sang together.

A tear rolled down Rosemary's cheek acknowledging all the pressure we'd been under, as well as the good news we'd just received. I pulled her over towards me and gave her a kiss on the cheek.

"I'm not sure if you're interested," I said, "but I watched closely while the sonographer was doing the scan. In the first trimester you can miss it, but I didn't see a talliwacker."

"You think it's a girl?"

"Just saying. We'll see what becomes."

Chapter 29.
THANKSGIVINGS

Rosemary wanted to share the news of her pregnancy. We decided to visit her parents for Thanksgiving in Basking Ridge, New Jersey. At a brief, but formative point in my childhood, I'd been a Southern Baptist Royal Ambassador. Baptists are well-schooled in original sin. I had an adolescent's fear of meeting Rosemary's parents. I'd allowed the devil to do bad things with my idle hands. Rosemary's tiny belly was essentially a confession. Happily, the Winslow family didn't seem to be worried about such things. Being Catholic, they thought more along the lines of blessings, rather than transgressions. It was refreshing.

The last Southerner to visit the Winslow home stole their daughter away, trashed her bright legal future in New York City, cheated on her and savaged her confidence. I walked into the Winslow home behind the eight-ball, courtesy of a Porter-boy ass-hole that Rosemary married and followed south. I hoped for a fair shake, but worried that my best behavior wasn't going to be enough.

Rosemary's father was the lead scientist at Hoffman-LaRoche Pharmaceuticals. Her mother taught history at a prestigious all-boys boarding school. It was easy to see where Rosemary got her smarts. Intellectually overmatched, keeping up with the conversations required my full attention. Being a baby-catcher didn't cut me any special status.

Rosemary's dad attended Seton Hall as an undergraduate, so we talked about the Pirates and their prospects for the upcoming year. Rosemary's mom, the history professor, was interested in my take on the Civil War, and its legacy in the South. I tried to be funny. Charlestonians were proud of the fact that they'd started the war that ended slavery. I didn't get the chuckle I'd hoped for.

I tried to rebound with something more thoughtful. I opined that, despite all the years, Southerners had never really come off their Calhoun inspired belief in state's rights. Resentment of the Federal Government runs deep in the South. It's the anchor that slows all progress. Frustrated state's rights, along with thick vein of racism, fostered Jim Crow, propagated segregated schools, the rise of George Wallace and the success of Lee Atwater's Republican Southern strategy.

I'm not sure if it was with that answer, or sometime later, when Rosemary's mother decided I had more to offer than the last bo-hunk Rosemary brought home. Or, at least, she decided to give me the benefit of the doubt.

Thanksgiving dinner was delicious. A far different experience than I'd grown up with. The Winslow Thanksgiving is more about the conversation than the stuffing. Thanksgiving at the Murphy's involved heated arguments over the relative merits of herb versus mushroom stuffing and pumpkin versus pecan pie. While it had its charms, the Murphy Thanksgiving always ended with me unconscious on the couch. The Winslow Thanksgiving was stimulating. Rosemary shared how we'd met over a legal case and recounted our adventures in exposing Paris and Hector Laveau. For some disturbing reason, my getting my ass kicked at BeBops Ice House in Lake Charles was always Rosemary's favorite part of the story. In her retelling, I came off as a dundering Don Quixote. Rosemary, of course, was the johnnie-on-the-spot rescuer. Rosemary's remembrances of the Board of Trustees meeting were hilarious. Rosemary's mother loved the part about "the best ball man in Charleston."

Madelyn and Bill Winslow were extremely proud of their daughter. They had every right to be.

Rosemary and I decided ahead of time to not discuss the threats we'd been receiving from Paris Laveau, or the murder of Lou Guillette. Those stories would only spoil the news of Rosemary's pregnancy. We wanted to enjoy our brief vacation without Paris Laveau intruding. The long Thanksgiving weekend with Rosemary's family was everything we hoped it would be. Rosemary's family was thrilled with her news.

We visited several of Rosemary's extended family. We relaxed one evening with a few of Rosemary's high school friends who were in town for the holiday. I wasn't surprised to discover that each were fascinating and accomplished. I begged them for embarrassing high school stories about Rosemary, but they stood shoulder to shoulder. The day after Thanksgiving, we drove to Jimmy Buffs for a hot dog. It wasn't the best hot dog I'd ever eaten, as Rosemary had promised, but it was damn good.

I also insisted that we take a day trip down to Asbury Park to experience the weathered beauty of the boardwalk. Mainly, I wanted to visit the seaside clairvoyant, Madam Marie Castello, and have my fortune told. Madam Marie's tiny Temple of Knowledge had been on the boardwalk since 1932. Her Temple was next door to the Stone Pony where Bruce Springsteen got his start.

Jersey Shore legend has it that Springsteen went to see Madame Marie for a reading when he was seventeen years old. Madame Marie foretold tremendous fame for the young Bruce Springsteen. In return, Springsteen immortalized her in "4th of July, Asbury Park (Sandy)" on his debut album in 1973. Every Springsteen fan knew that "the cops finally busted Madam Marie for tellin' fortunes better than they do."

Thanksgiving was not high season for the day trippers and the boardwalk was almost deserted. November on the Jersey Shore was blustery and frigid. Most of the boardwalk stores were closed, and watching the seabirds was the only open attraction. Except, of course, for the gypsy queen of the boardwalk. If it hadn't been for the chance to get out of the wind, I doubt I would've been able to get Rosemary into the back room of the Temple of Knowledge for a reading.

As we entered , Rosemary whispered, "If she pulls out any tarot cards, I'm walking out."

"Don't worry. Madam Marie reads palms. She would never stoop to the chicanery of tarot cards. Madam Marie is a real deal fortuneteller."

Thirty dollars later, we learned that our future was bright. We looked at each other when she noted that we had potent enemies that would not favor our marriage. Marie quickly added, however, that despite their efforts, we would rise above their opposition. As we left, I looked at Rosemary again and nodded.

"Pretty amazing, huh. Things are going to work out. The gypsy queen knows all."

"Get serious. That was like a fortune cookie. She might as well have told us that 'our efforts will be rewarded' or that 'tomorrow will be a new opportunity.' You know what, wait, I'm having a vision. We're going to feel a cold chill as we walk down the boardwalk."

"Very disappointing. Only a lawyer could be so cynical."

As we were buttoning up our jackets, Madam Marie stuck her head out of the door to the Temple's inner sanctum. "My friends, something I forgot to mention. Congratulations, it's going to be a little girl." She grinned a toothless grin and disappeared back inside. Rosemary was slack-jawed.

"Did you say something to her?"

"Not a word." I repeated myself. "The gypsy queen of the boardwalk knows all."

Rosemary stared silently out the window for most of the drive back to Basking Ridge. Anxious to talk, I asked Rose if she was pleased that our baby was going to be a little girl. Rosemary sighed and took her time in answering.

"I don't know what to think. We've got a Voodoo queen trying to kill us. A gypsy queen that says our love will overcome our adversaries. I'm not trained to process this kind of data. There weren't any courses in soothsaying or augury at NYU. I can tell you this. If it's not a little girl, I'm going to kick your ass."

I decided not to bother Rosemary again for the rest of the drive.

Rosemary's parents never once asked about our plans for marriage. We had an answer but were embarrassed by its lack of romance. Our lives had been too chaotic to give marriage plans the attention they deserved. We loved each other. We would eventually give our child a birth certificate she'd be proud of.

To be honest, we had discussed marriage plans quite a bit. Rosemary had no interest in a fancy spring wedding, with a designer gown cut to accommodate a third trimester pregnancy. Given the circumstances, she preferred a shot gun, justice of the peace wedding right away. For friends and family, she agreed to a full tilt boogie church wedding next fall. We'd figure out the details as soon as we had a chance.

I didn't care when it was scheduled, but I did want a church wedding. My previous marriage to Helene was also a courthouse affair because of the estrangement from her family. A marriage without family was bad luck. If Rosemary wanted to wait until after our baby was born, I was okay with that. Enough people considered me a bastard already. I didn't see a problem with adding another one to the family tree. I appreciated that Rosemary's parents were giving us the space to make whatever plans we settled on.

We weren't going to get that same consideration from my parents. Rosemary was uncomfortable with telling her parents, while keeping mine in the dark. She didn't yet know Marjorie Grace Murphy. My mother wasn't a proponent of giving space. If Rosemary and I wanted to have any say in our marriage plans, then we'd better come up with something solid, and fast. Marjorie Grace was an army officer's wife. There was a right way, and a wrong way, to do things, and my mother kept the instruction manual. If options were important, then the army would have issued you some.

That may be a bit too harsh. I appreciated that my parents had been through a lot. My mother and father loved Helene, ever since they'd known her in high school. Despite her privilege, they always felt sorry for her. Her death devastated them. That devastation was compounded by the depth of my despair. Marjorie Grace tried to engage me in numerous family activities. My excuses became increasingly tenuous and tiresome. I started avoiding her phone calls which was unbelievable within the context of the Murphy family.

Over the past couple of months, I engaged more with my mom and dad. I told them I was seeing someone new that I thought a lot of. Marjorie Grace dug for information, but I deflected. However, she put two and two together and knew something serious was happening. She hinted broadly, regarding her excitement to meet my new girlfriend. "Soon, mom, soon."

Rosemary wanted to make "soon" sooner than I had planned. I convinced Rosemary it would be best to plan Christmas with my mom and dad at their house in Columbia. That'd be a good time to let them know about the pregnancy. Serious marriage planning would begin within minutes of that announcement. On the plus side, once we tell them about the pregnancy, mom might let us sleep together. Rosemary laughed, but I was serious.

I sat in the Winslow living room and watched Rosemary and her mother working together in the kitchen on the family spaghetti sauce. I wondered if someday down the road, our daughter might be working with her on the same family recipe. It brought a smile to my face that Rosemary noticed. She asked what the hell I was grinning about. I just shook my head and smiled again.

Watching Rosemary with her mother, and carrying our child, filled my heart. I couldn't control either the smile it brought to my face, or the tears it brought to my eyes. I thought about Helene. She'd be smiling too. It was an undeserved gift to have loved, and be loved, not by one, but by two, of the most amazing women I'd ever known. I hoped that Rosemary's parents could sense our affection for each other. It had to be a shock to meet your daughter's new boyfriend and grandchild on the same weekend. They seemed to be handling it all extraordinarily well.

Despite my happiness, I was never completely free of the dark thoughts that haunted me during the quiet hours. I knew that Helene's HIV was not my fault. However, my abandonment of her in high school facilitated her drift into the world of the Jackpot drug smugglers. A lifestyle that exposed her to HIV, even before it even had a name. In the early days, the disease was called GRID. Gay-Related Immune Deficiency was the scourge of the San Francisco gay men's bath houses, not a death sentence for an abused and disenchanted heterosexual girl. Intellectually, I understood that the high school girl in the back of my Camaro was many steps removed from the adult drug mule that contracted AIDS. Still, every Rube Goldberg mousetrap started with a bucket getting kicked over somewhere far back down the line.

As I watched Rosemary chopping up the Holy Trinity, I brushed those thoughts aside. I promised myself that I was going to be a faithful husband and father. I wasn't going let to Rosemary down.

Whatever my deficiencies were in the past, my devotion to Rosemary would never waver. My connection with Rosemary was stronger than anything I'd ever experienced. I believed that Rosemary felt the same. I hoped others could feel that bond between us. As an alchemic principle, chemical bonds forged under high intensity are powerful. Our pregnancy had made those bonds even stronger. When we left on Sunday, Rosemary's mother and father gave me hugs that confirmed my hope. They'd seen the love that Rosemary and I shared.

While we may be a bit wobbly from time to time, this child was going to have some incredible grandparents.

Chapter 30.
CHINA GARDEN

December is a busy month in Ob-Gyn anyway. Gynecology patients arrange elective surgeries to take advantage of paid deductibles. Obstetrical patients try to talk their way into labor inductions for new dependent tax deductions. Rosemary and I both faced a busy week after our return from New Jersey. Our failure to make any preparations for Christmas, much less a new baby, only added to the do-list.

Rosemary had a late Friday afternoon OB appointment with Bobby Richmond. I'd hoped to attend every appointment, but I couldn't today because of a packed office. Rosemary would pick me up after her appointment. We'd set a modest goal of finding a nine-foot Christmas tree for our front window.

I didn't expect her until about six p.m. assuming everything went smoothly. It wasn't going to be a good night for Christmas tree shopping. It was already dark, and the overcast day turned into a drizzling night. The thermometer dropped noticeably once the sun went down. The blowing mist made it feel even colder. I never leave the house with the right weight of coat.

The drizzle on the road summoned the oil out of the microscopic canyons in the asphalt. The wet, slick road was made more dangerous by the notoriously poor illumination on Folly Road, and the distracting lights of the gas stations, automotive repair shops, franchised fast food and convenience stores. On a Friday afternoon, the darkness and wetness would turn rush hour on Folly Road into a Demolition Derby. I wished Rosemary hadn't made me promise to catch up on our Christmas preparations. My suggestion to put it off would be met with exasperation and accusations of procrastination. In the end, the fender bender would be less painful.

By six thirty, the office was empty except for Homer Lahr and me. I peeked out my office window periodically at our parking lot for

Rosemary's arrival. Homer stuck his head in my door. He was going next door to the China Garden and wondered if I wanted to join him. They had a sixty-eight-item buffet. Homer long ago made a deal with the owner for meals and food scraps for Dogue, in exchange for gynecologic care for his wife and daughters.

"Rosemary and I are going Christmas tree shopping. Thanks for asking though. Going in for dinner, or just take out?"

Homer grinned, "Both," and then held up the black bucket he used to collect his dog scraps. "Turns out Smokin' Joe likes Chinese even more than Dogue."

"I'm amazed that Smokin' Joe doesn't have the squirts all the time."

"Naw, he loves the stuff. I think he has a little gook in him."

"Maybe so. If Rosemary comes before you get back, have a great weekend. Do something that makes your blood pump. Monday rolls around again too soon."

"Will do, podna," and he was gone.

Fifteen minutes later, I saw Rosemary's headlights turn into our parking lot. I hurried to finish up the last of the charts on my desk. After several minutes, I looked up, surprised that Rosemary had not yet come into the office. Rosemary always came in through the back door. If it was locked, she would've rung the bell.

I opened the back door to find Rosemary collapsed in the monkey grass beside the back stairs. Blood flowed down the side of her face, pooling on the flagstones. I knelt beside her and gently turned her over. I cupped her head. I felt the unmistakable warm slickness of blood on my hands. In the dim yellow light of the back-door lamp I could see that Rosemary was bleeding briskly from a nasty gash at the back of her head. She was unconscious, but I could feel the carotid pulse. I put a free hand on her chest and felt her respirations.

I gathered myself to pick her up. I caught a glimpse of movement out of the corner of my eye. My right arm shot up in an instinctive move of self-defense. The knife buried deeply into my triceps muscle, rather than the intended chest. I rolled away and came to rest on my butt with my back against the office wall.

Standing over both Rosemary and myself, was a large, heavily muscled white man dressed in black jeans, with a black leather jacket and black army boots. He looked like a ninja with fine textured black gloves and a black gubalini. I'm six feet four inches. This guy looked every bit my size. He moved with the unmistakable grace of a predator, nimbly, silently, and with purpose.

The knife was a military style K-Bar. He came toward me with the knife held low in his right hand. He was planning an upward stab to the gut, then he'd yank it up through the diaphragm into my chest and heart. I held my right triceps with my left hand to staunch the bleeding and pulled up my knees to protect my stomach. The necessary connections between my eyes, mind and sense of mortality were far too slow. My death was playing out in a frame by frame progression. Yet, despite that recognition, I was incapable of responding in any meaningful way. All I offered in response was a confused look and an open, soundless mouth. The predator greeted my incredulity with a slight smile and a raise of his eyebrows. I had the oddest inexplicable thought that he seemed like a friendly guy.

I watched my killer swing his arm back, but it never came forward. I saw my attacker's brow furrow with the same question. Homer Lahr appeared out of the darkness and grabbed my killer's right arm on the back swing. He forced the knife towards the ground and wrapped his left arm around my attacker's upper arm, locking it in a hyperextended position. Moving more quickly than I'd believed Homer capable, he delivered an upward knee strike to the hyperextended elbow joint. The elbow bones were forced in a direction they were never meant to go and snapped like a twig.

The knife dropped from the now non-functional limb. My assassin went to his knees screaming in pain, trying to support his dislocated elbow. The last words out of his mouth were "Jesus Christ" just milliseconds before Homer smashed him upside the temple with a black plastic pail of Chinese slop.

Homer gave my right arm a quick look. It wasn't life-threatening. He turned his attention back to our attacker who lay moaning on the sidewalk, searching with his left hand for his knife. Homer calmly stepped on his fingers and picked up the K-Bar. After tossing the knife away, Homer grabbed ninja-boy by his leather jacket, picked him up like a rag doll, and spun him around. Homer wrapped his Popeye left arm around the guy's neck and locked it down with an overwrapping right arm. Sounds from the assassin's throat stopped instantly. All kicking and struggling stopped about forty seconds later, as the man in black fell asleep.

"Bring Rosemary inside," Homer said, as he kicked open the back door. He carried the unconscious attacker inside over his shoulder.

Homer secured our assailant by lifting him onto the outpatient surgery table and putting him in a lithotomy position with his feet in stirrups. Homer restrained him with an efficient combination of leather surgical straps and duct tape. After he was fully secured and searched, Homer returned to Rosemary and me. Homer inspected my wound once again to make sure there wasn't any arterial bleeding. He tossed me a wad of gauze to mash into the laceration.

Rosemary responded to an ampule of smelling salts. Homer delicately stitched up her scalp laceration. Her eyes were glazed, but Rosemary nodded that she was okay. He washed out my wound with sterile saline from a spritzer bottle. The bleeding had almost stopped. Homer injected some local anesthetic and proceeded to sew up the muscle and skin in layers. He wrapped my arm in Kerlex and popped a tetanus shot in my butt, chuckling when I flinched. Deeming me fit for duty, Homer gave me a menacing look. "Let's go find out who the fuck this guy is."

"What do you mean?" The look on Homer's face made me nervous.

"Look bubba, Lou's airboat got blown up. An innocent College of Charleston student was eaten by gators. Rosie gets her head busted open, and that dude in there was planning to filet you like a fish. He ain't a street thug either. He's not carrying any identification at all. He's got military tats, military gloves, a government issue knife and boots. Nothing about him suggests that he's a Laveau family friend. Somebody paid this guy serious money to find you and kill you. I'm interested in knowing who."

"Homer."

"And, he killed Dogue. I want to know who thinks he can get away with killin' a man's dog. That was a bad decision and I plan to make sure he understands that retribution can be a real bitch."

"You didn't find anything on him?"

"Only a nasty switchblade hidden in the top of his right boot."

"You know what I'm asking about."

"Yeah, I know. I found one of those tarot cards in his back pocket. Same as the other ones. This guy's been a busy little beaver over the past couple of months."

"I didn't think that Paris Laveau would take things this far. We need to call the F.B.I. They'll figure out the link between him and her. We need to find his car. It'll be a pick-up truck. Jesus, we need to make sure that he doesn't have a partner."

"No partner. This isn't the kind of guy that would have a partner. He's a lone wolf killer. I'd bet my life on it."

"I think we already have. If he's the type of killer you think he is, that's even more reason to call the police. Laurence Nodeen gave me the number for the local F.B.I. field chief."

"Calling the police is a mistake. This guy's military and he's professional. He knows how to keep his mouth shut. There'll be a back-up plan. Whoever sent him will take care of any loose ends."

"I don't know, maybe."

"No maybe about it. Jail time is part of this guy's job description. Right now, all we have on him is simple assault. Unwitnessed. At worst, he gets light time. If he keeps his mouth shut, and carries the weight, his jail time will be the best paying job he's ever had."

"What's the alternative?" I was afraid to hear what Homer was going to say next. Homer was a fearless man, for whom a little fear would probably be a good thing.

"He's here, we're here, and we've got all night. All weekend if we need it. That pissant is going to talk to me, and he's going to tell me everything we need to know. I'm tired of wondering who's pulling the strings around here."

"Yeah, but what's your plan?"

"I plan to flip the script. We're going to incentivize this mercenary to talk, instead of incentivizing him to keep his mouth shut. He's in my world now and I've convinced more than my fair share of hard cases to speak freely. I'm confident in my persuasive skills. You don't have to get your hands dirty. I'm happy to handle this. That asshole killed Dogue."

"Homer, you know that I don't mind getting my hands dirty, but what you're planning can have a lot of blow-back for us. We could lose our practice. For God's sake, Rosemary is an officer of the court."

"Legal hasn't gotten us very far. They don't even believe this guy exists. In fact, they don't ever need to know that he does exist. We can keep this between us and Paris Laveau."

"Homer, we can't vigilante this. We have to involve the police."

"Declan, you need to listen to me on this. That's what he's hoping for. This guy's a professional killer. He ain't no backwoods Cajun. Professional hit-men don't have anything in their pockets or any labels on their clothes. Professional hit-men wear high performance shooter gloves and carry razor sharp K-Bars. If he doesn't talk to us tonight, he ain't talking to anyone. He came here to kill you. He planned to kill you, your girlfriend and your baby. You okay with that? I'm not, plus, like I said, he's going to answer for killing my dog."

"Of course, I'm not okay with that, but there're limits on what we can do. This isn't something that we can take into our own hands."

"Don't be a fool. It's in our hands. What makes you think you can get through life without compromise? You wouldn't be working with me now if you hadn't made some major compromises."

"This is a lot more than a compromise."

"I understand that. I just don't care."

"I do."

"I know. That's why you need to stay out here with Rosemary. One of the most critical factors in getting information from people is for them to know that you don't care. He can't know that anybody else cares either. The first thing I'll explain to him is that we have absolutely no plans to call the police. Sooner or later, he'll figure out that he won't be leaving this office until we've finished talking. It's his choice whether he leaves here with or without all of his bits and pieces."

"Come on boss man, we can't do that."

"The hell we can't. I've got him strapped to an operating table right now. I've neutered every dog I've ever had. My operative skills are a lot finer than what he planned for you." Homer pulled the K-Bar out of the back of his pants. He dropped it on the floor. The metallic clang was startling. I knew that Homer was serious.

"He planned to take your heart. I'm just going to take his manhood. Unless, of course, he decides that he wants to talk sooner. I suspect that's unlikely. From experience though, I can tell you that once you start workin' around in the root cellar, virtually everyone becomes a chatty Cathy."

Homer wasn't the type of man who blinked. Besides driving a swift boat on the Mekong River, Homer was also a tunnel rat. Rats were the guys who went into the Viet Cong tunnels when they were discovered. Sometimes the tunnels were deserted, other times, there was a battalion waiting down there for you. It was the only duty in Vietnam that had a shorter life-expectancy than a helicopter pilot.

The rats went into the tunnels with a pistol and a flashlight. Rule number one was never turn on the flashlight until after you shot. The tunnel rats crawled through the dank stinking tunnels in absolute blackness, listening for the sounds of any other living creature. When you heard it, you shot it. Turning on your flashlight, not only made you a target, but also meant that you'd lost your nerve. Once you lost your nerve, you were done as a tunnel rat. Homer had flushed more than his share of rats from their tunnels.

It takes a lot to supersede the instinctual desire to survive. Marines are taught how to prevail in battle, and they are one of the most feared fighting forces in the world. However, you must experience the horror of battle to learn about anonymous retribution. Tunnel rats were never the new guys. The rats were a volunteer service and were always the older Marines who'd accumulated numerous scores to settle. When they went into a tunnel with a pistol and a flashlight, they also took an emotionally empty bucket. They never stopped working the tunnels until that empty bucket was filled with blood.

I didn't doubt for a second Homer's capability, or willingness, to interrogate our assailant just as he said he would. Homer wasn't looking for my permission. Homer also wasn't interested in any more debate on the question. This guy shouldn't have killed Dogue.

It troubled me that I wasn't in total disagreement with Homer. Everything Homer said was the truth. This guy attacked Rosemary because she either got in the way, or was on the hit list as well. Either way, he wasn't going to leave her and our baby alive. He'd intended to kill me by driving a thick piece of cold steel into my heart. I would've died quickly, but not instantaneously. He'd also killed Lou and Margaret McGinley because he believed I was also on board with them.

If it were just Homer and me, I'd be all in. My concern was for Rosemary. She swore to uphold the law. What Homer was planning would get her disbarred. She'd never be able to accept the savagery of what would be needed. Rosemary had been following the conversation but had yet to say a word.

I looked at Rosemary for her thoughts. I was certain she'd counsel caution. Rosemary knew what I was expecting, but she shook her head.

"Homer is right. If we call the police, it's likely that we'll lose our best chance of shutting this thing down and getting that bitch off our backs."

Rosemary read the shocked expression on my face.

"Sorry. This doesn't have anything to do with him splitting open my scalp. I know how the system works. He'll lawyer up as soon as the police get here. There'll be a lawyer waiting for him by the time he gets to the police station. The lawyer will demand that his client get immediate medical attention. He'll spend the night at MUSC. In the morning, he'll go before a judge, and the initial charge will be first offense assault. The judge will set bail which someone will pay. He'll be out of state by sundown, well before anyone figures out that his name and backstory are bullshit."

Each of us looked at the others. Rosemary and I both nodded at Homer. The shame of it was that this sad plan represented our best option.

We followed Homer into the procedure room. Homer stuffed a broken ampule of ammonia up our assailant's nose. When that didn't elicit anything more than a groan and turn of the head, Homer put all his weight on our attacker's swollen right elbow. The groan turned into a scream, and his eyes popped open like a Sleepy Time doll that had been sat up.

"Time to wake up, buster. We've got some things to talk about."

Our assailant thrashed around, struggling against his restraints. The procedure table had attachable arms that Homer locked in place. The hit-man's arms were duct taped securely to the arm board at the biceps, forearm and wrist. The restraint on the right arm was redundant. That arm was already done. Broad leather straps encircled his chest and waist. His black jeans were tucked into high laced, military style black combat boots. The combat boots had been heavily duct taped to the obstetrical stirrups, which had been pulled out from the end of the examination table. He could struggle all he wanted, but he wasn't going anywhere.

Homer waved the spirit of ammonia ampule under his nose once again. Once aroused, Homer slapped his face to get his attention. "Hey, are you with me yet? You're gonna want to pay attention because I've got some breaking news for you. Consensus is, you made a big mistake by not noticing that Lucy was still in the parking lot."

Our assailant didn't respond. He gave Homer a contemptuous look and continued to thrash against the arm and leg restraints.

"You need to calm down big guy. You need to save your energy. You're going to need it later."

Our assailant just grunted and uttered his first words. "Fuck you."

"What's your name, bad man? We're going to need to know what to call you, especially later when things get ugly."

"You must have shit for brains, old man. Get me the hell out of this thing, or you're going to be sorry you ever met me."

Homer calmly slapped him again, but harder. "I'm already sorry. However, since we've been forced to become acquainted, I should, at least, know your name."

"Go to hell."

"I have to tell you, that's not an attitude that's going to serve you very well. Since you don't seem to be interested in cooperating, I think I'm going to call you Pat."

"Fuck you, fat man."

"No so fat that I couldn't take you down. When I snapped your elbow, you screamed like a little girl. I'll be surprised if we don't hear that girly scream again. You're in my house now, and I've got some work to do."

Rosemary and I could tell that the conversation wasn't going in a good direction.

Homer just chuckled. "Have it your way. If you don't want to tell me your name, that's okay. I'm happy to stick with Pat. Pat can be short for either Patrick or Patricia. Which one it turns out to be, well, that's up to you."

Chapter 31.
FORMALDEHYDE

Homer busied himself, collecting instruments and placing them on a stainless steel surgical table. He dropped each instrument on the metal table as loudly as he could. With each ominous metallic clang, Pat cursed and struggled harder against his restraints. He twisted and pulled but accomplished nothing other than to exhaust himself. Gradually he calmed down, and his eyes started following Homer around the room. He paid rapt attention to Homer's obviously purposeful activities.

"Hey, you busted my elbow. You need to call an E.M.S. truck. It's dislocated. Dislocations need to be reset as soon as possible. It's going to go bad for you guys if you don't get me some medical attention right away."

"We're just going to have to risk that, Pat. I'm afraid that we're not yet sure what we'd tell the E.M.S. responders. At this moment, the full extent of your injuries is unknown. We don't want to jump the gun by calling for an ambulance when you might not need one. Plus, Declan and I are fully trained physicians and surgeons, but I think you already know that. You're getting ready to receive far more medical attention than you've bargained for."

"It's a God-damn dislocated elbow you idiot."

"Oh sure, I know your elbow is dislocated. I was there when it happened, in case you've forgotten. I'm also going to be here when your other injuries are discovered. How many there are, and how long it takes to find them is up to you."

"Mister, you're in way over your head. I don't have any issue with you. If you're smart, you'll let me go. I'll walk away, and everyone goes home safe and sound."

Homer chuckled again. "Ain't nobody ever accused me of being smart." Homer dropped a metal scalpel from a sterile plastic wrapper onto the surgical stand before continuing. "However, that is an enticing offer. The trouble is, we're all tired of being dull creatures of survival. A lot of bad stuff has been happening around here, and we're sick of it. When I was a younger man, I liked to follow around the Grateful Dead. Bob Weir summed it up for me in "Truckin." I'm tired of being knocked down like a bowling pin. Pat, your welcome around here has worn thin. You've got information that will help us finally get to the bottom of all this crap. You will give us that information tonight."

"I ain't talking to anybody but the police."

"Well, that's ultimately up to you, but I don't think that's going to turn out to be true. Before becoming a doctor, I spent a misguided youth in the jungles of Vietnam. The Marines are some of the meanest sons-of-bitches in the world, but we got our asses kicked. We underestimated how tough those little gooks were. They've got foot rot over there that'll eat a man alive. Doesn't bother them at all. They'd lay in the rice patties for three days at a time, without food or water, just so they could slit the throat of one of ours. They did it knowing they'd be blown away immediately after getting the kill. Didn't give them a moment's pause.

When we did catch them, they never thought they had anything to say either. I've done this dance a dozen times. You know what though, eventually, they all talked to me. Sometimes it took them a while to realize how seriously I valued a good conversation. But they all figured it out, sooner or later. You want to know one other thing? You aren't nearly as tough as those little motherfuckers in Vietnam."

I could tell that Pat's bravado was flagging. His eyes were darting around like a trapped animal. Despite the surgical suite being cool, beads of sweat were forming on his forehead. Homer's ominous presence, and surreal calm, had broken Pat's confidence. It's a poignant instant when you realize that you're no longer in control. Homer was in charge and was far more dangerous than anticipated.

"We want you to tell us everything you know about Paris Laveau. What you've been up to, and what your plans were. I want you to start with the day you poisoned my dog, and finish with what you were planning to do tomorrow. It'll be best if you don't leave out any details. We'll be recording your story, so please speak clearly."

"Fuck you. I don't know anyone named Paris Laveau." Homer and I both recognized that the conviction in his voice was gone.

"Pat, I have a lot of faults. I've been accused of not being the sharpest tool in the shed. But even a slow learner eventually figures things out. We found the tarot card in your back pocket. We've seen those cards before. You're also going to find out that one of my other faults is a lack of patience. I wouldn't recommend testing me with any more bullshit."

Pat's response was to scream. He'd regret that decision. Homer wrapped a big wad of white surgical tape around a tongue depressor. He jammed it in Pat's mouth between his teeth, as if he was having a seizure. Once in place, Homer secured it with some more surgical tape wrapped around his head. Homer wasn't bothered that the tongue depressor was causing Pat to gag and his eyes to water.

"There's no use in screaming, This is a finely built Craftsman style home from the 1920s. No cheap-ass sheetrock. Thick brick walls and real wood paneling. On one side of us is a Pep Boys that's now closed, and the China Garden is on the other. The screaming in that kitchen is far louder than anything you could muster. Nobody's hearing anything out on Folly Road, and there's nothing out back but a parking lot and woods. But you already know that , since you've been stalking us for a long time."

Pat tried to scream again, but it was muffled. He quickly quieted when he realized it was useless.

"Pat, the bottom line is this. You killed my dog. You're not going to find any sympathy or relief within these four walls. It isn't a question of whether this is going to be bad. It's a question of how bad."

Pat was now quiet and staring intently at Homer Lahr hovering inches from his face.

"Okay, so now that I have your attention, let me tell you what we're going to do. I'm going to take this scalpel, and slowly take you apart while you watch." Homer tapped the blunt end of the scalpel against Pat's groin. "We're going to start here. I'm going to dissect out your ball sac and testicles. Just like I did when I neutered Dogue. Once the twins are gone, then I'm going to remove your Johnson. I haven't done that before, but I can figure it out on the fly. Just a heads up, there'll be a lot more blood with the Johnson than with the nuts." Homer paused to let Pat contemplate the arc of his upcoming life.

After watching Pat blink and swallow hard, Homer continued. "I'm going to put all your bits and pieces into a formaldehyde specimen jar and donate them to the Pathology department over at the medical school. Nobody over there's going to ask any questions about where they came from. I'll even get a nice thank you note from the Pathology chairman."

Pat's eyes were now wide with the intended terror. He was shaking his head, and trying to talk, but it was unintelligible.

"Not now, Pat. Don't get frantic. We've already had plenty of opportunity to chat. I think we'll do some work first, and then, maybe, take a break to gossip a little later."

Pat's muted gibberish became louder.

"Pat, Pat, Pat, shhhh. No need to get overwrought. You're going to be contributing to the education of the next several generations of young physicians. The Pathology lab is lined with formaldehyde jars, just like the one we're going to send them with your little parts. Don't worry about the bleeding either. I can control that without too much difficulty. Sorry, I can't say the same about the pain. You killed my dog."

Pat screamed again. Pretty loud considering the tongue blade and tape over his mouth.

Homer calmly walked down between Pat's legs. He showed Pat the scalpel. Pat's thrashing stopped when he realized it might be safer to hold still. Homer inserted the scalpel just over the anus and incised the black jeans straight up the seam and around the zipper. He did the same with the white cotton boxer briefs. Pat's genitals tumbled free. At this point, Pat's screams had been reduced to whimpers and tears.

Homer picked up Pat's ball sac with DeBakey surgical forceps and moved his penis to the side with the blunt-end handle of the scalpel.

My gut was churning, my face was tingling, and I was numb around the mouth. I recognized the signs of hyperventilation. I didn't want Homer to do what I knew he was planning to do. If we mutilated this guy, we'd be crossing the Rubicon. There wouldn't be any crossing back."

I didn't see Rosemary cross the room. She put her hand on Homer's right forearm. "We don't need to do this. It's not you. It's not Declan, and it certainly isn't me. I don't care what happens to this ass-hole, but I do care about what this will do to you, and to us. You're a better man than he is. Don't lose yourself in this pile of dog shit."

"You're wrong, Rosemary. This is me. I've done far worse things. I'm not proud of those things, but they all served a purpose, and so does this. He's whimpering right now, but as soon as we back off, he reverts to being a hard guy. Our friend Pat is a professional. He was sent here to kill you and Declan by a psychopathic bitch. Who, by the way, is now working with some of the most prolific killers in the world. This is high stakes, and we can't lose our nerve."

"I understand all that. It scares the hell out of me. I'm worried about myself, Declan and my baby. I also know how the law works, but this can't be the way. If we castrate this guy, then Paris will have turned us into the same type of monster that she is. Yes, he'll lawyer up as soon as the police read him his rights. But, we can make sure the police understand who this guy is working for, and we'll call the F.B.I. number that Declan has. I'll make sure that he doesn't get bail. Law enforcement has been looking for a break just like this. It'll take longer, but the legal system will get what we need from him."

"Even if they hold him, that doesn't mean he's talking. More than anyone else, Pat knows what Paris Laveau is capable of. He knows what he was hired to do. The possibility of jail time isn't going to make this hard case talk. Next week, next month, or next year, Paris Laveau, or her new Mexican friends, will come back to finish up whatever business Paris believes she has with you. We've got to prepare for that. This guy knows how she operates, how she communicates and how much she's willing to pay. He might know what other resources she has to follow up on his failure. We have to know everything he knows, so we can be ready the next time Paris Laveau comes at us."

"But, not this way. There has to be another way."

"Does Paris Laveau seem like the type of woman who'll back off because the work is getting ugly ?"

"No, she doesn't," I interjected. "Rosemary and I are on her shit list. Homer is right. Paris Laveau's going to keep coming. We must learn everything he knows, and we need to know it now. Even if we can keep Pat from getting bail, you can look in his eyes and know he isn't talking."

I was sickened by what Homer was about to do. At the same time, I was furious with what Paris Laveau had done. She'd murdered Lou and Margaret McGinley and had now come after Rosemary and my baby. If we had to cut off this guy's balls to get the information we needed, I could deal with that. To be honest, I didn't care if we cut him up into a thousand pieces.

Little boys don't grow up in the south without doing some mean things. It might be the Rubicon, but I didn't have any qualms about doing whatever was necessary to protect my family. My only concern was how this would affect Rosemary. Rosemary's conscience didn't have the same soft pliability that allowed mine to make peace with the dark path we were taking. I didn't consider myself short on moral fiber. However, I knew what I was. I was part of the maddening crowd that allowed self-serving practicality to trump moral direction. Rosemary was not.

I looked at Rosemary. Her eyes were welling up. "I can't do this, Declan. I know we have to, but I can't. I'd rather be murdered than wake up every morning knowing I castrated a man with a tongue depressor jammed down his throat."

The look on Rosemary's face told me what I already knew. There are sins for which you'll never be forgiven.

I looked at Homer. He looked at Rosemary. "I'll do it. I've already given away that part of myself. Go home. You don't even have to be here."

"I'm still involved. It won't matter whose hands are on the scalpel."

"What if we can do it another way?" I asked. "I think we can interrogate him without putting his Johnson in a formaldehyde bottle. Homer put down the scalpel. I know another way."

"What other way?"

"Hold the phone. I'm going to get the nitrous oxide machine."

Chapter 32.
O, EXCELLENT AIR BAG

Homer liked the idea. I could see it in his eyes.

In 1967, Homer had an old brown Victorian on Clayton Street in the Upper Haight. He didn't miss a day of the summer of love in Golden Gate Park. Nobody knew more than Homer about "hippie crack." Anyone walking through the parking lot of a music festival has heard the unmistakable hiss of a nitrous canister being discharged in exchange for cash. Spent balloons strewn across festival grounds do not mean that a children's birthday party preceded the concert.

Homer was the office expert in using the nitrous oxide machine. Homer had been doing his own independent research with our new anesthesia machine. I made a point of never checking the invoices for nitrous canisters. There wasn't that much new to learn. Nitrous oxide was still being used in the same form and quantities that spun the needle two centuries ago.

Before drifting down to the hippies and the working class, nitrous oxide was the party drug for the British upper crust and academics.

Humphry Davy was a 20-year-old rising star in the British scientific community in 1799. He'd already invented the mining lamp and would later become the President of the British Royal Society. Davy was a chemist at the Pneumatic Institute in Hotwells, a former spa outside the western coastal city of Bristol. Hotwells took its name from the hot springs that bubble to the surface through the antediluvian rocks of the Avon Gorge. The well-to-do of western Britain, in the Georgian era, traveled to Hotwells to rejuvenate themselves in its milky warm waters.

The brilliant physician, Thomas Beddoes, founded the Pneumatic Institute in Dowry Square in Hotwells. Free treatment was offered to locals suffering from consumption, asthma, dropsy, "obstinate venereal complaints" and scrophula. Beddoes experimented with new gasses he believed would revolutionize the practice of medicine. Thomas Beddows recognized Davy's talent, and hired him as a laboratory assistant charged with designing the necessary machinery to generate and capture chemical gasses.

Davy's interest was the chemical reaction which followed the heating of nitrate of ammoniac in the belly of the reactor system. As the compound gently boiled in the heated retort, a colorless, odorless, and non-flammable gas bubbled up. The escaping gas was collected by hydraulic bellows and allowed to seep through water into a reservoir tank. The stored gas was then transferred to the signature oiled green silk bags of the Pneumatic Institute.

To test his new gas, Davy built a sealed chamber, designed by James Watt, for controlled inhalation. On Boxing Day, 1799, a shirtless Humphry Davy placed a thermometer under his armpit, and entered the sealed chamber under the supervision of his physician, Dr. Robert Kinglake. Engineer Watt was instructed to pump twenty quarts of nitrous oxide into the chamber every five minutes as long as Davy retained consciousness.

The gas tasted slightly sweet, which was followed by increasing pressure in the head and chest. Those feelings of pressure were followed by the rapid onset of intense pleasure. Inhaling much higher concentrations in the sealed chamber, Davy began to have sensations not previously experienced. The pleasure became more vibrant and euphoric. The color of objects around him became brighter and more distinct. The space within the chamber expanded into larger, unfamiliar dimensions. Davy believed his auditory acuity had increased fantastically, allowing him to hear things well beyond the confines of his sealed cubicle. He heard a vast and distant hum that he thought might be the vibration of the universe itself. Objects within his vision began to disintegrate into packets of light and energy. Davy described the experience as irresistibly funny, causing him "a great predisposition to laugh" as his senses struggled to understand their new limitless capacity.

As the nitrous oxide concentrations accumulated in his blood, Davy's hallucinations amplified. He became further dissociated from what he'd previously recognized as reality. Objects reached dazzling intensity of color, sounds were transformed and echoed, and sensations magnified. Within this new realm of consciousness, sounds, sights, sensations and thoughts jumbled together to produce images and perceptions that were totally novel.

Davy theorized, and Timothy Leary would agree, more than one hundred and fifty years later, half a world away in the Haight-Ashbury district of San Francisco, that the altered parameters of this new reality would permit discovery of new insights and revelations.

After what Davy believed to have been an eternity, Dr. Kirklake extracted him from the inhalation chamber in a semi-delirious state, stamping his feet and jumping around like a whirling dervish. As Davy stumbled back from his new to his old reality, he screamed his fading insights to Dr. Kirklake, "Nothing exists but thoughts. The world is composed of impressions, ideas, pleasures and pains."

Davy began to recruit the elite of Britain's medical, scientific, literary, political and social strata to his new consciousness raising sessions. An early acolyte was Robert Southey, the future Poet Laureate of England, who ecstatically wrote, "The atmosphere of the highest of all possible heavens must be composed of this gas."

Southey later wrote to his brother Tom about his experience breathing nitrous oxide out of a green silk bag. "O, Tom! Such a gas has Davy discovered, the gaseous oxyd! O, Tom! I have had some, it made me laugh and tingle in every toe and fingertip. Davy has actually invented a new pleasure for which language has no name. O, Tom! I am going for more this evening; it makes one strong and so happy, so gloriously happy! O, excellent air bag."

The nitrous oxide experiments became a nightly event at the Pneumatic Institute. Sessions took on a hedonistic excess that would've made Hunter S. Thompson blush. The nitrous gatherings became fascinating scientific, social and philosophical theater.

Davy was obsessed by his inability to recount the nitrous oxide experience using conventional language. His volunteers made written narratives of their nitrous sessions. Their literary efforts revealed the difficulty in describing the imponderable existential alteration of their reality. One volunteer simply wrote, "I feel like the sound of a harp."

Needing help, Davy turned to Southey and Samuel Taylor Coleridge to help describe the sensations imprisoned in the green silk bag. Some of the nitrous conjured imagery made its way into their poetry, but even Southey and Coleridge expressed frustration in their inability to clearly convey the divine revelations of nitrous oxide. As Coleridge inhaled, and felt the warmth spread through his body, he stated that the sensation reminded him of "returning from the snow into a warm room." Nitrous oxide, Coleridge argued, allowed the consciousness to transcend the bonds of the physical body, and reveal the vistas beyond our perception.

Over the ensuing months, the number of nitrous oxide experiments dwindled as the novelty of the experience wore off. Discoveries of expanded consciousness became less frequent. To his credit, Humphry Davy did not succumb completely to the siren's song of the green silk bag. Davy initiated a coherent and intellectually worthy dissertation on his new gas.

By Easter of 1800, Davy completed a 580-page treatise entitled *Researches, Chemical and Philosophical; chiefly concerning Nitrous Oxide, or dephlogisticated nitrous air, and its Respiration.* In a stunning final section, he described the subjective effects of nitrous oxide intoxication experienced by himself, Beddoes, Coleridge, Southey and dozens of other subjects. The monograph merged the dense scientific language of organic chemistry with the poetic and philosophical language of subjective thought. Homer Lahr owned, what was certain to be, the only copy of the Davy monograph in South Carolina.

"Hot damn, the nitrous machine. That's top drawer thinkin' right there," Homer said. "We'll spin up the nitrous, and this guy will tell us everything we want to know without any of the work." I couldn't tell if the smile on Homer's face was relief or excitement.

"Are you sure it'll work?"

"Fuckin' A. Give him fifty percent nitrous, and he'll tell us the names of everyone he's ever slept with. At seventy percent, he'll throw off all the ropes that keep him moored to the dock of reality. Once he's there, he won't even understand the concept of deceit. He'll share everything he knows, laughing like a drunken monkey while he's giving himself up. Turn it up to ninety percent for about ten minutes, and his brain will turn into porridge. Then we can send him back to Paris. A pant-shitting simpleton, too stupid to scratch fleas."

Rosemary and I looked at each other. We'd have to deal with those last ten minutes at some point, but neither of us wanted to address that just yet.

"Homer, we'll cross that bridge when we get to it. Let's find out if this is going to work first. Rosemary go get the Dictaphone unit from the front office. We'll record everything this ass-hole says."

Homer nodded, and then added in a much softer, confident voice, "It'll work."

Homer left his spot between our intruder's legs, making no effort to cover his exposed genitals. He walked to the head of the bed. The hit man's eyes were still darting around feverishly. His incoherent protestations were louder. There wasn't any stopping at this point to see if Pat might have changed his mind about becoming more interactive. He understood torture. I'm not sure he knew what to think about the portable nitrous oxide machine being rolled into the room.

Castration is about as serious an incentive as there is, but the hit man understood that we'd never go too far if he still had information to give. Despite being in a tough spot, he was familiar with the give and take nature of the negotiation that Homer initially proposed. Holding out bought him time and allowed him to take the measure of Homer. How far was Homer willing to go to learn what he knew? Only the insane would not recognize Homer as a serious negotiator.

However, the nitrous oxide machine was an unfamiliar variable. Could Homer really take what he knew without any parlay. Could the nitrous really melt his brain? I'm sure he was attached to his testicles. However, the look in his eyes suggested that even the possibility of castration didn't un-nerve him as much as the thought of becoming a vegetable, spending the rest of his life on rubber sheets.

Pat's body language expressed an urgent desire to open a dialogue. Homer made it clear that the time for negotiations was over. Homer leaned in close to Pat's face. "This ain't no fucking whippet, podna. This is medical grade shit. Too bad we don't know your name. In about thirty minutes, you won't know it either. Your toe tag is going to say Pat Doe."

Our assassin's face reddened, eyeballs bulged, and bubbles of snot appeared at his nostrils. He began to shake his head violently until Homer grabbed his chin with his king-sized right hand. "One other little thing, podna. After we gas you up, and get all the information we need, I'm still going to take your manhood and ball sac. I'm going to make a chew toy out of them for my new dog. The puppy that replaced the one you poisoned."

To emphasize his sincerity, Homer took his scalpel, and made a short smooth incision just beneath the hit man's right eye. A small pearl of bright red blood rose to the surface, and then trickled down his cheek admixed with a tear.

Chapter 33.
MARK “BUTTER” BLAND

It didn’t take but a few minutes to discover that Pat’s real name was Mark Bland, a heating and air conditioning contractor from Charlotte, North Carolina. Homer believed that Bland worked by himself. “This guy smells like a lone wolf.” With a few more questions, we confirmed that Bland didn’t have any partners lurking around in the bushes or waiting at the end of a phone line for a mission accomplished signal.

Once we got Bland’s nitrous concentration spun up to the right level we removed his face mask and met our new best friend. His speech was pressured, and he spoke with the animated fervor of a man with secrets he’d been unable to share with anyone in years. Homer backhanded him to get his attention. Contrary to popular belief, it isn’t possible to slap a stupid smile off someone’s face. God knows, Homer tried.

Mark Bland paid no heed to either the face slap, his grotesquely swollen and purple dislocated elbow, or that he was duct-taped to a gynecologic examination table with his balls hanging out. Mark was having one of the greatest nights of his life. The only challenge was keeping him focused on our questions rather than his many unseen distracters.

Bland thought that it was funny as hell that he didn’t know a thing about repairing broken heating or air conditioning systems despite what it said on the sides of his panel truck. He did love his business slogan, “When bad weather hits, hit back.” Bland repeated it endlessly, laughing hysterically at the cleverness of his double entendre. That bought him another slap across the face. When we asked him for the name of his employer, he laughed again. Mark Bland wanted to know if anyone thought it was funny that Taconic-

Pacific, in Georgetown, South Carolina hired a heating and air contractor from Charlotte, North Carolina. He found it a good bit funnier than we did.

Homer reapplied the nitrous oxide face mask. We walked to the next room in stunned silence, pole-axed by the realization that we'd been wrong from the get-go. Taconic-Pacific, not Paris Laveau, was behind all of this. These events had nothing to do with simple, sociopathic, but understandable, human retribution. It was soulless corporate criminality. An industrial polluter intent on silencing an environmental conservationist and, moreover, an influential scientist. This was about Louis J. Guillette, Jr. Ph.D. and his ability to impact their financial bottom line. Suddenly, that seemed far more malevolent than anything I'd imagined Paris Laveau capable. It also shook my confidence, that we'd been so wrong.

Not surprisingly, Homer wasn't cowed. "This doesn't change anything. We've still got to cut the head off the snake. Just a different venomous pit viper than the one we thought it was. That jack-leg laying in there still has the information we need. Knowing that Taconic-Pacific may be behind this makes it even more crucial we get all the evidence we can."

"I don't know, Homer. Paris is vicious, but if this is Taconic-Pacific, that's a horse of a different color. They're international. They have a much greater reach than Paris Laveau."

"No, Homer's right," Rosemary said. It was the first time she'd spoken since we'd decided on the nitrous oxide. "Now, more than before, we have to know what's going on. Taconic-Pacific will have unlimited resources to cover their tracks. They'll have the one thing that Paris never did. Deniability. With Paris, we just had to find her. With Taconic-Pacific we're going to need evidence, convincing evidence, and by any means necessary."

Rosemary was right, and we returned to the procedure room where Mark Bland was giggling, drooling and staring at the surgical lights. Homer removed his mask, and we resumed our interrogation.

Bland bragged about his large house in an upscale north Charlotte neighborhood. His two daughters attended the prestigious, and pricey, Charlotte Christian School. He laughed like a hyena when we asked him how he afforded those things on a repairman's salary. Bland was a deacon of the North Charlotte First Baptist Church, taught Sunday school, led a class of Royal Ambassadors on Wednesday nights and played basketball on his church's adult men's basketball team. His church friends called him "Butter" because of his smooth jump shot. Among a much smaller circle of friends, Mark Bland was known as "Butter" because, when he had a contract, you were toast. Mark "Butter" Bland's promise keeper lifestyle was financed by a prolific career as a contract killer.

Mark learned his skill set at government expense. After high school, he escaped an abusive father by joining the army. He spent the last eight years of his military career as a Special Forces instructor at Fort Bragg. He was discharged from the army with distinction, and with multiple lethal aptitudes. He put those talents to work almost immediately. Over the next ten years, he built a highly successful personal services business, taking care of other people's problems. In the Southeast, the name "Butter" was known to everyone who needed to know such names.

The only serious moment in our nitrous oxide fueled conversation came when Bland warned us against letting either his wife or daughters know about his career as an assassin. Through a big smile, and behind a flushed, joyous face, Bland explained, that if we did, he'd have to kill us all.

A representative of Tacoma-Pacific contacted Bland about six months ago. Initially, he was only asked to find out what Lou was up to, collecting waste water samples in their dumping canal. He laughed. That's why he had to kill Homer's dog. After killing Dogue, Bland entered our Folly Road office on several occasions to go through Lou's computer and research papers. I worried that the mention of Dogue might prompt Homer to turn the nitrous up to brain puree. However, even with the laughing gas, it was clear that Bland regretted killing Dogue. The moral compass of a paid assassin spun wildly and unpredictably. His remorse probably saved his life.

Bland didn't understand the materials he'd found, but he copied and photographed everything. They were returned to his contact at Taconic-Pacific. Two weeks later, Taconic-Pacific transferred

$100,000 to Bland's off shore bank account. It was a fifty percent down payment for the murder of Lou Guillette. Bland happily added, "Not including expenses." Bland described the death of Margaret McGinley as unavoidable, but not regrettable, "collateral damage."

After Lou's murder, Bland was contacted again when it became apparent I was still planning to present Lou's research at the Gordon Conference. Bland chided us for making things harder than he'd bargained for. "I told them I wasn't a God-damned Winn-Dixie. I don't do BOGOs. If they wanted Murphy dead too, it was going to be full price. I should've charged more. It's a mistake to come back to a place where you've worked before." Because of the nitrous, that realization was just matter of fact. "I didn't plan for this big ape getting in the way. You move pretty good for an old fat guy. Are you ex-Special Forces?"

"Marines, you simpleton."

One thing that Bland had told us the truth about was his ignorance regarding Paris Laveau. About a dozen Tarot cards had been sent to him in a manila envelope. His instructions were to leave them all over the place. There wasn't any explanation as to why. Bland didn't care about why. He thought it was silly, and unnecessarily dangerous. Taconic-Pacific obviously knew about our history with Paris Laveau. Smart to cover their tracks by hanging the murders on one of the F.B.I.'s ten most wanted fugitives. A fugitive who just happened to have a vendetta against me, Rosemary and anyone else we might work with. We completely bought in.

Bland apologized about hitting Rosemary on the head. Her arrival at the office was unanticipated. He assured us that she wasn't part of the contract. He didn't do women or children, unless there were special circumstances. He giggled and admitted that he'd handled some special circumstances in the past, but the price was always higher. From the expression on Rosemary's face, I don't think she was sympathetic, or inclined to accept Bland's apology. I worried for a moment that she might also reach over and spin up the dial.

Bland dissolved into some mindless babbling and his focus drifted. The more irritating our inebriated hit-man became, the more I liked Homer's initial plan for extracting the information we needed. Homer smacked Bland upside the head again to get his attention. "Why should we believe any of this bullshit? Maybe you just like killing people."

Although still smiling and sniggering, Bland was hurt by this accusation. "Hey, I'm a professional. I'm a husband, father and a church elder. I wouldn't kill anybody without a contract."

"Remind me to call the Better Business Bureau and give you a positive review. Now, answer my question."

"I told you. I'm a professional. If I learned anything in the military, it was to keep detailed records. When the brass come by, you better have all your paperwork in order." Bland again deteriorated into some incoherent babbling. He mumbled something about his employers probably not liking the thoroughness of his business records. Bland's eyes darted around the room, appreciating colors and images that we weren't privy to. His fingers were continuously moving, trying to touch effervescent objects. The straps on his arms were no longer an issue in Bland's new reality.

Homer turned down the nitrous a bit and slapped him again across the face. It was a tooth rattling smack, but Bland just looked up and grinned. "Hey, that was hard, big guy. You might've broken my jaw. Are you ex-Special Forces?"

"I already told you. Marines, you candy-ass."

"Okay, okay, a jar head. You're lucky I'm restrained, otherwise I'd take you apart." A threat accompanied by the most inappropriate shit-eating grin on his face.

"Don't threaten me you imbecile. You're lucky that your balls aren't in that bell jar over there. So back on point, what do you have that proves Taconic-Pacific hired you to kill my friends?"

"Why are you people so dense? If they hadn't hired me, why else would I be here? I've missed some of our church league basketball season. I don't have anything against you people. From what I can tell, you guys are pretty good scientists, I guess, and you seem pretty cool. But, you've got those paper mill people steamed. People like them, know people like me. You probably shouldn't be fucking with them."

With a little more prodding, and less ambiguous questions, Mark "Butter" Bland told us all about his business enterprise. Rosemary recorded everything and took careful notes to make sure we had it down. It was clear that we were going to need hard copy evidence.

He gave us all the codes we needed to access his off-shore financial accounts. Bland also had a small fishing cabin on Lake Norman that even his family didn't know about. A hidden room in the basement was his armory. It was where he'd made the bomb that blew up Lou's airboat. The components were still there. It pissed him off that I hadn't been on the boat with Lou. It was supposed to look like I was the target. When Margaret McGinley died in my place, Bland began to get a bad feeling about the whole assignment. Bland figured that if I'd been on the airboat, he would've never come back to Charleston. Bland was so high, he believed I'd feel sorry for him because of his failure to blow me to pieces.

More importantly, Bland gave us the number of a storage unit he kept on the industrial east side of Charlotte. It was his business office, where he kept his records. If nothing else, he was a freak about organizational efficiency. All his contracts were filed separately, with supporting documentation. Bland was proud of the fact that he'd written up detailed 'after action reports' for each assignment. The reports were a military-like self-critique of his performance. He highlighted the strengths and weaknesses exposed on each contract. The storage unit also contained copies of all his financial records. Bland itemized who paid for what and when. He never overlooked an unpaid invoice.

Bland started laughing uncontrollably. He wondered if maybe he'd regret keeping such records. "I don't give a shit though." He licked his lips, looked at something happening to his right, and then added, "The military taught me that good paperwork usually keeps you out of trouble."

He looked at Homer, "You were in the Special Forces. You know what I mean."

"What a fucking idiot."

"Right, right. I meant the Corps. Ooh-Rah Marine."

"Save it, dip-wad. Nothing's going to save your bacon, podna." Homer's menacing tone seemed to momentarily penetrated Mark Bland's nitrous fog.

Bland looked at Homer, raised his eyebrows in a shrug of acceptance, and then dissolved into incoherent muttering, followed by unconsciousness.

Rosemary turned off the recorder, and we huddled to discuss all that Bland revealed. She reminded us that the audiotape would never be allowed in court because of the nitrous. At least, we now knew who was pulling the strings. Taconic-Pacific was going to do whatever was necessary to make sure that no one found out about their dioxin dumping into Winyah Bay. It would've worked too, if Homer hadn't come back from the China Palace with a bucket of slop for Smokin' Joe. The trick was to prove it without the audiotape.

Homer's plan was to leave Bland on the table after turning the nitrous up to the max. We'd remove the restraints and call the police in the morning. The police would assume that Bland was a thief or drug addict who'd broken into our office and overdosed on our nitrous. We'd put the tarot card back in his pocket, and, hopefully, the police would put together the puzzle pieces.

I looked at Rosemary for her thoughts. "The police are never going to be able to connect the dots between this guy and Taconic-Pacific without our help. We need to connect the police to those records that Bland is so proud of. I just hope they are as damning as Bland says they are." Again, we knew Rosemary was right.

As he always does, Homer took charge. "Here's what we're going to do, assuming that our churchy hitman is telling the truth."

"He is," Rosemary said. "He thinks he's talking to his best friends ever. He probably thinks that Homer is Jesus." That thought made Homer smile.

Homer continued. "What we're going to do is collect all the hard evidence ourselves. I'll hop in Lucy and drive up to Charlotte. I'll find his storage unit, and we'll get all his records. Once we have the goods, then we'll make a citizen's arrest. We'll hand Bland over to the police along with the paperwork, all tied up with one big bow."

I looked at Rose for her response. "It'll work. The court won't care how we came to get Bland's business records. If we turn them over to the police, they'll be admissible."

Homer continued, "If he's kept all of his communications with Taconic-Pacific, like he's said, then we should have everything we need to take them down. I'll also drive by his Lake Norman cabin. If the bomb making stuff is still there, that'll hang Lou's murder around Bland's neck. It's the stuff we need to make sure our new friend eventually gets the needle. I'm assuming that you guys aren't going to let me spin up the dial on this dog killer."

"I like new plan better. It's the right thing to do."

"It might be the right thing to do, but it's not the fair thing. The fair thing would be for me to give him a needle full of botulism. The fair thing would be for me to be staring into his eyes just when he realizes that his diaphragm muscles are paralyzed."

Rosemary recognized the need to change the subject. "How long do you think it will take to find Bland's stash?"

"At this time of night, I can be in Charlotte in three hours. Give me another three to find and check out his storage unit and cabin. When I have everything, I'll call you. It should be before sunrise."

"I'll go with you, Homer."

"No. You need to stay here with Rosemary. Don't forget for a second that this guy is lethally dangerous. He's been in tough spots before, but he's still here. My advice is to keep him asleep, but whatever you do, don't loosen those restraints for any reason. I don't care if he pisses himself or shits on the floor, don't do a single thing for him. If he gets loose, he'll be a handful, even with a busted arm."

"Ten-four, big man. Rosemary and I will keep this guy wrapped up until you get back. If you find what Bland says he has, I'll call my friend Nodeen at Justice. We don't want to explain any of this to the local cops. Crossing state lines to do contract killing sounds like F.B.I. anyway."

"We're going to need the F.B.I., and the Justice Department, if Taconic-Pacific is behind all this," Rosemary said. "They've already demonstrated what they're capable of."

"It's a plan then." Homer concluded with a clap of his hands. "I love it when a good plan comes together. Just make sure that he stays alive until I've got what we need. After that, I'm okay with anything. Don't worry about my feelings if you get tired of babysitting him."

"Homer, are you okay with an all-night drive? You get sleepy sometimes."

"Don't you worry about me. Lucy and I have taken a lot of midnight drives. If I happen to take a nap, well, Lucy just drives herself."

"Don't joke. We're in some serious shit here. We're counting on you making it back. We need you to make it back."

"No worries, Rosie. I'm good to go. If Lucy can't get me to Charlotte, I've got another girlfriend named Betty who can also get me there."

Rosemary and I both smiled. We knew that Homer took amphetamines from time to time to combat his narcolepsy. There was something about Homer that inspired confidence. Even when there wasn't any reason to be confident. I'm sure it was the same way when Homer was in Vietnam. He'd already saved both of our lives once tonight. We had no doubt that he was going to be successful finding what we needed in Charlotte. Homer Lahr could be accused of a lot of shortcomings, but when he says he's going to do something, he does it.

Homer packed up the stuff he might need, including some bolt cutters. Before pulling Lucy out of the parking lot, he pulled us over to the window. "Remember, don't get soft with this guy. Keep him strapped and gassed. He's acting like a circus clown right now, but that's the nitrous. He's a Special Forces trained, professional assassin. Don't take your eyes off him. Like a lone wolf, he'll chew off his own arm to get out of those restraints, and beat you to death with the severed limb."

"Well, Homer, when you explain it like that, I think we'll keep a close eye on Mr. Bland."

"Ooh-Rah. You and Rosie, no hanky-panky. Keep an eye on the prize. I'll call as soon as I know what I've got."

Rosemary turned the nitrous down to dental procedure level. We decided to both keep an eye on "Butter" Bland. After a busy evening, he was now unconscious most of the time. Occasionally, he awoke with some chuckling at a personal conversation or vision that Rosemary and I were not part of. Actually, it was getting irritating.

We weren't worried about falling asleep. Bland gave us a ton of stuff to assimilate. All of it sobering. We considered ourselves reasonably bright, but never saw this coming. We weren't even the primary target. This was about Lou's research. It made us angry that we'd been nothing more than elaborate straw men. Lives taken to protect a paper company's profits. It was going to take more than all night to wrap our heads around all this. As unimaginable as the biblical sins committed by Paris and Hector Laveau, the actuarial calculation that went into Lou's murder was even worse.

At seven a.m. Homer called. He had no difficulty finding either the storage unit or the lake cabin. Everything was just as Bland described. However, there was far more documentation than we imagined. Homer was waiting until 8:30 a.m. to rent a U-Haul trailer. Mark "Butter" Bland had been a successful businessman. The body count was going to be large. Bland compulsively catalogued each of his contracts, linking each murder to the person or persons who'd ordered it. Homer thought that he might be sitting on one of the largest databases of criminal activity outside of the Department of Justice.

The trip to Lake Norman had also been fruitful. Bland's armory was impressive. Multiple ballistic matches would ultimately be possible. More specific to us, the lake cabin had everything necessary to build a high energy explosive. There was even a diagram of Lou's airboat, indicating where the bomb was to be hidden.

I asked Homer if he was doing okay. He said he was, and so was Lucy. I told him to be careful getting home. Homer promised that he'd be safe and would be back by early afternoon. He told me I needed to call Nodeen and get him down here right away. There was urgency in Homer's voice that unsettled me. This was even bigger than I had imagined.

I got on the phone to Laurence immediately. I'm not sure that Laurence either believed or understood everything that I told him.

Still, he could tell that the feces had hit the space cooling device. He called the local F.B.I. field agents to come take custody of Mark Bland. Laurence Nodeen would be on a plane within an hour.

Chapter 34.
WOODS HOLE

The Gordon Conference convened at the rustic conference center at Woods Hole Oceanographic Institute on Cape Cod. The blustering wind and slate-gray sky contributed to a forsaken and somewhat ominous mood on the otherwise deserted seasonal island retreat. I'm sure the organizers were thrilled with the winter rates, but the shuttered stores, empty bars and buttoned-down fishing boats all bespoke a poverty of vigor. The desolate disposition of the island matched the melancholy temperament we brought with us to the Gordon Conference. We struggled with how to make our presentation a celebration rather than a lamentation.

After speaking with the organizers, they generously gave me two slots for an extended research presentation. Even though I presented, I listed Dr. Louis J. Guillette, Jr. Ph.D. and Margaret McGinley as the primary and secondary authors. I also added Dr. Homer Lahr to the author list. That violated several different publication ethics, but I didn't care. Without Homer's bravery, there wouldn't have been a research presentation. If that didn't fall into the category of "essential scientific contribution," then I didn't understand the process.

Homer was grateful. In his long meandering career, he'd never had a single research presentation on his *curriculum vitae*. He proudly announced to the staff that he was closing the office and would attend the conference. That was also remarkable. Homer had not attended a scientific medical meeting in more than twenty years. I worried a bit about how he might react to a critical question. I didn't want Homer to school anyone with the back of his hand, instead of waiting for me to parse a nuanced answer.

Despite the dreary surroundings, the fire in the conference hall's hearth was warm and the anticipation surrounding my talk was great.

Lou had been a vocal regular at the Gordon Conference, and a close friend of most of the attendees. As a speaker, he was pioneering, provocative and entertaining. My mood was tempered by the realization I'd never be able to match the charisma that Lou always brought to the podium.

Lou's death shocked everyone in the environmental health community and broke many hearts. Most believed that I'd been given the extra time to memorialize Lou. Many expected a montage of his inspiring nature photography. Any presentation of Lou's research guaranteed one of biggest crowds of the conference. The registered crowd would be swollen by a substantial F.B.I. presence, although I couldn't tell who they might be. Laurence Nodeen even sent me an inspiring note. He knew that the Gordon Conference was big time and was planning to drop by to see me "screw the pooch in front of some real scientists."

I did start the presentation with my favorite of Lou's nature photos. A picture captured at dusk, taken at water level across one of the lakes on South Island of the Yawkey Preserve. The wicked red eyes of hundreds of alligators dotted the water's surface. It was the first standing ovation ever given after a single image presentation.

I followed that slide with an enhanced map of Georgetown, the rivers feeding Winyah Bay, and the locations of the North and South Islands of the Yawkey wildlife preserve. The next slide was the same, except it now also highlighted the location of the Taconic-Pacific Paper Mill. The next slide identified the locations where we obtained our water samples, and the collection sites of our alligator samples and egg clutches from the two islands of the preserve.

Over the next twenty minutes, I documented the incredibly high levels of the dioxin, TCDD, in the black water discharged from the paper mill, retrieved from their waste water canal. Those levels, while attenuated, remained significantly elevated, over acceptable limits, in the water and fish samples collected down the Great Pee Dee River, into Winyah Bay and in the tidal wash bathing South Island of the Yawkey Preserve. I smiled to myself when I used the term "femtomolar amounts."

Due to the river currents and tidal patterns which I illustrated in several slides, there was virtually no detectable TCDD in the water or fish collected off the North Island. As lifelong inhabitants, and fishermen exclusive to either North or South Island, Lou's alligators reflected any other apex predator. They were what they ate. The TCDD levels, as well as several other paper plant contaminants, were exceptionally high in the hundreds of alligators sampled from South Island, mirroring the contaminated water and fish taken at the mouth of the South Island estuaries. The alligators from the North Island had TCDD levels that were minimal, or even below the limits of detection.

Lastly, I showed the results from Lou's alligator egg clutches. The most obvious difference was the reduction in the number and size of the egg clutches from South Island compared to North Island. On South Island, the male hatchlings had shorter, and more frequently abnormal, phalluses. The female hatchlings demonstrated a high incidence of multi-ovular oocytes. The hatchlings from the North Island were essentially unremarkable.

The "money slide" was the one that graphically depicted the exceptional correlation between the TCDD levels in the water, fish, maternal alligators and female hatchlings with multi-ovular oocytes and male hatchlings with penile anomalies. To further nail the association, Lou collected follicular fluid from the ovaries of the female hatchlings. Not surprising to Lou, the dioxin penetrated from mother to hatchling. The dioxin concentrated in the follicles of what would one day be the next generation of alligators.

It was a compelling presentation, and Lou deserved all the credit. He painted the entire canvas. The conclusions of the study were obvious, but I hammered them anyway. I also proposed the link, which Lou had suspected, between multi-ovular oocytes in alligators exposed to high levels of TCDD, and the epidemic of polycystic ovarian disease filling our infertility clinics. I then showed a picture of a young, handsome Lou Guillette. The self-satisfied smile on his face perfectly captured everyone's memory of the man. The Gordon Conference attendees once again rose to their feet acknowledging Lou's lifelong commitment to preserving both environmental and human health.

Even though people were applauding, I wasn't finished. I put up a slide with a timeline of Lou's research efforts starting with his first visit to the Taconic-Pacific waste water canal and ending with his death on an airboat explosion. Over the next several slides, I superimposed a timeline of Mark Bland's intersection with our lives, beginning with his hiring by Taconic-Pacific. Each subsequent point on Bland's timeline was illustrated by an audio recording of an unusually jovial Mark Bland describing his work.

There was silence in the room as Bland described the brilliance of the bomb he'd placed on Lou's airboat. Bland expressed his disappointment that I hadn't been on board as well. Bland laughed as he recounted how badly Taconic-Pacific wanted to shut Lou up. He didn't know what it all meant, but Lou was never going to present his research. A cool two hundred thousand dollars had made sure of that. "I've got two girls who'll be off to college soon. You know I never got to go. I think I might've been a scientist if I had." Then Bland degenerated into some more incoherent babbling.

It was the coup de grace. Homer, who'd been standing at the back of the room, made a fist, popped it into his open palm, and walked out into the hallway. Homer asked a security guard where he could find an open bar. He was looking forward to sharing a beer with Lou.

After the presentation, I participated in a planned question and answer session. The first one was obvious. Mark Bland was arrested on murder charges and had not receive bail. The Department of Justice organized an F.B.I. Task Force to investigate his role in other unsolved murders. The Chief Executive Officer of the Taconic-Pacific Paper Mill in Georgetown, the Chief of Security and a few other members of upper management had been arrested. The F.B.I. was also searching for any involvement by Taconic-Pacific International, but so far, had only discovered an avalanche of horrified, but implausible denials. The Department of Justice considered this one of the worst cases of corporate and ecological lawlessness ever encountered. Their intention was to pursue it relentlessly.

Someone else asked if the F.B.I. would be indicting Taconic-Pacific as a corporation for endangering the public health. I knew how Lou would've relished that question. "We're still a long way from that kind of law enforcement. However, the necessary first step is to get the attention of the Environmental Protection Agency and raise the public's awareness. That was Dr. Guillette's life work. When the public shares our passion for preserving the environment and realizes the health consequences of the failure to do so, they'll demand environmental protection and the enforcement of our public health laws."

I paused before continuing. "Despite the elegance of Lou's experimental design and findings, we know there'll still be doubters. Corporate scientists will question the potential role of other contaminants. Regulators will blather about the difference between association and causation. Politician will express 'grave concern', but also worry about the potential chilling effect on American manufacturing. We've heard it all before. But this time it will be different."

"How so?" another questioner asked.

"Because this time, there's at least one significant group who doesn't have any doubt about the implications of our findings. That group is the suits at Taconic-Pacific. They're so certain of our findings, they were willing to kill to prevent us from presenting this data here today. Shrunken phalluses, infertility and a murder for hire tends to grab the public's attention."

After the question and answer session, the Gordon Conference arranged for a press conference. *The Boston Globe, Washington Post, New York Times,* national television news and a film crew from *60 Minutes* were all there. That's when I knew this would never end. I'd be telling this story, and recounting this research, in one venue or another for the rest of my life. Lou had warned me on one of our first trips to Yawkey. Environmental research would spark a passion and draw you in. There was no more important work. As always, Lou was prescient. At the same time, I knew that every time I presented this work, I'd feel like a fraud.

The man delivering this message should be Lou Guillette. He was stolen from us before his work was complete. People were going to be held accountable for that.

EPILOGUE

The year following the Gordon Conference was one of the busiest of my career. In addition to writing the manuscript for publication, I received dozens of invitations to speak at other conferences. They had some interest in the research, but mostly, they just wanted to hear the Taconic-Pacific hitman story. Eventually, I began to decline them all. It was more important to disseminate the science. I knew that Lou would've agreed.

For decades, sperm counts have dropped in men, young girls have entered puberty at younger and younger ages, rates of polycystic ovarian syndrome and female infertility had skyrocketed, childhood obesity, hyperactivity and autism spectrum disorder are all now considered epidemics, and rates of prostate, testicular and breast cancer are rising. The scientists all say that the reasons are multiple, but endocrine disrupting compounds polluting our nation's waterways and food supply are undoubtedly contributing.

In the human body, endocrine disruptors, like dioxins, either mimic or interfere with the actions of the sex hormones and disrupts the normally finely tuned hormonal interactions that control puberty, fertility, pregnancy, and menopause. Environmental endocrine disrupting compounds are also capable of stimulating the growth of tumors in estrogen and testosterone responsive organs such as the breast, uterus, ovary, prostate and testicles. Rachel Carson in *Silent Spring* first raised the public alarm in the 1960s, and now Lou Guillette was murdered to cover up the extent of the damage that Carson had predicted. The American public desperately needs a wakeup call. A wakeup call that Taconic-Pacific was desperate to prevent.

It frustrated me that I couldn't maintain focus on the environmental challenges we were facing. Each presentation became a little more morbid than the last. The outrage and questions were more about the murders, than the risks of environmental contamination on human health. It was a sign of the distractibility of our news/entertainment cycle and the ever-shortening attention span of the American public. It was discouraging because I knew what they were missing. To see the bigger picture, we needed a messenger with the depth, charisma and passion of Lou Guillette.

I thought back to a conversation between me and Lou on the day we met. "Teaching is like performance art. Don't let anyone tell you different. If you're not a performer, then you aren't doing it right." I did the best I could, but I'd never be able to enflame America's passion for the environment as effectively as Lou. Even though they'd been caught red-handed, Taconic-Pacific had still accomplished their goal of silencing an unbelievably effective teacher. I knew I was just a caddy carrying Lou's bags. After a while, it became tiring, even telling the story of his greatest round.

One meeting that I didn't turn down was in Pittsburgh. Louis J. Guillette Jr., PhD was posthumously named the seventeenth annual recipient of the prestigious Heinz Award which honors visionaries who've made extraordinary contributions to the environment in the name of the late United States Senator John Heinz. I attended along with Lou's family who accepted the award. Teresa Heinz, chairperson of the Heinz Family Foundation, gave Lou a moving tribute, recognizing his groundbreaking research on the impact of endocrine disrupting compounds on the reproductive systems of alligators, and other wildlife.

Teresa Heinz concluded, "Dr. Guillette's research on alligators and other marine life created an in-depth model for understanding the effects of toxins in the wild and provides information we need to safeguard both people and wildlife. Dr. Guillette was a pioneer in exhibiting how wildlife can function as sentinels for adverse environmental contaminant exposure. Dr. Guillette's research has taught us the simple, but critical public health lesson, that even low-level exposure to one or multiple environmental contaminants during critical periods of fetal development can have long-lasting human health implications."

It was a moving ceremony, and it gave me renewed hope that in the long run, maybe Taconic-Pacific had not won after all. In the short run, I promised myself that I'd never buy off-brand ketchup again.

I also tired of all the legal crap. None of the law enforcement agencies or courts, which became involved in the Mark Bland prosecutions, approved of our interrogation techniques. Even Laurence Nodeen could only shake his head when he heard the story. I was sick and tired of hearing the lecture about the innumerable laws we'd broken. It was all bark and no bite. There wasn't any chance that law enforcement was going to allow our activities to compromise an investigation that was one of the biggest in Department of Justice history.

Rosemary's legal assessment had been spot on. The Bland audiotape was never allowed in court or ever even mentioned. Words like torture and coercion weren't popular with juries. However, the boxes of records that Homer retrieved from Bland's storage unit, and the physical evidence retrieved from his Lake Norman cabin were more than enough, many times over. Dozens of air tight cases would be systematically built from this treasury of documentation.

Bland's lawyer petitioned the Justice Department to initiate an investigation regarding the violation of his client's civil rights. That didn't go anywhere. Rosemary and I received a gift basket from Laurence Nodeen with a note that simply said, "You're welcome."

We were also threatened that Mark Bland would sue us for physical and mental abuse, assault, kidnapping, robbery and a handful of other personal insults. Rosemary laughed and told his lawyer that we'd take our chances in court. As it turned out, Bland was circling the drain so fast his only concern was finding a way to avoid lethal injection. We never heard anything else about a lawsuit. Even if we had, Homer and I were both confident in our representation.

Early on, Rosemary was threatened with action against her by an indignant BAR association. However, the state Attorney General, made that disappear. Law enforcement was intent on making sure that nothing interfered with the development of their cases against Bland and his many employers. Rosemary got a stern talking to by someone from Columbia, but nothing more. Still, it made her hopping mad.

Homer and I were used to being officially labeled as loose cannons, but Rosemary, not so much.

Over time, law enforcement began to warm up to us. However, they never once failed to give us that "why don't you stick to what you know" smirk. Surprising, given the titanic record of law enforcement futility contained in Bland's business records. We did feel good when a team from the F.B.I.'s Quantico Training Base showed up to interview us. They wanted to know the details of how we got Mark "Butter" Bland to be so talkative. They were fascinated with our portable nitrous oxide machine. They were horrified when Homer described his back up plans in case the nitrous failed.

I also spent too much of my time in depositions, and testifying before grand juries, about the cases that blossomed from Bland's journals. The only one I followed closely was the murder for hire case against the Chief Executive Officer, Director of Security and the Director of Process Technology for the Taconic-Pacific Paper Plant in Georgetown, South Carolina. I gave a deposition about our confrontation with the Taconic-Pacific security officers and our research. Conviction was a certainty. The defendants began to scramble looking for plea deals. Everyone suspected that the culpability went even higher in the Taconic-Pacific corporate structure. Sooner or later, an incriminating memorandum was going to show up. Then things would really get exciting.

Taconic-Pacific International professed ignorance of anything going on in the South Carolina backwaters. Like the scene in *Casablanca* when the local Moroccan police raided Rick's Café Americain, they were "shocked that gambling was going on in this establishment." Taconic-Pacific International announced the investment of several hundred million dollars into the Georgetown mill and the local community. Taconic-Pacific pledged to reduce the dioxin effluent by upgrading its bleaching process. In addition, they pledged to do it without any prolonged interruption in production or any reduction in work hours. Significant money would also be put into improving water quality and providing child health services in the community.

Those announcements helped Taconic-Pacific's local public relations problems. The local papers had already published a couple of puff pieces praising the new, environmentally-conscious, community-invested Taconic-Pacific. While their past performance would not win them any awards from the Nature Conservancy, the new bleaching technology would dramatically reduce toxic discharges over the next decade. None of the newspaper articles mentioned that the TCDD spilled in Seveso was still in the ecosystem more than twenty years later.

There was discussion of a class action lawsuit by members of the local community, alleging damages to health and property from the Taconic-Pacific pollutants. Rosemary was approached about her interest in representing the plaintiffs. She rightly declined, noting that her involvement would be a major conflict of interest. She suggested some alternatives but advised them that a high profile trial lawyer wouldn't be necessary. Taconic-Pacific would drag its feet, but it will never allow the case to go to depositions, much less a trial. Ultimately, Taconic-Pacific will settle, and that settlement will be very generous. There is almost no number that's unreasonable when a corporate patriot wants to avoid having to discuss under oath their role in a contract killing. Nor will Taconic-Pacific be interested in the public dissemination of statewide data on the rates of asthma, respiratory illness, pregnancy complications, fetal anomalies and cancer in the Georgetown watershed district. Smart Wall Street investors had already figured out that the cost of manila envelopes and cardboard boxes were getting ready to go up worldwide.

On the criminal side, things were white hot. Laurence Nodeen told me that the Justice Department re-opened almost two dozen unsolved murders. Bland's detailed register included the who, the what, the when, and where the bodies were buried. There was never any mention of why. That was an element of the crime that Mark "Butter" Bland didn't concern himself with.

The things that did concern Mark Bland was who paid for his work, how much and were they timely or delinquent. His financials were the proverbial "smoking gun." Dozens of arrests were made by the F.B.I. Task Force, and cases were being prepared against a dozen more. There was even a member of the United States House of Representatives who made his wife's lover disappear. The Department of Justice was supervising everything under the auspices of their interstate racketeering and conspiracy jurisdiction.

Laurence Nodeen sat at the top of the reporting pyramid. During one visit to Charleston, he asked Rosemary if she'd like to be a prosecutor on the Federal Task Force. Honored, she politely declined. She explained that she was busy enough trying to keep Homer and me out of legal trouble. Laurence agreed. A pair of misfits like us could keep any lawyer's plate more than filled. There was also the small matter of a new baby that was due pretty soon and would likely need her attention.

Laurence was gracious. He thanked Rosemary for considering. He made Rosemary's day when he said it would be his honor to work with her someday. Just before we left Laurence's temporary office at the Federal Building on Meeting Street, he asked if we were interested in an update on the Laveaus. Duh, of course we were.

"Hector Laveau was dead. He was shived multiple times in the exercise yard at Lieber Correctional. He was hit by one of the Mexican gangs at the prison."

"I thought he was under their protection?"

"He did too. I'm sure he died with a surprised look on his face. There was a change in wind direction and Hector was the last one to find out about it. It also made us wonder how things might be going for Paris south of the boarder. Our intelligence was that Paris promised to open Louisiana to Amado Garrillo Fuentes as a drug trafficking pathway into the United States. We intercepted a big shipment of cocaine destined for New Orleans, coming into the country through Houston. It may have been Paris' shipment."

"The cartels don't take disappointment well?"

"No, they don't. A couple of days ago, a white woman's body was found, along with seven others, next to a highway in Nuevo Leon state, between the cities of Monterrey and Reynosa. The cartels deal a lot of death along that road."

"Is it her?"

"Can't tell yet. The bodies were all decapitated. All her fingers were missing, and her teeth had been knocked out, but we think it was her. One of the guys with her was probably seven feet tall, if he had a head. We expect a video to surface sooner or later."

Rosemary and I both nodded but had nothing to say. I couldn't muster any sympathy for Paris Laveau. I didn't think that made me a lesser person. A gruesome end to a gruesome life. I did feel a bit sorry for Hector. Not once in his whole life did he ever see it coming. Even when the knife split his liver, he still had no idea that he was again getting the shitty end of the stick from his sister. As he bled out in the cinnamon-stained dust and dirt of the exercise yard, his final thoughts were the same as all his others. Why did this happen to him?

On the way home to Wappoo Heights from the Federal Building, we stopped at the grocery store in South Windemere. We needed some fusilli, fresh green onions, tomatoes, garlic and some Italian sausage to make Salsa Picante. At checkout, we got in line behind a black mother with a beautiful baby. The baby had a short, soft Afro, puffy cheeks and pursed lips, like only breast-fed babies have.

"What a gorgeous child," Rosemary said.

"Thank you very much. I have two other children that are nice, but this is my 'soft' baby. Everyone should have at least one 'soft' baby."

"Well, she's wonderful. What's her name?"

"Sarah, from the Bible."

Rosemary reached over and tickled her tummy. "Sarah, you're such a pretty little girl." Sarah smiled.

"It looks like you're expecting too."

"Yes, it isn't going to be much longer. We're very excited."

"Is it a boy or a girl? No, wait, don't tell me." She reached over and gently felt the soft, round fullness of Rosemary's tummy. Then she looked up at Rosemary's perfect glowing complexion. "It's going to be a girl. No doubt about that. And, it's going to be a 'soft' baby too. You're lucky. I had to wait for my third to get a 'soft' one. You got yours on the first try."

Then she patted Rosemary's tummy again, smiled and turned back to the cashier. Rosemary and I stared at each other with mouths open. "How did she know it was a girl, and that it was my first?"

I just shrugged. Despite years in Obstetrics and Gynecology, female intuition was still a mystery. Real, but inexplicable.

Rosemary placed her fingertip to her lip as if hesitating. “She’s moving. She’s going to be here soon. I want her to be a ‘soft’ baby. I want to call her Sarah, too.”

I smiled. “Let’s see what becomes.”

CPSIA information can be obtained
at www.ICGtesting.com
Printed in the USA
LVHW09s0422140818
586831LV00008B/1377/P

9 781945 181399